Royal Rebels

Royal Rebels: Seducing the Crown

JULES BENNETT

CHARLENE SANDS

SANDRA HYATT

MILLS & BOON

First Published in Great Britain 2021
By Mills & Boon, an imprint of HarperCollins*Publishers* Ltd
1 London Bridge Street, London, SE1 9GF

www.harpercollins.co.uk

HarperCollins*Publishers*
1st Floor, Watermarque Building,
Ringsend Road, Dublin 4, Ireland

ROYAL REBELS: SEDUCING THE CROWN
© 2021 Harlequin Books S.A.

Behind Palace Doors © 2013 Jules Bennett
A Royal Temptation © 2015 Harlequin Books S.A.
Lessons in Seduction © 2011 Sandra Hyatt

Special thanks and acknowledgement are given to Charlene Sands for her contribution to the *Dynasties: The Montoros* series.

ISBN: 978-0-263-30054-3

MIX
Paper from
responsible sources
FSC™ C007454

BEHIND PALACE DOORS

JULES BENNETT

I'm dedicating this fairy tale to my stiletto-wearing, tiara-worthy glitter sister, Kelly Willison, and her beautiful princess in training, Anna. You two are a bright, shimmering light in my life. The glow may be all the glitter, but I think it comes from your heart of gold. Love you both.

And also to my own little princesses, Grace and Madelyn. I love watching you grow into beautiful little girls. I can't wait to see you fall in love and live your own fairy-tale dream.

Prologue

"Ever tried skinny-dipping?"

Victoria Dane gasped as Stefan Alexander, Prince of Galini Isle, stripped off his shirt.

"Umm…" She swallowed, watching as an impressive set of abs stared back at her. "No. No, I haven't."

He toed off his shoes.

"You're not going to…"

His soft chuckle caused goose bumps to spread over her body. Even at fifteen, she was totally aware of this handsome prince, who was technically a man, as he was three years older.

They'd quickly become friends since her mother was filming on his estate, and she assumed her girlish crush was normal. But was he really going to strip naked?

"I'm not doing it alone," he told her, hands on his hips.

Her eyes darted to his chest. "You got a tattoo?"

With a wicked grin, he nodded. "My first of many, I hope."

"What is it?" she asked, stepping closer to inspect.

Would it be rude to touch? Probably, so she slid her hands inside the pockets of her swim cover-up instead. Still, she imagined her fingertips sliding along the new ink.

"It's my family's crest," he told her. "I thought it appropriate to have that as my first. Besides, my father might not mind as much since it's symbolic."

The afternoon sun beat down on her, but Victoria knew the heat consuming her had nothing to do with the weather. She'd been on location with her mother for almost two months now, and she and Stefan had clicked from the moment they met. Of course, he probably saw her as a little sister and had no idea she was halfway in love with him.

The boys back home were nothing like this.

"Has your father seen it yet?" she asked, using the tattoo excuse to continue to stare at his chest.

"Nah. I've been careful to keep my shirt on around my dad since I got it two weeks ago. He'll throw a fit, but it's done, so what can he say now?"

Victoria moved toward the pool, dropped to the side and let her feet dangle in the cool water. "You're so relaxed about breaking rules and defying people. Aren't you worried you'll get in serious trouble one day?"

"Trouble?" He laughed as he sat down and joined her. "I'm not afraid of trouble. I'd rather be myself and live my life the way I want. I don't want to be ruled by what is considered to be the right thing. Who's to say what's right or wrong for me?"

She admired his take-charge attitude about life. He reminded her of her brother, Bronson.

"Don't you consider that lying?" she asked, still studying him. "I mean, you knew you were going to do it, so why not just tell your dad?"

Stefan glanced over to her, those bright blue eyes holding hers. "Lying by omission doesn't count in my book."

"Well, it does in mine. Maybe that's a cultural difference."

He scooped a hand in the water and playfully tossed it up onto her bare thighs. Shivers coursed through her.

"I think it's the difference between towing the line and living in the moment," he joked. "So how about that skinny-dipping?"

"I tow the line, remember? No skinny-dipping for me." Smiling at him, she placed a hand on his back and shoved him into the pool.

One

Every little girl envisioned a fairy-tale wedding. The long white train, the horse-drawn carriage, like the magical coach from Cinderella of course, and the proverbial tall, dark and handsome prince, chest adorned with medals and a bright blue sash that matched his eye color perfectly.

And while Victoria Dane wasn't living the fairy tale herself, she did have the glorious job of designing the royal wedding dress that would be seen by millions and worn by the next queen of Galini Isle.

Okay, so being the designer wasn't even a close second to becoming a queen.

"Victoria."

The familiar, soothing tone of her old friend's voice had Victoria turning from the breathtaking emerald ocean view. With a slight bow as was custom in this country, Victoria greeted the prince.

With his tight-fitting black T-shirt tucked into designer

jeans, most people would have a hard time believing Prince Stefan Alexander—owner of the most impressive set of blue eyes and some new ink peeking beneath the sleeve of his shirt on one impressive bicep—was the next in line to reign over this beautiful land.

Those muscles seemed to grow between each of their visits. Muscles he acquired from his passion of rock climbing. Yeah, that would make for a beautiful picture. A golden Greek god, shirtless and dangling high above the ground by his sheer strength....

There was one lucky bride waiting for her prince. Victoria would be lying if she didn't admit, even if only to herself, that at one time she'd envisioned herself as the one who would finally tame the great Prince Alexander, but his friendship had been invaluable and something she'd feared risking.

Strong arms that she had missed for the past few years pulled her into a warm, inviting embrace. Yes, this was the connection, the bond that phone calls and emails couldn't deliver.

"Prince Alexander," she said, returning his embrace.

"Don't 'Prince Alexander' me." His rich laughter enveloped her, making her feel even more excited to see him after so long. "And for God's sake, don't bow. Just because we haven't seen each other in a while doesn't mean I've become some royal snob."

"It's so great to see you, Stefan." She eased back and looked up into those striking blue eyes. "When you called to tell me you were getting married, I was shocked. She must be someone very special."

"The most important woman in my life," he said, lifting one of her hands to his lips.

Prince Charming had nothing on Stefan, and a slight surge of jealousy speared through Victoria at the fact another woman would be entering his life…and not just passing through like all the others.

He gestured toward the settee and matching chairs with bright orange plush cushions. "Let's have a seat and discuss my beautiful bride, shall we?"

Stefan dismissed his assistants with a silent nod. A man of his position and power didn't need to use words, but to Victoria he was still that rotten teen who'd tried to get her to go skinny-dipping in the royal pool…while a dinner party had been taking place in the grand ballroom.

"I've brought sketches of several dresses for you and your fiancée to review," she told him, laying her thin portfolio of designs on the tile tabletop and flipping it open. "I can also combine styles or come up with something completely different if nothing here catches her eye. They are all classic designs but different in their own way. Any would be flattering for the next queen."

"I've no doubt you'll make the perfect dress." He laid a hand over hers, a wide grin spreading across his devilishly handsome face. "It's so great to have you here, Victoria. I've missed you."

She returned his smile, unable to hide her excitement about not only seeing him again, but also the fact he'd finally found true love…something she'd started to have doubts about. And yes, she'd once wished his true love had been her, but their friendship was more important. As his best friend, she was thrilled that he was so happy and in love. She needed that reminder that not all men broke their promises of engagement.

"It's my pleasure to design for you, and it gives us both a reason to set aside our busy lives and get some face time," she told him, sliding her hair over her shoulder. "Phone calls just aren't the same."

"No, they're not," he agreed.

That sexy, sultry smile remained. Heavens, but the man was literally a tall, dark and handsome prince, and that cotton shirt stretched so perfectly over his broad shoulders and chiseled biceps. She wondered what the new tattoo was of, but if she knew Stefan, he'd find a reason to shed his shirt in no time.

Yeah, he'd changed over the years, and definitely in all the right places. Rock climbing does a body good.

"These are remarkable," he told her as he fingered through the drawings. "Did you do these yourself or do you have a team?"

A burst of pride ran through her. She may be one of the most sought-out designers, but each client earned her undivided attention and she loved hearing praise for her hard work...especially coming from such a good friend.

"I have a small team, but these are all my own. I was selfish when it came to your bride." She moved one thick sheet to the side, eager to display the rest of her designs. "I'm partial to this one. The clean lines, the cut of the neckline and the molding of the bodice. Classy, yet sexy."

Very similar to the one she'd designed for own wedding. Of course that had been six months, a slew of bad press and one shattered heartache ago when her up-and-coming actor/fiancé decided to publicly destroy Victoria. But working with Stefan and his fiancée would help her to remember that happily ever afters do exist.

When she'd met him as a teen on the set of one of her mother's films, she'd developed an instant crush. He'd been a very mature eighteen years old, compared to her fifteen, with golden skin and a smile she'd come to appreciate that held just a touch of cockiness.

She'd been smitten to say the least, but they'd soon developed a friendship that had lasted through the years. Fantasies had come and gone...and come again where she'd envisioned him proposing to her and professing his hidden, undying passion. But those were little girl dreams. Besides, Stefan always had a companion or two at all times.

"You would look beautiful in that gown."

Victoria shook off her crazy thoughts and jerked her attention to Stefan.

"Sorry. I realize your own engagement is still fairly recent, but—"

She straightened her shoulders and stepped back. "No, it's okay. But let's not talk about that. I'd much rather focus on your happiness."

He reached out, cupped her shoulders and gave a reassuring squeeze. "I'm still your friend. I know you didn't open up that much over the phone because of the timing being so close to the passing of my father, but you're here now and I'm offering you my shoulder if you need it."

Warmth spread through her. Other than her brothers, this was the one man she'd always been able to depend on. Even as they'd gotten older, their lives busier, she knew Stefan was always there for her.

"I may take you up on that," she told him with a smile. "But for now let's discuss you."

Because she needed to focus on their friendship and her work instead of her humiliation, her eyes drifted back over the designs. "A dress should make a woman feel beautiful and alluring. I wanted to capture that beauty with a hint of fairy tale thrown into the mix. When I don't know the client personally, it makes designing the dresses a bit harder, so that is why I chose to bring very different designs for her to look at. Do you know when your fiancée will arrive?"

Stefan leaned a hip onto the table and smiled. "Actually, she's already here. I have a proposition for you, Victoria."

Intrigued, Victoria rested one hand on the table and smiled. "And what is that, Your Highness?"

He chuckled. "Now you're mocking me."

"Not at all," she retorted with a grin, loving how they fell back into their easy banter as if no time had passed. "You just sounded so serious. What's your proposition?"

He took her hands in his, looking her in the eyes. "It has to do with my fiancée…sort of."

Oh, no. She recognized that look. It was the same naughty, conniving look he had when he'd wanted her to be his partner in crime in their early twenties…like the time when he'd asked her to pose as his girlfriend for a charity ball because he had a somewhat aggressive lady who wouldn't take no for an answer.

God. The sick feeling in her stomach deepened. The man was up to something no good.

"Stefan." She slid her hands from his warm, strong hold and rubbed them together. "Tell me there's a real fiancée and you're actually getting married."

"I am getting married and there is a fiancée." He threw her a wide, beautiful smile. "You."

Stefan waited for her response to his abrupt proposal. Damn, he'd meant to have a bit more finesse, but time was running out and he couldn't afford to tackle this wedding in the traditional sense. Nothing about this situation was traditional.

She placed her hands on either side of her temples as if to rub the stress headache away…he'd had a few of those moments himself recently. He'd never pictured himself as a one-woman man. And the thought always sent a shudder straight through him.

"I'm sorry to pull you into this," he told her. "I couldn't trust anyone else right now."

He prayed he chose the right words to make her understand. She was, after all, still recovering from an ugly public breakup, and she had always been such a good friend, no matter the distance between them. They'd shared countless phone calls in the middle of the night, during many of which she'd told him her dreams and he'd listened, hoping one day all those dreams would come true. And perhaps he could help that along.

"Why do you need me all of a sudden?"

"Galini Isle will go back to Greece if I don't marry and gain the title of king. My brother isn't an option because his wife is a divorcée and the damn laws are archaic. I couldn't live with myself if I didn't do everything in my power to keep this country in my family. I won't let my people down." He hated being forced into anything. "I want my title, but I do not want a wife. Unfortunately, I've looked for a loophole and there isn't one."

Victoria sank to the patio chair. "Again, why me?"

"I want a wife in name only. And I can't let my country revert to Greek rule. It's been in my family for generations. I refuse to be a failure to my family's name."

"This is crazy," she muttered, shaking her head.

Stefan stepped closer. "You've recently had scandal in your life. Why not show this fiancé who jilted you and the media who exploited your pain that you are stronger, you can rise above this and come out on top? What better way than to marry a prince?"

"You're serious?" she asked, looking back up at him. "How could we pull this off? I mean, we haven't been seen together in public for a couple years."

Stefan came over and took a seat directly beside her in the matching wrought-iron chair with plush cushions. "My people don't know who my bride is. I've made sure they only know there will be a wedding. I've been very secretive about this, which only adds to the mystery of the romance."

Romance. Yeah, that was the dead last thing on his mind right now. Couldn't he just have the crown? He was the prince, for crying out loud. Didn't that give him some clout? Why did he need a marriage to claim it?

"Once they see you, they'll know why I kept the engagement so quiet," he went on, knowing he was rambling, but he had to make her see this was the only way.

Damn, he hated vulnerability and being backed into a corner. Not only that, he hated putting Victoria in an awkward position.

Victoria laughed. "And here all this time I thought you were letting your romantic, protective side show."

"You are one of Hollywood's most famous single ladies—a bachelorette, I believe your country calls it—and I will simply explain I was protecting you from even more scandal and we wanted to express our love on our wedding day and not exploit it beforehand. Besides, there are all those articles and pictures from when we were in our teens and twenties. The media practically had us engaged at your twenty-first birthday party when I bought you a diamond necklace. The history is there, and the media will eat it up."

"Oh, Stefan." She sighed. "This is such a big decision. You can't expect me to give you an answer right now."

Leaning back against the chair, Stefan nodded. "I'm asking for only six months, Tori. After my coronation I'll have my title as king and the country will be secured with my family again."

"Then what?" she asked, her eyes searching his.

He shrugged, not really worried about anything beyond getting married and gaining his title. "After that it's up to you. You can stay married to me or you can end the relationship. The control is yours. Who knows, you may like being queen."

True, he may be a playboy, but he could think of multiple circumstances that would be worse than being married to the stunning Victoria Dane.

She stared out across the estate toward the ocean. Victoria's beauty was remarkable and surprisingly natural. She came from the land of perfection brought on by plastic surgeons, yet she looked more stunning than the fake, siliconed women he knew. And he was damn lucky she was in his life.

"This is the craziest thing I've ever heard." With a slight laugh she looked back to him. "You're taking something as serious as a royal wedding, a wedding that will create the new leaders for your country, and turning it into a…a lie. My God, Stefan, this is really putting the pressure on our friendship. Do you realize how risky this is? I can't lose you."

He sat forward, dead serious. "You could never lose me as a friend. If I thought that was the case I never would've asked you. Just think of this as a long, overdue reunion. I need someone I can trust not to back out at the last minute or use me for money in the end."

"Why did you wait so long to ask me?"

"Honestly I thought I could find a way around this." God knows he'd exhausted every avenue looking for one. "When I realized I couldn't, I knew I had only one option. You are the one person in my life I'd ever trust with something so personal, so serious."

She laughed. "I'd do anything for you, Stefan, you know that, but this is asking a lot. What about the people of your country? Won't they feel let down if we end the marriage? And how will this work out after your coronation? Will the country still remain yours?"

"No, my people won't feel let down," he assured her. "I will still be their leader. I will still keep control over my country. I just need the title to do so, which is where you fit in."

"You've really thought this through, haven't you?" She crossed her legs and shifted her body toward his. "You can't expect me to put my life on hold for six months. I'm a busy woman, Stefan."

He'd always admired her take-charge attitude and the way she matched him in this volley of wills. Not to mention the fact the woman was classy and beyond sexy.

Just as when he'd been in his late teens, Victoria Dane made his gut clench and still made him want her as more than a friend. But years ago he'd attempted to pursue her into something sexual. She hadn't taken him seriously, so to keep his ego intact, he played it off like he had indeed been joking. And the second time he'd been ready to take charge, she'd been in a relationship. But now she was free.

"I know you're busy, and I'm not trying to take your life away, but I do have something to offer you." He edged forward, taking her hand in his. "You'll get to show the world that you are stronger than the poor, humiliated woman they are making you out to be. The woman the media has portrayed as being overshadowed by her brothers and jilted by her fiancé. If you do this, not only will you design your wedding gown for this day, this could help you launch that bridal line you've been wanting. Make a play off the fairy tale of being a queen, if you like."

Her eyes darted back to the ocean. The sun was just starting to set, and Stefan knew as far as proposals went, this was probably the least romantic. But her apparent inner war with herself only told him that she was indeed considering his offer.

"I can practically see your mind working." He hoped she was leaning toward a yes decision. "This is a win-win for both of us, Victoria."

"Your way of thinking is not very Greek," she told him. "Aren't you all known for love?"

He laughed, squeezing her hand. "I think you know how passionate I can be about something I want."

She looked down at their joined hands. His dark, tanned skin next to her pinker complexion made for quite the contrast. But when she looked up into his eyes, he knew she wasn't going to deny him.

"You've always been determined," she whispered. "That's something I can understand. With my recent scandal and public embarrassment, I was adamant to get back on track, to take control of my life."

He waited, not wanting to interrupt as she guided her own words down the path toward everything he wanted.

"And what about the sleeping arrangements?" she asked, her wide eyes seeking his for answers.

Stefan laughed. "You know, you live in Hollywood where sin flows as freely as wine in my country, and you're blushing at the subject of us sharing a bed. I'm wounded."

Obviously this was something she hadn't expected, but he wasn't going to push. Yes, he'd desired her for years, but he wanted her to come to him. To realize that maybe something spectacular could happen between them behind the bedroom door.

He stroked his thumb over the soft skin on the back of her hand. "We'll have to share a room to keep up the pretense with the staff."

Her heart beat hard against her chest, and Victoria couldn't help the image that immediately popped into her head of the two of them entangled in satin sheets in a king-size bed. She knew that his dark skin was part of his heritage and not from lounging by the pool—which meant he would be lean and golden brown all over. There were rumors of hidden tattoos—some she'd seen, some she hadn't. The man simply exuded mysteriousness and sex. He'd been her best friend as a teen, and even though circumstances had gotten in the way of them seeing each other the past couple years, their phone calls and emails had kept that line of friendship open.

"I just don't know," she muttered aloud. "I'm scared of what this will do to us."

"We'll be stronger than ever," he assured her with a devastatingly handsome smile. "We've spent too many of the past years apart. Let's just focus on the fact we'll be together like old times. I need you, Tori."

Was she really about to risk more scandal and the bond she shared with Stefan? Yes, because he meant that much to her, and if the tables were turned, she knew he'd drop everything to help her. Besides, she was a member of the prestigious Hollywood Danes; it wasn't as if scandal hadn't been part of her life before.

For years she'd been in the spotlight as the sister of Hollywood's hottest producer and daughter of the Grand Dane—her mother's Hollywood-dubbed nickname. The threat of scandal followed her family everywhere.

Stefan's family had also had their share of scandal surrounding his mother's death years ago. His loyalty to his family—and his country—to maintain control of the crown was everything to him. And she completely understood family loyalty.

As she thought about it, Victoria was liking Stefan's proposal more and more. How could she not consider showing the world she could still come out on top—and with a sexy Greek prince, at that?

When Alex had put a ring on her finger, she'd been so determined to have a lasting, loving marriage like her mother, her brothers. Victoria didn't want pity, didn't want people looking at her as though she may fall apart if they brought up the broken engagement. Unfortunately, that's exactly what her family and friends were doing. But Stefan faced the topic head-on and didn't back down. He wasn't treating her like some wilted flower, but as a woman who was tougher than what most people thought.

Victoria was determined to come out stronger on the other side of this scandal. She was going to prove to everyone, including herself, that her iconic mother and hotshot brothers were not the only ones who could rise above anything life threw at them.

She looked down at her hand joined with Stefan's, knowing they could help each other…just like always. The arrangement was just on a larger scale than anything they'd ever confronted.

This proposition Stefan blindsided her with may truly be the answer to get everyone to stop throwing sympathy her way, to see that she was fine and had made her life her own. Not to mention she could use the publicity to help establish her bridal line, as he'd suggested. What better way to launch it than to design the royal wedding dress *and* wear it?

"You're thinking too hard," Stefan joked. "Go with your gut, Victoria. You know this is going to work. I won't let anything happen to you."

She looked into his vibrant eyes, confident he would do anything to keep her from facing heartache again. And that made his proposal even more appealing.

There was no denying the man was beyond sexy. He'd been dubbed the Greek Playboy Prince by all the media outlets for years. But Alex had been just as handsome, just as cocky…until he'd confessed he'd been using her for her family name to help further his acting career. Of course the truth had only come out after he'd impregnated another woman and had to call off the engagement.

Oh, how could she even sit here and compare the two men? Alex wasn't even worth her thoughts, and Stefan was everything to her.

Another look into his smiling eyes and Victoria nearly laughed. Stefan had been up-front and honest with her because that's the type of friend he was. What he was proposing was nothing like what Alex had done to her. Other than this marriage, what could she offer Stefan that he couldn't get himself? He certainly wasn't a rising actor like Alex had been. How could she deny him when she knew he was in a vulnerable state and he trusted only her?

"I'd expect you to be faithful, even if this is pretend," she told him.

"I assure you, you will have my undivided attention."

Swallowing the doubts and throwing caution to the wind, Victoria smiled. "Stefan, I'd be honored to marry you."

Two

Stefan had invited Victoria to stay in the palace so they could get some alone time to reconnect in ways that phone calls and emails couldn't provide. They had to attempt to make this seem like the real thing because the media would definitely pick up on any uncomfortableness between them if every touch, every lingering gaze didn't look authentic—like they were secret lovers.

Pretending to be infatuated by Victoria's beauty would be no hardship. Her flawless elegance had only flourished since the last time he'd seen her, and he was damned grateful she'd agreed to his insane proposal.

Parading her around the grounds with the royal photographer, snapping some pictures as they rode on horseback, cuddled beneath the trellis of flowing flowers and walked along the private, pristine beach, would help fuel this fire of his romance with the next queen of Galini Isle. Though he'd asked the photographer to keep Victoria's face out of the snapshots to add an aura of mystery. He'd always been proud and ready to show off the women on his arm. Victoria was the first one he'd protected from the camera. So once the photos started going out, they would hopefully create more talk of his upcoming wedding in four weeks.

Their brief time alone had already caused so many memories to resurface. She was still a tender heart where her family was concerned but lethal when it came to business. The beauty Victoria brought back into his life by being there in person was immeasurable. Holding her, laughing with her, staying up late last night talking again was amazing, and he vowed to never let so much time go between their visits again...if she ended up leaving at the end of the six months.

All thoughts of reconnecting were swept aside as Victoria entered the intimate dining area he'd had his assistants set up on the balcony off his master suite's second story. Stefan's breath caught, and he knew that spark of desire he'd always had for her would only spread and burn hotter now that they were spending so much intimate time alone.

Yes, he needed her to keep his country, but he wasn't a fool. No way would he let this prime opportunity pass him by to show her just how much he believed becoming friends with benefits was a great idea. He may not be ready for a "real" marriage, but he was past ready to have Victoria see him in a different way.

But he had to keep his thoughts and emotions to himself for now. The last thing she needed was him pushing anything more on her. Besides the fact she was saving him, she was coming out of a humiliating engagement to some prick who didn't know what a treasure he'd had.

When Stefan had initially learned of the breakup, he'd

immediately called, but in typical Victoria fashion, she'd assured him she was fine…hurt and angry, but she'd be okay.

And looking at her now, she was definitely more than okay.

Her long, strapless ice-blue chiffon gown was simple, yet so elegant and so beautifully molded to her slender curves, Stefan's palms itched to touch her. Years of friendship prevented him. Added to that, they'd never ventured into anything intimate. Either she'd been in a relationship or he'd been…preoccupied himself.

"You look beautiful, Victoria." He extended his hand toward her, pleased when she took it. "You'll be the perfect queen."

Her smile was genuine, but her eyes instantly darted to the waiting servant in the corner wearing a black tux. "I was hoping to have some time alone with you."

While he loved those words coming from her mouth, he knew she just wanted to talk. He squeezed her hand and gave a nod to his employee. Once they were alone, Victoria laughed.

"That's the second time you've nodded and someone has done what you wanted. You sure this prince-soon-to-be-king title isn't going to your head?"

Stefan shrugged, leading her to the table for two on the balcony. "They know what my needs are, so words are usually unnecessary. Besides, I'd much rather spend my evening with my stunning friend than boring staff. I have too many responsibilities with my title. I want to have the down time with you."

"Wow, I'm one rank above boring and responsibilities. You're such a charmer, it's no wonder you couldn't get another woman to marry you." She patted his arm and sighed. "I just hope my family understands my actions."

"We can't tell anyone that this is a paper marriage, Victoria." He turned her to face him, making her look him in the eye to know just how serious this situation was. "I cannot risk my title on the slip of a tongue."

He knew the strong bond she had with her family, knew she'd want to tell them, but he had to at least caution her as to the importance of this arrangement. Other than his personal assistant, Hector, and his brother, no one knew of this secret.

"I have to tell my mother," she insisted. "Trust me. She will know something is up and she will badger us both until she uncovers it if we don't confess now. Besides, she's always loved you."

"As a friend, yes," he agreed, then laughed. "I'm not sure she'll love me to play the son-in-law role."

She looked into his eyes, and a tilt of her perfect lips proved she knew he had a point. "Well, she does consider you a playboy, and she's not too keen on all your tats. But she does love you, Stefan. And she knows how much you mean to me."

He raised a brow. "What about your brothers?"

"I can't lie to them, either," she told him. "But you should know, of all families, mine understands the potential for scandal when secrets slip."

Because he could see the battle she waged with herself and because he knew she wouldn't back down on this, Stefan nodded. "If you promise this goes no further than your immediate family, I will agree to your terms. I trust them as much as I trust you."

"All right, Stefan," she told him, seeing his shoulders relax on his exhale. "My mother will be the silent observer until she sees if I'm just making a rash decision. But, I should warn you, my brothers will have some serious doubts. They will be all over you, especially after what happened with Alex."

Stefan intended to speak with both of her brothers privately. He had a business proposition for them that they may not want to pass up regarding a documentary to clear his parents' names in his mother's untimely death. Some thought his mother had committed suicide, while others were convinced his father had hired someone to have her killed. Both were pure nonsense, and he wanted to go into his reign with no blemishes on his family's name. But he would also reassure Tori's brothers that he would keep her from any more heartbreak or scandal.

"If I had a sister, I'd be very protective," he said with a smile. "I assure you, I can handle them. But we still have to make sure they know our relationship will have to look real, which means they'll have to rein in their behavior when we're out in the spotlight."

Stefan stepped closer, calling himself all kinds of a fool for torturing himself with her familiar floral aroma, her tall, lithe body close to his. But he couldn't help himself. He needed that intimacy, that closeness only Tori could provide. He told himself it was to get used to making this "relationship" seem real. In truth, he wanted to touch her, kiss her…undress her. Possibilities and images swirled around in his mind. Years he'd waited to have a chance with her, and here he was nervous as a virgin on a wedding night.

Na pari i eychi. Dammit. The last time he'd seen her in person two years ago he'd flown to L.A. to attend a benefit art show to raise money for a children's charity. His father was supposed to have gone but had fallen ill at the last minute, so Stefan had stepped in, all too eager to get to L.A. and try his hand at seducing Victoria.

But when he'd arrived at her home, she'd introduced him to some up-and-coming actor whom she'd just begun dating. Stefan had been totally blindsided with the sudden serious nature of the relationship. They talked on the phone, emailed or texted several times a week and no mention had been made of this other man.

Because she'd been beaming with happiness, Stefan had kept his lustful feelings to himself and tried to maintain a physical distance. But now she was here because that jerk, Alex, had humiliated her and crushed her heart.

Stefan had every intention of helping her heal. And now he knew there was no way he could hold his desire back. Eventually, he'd have to confess that he wanted her intimately, paper marriage be damned.

As if just realizing how close they'd gotten, Victoria looked up at him and licked her lips, making them moist and inviting. "I still think we have our work cut out for us. We've never been anything more than best friends."

It was just the opening he'd been waiting for. "Then we better start now making this believable."

In one move, Stefan had his arms snaked around her waist and his lips crushing hers, swallowing her gasp. He hadn't meant to push, really he hadn't, and the second their tastes and bodies collided, he knew this was a bad idea. Now he'd only want her more. But if his life depended on it, he couldn't pull away.

After the briefest of hesitations, she exploded in his arms, kissing him back with a passion he hadn't expected, but he would definitely embrace. For years he'd wondered, dreamed, and here she was kissing him as if she thought of him as a man and not just a friend. Obviously he wasn't the only one who'd imagined this moment.

And that aroused him even more and left him with the knowledge this was something that would have to be discussed sooner rather than later.

Needing more and taking it, he parted her lips with his tongue. Her fingers gripped his biceps as she leaned against him a bit more. And just like he'd imagined for years, she fit against him perfectly.

But before he could take more and allow his hands to roam freely over that killer body, Victoria stepped back, her hand immediately going to cover her lips.

"We can't…that was…"

Stefan closed the gap she'd just created, but not to pick up where she broke off. He intended to reassure her that what just happened was not a mistake. Hell no, it wasn't. An epiphany, yes, but no mistake.

"Interesting how flustered you are after one kiss," he told her with a smile, still tasting her on his lips. "We've kissed before, Tori."

With fingertips still on her lips, Victoria placed her other hand on his chest. "Our kisses were never anything like that."

Because he was a gentleman, at least where the ladies were concerned, he didn't mention the groaning she'd done when his lips had touched hers.

He wanted her to think about what happened… God knows he'd never forget. Her taste and the feel of her body were all burned into his long-term memory. But he needed to move slowly and stay on track.

"My top chef has prepared moussaka for us." He ushered her toward a chair and assisted her into it. "I remember how much you enjoyed Greek cuisine the last time you visited."

Victoria didn't even look at the meal; she merely gazed at him from across the intimate table complete with a small exotic bouquet of flowers and two tall white tapered candles.

"Are you going to pretend that kiss didn't make an impression on you?" she asked, arching a perfectly shaped brow.

Her bold statement had him smiling. Why lie? She knew him too well.

"I wasn't unaffected, Victoria." He held her gaze, needing her to see how serious he was. "Any man would be a fool not to be physically attracted to you. And I'd be a liar to say I hadn't thought of kissing you before."

"I'm not quite sure how to respond to that." She glanced down, then cleared her throat and met his gaze again. "I have to say, it's no wonder you have the reputation you do when you kiss like that. If you pull that stunt in public, the media will never think to question the engagement."

"They'll see nothing but *eros* when they look at us."

"What does that mean?" She laughed. "You always show off by throwing out Greek terms I don't know."

"Passionate, erotic love." Yet again, he held her gaze. "Cameras don't lie, and I know that's what they'll see. I will have no problem making the relationship look real."

Victoria shook her head. "I'm afraid your cockiness and ego may overshadow me in any picture, but I've found that ego charming over the years—must be from growing up with a very alpha brother. Your pride stems from confidence, which is always a redeeming quality in a man. But I know there's a soft side beneath that tough-guy persona. Besides, I've been around onlookers and cameras since I was born, so I actually don't notice them much anymore."

But they notice you.

"I'm glad to hear the media doesn't bother you because we'll have to pose for several formal pictures once we're married," he told her, taking the silver dome lids off the dishes. "Though something you may not be as used to is servants. As queen, you'll have your own assistants who will do anything and everything—from dressing you, to preparing your meals and escorting you anywhere you need to go."

Victoria's perfectly manicured hand stilled on her wine-glass. "I don't need someone to dress me—that's literally my job. And an escort? Is that really necessary? I can't stay here after the marriage until the title is official, Stefan. I have a life, a job to get to. If we need to put up a united front, you'll just have to come to the States and be with me there."

"For how long?" he asked. "With no one reigning as king, I am technically the…stand-in, if you will."

Victoria jerked in surprise. "You're acting as king now? I didn't know this."

He nodded. "Nothing is official until the coronation, but it's law that when the king dies, the oldest son will step in immediately. If something were to happen to me or if I did not marry, the country would go back to Greece. So this is all temporary until I fulfill my duties."

"So do you have to stay here the entire time?" she asked. "Are we going to spend our marriage apart?"

Stefan laughed. "Not at all. We will actually need to make several appearances together both here and in L.A. once we're married to ensure the public believes this is the real deal. What's your schedule like? We will come up with something."

His cell rang, interrupting their conversation. He pulled it from his pocket, glanced at the screen and hit ignore before sliding it back in his pocket…but not before Victoria saw the name of the caller. Hannah.

"Am I going to have to compete for your attention from your harem?" she asked with a laugh, even though inside she was dead serious.

"You will never have to compete for my attention, Tori." His eyes locked on to hers. "You're the only woman in my life right now. Let's get back to your schedule."

She wanted to believe him, so she did. He'd never lied

to her before, and she knew if Stefan told her not to worry, then she shouldn't. But no matter what his actions were, he couldn't force the other women to stop calling him. Surely once they were married the calls would stop. She hoped.

God, she was so skeptical. Damn Alex for making her that way. To doubt Stefan and his loyalty was laughable. He was going to great lengths to keep his country in his family. That act itself spoke volumes of what the word loyalty meant. So, no, she didn't think Stefan would do anything to betray her trust. He was the polar opposite of Alex.

"My workload is crazy." She ran her upcoming schedule through her head. "I'm swamped, but to be fair I'd say we should at least split the time between my home and yours."

"That shouldn't be a problem. I love your family and I love L.A." He moved around the table, unrolled her napkin and placed it in her lap, waiting until her eyes sought his. "But the first two weeks of our marriage, we are to remain in the palace. It's a tradition since the first king of Galini Isle. The country refers to it as the honeymoon phase."

Those expressive blue eyes widened. "I thought a honeymoon was when the couple went off to some undisclosed location to have privacy."

He tried to block the image of having her all to himself for two weeks. The instant erotic thoughts had him shifting back to his seat before he did something really embarrassing.

"This country prides itself on rituals. The *ethos,* or practice, is not to be dismissed."

Victoria stared at him from across the table. He could tell she was getting nervous, so he wanted to take her mind off what was to come.

"Tell me about what you're working on now, other than your own wedding dress," he added with a smile he knew would put her at ease.

In an instant her face softened, the corners of her mouth tilted up into a genuine smile and, yeah, he felt that straight to the gut. How would she look smiling up at him, hair spread across his pillow as he slid into her?

Damn. Now more than ever, he wanted her in his bed.

But he wouldn't pressure her. He'd wait until she was ready to come to him. And he had a feeling from that scorching kiss she'd be more than willing sooner rather than later.

Victoria was different than most women he dated, bedded. She was genuine. Rare in this world to find a woman this sexy and beautiful who didn't flaunt her body or use it to work her way through her goals. He'd always admired how she created a name for herself without riding on the coattails of her iconic family name.

"My brothers are working together on a film depicting our mother's life through the years. And I have to say they've gotten along so well since they put their differences aside and focused on our mother and this movie." She laughed, tossing her golden hair over one shoulder. "They're getting along so well, they even spend off hours together with their families. The kids at least provide a buffer and something else they have in common."

Stefan still couldn't wrap his mind around the fact Victoria's mother, the Grand Dane of Hollywood, gave up a child for adoption nearly forty years ago and the baby turned out to be Anthony Price, the long-time heated rival of Victoria's legitimate brother, Bronson Dane. Talk about confusing.

"I'm sure discovering Anthony was your half brother was quite a shock. I apologize for not being there more for you, but with my dad battling cancer then..."

"You were needed more here, Stefan." Victoria sipped her wine then picked up her fork. "I admit I was shocked, but my brothers took it the hardest. Mom gave Anthony up for adoption when she was starting in her career because she wanted him to have a good life and she wasn't ready for motherhood."

"That's a mature decision."

Victoria's eyes darted to his, and that sweet smile widened. "I knew you'd understand. You were always so open-minded. So many have called her decision selfish."

He shook his head, reaching for his own wineglass. "Selfish would've been keeping the baby, knowing she would put her career first."

She looked as if she wanted to say more, but she cut a piece of her meat and slid the fork between her perfectly painted pale pink lips. And like any man infatuated with a woman—or any man who had breath in his lungs—he agonizingly watched until the fork disappeared and she groaned with delight as her eyelids fluttered. Just when he thought his arousal couldn't get any stronger...

"This is still so amazing," she told him. "You have no idea how grateful I am that you remembered my favorite food."

He knew every single detail about her—her favorite color, the movies she'd seen countless times and even the old diary she kept all of her private thoughts in. He knew more about her than any other woman, which was why they had such a strong bond. He didn't mind listening to her talk about her life. Most other women talked about their lives in an attempt to impress him. Victoria impressed him simply by being there for him, making him smile and expecting nothing from him in return.

"So tell me about this film." He wanted to know more, wanted to support her. "What's your part?"

He also wanted to keep her relaxed, keep her talking all night—since that was his only option for now. Just like during their multiple phone conversations over the years, that sultry voice washed over him, making him wish for things he couldn't have right now. But at the end of this, who knew? Maybe they'd remain married. That would put quite a spin on the whole friends-with-benefits scenario.

He'd never had this type of arrangement before—even that would've been more of a commitment than he'd been willing to give. But for Victoria…hell yes, he'd be interested.

"I've never worked with my family before and never designed costumes for a movie, but I made an exception," she said with a glowing smile. "There's no way I could let another designer do this, not when it's so close to my heart."

"Sounds like you're going to be a busy woman," he told her, cutting into his tender meat.

"The designs are done since filming started a few months ago. But I'm needed on set in case of a malfunction or a last-minute wardrobe switch." She shrugged and sipped her wine. "My team back in L.A. is handling everything right now. My assistant may have to take on a bit more until our wedding is over, though. God, that sounds so strange to say."

He lay his fork down, reached across the table and took her hand. "Thank you for what you're doing for me, for my country. I'll never be able to express my gratitude."

"You've been my best friend since I had braces," she joked. "We may live far apart, but other than my family, you're the closest person in my life." She tightened her grip on his hand and tilted her head with a soft grin. "Besides, you've handed me a dream job designing the gown, and I get to play queen for a few months. Seriously, I'm getting the better end of the bargain."

Stefan laughed. "I wasn't sure you'd agree so easily. I should've known you'd stand by me."

"I admit I have reservations about lying to the public,

to my friends and employees." She shifted in her seat, breaking hold of their hands. "But I'm honored to stand by you. It's not often we find someone in our life we can truly depend on."

He hated the loss of her hands in his and the hurt in her tone. "I was afraid you'd be vulnerable since the breakup, afraid you'd shut this idea down before I could explain my reasons."

"Maybe I am still vulnerable." She chewed her lip, eyes darting down before coming back up to meet his. "But I won't let my heart get in the way of my life again, and I know I'm safe with you."

"Absolutely, Victoria." He'd die before he let her get hurt. "You know how much I care for you."

He admired Victoria for standing tall, not cowering behind her family when it would be so easy to do so after having her world ripped out from under her. He knew firsthand how hard life was to live in the public eye. The media was ruthless, and if the story wasn't there, they made one up and damn the consequences. Reputations could be damaged and ruined with just a small dose of ink from the written word and could take years to restore…if restoration was even possible.

Because of accusations thrown at his family after the death of his mother, he more than anyone knew how fast a reputation could be ruined.

The rest of the meal moved quickly through some laughter and easy conversation, but Stefan couldn't get his mind off that scorching kiss. He wanted his hands on her again, whether to torture himself or just have a brief moment of instant gratification, he didn't know. But he knew how to rectify the situation.

"Dance with me," he told her when she'd placed her napkin beside her now-empty plate.

"Right now?" She glanced around the spacious, moon-lit balcony. "There's no music."

He came to his feet, moved into the master suite and within seconds had the surround sound filtering out into the night. When he came back through the open double doors, he extended his hand.

"Dance with me," he repeated, pleased when her hand slid into his. "We should practice before the official royal wedding dance after the ceremony. It's been years since we danced together."

She came to her feet, and he took no time in pulling her body against his. Wrapping his arm around her waist, Stefan was more than eager to have her invade his personal space.

"No wonder you're the Playboy Prince," she murmured, her breath tickling his cheek. "You're very good at this. I can't imagine how you'd be pouring on the charm if I weren't an old childhood friend."

He eased his head back but kept their bodies flush and swaying to the soft, soothing beat. "I promised to keep this simple, to give you all control in the end. I never go against my word."

She smiled. "I'm sure you wouldn't, but I also know your reputation. And I was on the receiving end of that kiss."

"You weren't just on the receiving end...you were an active participant."

Victoria's breath caught. "That's a...pretty accurate statement, but we've been friends too long for us to let lust cloud our judgment. Sleeping together would not be wise, Stefan."

He leaned in close to her ear and whispered, "Who says?"

Her hand tightened in his as she turned to look him in the eye, their lips barely a breath apart. "I don't know if we're getting swept up into this idea of pretending or this physical pull is stemming from seeing each other after such a long time apart, but I can't risk losing your friendship just because of this sudden attraction."

"I don't know how sudden this is, at least on my end." He kissed her lips slightly and eased back. "I can't deny my desire for you, but I do promise not to do anything you don't want."

"I'm going to hold you to that," she told him. "I know this situation will be hard for you."

He laughed at her choice of wording. "You have no idea."

Three

Sliding a hand down the fitted satin bodice, Victoria stared at her reflection in the floor-to-ceiling mirror. The gown was perfect, and she was so thankful she'd made a handful of wedding dresses in her downtime just to keep on hand for when she decided to branch out and start a bridal line.

No one had seen any of the finished designs, but she'd told her mother where they were and to ship them all. Victoria had taken a couple apart and pieced them the way she wanted. Her mother had only grumbled and complained a little when she learned Victoria wouldn't be returning to L.A. before the wedding.

And that conversation was a whole different issue.

Of all the times she'd fantasized about her wedding day, both as a child and an adult, she'd never envisioned marrying Stefan under these extremely strange circumstances.

Yes, she'd pictured a few times how it would be if

they'd taken their friendship to another level. She wasn't too proud to admit that she'd fantasized his kisses a time or two…and that was *before* he'd taken her into his arms and captured her mouth, showing her exactly what she'd been missing all these years. How could she delete that arousing sensation from her memory? How could she get his taste from her lips?

And why would she want to erase such pleasure?

Because he was a playboy, and even though she believed him when he said he'd be faithful, that didn't stop his previous lovers from calling him.

So here she stood, confused, intrigued and ready to take a giant life-altering step toward marriage while two of Stefan's royal assistants adjusted the veil around her hair. Another assistant stood in front, touching up her blush and powder for at least the third time in an hour. Couldn't have the soon-to-be queen of Galini Isle looking peaked.

God, she sincerely hoped she didn't have to do this for every appearance as queen. Thankfully Stefan had assured her she wasn't required to do too much. Even though she was from an iconic Hollywood family, she didn't crave the limelight.

"Ladies, could I have a moment alone with my daughter?"

Victoria adjusted her gaze in the mirror to her mother, who stood just inside the arched doorway to one of the many suites in the royal palace.

Obviously comfortable with taking orders, the middle-aged ladies scurried away at Olivia's request. Once the door was closed, Olivia moved in behind Victoria and smiled.

"Are you sure this is what you want to do?"

Stamping down any doubts that rose deep within her, Victoria returned her mother's questioning smile. "I'm sure, Mom. Stefan needs me, and perhaps at this point in my life, I need him. He's my best friend."

"But in the past few years you've scarcely seen each other."

Victoria shrugged. "Distance doesn't matter. Not with us. You know we talk nearly every day, and it's nice to know I am the one he trusts. We have a bond, Mom. A bond stronger than most marriages, actually. This is just another chapter in our friendship. I was engaged for romantic love once. This time I'm doing it for another kind of love."

"That's what worries me, my darling." Olivia pulled the veil over Victoria's face, then placed her hands on her shoulders, giving a gentle squeeze. "As a mother I worry your heart will get mixed up in this. He's a wonderful man to you…as a friend. I worry that in the end Stefan will come out getting everything he wants and you will have just another heartache."

She'd hadn't told her mother she and Stefan had shared numerous scorching kisses. Opening up about that certainly wouldn't alleviate any worries. Best to keep some things private…especially until she could figure them out herself. Arousal and confusion combined made for a very shaky ground.

"I'm not worried at all," she assured her mother, knowing it wasn't completely a lie. "He's given me an open end to this marriage. I may love being queen or I may want to return to my life in L.A. once all this is over. We'll put in a few appearances once we're married and this will all seem legitimate. Neither of us will be hurt. We're both too strong to let this arrangement destroy us."

"You're fooling yourself if you think this will be that simple." Olivia tilted her head, quirking a brow. "I've seen Stefan's charm, Victoria. I've witnessed how he's looked at you since I arrived here. I've also taken notice how he's looked at you over the years. He's got an infatuation that I believe is beyond a friendship. There's no way the two of you can play house and not get tangled up in each other. He's one very attractive man. Lust clouds even the best of judgments."

Intrigued, Victoria wondered just what her mother saw over the years from Stefan. Lust? Desire? This past month had brought to light a deeper side to their relationship. Beyond the steamy kisses, Stefan had been attentive to each and every one of her needs. He'd had her favorite foods prepared, would bring her a freshly picked flower from the gardens as she was working, insisted on breaks to walk along the beach so she could relax. He'd been the prefect Prince Charming…all because he knew her better than she knew herself in some ways.

Victoria shook off the questions regarding just how deep Stefan's emotions were and the fact he'd made it perfectly clear he'd had thoughts of her as more than a friend.

"Mother, his appeal and his charm are nothing new to me. And no matter how you think he looks at me, I assure you we are only marrying for the sake of the country and to help launch my bridal line."

Though she knew from his promising kisses and honest words that was false. But since she was still reeling from that fact herself, that was another tidbit she'd keep inside. She had enough "what-ifs" swirling around in her mind without adding her mother's into the mix.

"Well, he'd be a fool not to think of you as more," Olivia retorted. "And since he's asked you to marry him, he's no fool. I've always wondered if the two of you would end up together. I can honestly say this is not how I'd envisioned it."

Nerves swirled around Victoria's stomach. As if having the title of princess weren't crazy and nerve wracking enough, she'd be sharing a bedroom with Stefan for months. There was no way to deny they had chemistry and no way she could lie to herself and say she hadn't replayed those kisses over and over.

Victoria turned away from the mirror, taking her mother's hands. "I'm going into this with my eyes wide open, Mom. With Alex I was blindsided, but Stefan isn't using me. He asked for my help at a time when there was no one else he could trust. And there's nothing that can damage my heart here because my heart isn't getting involved. Stefan won't hurt me."

Olivia looked as if she wanted to say something more, but Victoria squeezed her hands, unable to discuss this delicate topic any further with her mother. "Trust me."

With misty eyes full of worry, Olivia's gaze roamed over Victoria before she stepped back and sighed. "The last time I was at this castle I was playing a queen myself." She laughed. "I didn't even compare to how beautiful you look. Must be the difference between acting and real life. I can't believe how long ago that was."

Tears clogged her throat as Victoria hugged her mother, not caring about the crinkling of the silk fabrics.

"You were stunning in that film, Mom. Besides, I'm acting, too, aren't I? Playing queen for Stefan so his country will remain under his family's control. Ironic, isn't it? I always swore I'd never go into acting."

Olivia eased back, placing her hands over Victoria's bare shoulders. "You'll be queen for real, my darling. What happens inside the bedroom may not be real, but your title will be. Have you thought of that?"

As if she could think of little else.

Okay, well that was a lie. She'd thought immensely about the fact her fiancé/best friend had her stomach in knots. On one hand she was thrilled to be helping him obtain his goal as he helped with hers. She found herself admiring him for his determination to take what was rightfully his. Most other times she didn't think of him as a prince or king at all…and now, well, she thought of him as a man. A very sexy, very powerful man. Not powerful in the sense that he'd rule a country, but powerful in the sense that he'd dominate a room the moment he entered. He'd control any conversation, and he'd most certainly take charge in the bedroom.

And that path was precisely where her mind did not need to travel. She was letting her thoughts run rampant because of a few heated kisses. Very hot, very scorching, very toes-curling-in-her-stilettos kisses. Just because she'd once wondered "what-if," didn't mean that anything could stem from this arranged marriage. One day at a time is how she would have to approach this. She couldn't afford to let lust steal the greatest friendship she'd ever had.

But she knew her emotions were teetering on a precipice and it would take just a small nudge for Stefan to push her over the edge and right into his bed.

"Stefan and I have discussed everything, Mom." Victoria offered a comforting smile, hoping she wasn't lying to her mother. "I'm pretty sure we have this under control. He's assured me that he won't let me get in over my head. I'm basically an accessory for him at this point."

Accessory. She hated that term, but what else could a wife to one of the world's most powerful, sexy men be called? He didn't need her to do any public speaking or head up any charities, not in the short time they planned to be married, so the demeaning name, unfortunately, fit.

"I had to keep your brothers out of here, you know." Olivia stepped back, smoothing a hand down her raw silk, pale blue floor-length gown. "They insisted on making sure you were okay, so I had to assure them I'd check and report back."

Victoria laughed, turning to face the mirror and glance

at her reflection once more. "You can tell my self-imposed bodyguards that I am not having cold feet and I'm perfectly fine. They should be worrying about their wives standing up beside me in front of millions of people watching on TV. I swear, last I saw of Mia and Charlotte, they were so nervous I thought they were going to pass out."

"I'm going to see them now," Olivia said. "They will be fine, so I just want you to concentrate and worry about you. This is your day, no matter what the circumstances."

Olivia's hands cupped Victoria's shoulders as she laid her cheek against hers to look at their reflection in the mirror. "You're beautiful, Victoria. Stefan may change his mind about you having control in the end. He may not want to let you go once his title is secure."

"The Playboy Prince?" Victoria joked, using his nickname. "He'll let me go so he can shuffle back into the crowd of swooning women and place me back on that friend shelf."

Their kisses replayed once again in her mind. Could they go back to being just friends? Would she want them to? They hadn't even lived together for their allotted six months and already she had fantasized about taking those kisses further. How could she not? They were definite stepping stones to more promising, erotic things.

God, in heaven. What had she gotten herself into? She swore she wouldn't put her heart on the line again, but how could she not when Stefan needed her? Maybe she needed him, too. More than she ever realized.

Hundreds of guests filed through the grounds at Alexander Palace on the edge of the emerald ocean. Cameras were positioned at every angle to capture each moment as guests entered the Grand Ballroom. The world watched as the next king and queen of Galini Isle were about to wed in what the media had dubbed the most romantic wedding of the century. Obviously the mysterious bride angle had paid off.

Many of the headlines leading up to the nuptials had been amusing. Stefan's personal favorite: Playboy Prince Finally Settles Down.

The media could mock him all they wanted. He'd show them just how serious he was about this wedding...even if the idea of being wed scared the hell out of him.

He focused his eyes to the end of the aisle and his chest constricted, breath left his lungs.

Stefan couldn't think. At this moment, he couldn't even recall the exact reason he'd asked Victoria to marry him, but he was most thankful he had.

She floated—yes, floated—down the aisle like a glorious angel coming to rescue him, wearing an original-design gown that dipped just enough in the front to have his imagination running into overdrive, while still looking classy. Two strands of pearls draped over each of her toned biceps, hinting that they'd once been straps that a lover had slid off her slender shoulders. And damn if he didn't want to be that lover.

The dress cut perfectly into the curve of her waist and fell straight to the ground. A shimmery veil shielded her face, and Stefan couldn't wait to lift it, to kiss his bride and get another taste of the flavor he'd come to crave from her lips.

Stefan knew his best friend was a walking fantasy that every man would give his last dying breath for. Well, except for that bastard she'd been engaged to. Stefan straightened his shoulders and smiled. He hoped the jerk was watching his TV and regretting letting such an amazingly talented, beautiful woman out of his life.

Victoria's gaze met his, and Stefan's heart clenched as

a wide smile spread across her face from behind the iridescent veil.

"You've chosen a beautiful queen, Stefan. Victoria is perfect."

Stefan merely nodded at his brother's whispered compliment. Mikos Alexander stood as best man, and Stefan knew his brother breathed a sigh of relief when he'd discovered the country would remain under the Alexander name. Stefan had worried when his brother had married a divorcée, thus preventing him from claiming the throne, but Victoria was a perfect fit.

Never in his life would he forget how she'd stepped up to save him, selflessly and radiantly. Stefan moved forward, taking Victoria's hands in his.

She squeezed them before turning to the priest. In a blur their vows were said and the gold heirloom rings exchanged. As Stefan lifted her veil, Victoria chewed on her bottom lip as if nerves were getting the best of her.

"You may kiss your bride."

Stefan wasted no time in capturing Victoria's lips. Though he couldn't claim her mouth the way he wanted to, considering there were television cameras on them and millions of people watching to see how the Playboy Prince would act, he was still just as affected by that one, tender kiss as he had been when they'd been alone on his balcony and shared their first passionate encounter. He'd taken every opportunity since then to steal more…each one always sweeter than the last and leaving him wanting.

Easing her soft lips from his, Victoria's gaze landed on his. "Good thing we've been practicing," she whispered with a slight grin.

He smiled and placed a quick peck on her lips once more before taking her hand and turning to the crowd.

"I present to you Prince and Princess Alexander," the priest exclaimed. "Galini Isle's next king and queen."

Applause broke out and Stefan glanced toward Victoria's family seated in the front row. Her brothers were smiling, but a hint of caution clouded their eyes, and her mother, the grand Hollywood icon, had unshed tears and a smile on her face...a face full of worry.

Stefan couldn't feel any guilt right now. How could he? He was going to be king and Victoria was going to stand by his side. Finally he could explore his feelings further because while he knew he wanted to be with her in more than just a friendly way, he also wasn't sure just how much of a commitment he could offer after the six months if she decided to remain in their marriage. He did, after all, get his reputation for a reason.

Right now, though, he had to concentrate on his title and gaining his country's confidence by eliminating the black mark over his family's name. That was his first order of business. But seducing Victoria would certainly be a welcome distraction, even if a challenge, and one he couldn't turn down. Especially now that he'd had more than a few tastes.

As he and his new bride made their way back up the aisle, Stefan beamed knowing he'd just married the most beautiful, intelligent, sexy woman. And for the next six months, and maybe even more if she chose to stay, Victoria was not only his best friend, she was his wife...and possibly lover.

Arousal shot through him. He wasn't known as the Playboy Prince for nothing. Seduction had always been his partner in crime.

Victoria had never smiled so much in all her thirty-two years combined as she had tonight. Between the professional royal photo shoot with Stefan's brother and wife and Victoria's family and then of the two of them alone, then the grand parade after the ceremony where they were shown off through the entire seaside town, she'd almost convinced herself this was real.

Now they were at the reception back inside the grand ballroom of the palace, and Stefan held her in his arms as they danced their first dance as Prince and Princess Alexander.

The spacious room with high, stained-glass ceilings had been transformed from the ceremony and set up to host the reception in the hours they'd been gone for the traditional wedding parade.

A dance floor had appeared surrounded by elegant white silk draped between tall, thick columns. White silk also adorned each table, as did slender crystal vases with a spray of white flowers and clear glass beads in each.

Thousands of twinkling lights created a magical, fairy-tale theme. Ice sculptures and champagne fountains were in abundance. The ballroom had shifted into something from a dream and something fit for royalty.

And while so much beauty surrounded her, she couldn't think of anything else but the man in her arms. Her doubts, her confusion, it all slid into the very back of her mind as the slow, classical ballad played and she swayed against him.

His warmth, his familiar masculine scent and the powerful hold he had on her all made her want to put her head on his shoulder and relish the moment. So she did. He'd held her numerous times over the years. But she knew in her heart this time was different.

With a sigh, she closed her eyes, letting him lead in their dance, and rested her head just for a moment on one broad, muscular shoulder. The man was the proverbial good time, but right now she wanted to just lean on him, to draw from his strength and courage.

Her cheek rested against his smooth, silky sash. Victoria had known he'd wear his best royal dress for the ceremony, but her Prince Charming had truly been a sight to see, waiting at the end of the white-petal-covered aisle. It wasn't often in their years together she saw him in person dressed as a prince. Normally they were just hanging out in casual clothes. But with his tailored black suit with shiny gold double-breasted buttons, glossy black shoes, and a wide, blue sash crossing from shoulder to opposite hip, he exuded bad-boy prince. She knew beneath all the impressive gold buttons and fringe-capped shoulders lay a great deal of body art molding over and around his chiseled arms, chest and back. Sexy didn't even begin to describe her man.

Medals, which stemmed from charity work to his family's crest and various other ranks, also adorned one side of his jacket. The blue from his sash matched his eyes perfectly, and he couldn't look more fit for a royal role than if he were the star in one of her brothers' films.

The designer in her should've made notes on how well the lines were cut in his suit, but the woman in her was too busy admiring the view. Hey, he may be her best friend, but he was still one magnificently built man and she'd be a fool not to notice. But she'd been noticing more and more in the past month leading up to their nuptials. Was she getting caught up in the wedding, or was she beginning to see him as more of a man? He'd always been charming, but recently he'd become…irresistible. And her desire for him was starting to consume her.

The glamorous ceremony was something she'd remember for the rest of her life. With celebrities, other royalty and every media outlet on hand to snap thousands of pictures, the scene was something out of a modern-day fairy tale.

"You made a beautiful bride, Victoria," he murmured. "I'm one lucky prince."

She raised her head, looked him in the eyes and smiled. "Oh, I'm pretty lucky, too. I'm living every little girl's dream by marrying royalty and living in a palace."

"Only for two weeks," he reminded her. "After our honeymoon phase, we'll travel to L.A. I'm anxious to see you at work and visit with your family. It's grown considerably since I was there last."

"I'm anxious to get back, too, but I don't mind playing hooky. Not when I'm living a fantasy life."

"Speaking of fantasy," he murmured, raking his eyes down to where her cleavage nestled against his tux. "Have I told you how amazing you look today?"

"You're letting your reputation take over," she joked, though nerves danced in her belly at the hunger in his eyes. "My eyes are up here."

"Oh, I know where your eyes are." He smiled, meeting her gaze. "But I'm enjoying the entire view of my beautiful bride."

He wanted her and he wasn't hinting anymore, which only made her even more intrigued.

Obviously the ball was in her court. Game on.

"And my reputation has nothing to do with what I'm feeling right now." He pulled her body closer to his as he spun her in a wide circle around the perimeter of the dance floor. "Trust me, I'm the envy of every man around the world. I nearly swallowed my tongue when you came down the aisle."

"As a designer, I take that as a compliment." She laughed. "As a woman, I'm thrilled to know I have that effect on someone."

He shifted slightly against her, a wicked smile on his face. "Oh, I'm not unaffected."

Mercy. No, he wasn't. How had this dance gotten so far out of control? And why did she care? How could she avoid the fact Stefan was so open with his feelings? Should she even attempt to hide that she'd been thinking of him in a new light, as well? Those "what-if" thoughts from years ago were now more realistic and...obtainable.

Did she dare try to move to the next level with Stefan? The idea made her nervous and excited and, most of all, curious. All of her giddy emotions overshadowed the fear and doubts.

Their wedding night was fast approaching. Only hours until the reception drew to a close and they would be alone. Perfect timing?

Well played, Fate. Well played.

"You're blushing again," he told her, stealing a quick kiss. "I know everyone is watching us and the cameras are still rolling, but that kiss was purely selfish. I'm finding it hard to keep my hands off you, Victoria."

"Stefan." Her heart beat against his chest. "I'm not sure...I mean, yes, I'm finding myself more drawn to you than just as a friend, but won't taking another step here make this arrangement more complicated?"

"We won't know unless we try," he told her, nipping at her lips again. "I'd hate to let an opportunity pass me by. What if sleeping together is the best decision we ever made?"

"Is that where we're headed?" she asked, already knowing what he'd say.

Unfortunately, she kept hearing her mother's warning about getting her heart entangled in this man. Fortunately her heart had already been trampled and crushed, so there was no more to break. And she knew Stefan would never hurt her.

"How much longer are we staying?" she asked as the orchestra slowed the song down toward the end.

He smiled. "Anxious to get me all alone?"

Considering they'd known each other for so long and he knew her better than most people, he had a love for his family that rivaled her own and his loyalty to his country made her heart melt, she may have a little trouble avoiding his charms.

Oh, the hell with it. Why dance around this attraction? Six months of torture would be pure…well, torture. People did friends with benefits all the time, right? Granted she never had, but Stefan was special and he so obviously wanted her, which was good because she couldn't deny it any longer.

"Maybe I am," she told him with a grin, knowing she was playing with fire.

As the song ended, he pulled her close, close enough she could feel just how turned on he was, and whispered in her ear, "I've been waiting for you to say that. What do you say we go start on our honeymoon?"

And with that thrilling promise, he tugged on her hand and they slipped through the crowd and out the double doors.

Four

As he led her through the long, marble hallways, Victoria didn't care about the doubts and fears swirling around in her head, nor did she care about the fact she'd just left hundreds of guests in the main ballroom.

What she did care about was how much farther they had to go until they reached their destination because she wanted Stefan, and the realization of just how much she wanted him both thrilled and scared her. This sexual tension had been brewing before she'd come to Galini Isle a month ago—there had to have been an underlying current or she wouldn't have been so eager to have his mouth on hers when they'd shared their first kiss…or the several scorchers that followed.

But she couldn't think about anything from their past now or she'd remember that this man was her best friend… and he was about to become her lover. Something about taking their relationship to a level of intimacy aroused her even more. She could analyze later all the reasons this wasn't a wise move…but right now she didn't care. She. Wanted. Him.

When Stefan pulled her through a set of heavy double doors, she blinked into the darkness, trying to get her bearings, and wondered if they'd just entered his master suite.

His room was on this floor, but she'd thought it was farther down the wing. She'd been in his suite a few times, but for purely innocent reasons…as opposed to now, when the reason was a bit more naughty.

She remembered his king-size bed with navy silk sheets. The bed had always sat in the middle of his suite, dominating the room.

A man like Stefan with his bad-boy behavior wouldn't have something as boring as a bed in a corner. He'd want that bed and all the action taking place there to be center stage.

Stefan eased the door shut and with a swift click, slid the lock into place. He immediately set the lights to a soft glow.

Good, that would help her nerves if she didn't have to have spotlights on her. While Stefan had seen her in swimsuits, he'd never seen her fully naked—not for lack of his playful trying at times, but she'd always written off his silly remarks as jokes. Had there been genuine want behind his words?

Victoria turned around, amazed at the room spread out before her, and she laughed. This was his idea of a romantic wedding night? Stefan never failed to amaze and surprise her.

"If someone starts looking for us, they'd check my wing first," Stefan told her. He slid off his jacket, flinging it to the side without taking his eyes off her as he stalked— yes, stalked—right toward her. "They'd never think to look in the theater."

How many women had he snuck into this room or any other room in this magnificent palace, for that matter? She knew the media really exploited his bachelor status and the fact that he enjoyed women, but she also knew most of their accounts were accurate. Stefan never made any apologies for the man he was, and that's perhaps why people loved him so much. He was honest to a fault and sinfully charming.

Past women didn't matter to her. He was her husband now, and what he did before this moment was ridiculous for her to even entertain. She wasn't a virgin, and they weren't committing themselves to anything permanent. They were adults, best friends, and they were acting on these newfound sexual feelings. So why analyze it to death when there was one hot, sexy, aroused prince standing before her looking like he wanted to devour her? No woman would be stupid enough to turn that invitation down... especially from her own husband.

Wedding night or not, this would be one experience she'd never forget. She needed the awkwardness and doubts to get out of her mind because she wanted to concentrate on the here and now.

"You look beautiful." He closed the gap between them, running a fingertip along her exposed collarbone. Shivers coursed through her at his provocative, simple touch. "The way this dress molds to your body makes me wonder if you could possibly fit anything between this satin and your skin."

Her eyes roamed over his bronzed face and his heavy-lidded eyes as his finger continued to tickle its way back and forth across her collarbone, teasing her, tempting her. If one finger had that much of an impact on her senses, who knew what a full-bodied touch would do.

"I'm a designer," she told him, reaching up to slide one

button at a time through the hole of his dress shirt. "It's my job to make things fit and create an illusion of perfection."

His hands glided down her arms, slid to her hips and tugged her until she was pelvis to pelvis with him. Chills raced over her body, the promise of what was to come making her shiver.

"I'd say fitting won't be a problem, and there's no illusion." His gaze dropped to her lips, to her breasts pressed against his chest and back up to her face. "There's plenty of perfection without the tricks you may practice as a designer. I've known you for years, Tori, and there's nothing imperfect about you."

The attack on her mouth was fierce and oh so welcoming. The man knew what he wanted, and the fact that he wanted her made her feel alive again for the first time in months. Maybe that made her shallow, but she needed to feel beautiful, sexy and, yes, even needed.

Stefan may be her best friend, but right now she wasn't having thoughts of friendship. Desire shot through her as she pressed her body against his.

How many times had she kissed him, hugged him? How could she have taken for granted such a hard body?

Victoria eased back, continuing her work on his shirt. Stefan slid her hands away and pulled it over his head, ignoring the last few buttons that weren't undone.

That chest. She'd seen it many times before, but she hadn't seen this fresh ink and his finely sculpted body in some time. Victoria glided her hands up over his chiseled abs and outlined the new tattoo over one of his pecs.

"How come every time I see you, you have new ink?" she murmured, tracing the detailed dragon.

"I like the art," he said simply. "Let's discuss tattoos later. How the hell do I get you out of this thing on your head and this dress without hurting one of us?"

Victoria laughed, thankful he'd lightened the mood. This is what she needed. The playful side of Stefan. The side that always made her smile. Of course, she had a feeling he'd be showing her another side that would make her smile even more in a minute.

She reached up, sliding several pins from her hair and placing them on the counter along the wall. After removing the diamond tiaralike headband and veil, she laid it out along the counter, as well.

She realized she was taking her time. In part she wanted this moment to last. But she also couldn't help being a little afraid of where this epic step would take them.

"I wish I'd designed a dress that could just peel off," she told him, reaching behind her. "But I'm afraid there's a zipper, and you're going to have to get it."

She turned, giving him her back but throwing him a glance over her shoulder. "Sorry I wasn't thinking ahead."

"Oh, this is my pleasure," he told her with a crooked smile and a wink.

When his fingers came up to her back and slid to the zipper, she couldn't suppress the shiver that raced through her. Arousal quickly overrode her awkwardness and doubts that threatened to creep in.

As the material parted in the back, Victoria shimmied her arms slightly so the dress fell down the front of her, leaving her standing in a strapless bustier that lifted her meager chest into something voluptuous and enticing...at least she hoped that's how he saw her.

Stefan didn't know which god deserved credit for making Victoria realize that the two of them sleeping together wasn't a mistake, but he'd graciously drop to his knees and thank him.

"Oh," he whispered when she turned around. "Had I

known you looked that good, I would've insisted you go without the dress during the ceremony."

Just as he'd hoped, Victoria laughed. That rich, seductive sound washed over him. As much as his body wanted hers, he also wanted her to be comfortable. He couldn't allow any uneasiness to settle between them.

"This royal wedding would've been talked about until the end of time," she joked. "Besides, since I'm the designer, I would've looked rather strange coming down the aisle without a gown."

"Strange?" he asked, tracing the top of the silk material that covered her tan breasts. "No. Sexy as hell and the fantasy of every man? Absolutely."

Victoria bit her lip but held his gaze.

"Don't," he told her. "Don't think. Don't worry. Just… feel."

She shivered beneath his touch, and Stefan wished she knew the effect she had on him was just as potent. He had shivers racing through his body just thinking of what they were about to do. God, he'd waited so long to make love to her and here they were.

Of course, all those times he'd envisioned them sleeping together, he never once pictured her in a wedding dress beforehand.

She inhaled, causing her chest to press deeper into his touch. The rustling of the dress had him pulling back just enough so she could step out of it.

"One of us still has too many clothes on." She smiled, picking up her dress, and, with great care, she laid it over the back of one of the oversized leather theater chairs. "Normally you're so eager to show off your body. Are you getting stage fright, Prince Alexander?"

A naughty smile spread across her face. She was literally a sinful sight before him, but he'd never been known for being a choir boy.

"Oh, I'm not afraid of anything." He wasted no time in stripping down to his black boxer briefs. "I was merely admiring the view of my sexy new wife."

When Victoria's eyes raked down his body, pausing at his throbbing erection, then back up to meet his eyes, she bit her lip. Nerves were getting to her and he refused to let her overthink this.

"You were starting to relax. Come on, Tori." He reached out, sliding his hands up her bare arms and stepping into her. "You've seen me in swimming trunks skimpier than this."

Her eyes locked on to his, her hands coming up to rest on his chest. "True, but this is so much different. I just don't want this to change us…you know, afterward."

He kissed her lips, gently, slowly. Kissed his way along her jawline, down the long, slender column of her throat, pleased when she tilted her head back and groaned. He'd dreamed of this moment for so long. Longer than he liked to admit, even to himself. He'd never allowed any woman to have such control over his mind or his fantasies.

"Nothing will change," he assured her between kisses. "Unless it's better. And I'm positive in the next few minutes, things between us will get a whole lot better."

Victoria's arms circled around his neck as her head turned, her mouth colliding with his.

And that's when the dam burst. His, hers. Did it matter? He'd wanted her for years, and whether she'd wanted him that long or she'd just decided it in the past few weeks they'd been together he didn't know, but he did know he was going to have her. Now. Here.

Stefan encircled her waist with his hands, slid them on down to the slight flare of her hips and slowly walked her to the bar in the back of the room. When he hoisted her up onto to the counter, she laughed.

"In a hurry?" she mocked with a teasing grin.

"I've waited for this for a long time," he told her, staring at her moist, swollen lips. "I always swore if we ever came to this moment I'd take my time. But right now I can't wait another minute."

Her smiled weakened as she held his gaze. "I think I've been waiting for this for a long time, too. I just never realized…"

Stefan didn't want a confession, not now. He didn't want her to explore her feelings…or, God forbid, try to uncover his. He just wanted Victoria.

He stepped between her gloriously spread legs, slid his palms up her smooth, bare thighs and thumbed along the edge of her white silk panties.

When she hooked her thumbs through the thin straps and shifted from side to side to ease them off, he gratefully helped her slide them down her long, toned legs.

She reached around behind the bustier.

"Leave it," he ordered. "I like how you look right now."

With tousled hair, bare skin from the waist down and that white silk bustier molded to her curves and pushing her breasts up…yeah, he liked her just the way she was. All sexy and rumpled and ready for him.

"I want to feel your skin on mine," she told him, still working on the back of her lingerie.

How could he argue with her defense? No man with air in his lungs would turn down bare breasts.

"Then let me help," he offered.

He eased his hands around and, one by one, each hook-and-eye closure popped open. Thankfully it was cut low, so there weren't very many. When the garment was fully open, he stepped back.

Victoria held on to the front of the material still covering her breasts. "You're sure?" she asked.

Without a word, he brushed her hands aside, took the bustier and threw it over his shoulder. And finally, she was completely and utterly naked. And completely and utterly his.

He palmed one breast in each hand as he captured her lips once more. Arching her back, Victoria leaned into his touch, his kiss, and let out a soft, low groan.

Her arms came around his shoulders, her fingertips toying with the ends of his hair on the nape of his neck. She shifted, scooting to the edge of the counter, and wrapping her legs around his waist. Stefan let go of her breasts long enough to shuck his boxers and kick them to the side. With her legs around him, he palmed her backside and lifted her off the bar until she was settled right above him.

His eyes searched hers as he walked a few steps to the nearest wall, where he rested her back. He stayed still, waiting for any hint of a signal that she was uncomfortable or not ready to go through with this.

Stopping would kill him, but even with his hormones in overdrive he'd stop if she said the word. But when he looked in her eyes, all he saw was desire. Heavy lids, half-covered vibrant blue eyes…eyes that were focused on his lips.

At the same time he sealed his mouth to hers, he slid her down to take him fully. The flood of emotions within him was indescribable. Her body all around his, the soft feel of her skin, the fresh, floral aroma and her tiny little gasps had him nearly embarrassing himself and drawing their first encounter to an abrupt, climactic halt.

He moved within her, slowly, then, when her hips rocked faster, he increased the pace.

She tore her lips from his. "Please."

If she liked things fast and sweaty, they could very well kill each other before the six months were up because she was speaking his language.

Victoria gripped his shoulders, flung her head back and closed her eyes. That long column of her neck begged to be licked, savored. He nibbled his way up, then back down and nestled his face between her breasts.

"Stefan...."

Yeah, he knew. She was close, which was a relief because so was he. He normally prided himself on his stamina, but one touch from Victoria and he was ready to explode. He didn't take the time or the energy to think that this had never happened before. There was something about his Tori....

Her legs tightened around his waist as her whole body stiffened. He grabbed her face, forced her to look at him and for the briefest of seconds, when their eyes met, he felt a twinge of something he didn't recognize. But he certainly wasn't taking the time to figure it out, not when he had a sexy, wild woman bucking in his arms, finding her release.

Capturing her lips while she came undone around him was all he wanted. His tongue slid in and out, mimicking their bodies. His own release built and before he knew it he, too, let go. He gave in to Victoria's sweet body, allowing her to take him—her welcoming arms enveloping him and her soft words calming him.

Never had he experienced anything like this before. But he knew that the next several months with his best friend-turned-wife would be nothing if not life-altering.

And that epiphany scared the hell out of him.

Victoria sat in the oversize cozy leather chair in the palace theater waiting for the movie to start and eating from a tub of popcorn. Only moments ago the man beside her rocked her world in a way she hadn't known possible, and now he pretended as if their giant step beyond friendship were perfectly normal.

After they'd nearly killed each other in a bout of heated, frenzied sex, she'd thrown on his tux shirt instead of her gown. He'd slipped back into his pants, leaving his gloriously tanned and tattooed chest bare. He nearly had a whole sleeve of tats on one sculpted arm. The swirls slid over his shoulder and stretched from his back over his pecs. And Victoria wanted to trace every line, every detail with her fingertip, then follow with her tongue.

God, he'd turned her into a sex fiend. Knowing Stefan, that had been his goal all along.

Who knew he had such...skills. Well, given the amount of women the paparazzi put him with over the years, she should've known, but she'd not thought of his hidden talents before. Shame that.

But she'd be thinking of them now. She had a feeling they would be in the forefront of her mind for quite some time. Would she ever get used to seeing, touching her best friend in such a way?

"So do we talk about this or just watch the movie?" she asked, reaching into the giant tub of popcorn he'd prepared.

He propped his feet upon the footrest of his own over-sized leather chair and threw her a smile. "I knew you wouldn't be able to just relax and watch the movie."

Relax? After what had just happened? Her body was still trembling and her orgasm had stopped twenty minutes ago. Yeah, definite skills. But even through the climax-induced haze, she had to know what he was thinking. She didn't care if that was too girly and mushy for him, she couldn't just pretend this moment hadn't changed her life.

"Do you feel different?" she asked, turning in her chair to face him.

A wicked grin spread across his handsome, devilish face. "Oh, yeah."

With a playful swat on his arm, she laughed. "Stefan, be serious. We're married and we just had sex."

"Just sex?" he asked, quirking one black brow.

Images of how they must've looked slammed into her. His golden, toned body plastering hers against the wall as she arched into his touch. Her glorious Greek prince staking his claim, dominating her.

"Okay, so it was amazing sex," she admitted as tingles continued to spread through her. "This isn't going to be weird now, is it? Because I really can't handle weird."

"The way you were groaning earlier and the way you're smiling now, I'd say you feel anything but weird."

Victoria rolled her eyes. "You're begging for compliments, aren't you? I already said it was great sex. I just don't want this to get uncomfortable between us."

He reached out, grabbed her hand and squeezed. "I care for you just as much as I always have," he assured her, all joking gone from his face. "You're still my best friend, but I've discovered that my best friend has a kick-ass body that I can't wait to take my time in savoring and getting to know better."

Chills and excitement coursed through her at his promise. If he was this confident, than why was she letting fear spread through her? Why borrow trouble when she'd just had the most incredible sexual experience of her life?

"I think this marriage is going to be one of the wisest decisions we ever made," she told him.

As the movie started on the screen, Stefan held on to her hand, occasionally stroking his thumb across her skin. The man had a tender side, and he wasn't afraid to express himself. They'd held hands before, but holding them after being so intimate took on a whole new meaning.

If the next six months of their marriage were anything like tonight, she'd certainly think twice about walking away. She may just be queen of Galini Isle forever.

"You picked my favorite movie," she told him as the title popped up on the screen. "You had this whole night planned, didn't you?"

He shrugged and grinned. "I actually had the movie planned because I thought you'd want to get back some sense of normalcy after the circus today. The sex was just a major added bonus."

"Oh, you have such pretty words," she mocked with a heavy sigh. "Watch it, Stefan, I may not find it in my heart to leave you after six months."

And while she was joking on the outside, inside her heart she feared she may have gotten in deeper than even she thought she would go.

Five

Victoria stood over the mahogany desk and sighed as she stared down at the scattered dress designs and random doodles. She'd started fresh sketches the day after her wedding and now, over a week later, she still wasn't happy with the results.

Nothing compared to her own lavish gown...of which many replicas were already being made by designers who only wished they would have had the initial idea.

And while that dress was her absolute favorite, Victoria didn't want to re-create it for resale. That unique design was hers, whether the marriage was real or not. She wanted to keep the gown special, but she would do others that were similar for future clients. And she knew she couldn't stop other designers from trying to mimic her gown, but they still wouldn't be the same. Hers was literally one of a kind.

Her thoughts circled back around to the "real" marriage.

She didn't know why she always put quotations around the word in her head. Her marriage to Stefan was as real as anyone else's marriage. In fact, she'd bet her entire year's salary that theirs was better than the majority of those living in Hollywood because she sincerely loved Stefan and would do anything for him…obviously a point she'd proven.

Not only did they share that bond and connection of their friendship, but the sexual chemistry was beyond amazing. Didn't married couples complain that after they said "I do" the light burned out on the passion? Yeah, there was no dimming the desire in the bedroom here.

After their initial lovemaking in the theater—and their movie night—Stefan had brought her into his master suite where they'd playfully undressed each other once again and enjoyed the benefits of the sunken garden tub in his master bath.

If this was how the whole friends-with-benefits thing worked, no wonder so many people jumped on board. Six months of Stefan attending to her intimate needs hadn't been part of the initial bargain, but it had become a surprising extra.

Unfortunately, her emotions were a jumbled mess. She had been stunned at what an attentive, passionate lover Stefan was, but when she started really thinking about their intimacy, she couldn't help but feel they'd passed the point of no return. After this six months, if she chose to leave, could they actually go back to just being friends?

Victoria turned her focus back to the pencil sketches staring up at her. Before her wedding she would've loved these designs, but now that she was technically a princess— still an odd term to grasp when referring to herself—she wished for all of her future brides to feel the same on their special day.

She wanted to launch her Fairy-tale Collection with magnificent gowns that women would love just as much as the one she wore, and if she was going to start this, she needed to stop coming up with garbage.

Raking her hands through her hair, she groaned.

"Bad time?"

She spun in the direction of the door to find Stefan entering their bedroom. In the past she'd always appreciated his fine build, but now that she'd seen, tasted and touched every delicious inch, she had a whole new admiration for her sexy husband...a weird sensation to associate with Stefan, but surprisingly a very welcome one.

Would it be too taboo for the prince to walk around naked? A shame, really, to cover such a magnificent creature.

If one didn't know he was a prince, they'd never guess from his attire. Though he did look mighty fine in his black T-shirt stretched over his broad shoulders and faded, designer jeans, it was the baseball cap pulled low to shield his face that captured her attention. Not often had she seen him in a hat, but he wore it well. And while he may look very American with his ensemble, he was every bit the Greek god she knew him to be.

"Perfect timing, actually." She turned away from her ghastly drawings and leaned back on the desk. "What's up?"

Those long legs ate up the space between them, and he rested a hip beside hers on the desk. "Well, I'm in the honeymoon phase and my wife is working. The tradition in my country is that these two weeks are for the husband and wife to get to know each other."

Wife. She didn't know if she'd ever get used to that term coming from Stefan's lips...especially when referring to her.

Victoria laughed. "I'm pretty sure we know each other quite well."

He reached around, fingering through her designs. "Still drawing random sketches?" he asked.

"Yeah. It's always easier to concentrate when I'm doodling and just let my mind relax."

He lifted a torn piece of scratch paper. "This looks like my family crest, but...are those initials?"

Victoria nodded. "I intertwined our initials together. Silly, isn't it?"

"Amazing how you're so extremely talented and still hard on yourself."

He took her hands in his and flashed a wicked smile. "Let's get out of here. Go down to the beach or have a picnic. Want to go for a ride on my new bike?"

"Is that a double entendre?" she asked, smiling. "How about we take a ride on the bike to the beach for a picnic?"

"And you'll lay off work the rest of the day?" he asked.

She watched him, those taut muscles beneath his shirt, the way the hat shielded those cobalt-colored eyes. As his best friend she hadn't been able to deny him anything, so as his wife and lover she definitely couldn't say no.

"Just today," she promised. "I really do need to get this line started, and these designs are crap right now."

Stefan pulled her up as he stood. "All the more reason you need a break. I know how you get when you're frustrated. Nothing will make you happy until you take a breather, refocus and come back to it. Besides, you're not sleeping well and I know it's because of work."

She jerked back. "How do you know I'm not sleeping well?"

"Because you normally snore like a train," he laughed. "All you've been doing lately is tossing and turning."

"I do not snore," she told him with a tilt of her chin. "You're lying."

He hugged her closer and nuzzled her neck. "Maybe I'm not wearing you out enough before bed."

The familiar masculine aroma that she always associated with him enveloped her. Amazing how their time apart didn't hinder his knowledge of how she worked. They may not see each other in person as often as she would've liked, but he still knew every layer to her. Even more so now since they'd slept together.

"If you want to ride my bike, in any form of the term, let me offer myself to your services."

Victoria laughed, smacking his shoulder. "I'm so glad you're willing to sacrifice yourself for my work."

With a loud smack, he kissed her on the lips. "Anything for my new bride."

"Let me change and I'll meet you in the kitchen."

His hand snaked up her shirt, his thumb skimming the edge of her lacy bra. "Do you need help changing?"

His touch affected her in ways she'd never known before, and she had to assume the chills and instant erotic pleasure that came from his fingertips stemmed from their playful, yet intense lovemaking.

"What I need is for you to get that picnic lunch prepared so we can go," she told him, swatting his hand away and taking a step back.

He shoved his hands in his jean pockets and smiled… Oh, the things that smile did to her insides, touching places she had thought dead since her exploited and humiliating breakup months ago.

She had known Stefan would be there to help her through the tough time, she just never imagined it would be with their clothes off.

Every time she thought of how fast, how thrilling their

new relationship was, nerves settled low in her belly. She was already getting too comfortable and she hadn't even put a dent in this six-month period.

Even though he'd given her control in the end, she couldn't help but wonder if he'd tire of her, physically, by then and if he'd be eager to get back to his old, playboy ways.

"I already had my chef prepare the food," he told her. "How soon can you be ready?"

"I'm just going to throw on some jeans and a tank."

Stefan rolled his eyes. "You are a fashion designer. You never 'throw on' anything. You'll go to the closet and think about it, try something on, discard it and start over."

Offended that he'd hit the nail on the head, she folded her arms over her chest. "For your information, I know exactly what I'm going to wear."

He quirked a brow and tilted his head. "Really? Then I'll just wait."

In her mind she went through everything she'd brought from the States. She hadn't had all of her things shipped since they were returning to L.A. after the two-week honeymoon period was over, so her options were limited.

"You're just waiting to see me naked," she joked, heading to her walk-in closet.

"An added perk," he agreed. "But I want to see you get ready as fast as you claim you can. This will be a first."

Victoria eyed her selection. If they were riding a bike, she would need pants, so she grabbed her favorite pair of designer jeans. Her eyes roamed up to the top rack of clothes where she'd hung her shirts. A little sleeveless emerald-green wrap shirt caught her eye—perfect. Sexy, cool and comfortable. She glanced to the shoe rack at the end of the closet and grabbed her gold strappy sandals. Not bike material, but perfect for the picnic and beach.

"Voilà," she announced, holding her items up in the air as she came from the closet, then stopped.

The man was lying across the bed wearing nothing but tattoos and a grin. He'd taken off his hat, too, leaving his hair messy and those cobalt eyes, beneath heavy lids, staring across the room at her.

"You don't fight fair," she told him, trying to remain in place and not attack her husband like some overeager teenager.

"Fighting wasn't on my mind at all." He laced his hands behind his head, forcing his muscles to flex beautifully beneath his tats. "Looks like you still need to undress."

Check and mate. And by the smirk on his face, he knew he had her. He'd played this scene perfectly.

How could she turn down such a blatant invitation? Even with their short time frame looming in her mind, she couldn't deny herself giving and receiving his pleasure.

She tossed her items to the floor, not caring where they landed. In a slow, what she hoped was sexy, striptease, she loosened the ties on her shirt and flung it off to the side, as well.

"Since I'm being rushed, I may need some help," she told him, sliding her thumbs into her jeans and sending them to puddle at her feet. She stepped out and smiled when his eyes roamed over her body…twice. "You want the job?"

"Sure, I'll help by getting you out of these."

He came to stand, all six-foot-plus glorious inches of him. He was beautifully tanned, magnificent and, for now, he was hers.

"Being with you like this should be awkward." She reached out, tracing his family's crest he had tattooed over his heart. "But it's not. I'm amazed how comfortable I've been being intimate with you."

"You're not going to want to leave me at the end of this six months," he joked, sliding the strap of her bra down one arm.

She reached around, unhooking the unwanted garment, and smiled. "Maybe not. We may just like being married to each other. This is the best relationship I've ever been in."

"You're just saying that to get me into bed," he told her, his hands coming up to cup her breasts.

"Yes, because it is so hard to get you naked and horny." She laughed.

The corners of his mouth kicked up at the same time he scooped her up and tossed her onto the bed. She bounced once before he was on her, pinning her hands above her head.

"I don't know why, but that smart mouth of yours has always been one of the things I love most about you."

She knew he loved her the way best friends loved each other, but when he said it like that, especially now that they were practically naked, the words sounded a bit more intimate and almost…awkward. She so did not want awkwardness to enter into this marriage or friendship. She enjoyed this friends-with-benefits arrangement they had. Her heart couldn't handle any more.

"You're thinking," he murmured, looking down. "None of that here. Work and everything else stays out of this bed."

She smiled, knowing he was the proverbial "fun guy," but he also knew when to be serious and when to work. The media had just caught him mostly in those "fun guy" moments.

But she knew the man beneath the playboy persona.

"Not thinking right now is perfect," she told him, looping her arms around his neck. "Marrying you was good for my creative mind."

He laughed. "Let me show you how creative I can be."

Six

Stefan's cell went off again. And again, he ignored it.

"Whoever is calling you must want you pretty bad," Victoria told him. "Why don't you just answer it?"

Because he wanted to ignore the fact that certain people did not believe this marriage was real and that he was officially off the market.

"Could be important," she went on as she slid her dainty feet back into her sandals and strapped them around her ankles.

After an intense bout of sex, a ride on his bike and a picnic at the beach, the last thing he wanted was an interruption to the day—especially by answering phone calls from past lovers. He had his best friend-turned-wife with him, and he was happier than he'd been in a long time. All of his goals were within his reach, and he didn't want anything to dampen his mood.

He'd promised Tori he'd be faithful, and he wasn't going

back on his word. Never before had he promised to be exclusive, something he made sure his lovers knew up front, but with Tori warming his bed, he didn't mind at all. He kept waiting for that feeling of being trapped to overtake him, but so far he'd not felt anything but complete and utter happiness.

"They'll leave a message," he told her, not really caring if they did or not.

Victoria leaned her hands back in the sand, shook her head and allowed her hair to fall past her shoulders and cascade down her back. As her gaze settled on the emerald waters before them, he smiled. It wasn't every man who could say he married his best friend…a hot, sexy, centerfold-material friend. Damn, he'd lucked out. An open-ended marriage was absolutely the way to go. Once the crown was his in a few months, he'd seriously have everything: title of king and Victoria in his bed with no major commitment to marriage.

And hopefully he could also convince her brothers to work with him on a documentary to clear his father's name.

"I'm not jealous, you know," she said, her eyes still on the orange horizon as the sun set.

He eased closer to her, drawing his knees up and resting his arms on them. "Jealous of what?"

"The women calling you. I'm sure that's why your phone vibrates and rings every half hour."

Stefan laughed. Victoria had never been one to mince words or back away from any uncomfortable topic. She was also very confident, like most American women were. He found that quality extremely sexy. What had that jerk Alex been thinking? Stefan only hoped they didn't run into the guy once they were back in L.A. Or if they did, he hoped the media wasn't around. The last thing he needed was a picture of him popping the other guy in his pretty-boy face.

"Go ahead and laugh," she went on. "But I know that's your entourage calling."

"And how do you know this?" He chuckled again, now at her description.

"Because if it had been your brother, one of your staff or anyone else important, you would've answered it."

He shook his head. "Possibly."

With a wide, sinful smile, she turned to face him. "So you admit your harem has been calling?"

"Maybe, but with the way you can't keep your hands off my body, I don't have time for others."

Victoria's laugh washed over him. "Your ego is even bigger than your bank accounts. I think we both know who initiated the sex this afternoon."

"You were the one who insisted on changing clothes. In a man's mind, that's code for 'I'm getting naked and you should join me.'"

"Oh, please." She rolled her eyes, still smiling. "If a woman says 'I'm going to the grocery store,' a man thinks that's a code for 'let's get naked.'"

Stefan didn't want to feel guilty about the women calling him. He couldn't help it. The fact he was married wasn't exactly a secret; it had been televised for the entire world to see. But a few of the women from his past knew him too well and had convinced themselves this marriage was a lie.

"Are you just a little jealous?" he asked, throwing her another smile.

Part of him wanted her to be, but the other part of him hoped she kept their relationship light and carefree.

Yes, he'd wanted Victoria on an intimate level for years, but now he had her where he wanted her. He didn't need emotions or anything too deep to creep into this new relationship they had discovered.

"I'm not jealous." She looked him dead in the eye, no smile, no glimmer of amusement. "But I won't be the other woman or played to look like a fool ever again."

Stefan turned, grabbed her by the shoulders and met her eyes. "There's no way in hell I'd ever treat you that way, Tori. And I'm not that jerk you were engaged to. Remember that."

He'd be damned if he'd let that bastard play the third wheel in their relationship, no matter their carefree set-up.

On a sigh, her head drooped. "I'm sorry. I don't have trust issues with you, Stefan. My mind just instantly ventured in the wrong direction."

"Hey." He placed a finger beneath her chin and lifted her face to meet his once again. "This marriage may not be a traditional one, but I say from here on out we keep your ex and my past out of it. Deal?"

"Deal."

The quick snapping of an automatic camera had him jerking his attention around.

He spotted a man crouched in the lush plants surrounding what was supposed to be the private beach to his family's palace.

Stefan jumped to his feet and took off after the unwanted intruder. "Stop," he yelled.

Hot sand squished beneath his feet, making him slide with each step. By the time he'd gotten to the area where the man had been in hiding, the guy was gone.

What the hell had the intruder overheard?

Stefan pulled his cell from his pocket and punched a button. "There's a man on the grounds," Stefan said before his security guard could utter a word. "If you find him first, take his camera. Then call the cops. I'm looking near the beach. Take the front of the palace."

Knowing Victoria would be fine for a few minutes, Stefan moved through the foliage in the direction the trespasser took off. No way in hell was he letting someone invade his privacy, and on his own secluded beach, as well.

Even though he knew without a doubt that Victoria didn't think anything of flashing bulbs and media circuses, he wanted their marriage, their life to be private. The bond they shared was so special, and even though the paparazzi had them practically married as teens, he didn't want their engagement or wedding tarnished. What transpired between him and Victoria was nobody's business.

But he had to find the guy and find out exactly what he'd overheard and take that damn camera. He couldn't afford for this secret to get out before the coronation. This country was his, damn it, and he'd do anything to keep it.

Besides, he wanted Tori all to himself...he was selfish like that. He wouldn't share her with the public any more than necessary.

More than anything, though, he wanted to shield her, protect her from any more pain. Because he cared for her more than any other woman in his life, he wanted to be the one to ride to her rescue and keep her life worry-free and happy.

Stefan spotted footprints in the sand and followed them up the embankment toward the tiny village. Sweat trickled down his back, but the heat was nothing compared to the anger in knowing someone had infiltrated his home. What the hell had his guards been doing? A discussion he'd be taking up later with the head of his security.

Stefan stopped when he spotted the man crouched down on the sidewalk, holding his camera, and from what Stefan could see, the man was looking through his shots. Probably checking to see if he needed to come back for more.

Without a sound, Stefan moved in from behind and wrapped an arm around the guy's neck, hauling him up to his feet.

"Drop the camera," Stefan growled in his ear.

Immediately the camera clattered to ground. With his free hand, Stefan pulled his cell from his pocket and dialed security to come collect the trash.

"You made a mistake in trespassing," Stefan told him, tightening his grip. "I don't take kindly to people invading my wife's privacy."

"I'm sorry," the man choked out. "Please."

"Whatever you *think* you overheard, forget it. If I even suspect you've gone to the media with lies, there won't be a place you can hide that I won't find you." Stefan loosened his hold but kept the guy in a lock until backup arrived. "I better never catch you on my property or even looking in my family's direction again or a smashed camera will be the least of your worries."

The heavy pounding of footsteps had Stefan shouting for the guards. "Over here," he yelled.

Once the guards had the trespasser secure, Stefan stepped around to get a good look at the man's face so he could remember it. Then he crouched down, picked up the broken camera and pulled the memory card out, sliding it into his pocket.

"Take him to the front while you wait for the cops," Stefan ordered his guards.

Tamping down his anger and wiping the sweat off his forehead, Stefan made his way back to Victoria. Her long, golden hair danced around in the ocean breeze, her face tilted up while she watched the water as if her privacy hadn't just been invaded.

"We secured the guy. Cops are on their way, and I personally confiscated the memory card." Stefan took a seat beside her. "Sorry about that."

With a shrug, Victoria turned to face him. "I'm used to it. Privacy really means nothing to me. I wouldn't know what to do with complete seclusion."

Stefan knew with her family she came into this world in the spotlight, but something about her statement struck him. She wasn't asking for privacy; no doubt she thought that was something she could never have. But why couldn't he provide her a little escape?

"What did he overhear?" she asked.

"I didn't give him the chance to say, but I made it very clear he's not to repeat anything or he will be found and dealt with."

Tori gasped. "You threatened him?"

"What did you want me to do? Ask him over for tea?"

On a sigh, Victoria shook her head. "I don't know. I just hope he didn't hear us. Pictures are one thing…"

Stefan wouldn't let some overeager cameraman ruin his future, or Victoria's. No matter the cost. He also wouldn't let the bastard ruin his day with his wife, either.

"Remember when we first met and we were trying to hide from all the cameras and crew for the film your mother was in?"

A genuine, beautiful smile spread across her face. "That was fun. We were purposely avoiding anybody so we could do whatever we wanted."

Stefan pictured the time in his mind, so clear and vivid. "I believe that's when I introduced you to alcohol."

On a groan, Victoria closed her eyes. "Don't remind me. I was so set on impressing you, I didn't want you to know I hadn't drank before."

"The look on your face after your first sip of whiskey kind of gave you away," he told her.

"You probably thought I was such a loser." She laughed, lying back on the blanket and looking up at the clear, blue sky.

"A loser? Nah. I thought you were innocent, and that's the kind of girl I was interested in."

And he had been…well, as much as a teenage boy could be interested in a girl. She'd been California fresh with all that silky blond hair and tanned skin. He'd instantly had a crush but had to play it cool.

So he did what any good boy would do. He'd plied her with alcohol and tried to talk her into skinny-dipping.

"You mean the kind of girl you were interested in corrupting?" she asked with a low laugh that made him pause to enjoy such sweetness.

There was just something about her that always made him smile. Their friendship never had any speed bumps, and for years he'd found himself wondering what something more with her would be like.

Of course, marriage to anyone never entered his mind, but so far being married to Tori really had its perks. She was playful in bed, and he appreciated the fact she wasn't getting too involved on a more heartfelt level.

"Maybe a little corrupting," he agreed. "I never did get you to go skinny-dipping."

Victoria shook her head. "That's something I've never done. It just sounds so…cold."

His eyes roamed over her body. She'd forgone the jeans and shirt and had ended up donning a beautiful pale blue strapless romper, and he wanted to slide his fingers between her breasts, loosen the knot and see the material puddle to the ground.

"Trust me." His eyes came back up to meet hers. "When I get you naked in the water, you'll be anything but cold."

Her breath hitched as she bit her lip and dropped her eyes to his mouth. Hell yeah. She was sexy personified, and she was all his for the next six months. After that... well, that ball was in her court. Going back to dating, and bedding, other women surprisingly wasn't a priority, not with Tori matching him both in bed and out.

Stefan slid one hand through her hair, his other hand cupping the side of her face. With the utmost care and tenderness, he tilted her head and secured his lips to hers. With gentle persuasion he coaxed her lips apart, pleased when she accommodated him. Her soft moan as she eased into his body aroused him more than all their frenzied kisses. Those fast-paced kisses were stepping stones to sex. This gentle, passionate kiss was a stepping stone to...what?

He told himself he was just enjoying the moment and not getting deeper intimately with her. Stefan didn't want to go down that path. But he did want to keep savoring his wife. He wanted to slowly strip her and see her body in the sunlight on the beach as he...

His cell phone chimed, breaking the moment. With a muttered curse, he eased back from those tender, swollen lips.

After jerking the phone from his pocket he answered, "Yes?"

"The police are here," the guard told him. "Would you like to come and talk to them or do you want me to take care of it?"

Stefan stared at Victoria. The moment of reminiscing had turned intense...something he hadn't counted on. Sex was one thing, but that flutter in his chest was not welcome.

Na pari i eychi. The woman was almost too perfect for

him. He couldn't afford to let himself get all emotional about their arrangement. He was a man—one known for his physical relationships. He had to remember that here.

"I'll be right there," he said before disconnecting the call.

Stefan came to his feet, put his hands on his hips and looked down at Victoria. "Police arrived. I'm going to go talk with them."

Still staring into his eyes, as if searching for answers about what had just happened, Victoria nodded and remained silent.

What *had* just happened? He didn't even know himself, but it was far too much. Besides, he couldn't focus on that right now.

"I can send someone to pick up our picnic later," he told her. "Are you staying here or coming back with me?"

"I think I'll stay here."

He studied her, trying to read if she was uncomfortable or just confused like he was. Was she feeling something beyond their friendship and sexual desire?

"Then I'll send someone down to make sure you're all right by yourself."

Victoria smiled. "I don't need a sitter, Stefan. I'll be fine. Go on and talk to the police. But you have the man's memory card, so don't be in a rush to press charges."

That was his Victoria. Always wanting the good in life to override the bad. She was a special woman and for now she was not just his best friend, she was his wife. He refused to delve deeper than that.

Victoria slid into her red silk nightgown and smoothed her hair back over her shoulder. The phone calls Stefan had been receiving shouldn't still be in the forefront of her mind, but they were, and she hated the fact she let the jealousy settle there for so long.

Stefan wasn't Alex. Stefan was the most loyal friend she'd ever had and no way would she compare the two men because Alex didn't even deserve the time of her thoughts.

What did deserve her thoughts were those blasted designs. Something just wasn't clicking. She'd never encountered this before, where all of the drawings weren't up to her own standards of perfection. Granted, they may be okay for some designers, but Victoria prided herself on flawless, shockingly stunning designs before she let anyone see them, and she wasn't going to change her ways with this new bridal collection.

She wanted her team back in L.A. to gasp with awe when they saw what she'd come up with. Unfortunately, if she took these current drawings to the table, her associates would only gasp in fright.

On the bright side, her random drawings of various forms of the Alexander family crest were quite impressive, if she did say so herself. Too bad that wasn't her main focus.

Soon-to-be brides around the world were waiting with high expectations to see what Victoria Alexander, Princess and almost Queen of Galini Isle, would come up with for the launching of her new line.

Maybe if she added a touch more lace. Lace said romance, but too much could scream tacky. Perhaps longer trains like so many girls dreamed of. Grown women still kept that little girl fairy tale in their mind. Their wedding day was supposed to be magical, and it all started with the dress because it set the tone.

Warm, strong hands cupped her shoulders and Victoria jumped.

"Easy."

She turned in Stefan's arms and smiled. "I didn't hear you come in."

His eyes dipped down to the V in her nightgown and a wicked grin spread across his lips. "Why cover up? Inside this room there should be a no-clothes rule."

Victoria rolled her eyes. "I barely get them on before you take them off."

"Exactly," he agreed, squeezing her almost-bare shoulders. "It's a waste of time. So tell me what had your mind so preoccupied?"

Reaching up, Victoria grabbed his forearms and held on. Sometimes it was just nice to have his strength, his shoulder to lean on. He never judged her and always listened with the compassion that only a best friend could.

"I've just hit a rough spot with the designs." Fear gripped her at the thought of being stuck in a rut, at the idea that she may be tapped out at the moment in her career she needed her creativity most. "This has never happened."

"You're stressing yourself," Stefan told her. "Take another day off to think about it. For that matter, take the rest of our time here off. Maybe once we get back to L.A., when you're in your element, the ideas will flow."

She hoped, but she couldn't count on what-ifs to get her through her career. Idly sitting by while waiting for something spectacular to jump in her mind wasn't how she worked. But taking a few days off couldn't hurt. It's not like the designs could get worse.

Offering a smile, she nodded. "You're right. I probably just need to get home."

Stefan slid her straps down her arms, the feather-soft touch of his fingertips she'd so quickly grown used to sending shivers all over her body. And her body never failed to respond to him since they'd first made love in the theater.

Made love? Yes, she felt confident using that phrase—

though she doubted Stefan would be. She loved him as her best friend, and the special relationship they had was unique. Granted this marriage may not be like many others, but at least they had a strong bond that was lacking in so many other couples.

"Now, since we have through the end of the week to enjoy this honeymoon phase," Stefan said, backing her toward the four-poster bed, "what do you say we continue making use of this alone time?"

And who could argue with a sexy Greek prince?

Seven

Stefan knew he wouldn't get out of Galini Isle without his entourage following him. While he was used to the guards being underfoot, now that he was king—or very soon to be—they took the role even more seriously.

Victoria didn't seem to mind the extras at her impressive Hollywood Hills home. Then again, her mind hadn't been on much else other than her designs. She'd drawn on the flight, she'd stayed up all hours of the night back in Greece, and she was still struggling.

Stefan hated to see her being so hard on herself. They'd been back in L.A. for only a few hours and she was already downtown at her office speaking with some of her staff.

The woman was a workaholic, but he admired her more than nearly anyone he knew. He also had a little surprise for her, hopefully to help get her creativity flowing in the direction she needed.

"Sir."

Stefan turned from the view of the city and faced the open living area to see his assistant, Hector, standing in the arched doorway.

"Yes?"

The man, who had been assistant to his father before his death, stepped forward.

"If you have a moment, Sir, we need to go over your schedule of events while we are in the States."

Stefan nodded. "Has something changed, Hector? I know Victoria and I are scheduled for the homeless shelter and a library appearance to help with funding."

"Yes, sir, but Her Highness's alma mater called and wanted to know if you both could put in an appearance. They were hoping to have a special dinner to honor the two of you. It won't be for a couple of weeks if you agree, because we'd need time to set up security."

Stefan sighed. "Let me ask her, but I don't think it will be a problem," he told Hector. "I can let you know by this evening. I don't want to disrupt her while she's at work."

Hector bowed. "Of course, sir. I will check for a spot on the schedule that will accommodate both of you should she agree."

When Hector quieted but remained standing and staring, Stefan smiled. "Is there something else?"

Hector's lips barely lifted into a grin, but he merely nodded. "You know I don't like to put my nose into anyone's business, but—"

Stefan chuckled. "It's your job to do so, yet you apologize for it every time you interfere. There's always a valid reason, so let's hear what it is."

Stefan gestured to the wraparound sofa and took a seat. "Something is on your mind because you've waited until Victoria left to come to me."

The elderly man sat, not fully relaxing because he remained on the edge of the cushions. "With Victoria gone, perhaps this would be a perfect time to call one of her brothers."

Stefan shrugged. "I will. But, I'd like to see them in person. They don't normally do documentaries, so I need to present all the facts before they can make a decision."

"Have you told Victoria about your idea yet?" Hector asked.

Shaking his head, Stefan replied, "No. She's so busy with work, and this really doesn't involve her."

Hector came to his feet. "Everything in your life now involves her. I wouldn't keep this to yourself too much longer, Your Majesty."

As was custom, Hector bowed before leaving the room.

His loyal assistant was under the illusion the marriage with Victoria was genuine, so of course he thought this idea involved her. Stefan would tell Victoria if her brothers agreed to the film. But right now she was busy and she'd already done so much by taking on this marriage and title. He wasn't going to pile more on her plate. He had to speak to Bronson and Anthony first, and he didn't want Victoria to feel as if she were obligated to help or caught in the middle.

Would they even go for something like this? Stefan didn't know Anthony very well, but he knew Bronson well enough to ask if he would entertain the idea.

A documentary with the Dane and Price names behind it would no doubt kill any suspicion that the film wasn't thoroughly researched and executed. That reputation of the filmmakers would certainly carry a lot of clout in clearing up the speculation of his father's involvement in his mother's untimely death.

Just because his father had admitted an extramarital affair, that didn't mean he'd planned an accident to remove his own wife from the picture so he could be with his mistress. Nor did it mean his mother had taken her own life. The curvy roads were slick, the brakes needed changing—a fact that had come out later from the police report—and his mother had insisted on not using a driver that day. The series of events led up to a tragedy, but Stefan refused to blame his father.

Oh, he'd blamed him at the time. Yelled and cursed at him for not loving his mother enough and for going around having an affair, but once Stefan saw the grief, the anguish that his father had gone through, even up to his own death, Stefan realized that his father was only human. His father may have strayed from the marriage once, but the man had been completely in love with his wife.

Stefan came to his feet again and moved to the floor-to-ceiling window, where he admired a view of the city in the distance. Somewhere in the crazy overpopulated town was his wife, his best friend. He wanted her opinion, but she had so much on her plate already and he hated to bother her with his own issues. Wasn't she already going above and beyond by helping him secure the crown and keep his country independent? He didn't want to make her feel like she needed to step in and persuade her brothers to agree to the film. Besides, as of this point, taking the blemish off his father's reputation didn't concern her.

Right now he wanted her to concentrate on her designs, on letting her creativity flow and her natural spirit shine through. She'd already done enough for him, and he wasn't going to ask for another favor for a really long time…unless he asked her to don a certain type of lingerie, and that didn't count as a favor when the enjoyment was mutual.

Raking a hand through his hair, Stefan recalled that Victoria's mother was planning a dinner party tomorrow. If the right time presented itself, he'd approach Bronson, but this wasn't something he'd announce at the table. He really did want to keep this quiet until he knew for sure this was a project Bronson and Anthony were willing to take on.

As the next king of Galini Isle, Stefan felt it was not only his duty as the son of a man wrongfully accused, but he also knew telling the truth was the right thing to do to keep his family's name and honor one of integrity.

And he hoped like hell that intruder on his property had taken the threat seriously, otherwise he'd have a whole new mess on his hands. He already had enough to deal with without worrying if his country was secure. So far this marriage was getting him closer and closer to his title. He couldn't lose it now.

As he glanced around the spacious, brightly decorated living room, he couldn't help but wonder what would happen at the end of the six-month period. Would Victoria stay with him? He had to admit, being married to his best friend was much better than he ever would've dreamed. And once they put in a few royal appearances now that their honeymoon phase was over and they were in L.A., Tori would get an even better sampling of what being royalty truly meant. Perhaps she wouldn't like all the hype and responsibilities.

He moved to a built-in bookcase and gazed over the snapshots of Victoria with her family and friends through the years. There were even a couple shots of the two of them together. In one they were laughing, Victoria's hand on his chest. The captured scene ran through his mind and he recalled that day so vividly. He'd come to visit her—it was actually one of the times he'd been about to tell her he wanted to explore a physical relationship. They'd been at a restaurant opening for a mega-movie star who had started a chain, and the media was swarming, waiting to get pictures of all the rich and famous.

He'd pulled her aside and asked her if they could skip the event. When she'd told him it was rude, he told her he'd rather be having a root canal without painkiller and she'd started laughing. Someone in the press had snapped the picture, and it had ended up in several media outlets with speculation that the two of them were more than friends.

But now fate had handed him this opportunity, and he didn't intend to screw it up. While he may not have married Victoria for love, he did respect her, and she was a perfect match for him. After all, she'd grown up in the spotlight as well, and they knew going in that their privacy was limited.

Besides, Victoria had her own life goals and issues to keep her occupied. Which was why he'd keep this documentary idea to himself until he found out if anything more would come of it.

He hoped the opportunity would arise tomorrow night to discuss possibilities with Bronson so he could finally bury his parents in his heart with the respect they both deserved.

Frustrated didn't even come close to describing the emotions swirling inside her.

Victoria let herself into her Hollywood Hills home and smiled at Stefan's permanent bodyguard/assistant positioned by the door. That would take some getting used to, but she was technically on her way to being a queen, so just one more thing she'd have to deal with...eventually. Right now she'd put it on the back burner because she didn't have the time or the energy to even think about her royal crown or any of the duties expected of her.

Her wedding gown designs were improving but still not to the point where she was ready to start whipping out her needle and thread.

Her team had bounced around ideas all day, and by the time four o'clock rolled around, Victoria was ready to strangle herself with a bolt of satin.

She bypassed the living area and headed straight up the wide, curved marble staircase that led to the second-story bedrooms. She assumed Stefan was around somewhere because his guard was at his post.

When she went into her walk-in closet, she slid off her Ferragamo pumps and sank her toes into the plush carpet. After unzipping her sheath dress, she folded it onto the shelf, where she had a pile that needed to go to the cleaners. Obviously something she'd forgotten to have done before her whirlwind proposal, marriage and step up the royal ladder.

Did royalty even worry about such mundane things as dry cleaning? Of course, people may think a member of the prestigious Dane family didn't, either.

Bracing her hands on the shoe island in her closet, Victoria bowed her head and sighed. She'd never felt out of control, never felt so overwhelmed that she wanted to burst into tears, but she was definitely there now.

How had her life become so out of control? How had all of her decisions, goals and dreams slipped away and turned into something else she didn't even recognize? She'd never had a problem designing before. But now that she was married and struggling with her rapidly growing emotions, she just couldn't concentrate.

Between work and Stefan, she was a mess of jumbled-up nerves.

Tears pricked her eyes, her throat burned and she shook her head. No. Tears solved nothing and feeling sorry for herself wouldn't help put life back on track where she was comfortable.

"Well, this is nice to see." Stefan entered the closet,

eyes roaming over her matching lace bra and panty set she was left standing in. But when his gaze landed back on her face, all joking and sexual looks vanished. "What's wrong? Are you okay?"

He closed the gap between them, taking her in his arms and holding her against his chest. And wasn't that just like him? Always ready to comfort, always ready to rescue the distressed damsel?

Victoria sniffed. "I'm just being overly dramatic today. Chalk it up to being female."

"Well, honey, you've been female the whole time I've known you, and it takes a lot to bring a strong woman like you to tears." He eased back, swiped at her damp cheeks and stared into her eyes with the compassion she'd always known from him. "Want to talk about it? Is it work?"

She had to be honest. He was her husband, after all, so they should share everything. And in some ways he knew her better than she knew herself, so he would most likely know if she was holding something back.

"I think everything just hit me," she told him. "Work, marriage. It's all moving so fast, I don't feel like I'm in control anymore."

He kissed her forehead. "You're in control, Tori. You just always put this pressure on yourself to excel and be the best, which is great, but sometimes you need to give yourself a break."

She studied his face, that handsome face that so many women dreamed about, and smiled. "Is that what you would do? Take a break?"

He shrugged. "Probably not, but I don't like to see you upset."

"You don't get upset?"

"Upset? No. I do get angry, which fuels me to work harder."

Her smile spread wider and she tilted her head.

"I get it," he said, laughing. "Those were angry tears?"

"Frustrated tears," she corrected. "But at this point, same thing."

He leaned forward, kissed her gently and stepped back. "Why don't you throw on some clothes and meet me downstairs."

Comfortable with her body, Victoria placed her hands on her hips. "Now I know the honeymoon's over." She laughed. "I'm standing here nearly naked and you're telling me to throw on clothes."

Heat instantly filled his eyes as he raked his gaze over her. "Oh, believe me, I'm having a very hard time being noble here, but sex isn't what you need right now. Just get dressed and come downstairs. Or wear that, but my guard will see more of you than I'm willing to share."

Stefan turned and left, leaving her staring after him.

Some married women didn't have a tenth of the connection she had with Stefan. And even though they married under less than traditional circumstances, she knew she had a good thing going…if she could just keep her emotions in check.

She threw on a pair of white shorts and a flowy green top. After sliding into a pair of gold sandals, she made her way downstairs. She didn't see the guard by the door, but she knew he wasn't far. Thankfully he did try to stay out of sight and give them privacy.

Victoria saw Stefan through the patio doors. She crossed the living room and walked out the open set of French doors to the warmth of the evening SoCal sunshine.

Stefan sat on one of the plush outdoor sofas she'd recently added and Victoria took a seat next to him.

"What's that?" She pointed to the small folder he held

on his lap. "Did you draw some secret, magical designs you're willing to share with me?"

He laid the folder on her legs. "Open it."

Intrigued, she pulled back the cover flap and gasped. "Stefan…" Page after page, she shuffled through designs and even some of the crazy doodling she'd done as a teen. "Where did you get these?"

"I kept them."

She eyed the papers, yellowing around the edges, and looked at him. "But…why?"

With a shrug, he turned to face her. "When you came to visit, you were always doodling and talking about being a designer. Sometimes I'd keep the papers you left laying around. I knew you'd make a name for yourself because you've always been so determined. You had such *pathos,* a passion, for designing." He laughed. "Even then you would sketch random images to help you think clearer."

Emotions clogged her throat and, dammit, for the second time today she was going to cry. Even all those years ago he'd had faith in her.

"These are, well…terrible." She laughed through watery tears.

He put a hand over hers, taking his other hand to cup her chin and hold his gaze. "They may be terrible to you, but they were your dream, Victoria. Look at them. Look close. You may see something ugly, but I see a promise that a young girl made to herself."

Oh, God. How did the man always know what to say?

"You're right," she whispered. "I just can't believe you kept them."

His hand dropped from her face. "Maybe I wanted to keep them so that when you became famous I could sell them."

A laugh burst from her. "You're so rich, you never would've thought to sell these."

His eyes settled on hers, and the heat she saw staring back at her had the smile dying on her lips.

"Maybe I saw the talent," he told her. "Maybe the crush I had on you prompted me to keep them."

Victoria's heart clenched. "Stefan, you didn't have feelings for me then."

"I did," he confessed. "I may have been young and foolish, but I did care more for you then than any other girl I knew."

Victoria couldn't handle this. Couldn't think what that revelation could've meant for the course of their relationship had he told her his feelings at the time.

"I'd hate to think if we dated seriously as teens or in our twenties we would've lost each other as friends. Besides that, you would've disappointed all those ladies," she joked. "Good thing you grew out of it, huh?"

Something she didn't recognize, or didn't want to recognize, flitted through his eyes. "Yeah, good thing."

As Victoria looked down at her designs, she remembered dreaming as she'd been drawing them. Dreaming of her wedding day, of her groom waiting at the end of the aisle.

And in all her dreaming, that man had been a prince. A prince who knew her inside and out, who cared for her as a friend and lover, who would do anything to make her happy.

Victoria could no longer deny that she was teetering on the edge of falling in love with her husband, and that out-of-control emotion scared her to death.

Eight

Stefan sat back and watched the chaos—otherwise known as dinner with his in-laws—which was becoming a little too hearth and homey to him between the newlyweds and the babies.

Bronson and his wife, Mia, took turns holding and feeding their little Bella, whom he believed Victoria told him was almost a year old now.

Victoria's other brother, Anthony, was holding histwo-month-old baby girl as Charlotte fed the eighteen-month-old Lily in her high chair.

And through all the cries, spit-ups and diaper changes, the Grand Dane of Hollywood, Olivia Dane, sat at the head of the long, elegantly accessorized table and smiled. Either the woman didn't realize that in a year or so her immaculate Beverly Hills home would be a giant playground or she was so in love with her family she didn't care that her fine china could end up in millions of shards on her marble floor.

"Bella, no, honey."

Stefan glanced to the other end of the table where Bella was throwing some orange, liquid concoction onto the floor. Why did all baby food look like already recycled dinner in a jar?

"Oh, don't worry about it." Olivia waved a hand. "Marie can clean it up when she clears the table later."

"No, I'll get it." Mia came to her feet and whipped out a bunch of wipes from who knows where. Obviously moms had a knack for always being ready for anything.

"I think Carly needs a diaper change," Charlotte said as she came to her feet, holding her baby to her chest. "I'll be right back."

Anthony stood, taking the infant. "Let me. Go ahead and finish eating."

Victoria laughed. "I love seeing my big strong brothers taking care of baby poop and puke."

Stefan dropped his fork to his plate with a clatter. "And that's the end of my dinner."

Patting his leg, Victoria laughed. "Oh, toughen up, Prince. Your day will come."

A shudder coursed through him at the thought of children being written into the archaic laws of his land. To be honest, he was surprised they weren't, but at the same time he was thankful.

And just as quickly as that shudder spread through him, another took over as he glanced to Victoria's smiling face. An image of her swollen with his child did something unrecognizable to his belly, his heart. He didn't want to examine the unwanted emotions any further because if she were ever swollen with a baby, it more than likely wouldn't be his.

She was on birth control. Besides, they hadn't even discussed kids. They hadn't discussed beyond the six months, other than to joke, much less anything permanent or long term.

"You okay?" Victoria asked in a low whisper. "You're staring with a weird look on your face."

He shook off the thoughts and returned her warm smile. "Fine. I admit I'm not used to babies, so all of this is new to me."

"We weren't, either," she admitted, placing her cloth napkin onto the table. "But we adjusted quickly, and I couldn't imagine our lives without all these little cuties."

He studied her face once again, wondering if she did indeed have babies in her dream for life. Had he put that aspiration on hold when he'd selfishly asked her to be his wife? Hell, he hadn't even asked, he'd basically begged…a moment he wasn't very proud of, but nonetheless he'd had no choice. Once she'd mentioned wanting a family someday, but was that still a desire? And if so, where would that leave them and their marriage?

Discussing her fantasies of a family would have to wait. For one thing he didn't think the topic was appropriate conversation at the dinner table with her family, and he had to speak with Anthony or Bronson, hopefully both, about his documentary idea.

Unfortunately, the right time had not presented itself.

Olivia scooted her chair back, the heavy wood sliding over the dark marble floor. "If everyone is done eating, we can go into the living room where the kids can play on the floor."

Stefan came to his feet and pulled Victoria's chair out for her.

"You married a prince and he pulls out your chair," Mia said, then turned to Bronson. "Are you taking notes?"

Bronson laughed, and glanced at Stefan. "Give a guy a break, would ya? You're making me look bad."

Victoria wrapped an arm around Stefan's waist and squeezed. "Can't help it if my man is always a gentleman, Bron. Looks like you need to step up your game."

Stefan didn't miss the way Bronson studied how Victoria was holding on to him, and he didn't miss the way the look of surprise resonated when Victoria said "my man."

Just where were they headed? And why the hell was it important for him to know? He was a man for crying out loud. The sex was amazing, she wasn't demanding of his time and she hadn't asked him for anything. Why was he suddenly analyzing everything like a damn woman?

Anthony came back in as they were all moving from the room. "She's all ready to go," he announced, handing Carly back to Charlotte.

Olivia went to get Lily from her high chair when Bronson spoke up.

"You ladies go on ahead," he said. "I'd like to talk with Anthony and Stefan."

Okay, so now the moment of opportunity had presented itself, but Stefan had a feeling this wasn't going to be the time to bring up his favor, not with the look Bronson was giving him.

Because he tended to be spiteful, Stefan leaned down and gave Victoria a kiss—and not a simple see-ya-later peck.

What he and Victoria decided to do with their marriage was nobody else's business, and he would fight for their privacy no matter who he went up against.

"Fine with me," Olivia said. "I'm just glad you're all not talking about the film."

"We just haven't gotten to it, yet," Anthony piped up.

"We will. Don't worry. We're only a few months into the shoot, still plenty to discuss."

"Yes, I'm aware of the time frame." Olivia rolled her eyes and adjusted a wiggly Lily in her arms. "I should've known better than to think we'd get through the night without shop talk."

"Play nice with the other boys," Victoria said with a wink.

Obviously she missed the way Bronson was throwing daggers. "Always," Stefan promised.

Once the ladies and babies were gone, Bronson crossed his arms over his chest. "What the hell kind of game are you playing with my sister?"

"No game." Relaxed, Stefan rested a hand on the back of his chair. "And before you get all big brother on me, let me tell you that I will not share how Victoria and I treat this marriage. It's none of your concern."

Anthony cleared his throat. "Excuse me, but did I miss something in the two minutes it took to change a diaper?"

"Stefan seemed to be on more than friendly terms with Victoria," Bronson supplied. "I'm just trying to make sure he's not playing a game with her. She's been hurt before."

"Bronson." Anthony sighed. "Simmer down. Stefan and Victoria are grown adults. If they want to…whatever, then that's their business."

Bronson cursed. "Did either of you pay attention when that jerk broke her heart? Did you hear her crying? See the way her self-esteem lowered? I won't watch someone I love go through that again."

Guilt tore at Stefan that Victoria had gone through all of that and he hadn't been able to help her more. But with his father's illness and death, there was just no way to be in two places at once.

Just the thought of her crying over some jerk who wasn't

worth her tears made his gut clench. She deserved all the happiness and love life could give.

"Listen," Stefan said. "We know what we're doing. Yes, we've grown closer than just friends, but that's our business. I won't explain our actions to you or anyone else."

Anthony chuckled. "Guess that settles that discussion."

Refusing to back down, Stefan continued to stare at Bronson. No, he hadn't heard the cries from Victoria because she'd always been so strong on the phone, but he knew she'd been hurt. A woman like Victoria who loved with her whole heart and was loyal to a fault couldn't come out of a relationship like that and not be scarred.

And he was no better than Alex. Wasn't he using her as well to gain a title? The only difference was he'd told her up front.

"I won't let her get hurt again," Bronson said. "I hate to sound all big and bad, but I had to tell you where I stand."

Stefan nodded. "Duly noted."

"If you two are done kissing and making up, can we get back to our family night?" Anthony asked.

Stefan knew an opening when he saw one. "Actually, I'd like to run something by you two since I have you here together."

Bronson gestured toward the doors. "Let's go out on the patio then."

Bronson led the way out the glass double doors and onto the stone patio surrounded by lush plants and flowers and a trickling waterfall.

Stefan took a seat in one of the iron chairs and waited for Victoria's brothers to get comfortable on the outdoor sofa across from him.

"What's up?" Bronson asked.

"I know you're both aware that my mother passed away when I was younger and there was speculation that she ei-

ther committed suicide or my father may have had something to do with the accident."

When both men nodded, Stefan went on. "I have wanted
to clear my family's name because my father never would
go public before. He just wanted the rumors to die down,
and he feared if he kept bringing it up people would assume he was covering his own tracks. Well, now that he's
gone, I want to shed some light on the situation and prove
that he had nothing to do with her accident, nor did she,
and they did indeed love each other very much."

Anthony eased forward in his seat. "What do you have
in mind?"

"I know that you two don't normally take on projects
like this, but I was hoping we could discuss working on a
documentary." Stefan wanted to hold his breath and wait
for a response, but at the same time, he wanted to keep
talking to convince them. "I have proof my father had
nothing to do with the accident and that my mother wasn't
depressed or suicidal. There's not a doubt in my mind that
while, yes, he had an affair, he was not trying to get rid
of my mother. The affair had been years before the accident, and when she died, I saw him go through pure hell.
I just want to clear his reputation and go into my title with
a clean slate for the Alexander name."

"You sound certain that this was an accident," Bronson said. "I'd be willing to discuss this further. I may not
typically do documentaries, but that doesn't mean I'm not
open to the possibility."

"I agree," Anthony said. "Could we set up a time to talk
about this in greater detail? I mean, we'd have to look at
the police reports and interview credible witnesses who
are willing to come forward."

"I can provide you with anything you need." A spear
of relief spread through Stefan. "Victoria and I are going

to be here for another few months, so whenever you two are free, let me know. We have a few engagements coming up, but our schedule in the States is still pretty light. I can work around your shooting times."

As Victoria's brothers discussed their upcoming schedules, Stefan couldn't help but be overly thrilled. He had no idea they would be so open to the idea and respond so quickly. Though they hadn't agreed to anything, they hadn't shot down the idea.

Moving forward with this project and his coronation, Stefan knew that if everything fell in the right place, his life would be just as he'd pictured it. Clean family reputation and his country secured in the Alexander name.

What more could he want?

Nine

"So what did my brothers talk to you about?"

Victoria's fingertip circled the top of her wineglass as she eased forward in her seat. Stefan had taken her to her office, then afterward she wanted to show him a new restaurant that had opened. They were just having drinks and a dessert, but sometimes it was nice to get out of the house and enjoy society like a normal person—or as normal as one could be between her iconic family and her royal status.

With the outdoor seating and sunset in the distance, the ambiance screamed romance…even if a bodyguard was seated a few tables away trying to blend in.

Yeah, this was now her "normal" life.

Stefan shrugged. "Nothing much."

Victoria glared at him across the intimate table. "You're lying."

His eyes came up to meet hers as he reached across and

took her hand from her glass. He kissed her fingertips one at a time, and she relished the familiar shivers that crept over her body at his simple, yet passionate actions. But she wasn't letting the question go.

"Stefan?"

Lacing his hand through hers, he smiled. "Yes?"

"You've never been a good liar, and all this charm isn't working on me."

He quirked a dark brow. "Oh, yeah? I guarantee your heart rate is up, and I know you want to kiss me because you're watching my lips."

Busted.

"I'm watching your lips because I'm waiting for the truth to emerge from them." No way would she admit that he could do so little and turn her on. "Did Bronson get too protective?"

"We simply had a misunderstanding, and now we don't," Stefan said. "Men don't stay upset like women. He just wanted to discuss something, and it's over."

Victoria would make a special trip to Bronson's house. No way was she going to be sheltered or coddled by her brother.

"What was Anthony there for? Peacemaker?"

Stefan smiled. "He is quite a bit more laid back, yes?"

"He wasn't when Charlotte left him," Victoria replied. "I'd never seen a man so relentless on keeping his family together. He would've walked through hell for her."

"I'd do the same for you."

Victoria jerked at his automatic, non-hesitant response. Surely he wasn't developing feelings for her...not like she had for him. God, if he ever found out she'd fallen in love with him their friendship would be strained. Right now, with the playful sex and always hanging out, they had a good thing. No way would she put this relationship in jeopardy by revealing her true feelings.

"Stefan…"

"I realize their marriage is quite different from ours," he told her, stroking the back of her hand with his thumb. "But you're the one woman in my life that I would sacrifice anything for."

This was the point in a conversation where some women would think this was a major confession of love…Victoria was not one of those women. She knew Stefan better than any other woman did. He was a charmer, a playboy, but most of all, he did love her. In the way all best friends love each other.

But the romantic in her, the smidgen of a sparkle that hadn't been diminished by Alex, sighed and smiled internally at the idea that her husband would sacrifice anything for her.

"I'm ready to head home," he said, giving her a look that she knew had nothing to do with friendship and everything to do with lust. "Why don't you finish that drink."

"Forget the drink," she told him with a slight grin. "I have wine at home."

She grabbed her bag off the back of the iron chair and stood at the same time he was there to help her from her seat. When she turned, their lips were a breath apart and Stefan sealed them together briefly but firmly, loaded with promise.

"We need to leave before I really give the media something to print," he murmured against her mouth.

She swayed slightly and his warm, strong hand came around and settled firmly against her bare back where her summer dress dipped low. The heat from his touch did nothing to help her wave of dizziness brought on by pure desire.

She'd never had even a fraction of this passion with Alex. Mercy, she was in trouble.

"I've got you, Victoria. Always."

The heat in his eyes made her wish this were more than a marriage of convenience or a businesslike arrangement. But she was too afraid to explore that deeper level of emotion until she could see just where they stood at the end of the six months.

With a smile, she nodded. "I'm ready."

He led her from the cozy outdoor restaurant to the car that was waiting for them at the curb. Victoria's driver had been replaced with one of Stefan's guards, and the man instantly appeared, opened the door and let them into the backseat. As she slid across, her dress rode up high on her thigh. Stefan came in beside her and placed a hand over hers before she could pull the material down.

"Leave it," he said, hitting the button to put up the soundproof one-way window divider. "I have the best idea."

Oh, Lord.

As the guard brought the engine to life and pulled from the curb, Stefan turned on the intercom to tell the man to take his time heading back to Hollywood Hills.

An hour in the backseat of the limo with a man as seductive and sensual as Stefan? Victoria's body hummed and tightened in anticipation.

When he clicked the button off, he turned, sliding his other hand up her thigh and pushing both sides of the dress to her hips.

"Convenient you wore a dress," he murmured, staring down at her bare legs and the peek of yellow satin panties that were exposed. "Hate to waste this opportunity."

As his hands squeezed her thighs, his lips captured hers. The wine they'd drank tasted so good on his tongue, intoxicating her to the point she didn't care they were in the back of her car getting ready to have what she hoped was hot, wild sex.

When her hands came up around his neck, he eased back.

"Scoot down in the seat," he whispered. "I want this to be all about you."

And there was no woman in her right mind who would turn down an invitation like that.

Victoria did as he asked as he eased her legs farther apart. In his strong grasp, she felt the tug on her panties until she heard the material give way and tear.

"You owe me a pair of panties," she joked.

As he settled onto the floor between her legs, he gazed up at her beneath heavy lids. Bright eyes pierced hers as he said, "I prefer you without them."

With his wide shoulders holding her thighs apart, Victoria wondered if they were really doing this. Were they actually going to get intimate in the back of a car? And not only that, but this was far more personal than sex. Was Stefan taking their relationship to the next level? Obviously yes, but was he even aware of how personal this act was?

She didn't care and couldn't think anymore the second his finger slid over her, parting her a second before his mouth fixed on her.

Instinct had her sliding down even more. The way he made love to her with his mouth had her gripping his shoulders, the edge of the seat, the door handle, anything to keep from screaming at the overwhelming sensations rocketing through her.

In no time, her body quivered, bursts of pure bliss shooting through her. Stefan stayed with her until the last of her tremors ceased.

Reality hit her as he literally crawled back up her body.

Those talented hands slid over her curves, and he took a seat next to her, lifting her up to settle on his lap. As he nestled her into the crook of his arm, she tucked her face against his warm neck.

"You're not seriously going to try to hide the fact you're completely turned on, are you?" she asked.

His soft chuckle vibrated against his hard chest. "Kind of hard to hide it, but I wanted this to be about you. We can continue at home if you'd like."

Victoria lifted her head, wondering if Stefan realized how this moment, even though it was in the back of a car, had changed the course of their relationship. Did he get this intimate with all of his women? She closed her eyes briefly, trying to block out the instant mental images. If she had anything to say about it, he'd not be with any other woman ever again. He'd put the ball in her court at the end of the six months, and she was seriously considering staying, making him see just how this marriage could and should work for all the right reasons—which had absolutely nothing to do with his title.

But if she stayed, could she be a loyal, devoted queen and still design? She couldn't give up her own goals to cater to his, but she wanted this marriage to work. There had to be a way.

Stefan stared down at Victoria. Holy hell. What had just happened? He'd meant to be giving, passionate, but something changed…something he couldn't put his finger on. The way she looked at him with her face flushed and her lids heavy made him want to rip off both their clothes and satisfy her once again before finally relieving himself of this constant state of arousal he seemed to have around her lately.

"I want to make you happy, Stefan," she told him, stroking her fingertip down his cheek and along his jawline.

Yeah, something definitely changed. She wasn't smiling, wasn't playful. Her words, her actions were from the heart.

Was she sinking more into this marriage than she should? Granted, he'd always wondered how they'd be together, but if she was falling for him, could he ever give her that deeper, loving, marital bond in return? He honestly didn't think he had it in him.

God, he didn't want to hurt her. Right now all he wanted was to enjoy the way they were living together. Why couldn't that be enough?

"You've made me happy by helping me, Victoria."

"You know I could never tell you no," she replied, flashing him a sexy grin. "Besides, I'm getting what I want, too."

Friends and business. That's what this had to be…no matter what flutter he thought he felt in his chest earlier. The emotion had to be ignored. Victoria was too important to him to risk their bond on something as questionable as love.

As the driver wound his way up the Hollywood Hills, Victoria sat nestled against his side. He loved the familiar lavender scent that always surrounded her and the sexy way she would sigh as she crossed her legs and curved her body more into his. And now that he knew she wore nothing beneath that dress, well, *sexy* was a vast understatement.

He would let her show him her appreciation when they returned home. For now he needed to come to grips with the fact that he didn't want to get too involved in this marriage on a foundation he couldn't control, but when he'd taken their lovemaking to another level only moments ago, he'd done just that.

And he had no one to blame but himself.

Ten

Victoria's smile never faltered, and they'd been serving meals to homeless veterans for the past two hours. Her beauty radiated throughout the entire gymnasium of the old school where the Vets chatted and tried to capture a piece of her time.

He didn't blame them. Victoria was so easy to talk to, so easy to be around—the crowd would've never known that minutes before they'd come in she was nervous about fulfilling her first royal duty. He'd told her to be herself because she was a natural.

As she put the group at ease with her thankfulness for their services and the occasional gentle hug, Stefan continued to refill plates and cups. He let her use her charm on the room, and all the while the cameras were eating this up and proving to the world that she was the perfect woman for this position.

"Sir." Hector came up behind him and whispered, "The

cameraman would like you to stay closer to Victoria so he can capture your charity work together. That was the point of the visit."

Stefan glanced around the room of men and women who had given their all for their country…something Stefan could relate to. Guilt weighed heavily on his shoulders.

"I'm not here for a photo op, Hector." Stefan turned to face his assistant and lowered his voice. "I'm here to assist these people and show them that my wife and I care about them. I don't give a damn about the photographer. If he wants a good shot and story, tell him to take pictures of all these people who have been forgotten."

Hector folded his hands in front of him. "Sir, the whole reason for coming was to showcase your role as your country's leader and so the world could see you and Victoria as a united front."

Stefan sighed. "We are a united front, Hector. Tell the photographer he can nab a picture of us when we're done. We'll pose for one then. Until that point, we are here to help, not for some show for the world so they just *think* we are helping."

Hector nodded with a slight bow and walked off. When Stefan turned back with the pitcher of tea, an elderly man wearing a navy hat with his ship's name embroidered across the top was looking at him with tears in his eyes.

"Thank you," the man said.

Stefan looked down at the elderly man, who had scarred hands and a weathered face. "Nothing to thank me for, sir. I'm the one who needs to thank you."

The man used the edge of the table and the back of his chair to come to his feet. Stefan stepped back to give him room.

"I've never met royalty before, sir," the man said. "It is an honor to have you and your beautiful wife here. And for you two to be so caring…well, it just touches an old guy like me to know there are still people who give a damn."

Stefan held out his hand, waited for the man to shake it. "What's your name?"

"Lieutenant Raymond Waits," he replied, straightening his shoulders.

"I will personally see to it that this shelter is funded for as long as possible." Stefan would make it happen no matter what. "I will also make sure my wife and I schedule a stop here twice a year when we are in the States."

The handshake quickly turned to an embrace as Raymond put his free arm around Stefan. He hadn't meant to get on a soapbox, but dammit, he understood loyalty to a country, and these vets deserved respect and love.

"Now, I better get back to refilling drinks or you'll be my only friend here," Stefan said when the vet pulled back, trying to look away as if embarrassed by the tears in his eyes.

Raymond nodded, taking his seat. As Stefan moved on, he glanced up to see Victoria watching him from across the room, and he didn't miss the moisture that had gathered in her own eyes. Obviously she'd seen the emotional moment.

Stefan smiled and winked at her, trying to lighten the mood because the last thing he wanted was for her to believe he was some sort of hero. He was just doing what was right.

By the time they needed to leave to get across town to the library for a fund-raiser, Stefan had already discussed the funding with Hector, who was putting a plan into motion. Now this is what being powerful was all about. Why have such control if you couldn't use it for the greater good?

They posed for just a few pictures with some of the soldiers and promised to return. Stefan hated that a piece of his heart was left with this group of remarkable men and women. He wanted to rule his country while keeping his emotions in check, not tear up when he came across charity cases.

Victoria swiped tears away as they headed to their waiting car. Once settled inside, he pulled her against his side and sighed.

"You okay?" he asked.

"You're amazing." She sniffed. "I don't care if the media portrays you as a bad boy, Stefan. I know the truth, and you've just revealed it to a room full of thankful vets."

He didn't want to be commended for doing what was right and good. "I wish I could do more," he said honestly. "But we'll do what we can where we can."

Tori reached up, cupping his cheek, and shifted to face him. "You're one amazing king, Stefan."

She touched her lips to his, briefly, tenderly. But he didn't want gentle, he wanted hard, fast. Now. He wanted to feel her beneath him, feel her come undone around him.

His hand slid up her bare thigh and her breath caught.

"Didn't we just do this the other day?" she asked, smiling against his mouth.

"Glad I could make an impression," he murmured. "But I plan on torturing you until we get to the library. It is across town, you know. I may even continue for the ride home afterward."

She slid a hand up over his denim-clad leg and cupped him. "Torture can be a two-way street, you know."

"I'm counting on it."

As his mouth captured hers again, his hand snaked up beneath her dress. When his fingertip traveled along the edge of her lacy panties, her legs parted. Yeah, he wanted what she was offering, but foreplay was so much fun, and he wanted to relish these next few moments of driving her wild. He'd always considered himself a giving lover, but with Victoria he wanted to focus on her and her pleasure. Everything about touching her, kissing her was so much more arousing than seeking a fast release.

Her palm slid up and down over the zipper of his jeans…a zipper that was becoming increasingly painful.

He tore his lips from hers. "Tori, you're way too good at this game."

When she put both hands on his shoulders and slid to the floor between his legs, he swallowed hard. "Way too good," he repeated.

And thankfully he'd put the divider up between them and the driver because she was reciprocating the favor he'd given her a few days ago.

How was he ever going to get over all of this if she chose to leave?

Victoria couldn't stop smiling. Finally, she'd managed to take control, shut Stefan up and make him lose his mind all at once. Yeah, she was pretty proud of herself.

The ride to the library and then home was quite memorable…for both of them.

As they walked up the brick steps toward her front door, a car pulling into the circular drive had her turning back to see who the visitor was.

Her heart stopped, her body tensing at the unwelcome guest.

No. This couldn't be happening. What was he doing here?

"Victoria?" Stefan touched her arm. "Who is it?"

Before she could answer, the car came to a stop and Alex unfolded himself from the two-door red sports car.

"I'll talk to him," Stefan told her, jaw clenching. "You can go inside."

Victoria held up a hand and shook her head. "No, you go on in."

"Like hell," she heard him mutter as she descended the steps to see what her ex could possibly want.

Victoria didn't want to play the alpha male drama game so she ignored Stefan's remark. All she cared about now was why Alex had showed up here like he still had a right to.

"Victoria," he greeted her as she came to the base of the steps. "You look beautiful as always."

Crossing her arms over her chest, she thanked God that seeing him did absolutely nothing for her.

"What are you doing here, Alex?"

His eyes darted over her shoulder, then back. "Can we talk privately?"

"You're kidding, right?" Stefan asked from behind her.

Victoria turned, gave him the silent "shut up" look, and turned back to Alex. "Whatever you want to say, say it so Stefan and I can go inside."

For the first time in his life Alex looked uncomfortable. Once again his eyes darted from Stefan to Victoria, and she knew he wasn't going to say anything as long as Stefan was around. This bulldog stare down could go on all night, and she had other plans, which involved her husband getting naked and staying that way for a long time. She wasn't going to let her ex who destroyed her ruin her evening or her life.

Victoria spun back around and walked up a few steps to Stefan before whispering, "Give me five minutes. He's harmless and he won't talk if you're glaring at him like my bodyguard."

"He hurt you, Victoria. He has no right being here."

Funny how Stefan wasn't being territorial. He was upset because Alex had broken her. God, her heart melted even more. Did he have any idea how romantic, how sexy that was?

Stefan eyed her and she was positive he was going to argue, but he leaned forward, kissed her slightly and said, "He can't touch you now."

Stefan turned and walked up the steps into the house, leaving Victoria even more stunned. But she couldn't think right now about all the amazing ways Stefan was showing her love. He may not even know it yet, but he was falling for her.

It ticked her off that her ex stood behind her. She was supposed to be seducing her husband, showing him just how good they were together. Instead she was dealing with the one man who'd used her, cut her down in public and tossed her aside as if she were useless.

Shoulders back, head held high, she faced him once again and met him at the bottom of the steps. Stefan was right; Alex couldn't hurt her again. She refused to let him have an ounce of control in her life anymore. She took pride in the fact she was stronger now, thanks to Stefan.

"You have five minutes," she told him, resuming her stance and crossing her arms.

"I made a mistake." He took a step toward her, reached out to touch her shoulder, and Victoria jerked back. "Please, Tori."

"You've got to be kidding me. First of all, I'm married."

Alex shoved his hand back in his pocket. "You don't love him like you did me."

Victoria smiled. "You're absolutely right. What I feel for Stefan is completely different. I would do anything at all for him. I've never felt so appreciated and treasured as I do with him."

"Is that the money and title talking?"

Before her mind could process what she was doing she found her open palm connecting with the side of his face.

"I will not defend myself to anyone, especially you," she told him, rubbing her thumb over her stinging hand. "Now get out of my sight before I let Stefan come back out and settle this in a very old-fashioned, clichéd way."

She didn't need to tell Alex what that was. Any man would know.

He rubbed the side of his cheek. "I didn't come to argue with you. I wanted to know if your marriage was for real, and I just couldn't imagine you fell in love with someone that fast and married. I mean, you always told me you two were only friends."

"We *were* always friends. Now I realize that Stefan was the only man for me. And this marriage is more real than anything you and I ever shared."

She didn't wait for him to respond. Victoria pivoted on her heel and marched up the steps, running smack into a hard, familiar chest, instantly enveloped by a scent she'd come to associate with her husband.

Strong hands wrapped around her biceps and pulled her flush with his body.

"It's okay," Stefan whispered. "I've got you."

He walked her into the house and she realized tears were streaming down her cheeks. Had he heard everything? Fear and worry took the place of the anger she'd felt only moments ago. She didn't want him to know how she felt yet. She couldn't chance ruining their relationship.

Any and every feeling she had for Stefan totally overshadowed anything she'd ever had for Alex.

"We need complete privacy," Stefan murmured.

"Yes, Your Highness," one of the guards stationed inside the door replied.

Stefan swept Victoria up into his arms and she settled

her face against his neck. Alex's presence had awakened something in her, something she thought she'd never feel again. Love. But not love for her ex. No, she was utterly and completely in love with the man who carried her, the man who knew when to let silence express his care for her, the man who showed his tender, compassionate side at the shelter only an hour ago. The man who'd taken such joy in pleasuring her, in the bedroom and out.

Her husband. She knew she'd fallen for him, but this moment solidified the fact she was completely in love. And perhaps she'd been in love with her best friend since they met. On some level she knew that to be true. But now she knew without a doubt that she loved him wholeheartedly and without any reservations.

He'd given her the control over the end of their marriage and, to be honest, she wanted to make this relationship permanent. And not just permanent because they were friends and they got along in bed, but permanent because she knew Prince Stefan Alexander was her soul mate.

And Fate had given her the chance to see just how a marriage, a love life should be. Now she just had to show Stefan.

Eleven

He was the only man for her?

Dear God, what a bombshell. When the hell had she decided that? If she were having any notions of love…he couldn't even fathom where that would put them.

Stefan kicked the bedroom door closed, crossed the spacious room and gently laid Victoria on the chaise chair in front of the balcony doors. Sunshine streamed in through the windows, bathing their bedroom in bright rays.

"I'll get you some water," he told her, his voice rough.

"No." Victoria wiped her damp cheeks and sat up straighter. "I'm fine. Sorry for the tears. I was caught off guard."

Stefan stared down at Victoria, surprised that he was jealous over the ex, who was obviously out of her life for good, she was shedding tears over.

"I'm sorry it upset you to see him," he told her, easing

down on the edge of the chaise beside her hip. "I'll advise my staff to keep him away if he returns."

Victoria smiled. "I appreciate that, but I doubt he'll come back. He hates having his pride hurt, and my refusal to accept his lame apology and rush back into his arms really damaged his ego."

Her silky, golden blond hair lay over one shoulder, and his fingers itched to mess it up, to see it fanned out on her white, satin sheets as he made love to her again. She was always a stunning woman, but since they'd become intimate, her beauty had taken on a whole new level of sensuality.

But he couldn't pick up where they'd left off in the car, not when she was so upset and certainly not with the revelation he'd just heard.

"I wish you wouldn't cry," he told her, trying not to think about what he'd overheard. "That's one thing I cannot stand."

"My emotions are harder to hide than yours," she explained. "I can't just close them off, Stefan. I have feelings and sometimes they come out when I don't want them to."

He rubbed his hands over his thighs in an attempt to keep from reaching out to her. Treading lightly during these next few minutes was a must.

"I'm okay," she assured him, wiping her cheeks and pasting on a smile. "Really. Don't let Alex ruin our day."

Alex hadn't ruined the day, but her verbal epiphany had sure as hell put an unexpected spin on where they stood with this marriage—and its open ending once the six months were over.

He hated to bring up what was such a humiliating time in her life, but since Alex showed up, that had to be playing through her mind. What type of bastard would purposely have pictures taken with his new girlfriend, a pregnant one at that, while still engaged to another woman?

He was quite convinced Victoria's ex wasn't a man, but the lowest form of life for treating her the way he had. Stefan felt he deserved a shiny gold medal to add to the collection on his royal coat because he hadn't busted the guy in the face.

She turned her head, looking out the double glass doors that led to her balcony. As he watched her profile, he saw her eyes fill up again.

Well, hell. Now what had happened? This was precisely why he never got too involved with women. He just plain didn't understand the emotional roller coasters they seemed to always be on.

"I just had a bit of an epiphany, and it hit me harder than I expected."

A tight band formed around his chest and squeezed. Did that mean she truly felt what she'd told Alex about their marriage? Was she going to discuss it now? He sure as hell wasn't going to bring it up. Yeah, he was being a coward, but there was a first time for everything.

"Since you're so quiet, I'm assuming the mood is gone."

He nodded and sighed. No way could they become intimate right now, not with her emotions so high.

"I think we need to take a breather for today."

Hurt flashed in her eyes before her defiant chin lifted. "You've never been known for running away."

"I'm not running." He was sprinting. "You need some time to think." Some time to come to grips with her emotions that scared the living hell out of him.

Before she could guilt him more with her expressive blue eyes, he came to his feet, walked out into the hall, closed the door and leaned back against it. His chest ached, like someone was squeezing the breath from his lungs.

They'd only been married over a month. How in the world would they make it to the six-month mark with their feelings so at odds? Something about seeing her ex made Victoria realize her emotions were deeper than he'd thought. He only hoped she was just shocked by seeing Alex and once she truly thought about what she'd said, how she was feeling and where they needed to go from here, she'd see that maybe what she thought was romantic love was just a deeper level of friendship.

He rested his head against the solid wood door and closed his eyes. Sleeping together had changed things, but he'd had no idea Victoria would fall for him.

Stefan didn't have a clue about how to proceed from here, but he did know that if Victoria cared for him the way she thought she did, he was going to have one hell of a problem on his hands. And it had nothing to do with the crown or the documentary.

Love wasn't something he had ever experienced outside his family or his country. He certainly wouldn't try it out on the one person who meant the most to him. He couldn't risk losing Victoria's friendship by mucking it up with an emotion so questionable.

Love had no room in this marriage.

"So based on the information you sent us, we completely agree that this story shouldn't be kept silent."

Relief speared through Stefan at Bronson's statement. He'd called Victoria's brothers to see if they had time to meet last minute, but Bronson was the only one available. Anthony had to stay home with the kids because the baby was napping and Charlotte was out.

He'd had to leave the house. He couldn't face Victoria right now, not with her emotions so raw, so...gut wrenching. They needed a break and he needed to focus because sex and tears could cloud his vision.

He'd cut off his arm before he intentionally hurt her, but if she had feelings that deep for him, he wasn't sure how he could avoid damaging her already battered heart.

"Stefan?"

He focused back on Bronson, who had switched television shows for his sweet little girl, Bella. She was now enthralled in another program with crazy characters singing and dancing across the screen, making silly faces to get the toddler audience to laugh.

"Sorry," Stefan said. "Does Anthony feel the same way?"

"Absolutely." Bronson sat down on the leather sofa and stretched an arm across the back of the cushions. "We both believe that this story, if told the right way, would have the impact you want to make. Your father was simply the victim of bad timing, from the affair, to the public argument, to the death of your mother."

"So you'll take on this project?" Stefan asked, hopeful.

"If you trust Anthony and me to do the documentary justice, we'd be happy to. But, keep in mind we've never done this type of film before."

Stefan knew the two perfectionists wouldn't let him, or his country, down. Stefan wanted his people to see his family in the way he did, to see that his father was not a murderer, but a man who was grieving, a man who'd lost his wife after such a public scandal and had instantly gotten a less-than-stellar reputation.

With the beginning of his reign, Stefan wanted to wipe the slate clean and remove the dark stain from his family's name.

"You have no idea what this means to me," Stefan said. "I owe you."

Bronson eased forward in his seat across from Stefan and nodded. "You can pay me back by telling me why my sister called here in tears and my wife is currently on the phone with her."

Na pari i eychi. He should've known that this meeting wouldn't be simple.

"Victoria had a very emotional day." And wasn't that a vast understatement. "Whatever she wants to share with Mia, or you, is up to her."

Bronson sighed. "I probably don't need to tell you that Victoria is in this marriage deeper than you think."

Stefan swallowed the lump of guilt and fear that crept up. "No."

"And I'm the last person to give advice on how to go about keeping a woman happy, but try not to hurt her."

Could be too late for that.

"Can you at least tell me what happened today that got her upset?"

"Alex came by."

Which wasn't a lie, but it was a combination of Alex's appearance and her revelation that had her so distressed. Was she upset because she didn't want to love him? Or was she upset because she knew in her heart that he couldn't love her that way in return?

"What the hell did that bastard want?" Bronson all but roared.

Stefan shook his head. "I let Victoria talk to him alone, but she claimed he wanted to apologize. He didn't believe our marriage was real and thought she would take him back. I didn't hear what all was said, but I did see her give him an impressive slap."

Bronson chuckled. "She's only been that angry twice: once when we were kids and I tried to put her Barbie dolls' heads in the garbage disposal and once when I was being an ass to Mia. Victoria loves with her whole heart, and once it gets bruised, she's like a bear. You don't want to cross her."

Well, damn. Victoria hadn't come right out and said she loved him, but the implication was there. God, he couldn't do love, had never wanted to. So how the hell had he allowed this to happen? He'd told Tori going in that this wasn't about love, that the marriage was only about his country.

Why had she done this to herself and how had he not seen this coming?

Twelve

"Guess I had my first emotional breakdown."

Victoria sat on the simple white bench across from the guest bath where Stefan had showered after his early morning run. They hadn't spoken since her crying jag last night. He'd never come to bed and she assumed he'd slept in the spare room, but she couldn't go on with all this tension inside her body or her home.

"I guess so," he replied.

Stefan leaned against the door frame, all tanned and gloriously misty from the shower. One crisp white towel sat low on his hips, and he'd draped another around his neck. Muscles covered with beautiful tattooed artwork stared back at her, mocking her. No matter her heart's emotions, her body wanted him and instantly responded.

"I'm sorry about yesterday," she told him, bringing her eyes back up to his face. "Seeing Alex threw me off."

Stefan's dark brows drew together. "Why be sorry?"

Victoria resisted the urge to look down at the floor. Instead she tilted her chin, held his gaze and shook her head. "Because I made you uncomfortable."

The muscle in his jaw clenched, and she knew he was still uncomfortable. Was it just Alex's presence and her emotional breakdown that had made him ill at ease, or was it more? Had he heard what she'd said about their relationship?

The implications of her outburst to Alex were something Stefan was not ready for. She wasn't even sure she was ready herself, but she could no longer control her feelings toward her husband. Her heart clenched as if trying to protect itself from the inevitable hurt that would surely consume her once they discussed what her emotions meant to their marriage.

Stefan walked toward her, squatted down between her legs and took her hands in his. "I just have a lot more to deal with than I first thought. I can't take on more than protecting my country and gaining my title."

"I know, and I didn't mean to add to your worry."

His gaze traveled down and settled into the V of her silk nightgown before coming back up to meet hers. Shivers raced through her. So she hadn't completely scared him off.

But he let go of her hands, and that giant step back from intimacy spoke volumes. He was pulling away. Maybe the hurt would slither its evil way in sooner than she'd thought.

A chill crept over her.

Seduction had been on her mind when she'd dressed for bed last night, but he'd never come in, and now, catching him fresh from his shower, it seemed her efforts were moot. He was obviously having no part of her plan.

Was this how the rest of their marriage would play out? They'd dance around each other all because Stefan was afraid to confront her emotions—or his, for that matter?

She didn't believe for one second that he wasn't feeling more for her. She did believe, however, that he was going to fight that feeling for as long as she'd allow it.

"Come back to bed with me," she told him.

His eyes remained locked on hers. "I have some work to go over with Hector."

The steel wall had been erected in a matter of seconds, and he was making no attempt to let her in. But in his defense, he'd told her up front this could be nothing more and like a damn fool she'd been on board with the preposterous plan.

Stefan came to his feet, the subtle movement sending his fresh masculine scent wafting around her, enveloping her, and she knew that's as close as she'd come to being surrounded by her husband right now...and maybe for a while.

"Maybe I'll see you for lunch. I have a lot to do so don't wait on me."

And with that, he headed down the hall.

Victoria wasn't naive. She knew if Stefan could've gotten that title and crown any other way besides marriage, he would've jumped at that opportunity without question. But he couldn't get around it and he *did* need her. No, he was not the marrying type, but he was the type who thrived on loyalty, honesty and integrity...all a good base for marriage and love.

Since she couldn't actually say the words without him pulling back even more—if that were possible—all she could do was show him her love, show him they were meant to be.

With his upcoming coronation and responsibilities on his mind, he'd never complained, never even spoken of worries. He'd been right here with her, trying to help her get her line started, trying to get her to open her mind and really create some spectacular pieces.

Of course when he wasn't being loyal and helpful, he was being sexy and impossible to resist. How could she not love a man like that? And how could he not see that he loved her?

Stefan had been gone all day, but he was due to return home soon. Victoria had requested Hector remain in the front of the house and only to come around back in a dire emergency.

With a deep breath, she set her plan in motion by dipping her bare foot into the pool and gliding it along. Yeah, that would be refreshing once she submerged her entire body…nude.

Okay, so maybe there was a little bit of a reckless side to her, but Stefan brought it out. No way would she ever have thought to get into her infinity pool overlooking the L.A. skyline while wearing nothing but a suntan and a hair clip.

And no way in hell would she ever have done something like this for Alex.

Looking back she could admit that she'd been in love with Stefan for years, but it took the intimacy, the devotion, to finally open her eyes to her true Prince Charming. But she'd never really thought of him as a prince. To her he was her best friend, her confidant, now her lover and husband.

This afternoon they'd ended up sharing a strained lunch and he'd informed her he'd be busy the rest of the day—but at least he'd come for lunch. He had gone into her spare office to check emails and talk with Hector about the coronation. She let him do his thing because that whole royalty territory wasn't her forte. But she was going to have to get more comfortable with it because she intended to stick out this marriage, title and all. And while she was afraid of what being a queen truly meant, she wasn't afraid to sacrifice herself for the man she loved.

While she'd never played the meek and mild woman before, doing so with the title of queen wasn't even an option. She loved being able to assist with charities and use her name and title to help others. And when Stefan had taken charge with the Veterans' Homeless Shelter, her heart had melted. That's the type of work she wanted to get behind. That's the part of being royalty she could completely embrace.

Victoria slid out of her short silk robe and let it puddle next to the steps. The thick candles she'd lit all around the pool added just that extra bit of romance. When Stefan stepped out onto her patio, she wanted him to take in the scene: discarded red silk robe, flickering candlelight and his wife naked in the water.

She may be uncomfortable with this, but she was a Dane and everything was about setting the stage to pack a punch with the audience. And there was only one audience member she cared about.

Now all she had to do was float lazily on her back, wait and fantasize about how spectacular this night would be. Hopefully Stefan would see the way she stepped outside her comfort zone for him, and if he did, surely he'd realize that her love knew no limits.

And perhaps he could step out of his comfort zone, too.

Stefan raked his hands through his hair. His coronation was scheduled to take place in a few months and he was trying to get a start for this documentary so he could at least assure his people that a new era was going to begin, starting with the truth, to remove the black mark hovering over his father's name.

His investigators had found several people who were

willing to speak on camera if a film was produced. Hector had been working behind the scenes, as well, jotting down key things he remembered from that time...after all, the man had also been the assistant to Stefan's father and knew more than most.

But right now his mind was still plagued by the awkwardness with Victoria. He knew she'd picked up on the distance he'd put between them, but he needed the time to process everything. And he still hadn't come to a damn conclusion.

He made his way up to their room, where he fully expected her to be, so he was surprised to see a note resting on her pillow.

Meet me at the pool.

Intrigued, he tossed the note aside and headed back downstairs. When he stepped through the double glass doors, he stopped, taking in the ambiance all at once.

"I'm dreaming. No way is the prim and proper Victoria Dane skinny-dipping out in the open."

She moved through the darkened water like she had all the confidence in the world. "You've been trying since we met to get me here. I thought I'd put you out of your misery."

Arousal shot through him even harder as she flipped, floating on her back with those breasts poking out of the water. His palms itched to touch them. He'd been without her for two days. Way too damn long.

He pulled his T-shirt over his head and tossed it aside. After toeing off his shoes, he unfastened his pants and slid his boxer briefs down, then kicked them aside, as well. There was only so much willpower a man could have.

For a moment he simply stared. Finding a naked woman in a pool was every man's fantasy, but he wasn't stupid.

He knew how her mind worked. She was trying to draw him back into her web and she was spinning it beautifully.

"Are you going to stand there all night?" she asked. "I'm pretty lonely in here."

Like he needed another invitation.

Stefan didn't even bother with the steps. He dove right in, making sure he reached his hands out toward her body. As he came up, he glided his palms over every wet, luscious curve.

"You feel amazing," he muttered when his face was next to hers. "It takes a lot to surprise me, Tori. I honestly never dreamed you would've given into this skinny-dipping thing."

A naughty smile spread across her lips. "Well, when you first asked me, you just wanted to see me naked. Then it just became a game to see if I'd cave. But you've been working so hard, I thought you deserved a reward."

He nipped her chin, her jaw, all the while keeping his arms wrapped around her waist. "Reward, huh? I think I'll reward you for making a part of my fantasy come true."

Her gaze locked on his as her brows drew together. "A part? What am I missing?"

"I wanted you in the palace pool. On my turf."

Victoria rolled her eyes. "No way. Do you know how many staff members you have? There's never a moment of privacy there. At least here I only had to tell Hector to stay out front since the other guard is off for the night."

Stefan smiled. "I'm not complaining."

Resting a delicate hand on his bare chest, Victoria smiled. "I just want to enjoy our time together. However long it may be."

Something flipped in Stefan's heart—something he didn't want to explore or identify.

His arms tightened around her waist. Her vibrant blue

eyes, sparkling from the candlelight and full moon, studied his face. She bit her bottom lip as her gaze darted down.

"What is it?" he asked, tipping her chin up so she would look at him again.

"What will happen after the coronation?"

A sliver of fear slid through him. Was she thinking of staying at the end of the six months? Surprisingly, he wanted her to, but he didn't want her love...not in the way he feared she was heading.

Damn it. He was a selfish bastard. He couldn't have it both ways. He either had to let her go after the coronation or step up and face her feelings. He wasn't crazy about either of his options.

How could he love someone forever? He'd never thought that far ahead when it came to a relationship. Living in the moment was more his speed. What if he tried loving her and a year into the "real" marriage he decided he wasn't cut out for it? She'd be even more hurt. And Victoria deserved better than that.

Why did he have to choose? Hadn't he laid out a fool-proof, simple plan before they married?

"I don't want to put a damper on this party," she told him. "Forget I asked. Just tell me what you want right now."

Everything she was willing to give.

She deserves better than what you're willing to give. She's sacrificed everything for you. Her heart is yours if you'll take it. If not, she'll get tired and leave, you selfish jerk.

Her wet body molded against his and her hips rocked against him as her arms encircled his neck. He wasn't going to explore further than right now. He didn't want to keep seeing that hurt seep into her eyes.

For now he would be a self-centered bastard and take

what she offered. In the end, when she realized she couldn't change him and needed more, she would walk away. And he would get what he deserved. But until that day, he'd enjoy every moment of being married to his best friend.

Victoria was just too damn sexy and tempting to turn away. And he knew by taking what she was offering, he was damning their friendship because he had a feeling she'd be leaving soon.

Thirteen

The shrill ringing of the phone jarred Victoria from an amazing dream. The second ring had her slapping a hand over the cell that sat next to her bed only to realize the ring wasn't coming from her cell, but from Stefan's.

If this was another woman…

Surely not. Those calls seemed to have either died down, or Stefan was doing a good job of intervening before she knew.

She glanced over, noting the man was completely out—if his heavy breathing meant anything. And he claimed *she* snored? Reaching across him, she grabbed his cell and answered it.

"Hello?"

"Victoria?"

"Yes." Not recognizing the woman's voice, she moved away from the bed and toward the balcony doors. "Who is this?"

The lady on the other end sniffed. Was she crying?

"This…this is Karina. Mikos's wife. He's been in a rock-climbing accident." Karina wept, and static came through the phone before she continued. "I need Stefan to come home."

Panic gripping her, Victoria looked back to her husband, knowing when she woke him she'd have to tell him news that could possibly change his life forever. This could not be happening.

"Of course," Victoria agreed. "We'll be there as soon as we can."

"Please hurry. The doctors aren't hopeful," Karina cried. "His injuries are substantial. He's in surgery now."

A sickening pit in her stomach threatened to rise in her throat. What would Stefan do if he lost his brother? He'd just lost his father. Fate couldn't be this cruel. Besides, Stefan and his brother were expert rock climbers. What could've gone wrong?

"As soon as my pilot is ready we'll be on the plane," she assured Karina. "Please keep us updated and try to be strong."

Her sister-in-law said a watery thank-you and hung up. Victoria stepped onto the balcony to call her pilot. Even at five o'clock in the morning, he wouldn't mind. He'd been a loyal employee to her family for years, and last-minute things occasionally arose.

Once she had the pilot readying the plane, she took a deep breath and bolstered up her courage to wake Stefan and tell him the news. She needed to stay strong and positive and be there for him no matter what.

When she sank down on the edge of his side of the bed, he roused and his lids fluttered. He flashed that sweet smile she'd grown to love waking up to, and she tried to return the gesture, but her eyes filled with tears.

So much for being strong.

"What happened? I thought I heard the phone ring." He glanced at the clock on the nightstand then back to her as if realizing early morning calls were almost never good news. "Victoria?"

"Your brother was in an accident. We need to get back home."

Stefan jerked up in bed. "What kind of accident? Who called?"

"Karina called and Mikos is in surgery. He was in a rock-climbing accident. That's all I know."

Stefan closed his eyes, shaking his head. "I need to call your pilot."

She laid a hand on his arm, waiting for him to open his eyes and look at her. "Already done. Now get dressed and let's go."

"Wait." He grabbed her hand as she started to rise from the bed. "You don't need to go."

Hurt threatened to seep in. "You don't want me to?"

"Yes, I want you to, but you're so busy here designing your bridal collection, and your brothers may need you on the set."

She'd drop everything without even thinking for the man she loved. Didn't he realize that?

"Do you think I'd choose any of that over family?" she asked.

He studied her face, then nodded. "No, I know what's most important to you." He lifted her hand to his lips and kissed her knuckles. "Thank you for making my family yours."

"We're a team, Stefan." She came to her feet. "Now let's get changed and I'll throw some things into a suitcase."

They worked in a rushed silence to get out the door and to the airport. By the time they boarded the plane, along with the guards, she could tell Stefan was a ball of nerves. He hadn't spoken, hadn't even really glanced her way. He was lost in thought and she had no doubt he was not only feeling helpless, he was reminded of the fact that his mother was gone and his father had just passed away eight months ago.

"It will be okay," she assured him, placing her hand over his during the takeoff. "Once we arrive and you can see him, you'll feel better."

Stefan merely nodded and Victoria knew he wasn't in a chatty, lift-your-spirits type of mood, but she wanted to stay positive for him and wanted him to know she was there.

"I know you're trying to help," he told her, squeezing her hand. "But you being here is really all I need right now."

Victoria swallowed her fear. "I wouldn't be anywhere else."

Stefan held on to Victoria's hand as they made their way down the hospital corridor. The gleaming white floors and antiseptic smell did nothing to ease his mind. He wanted to see his brother. Wanted to see that he was going to be okay and know what the hell had happened. He and Mikos had practically been raised climbing those rocks in Kalymnos. They climbed the hardest, most dangerous rocks for fun, and people had always tried to warn them they were risking too much.

He couldn't lose his last family member. He refused to believe fate would be that cruel to him.

As he approached the nurses' desk to ask where his brother's room was, Karina came rushing toward him, throwing her arms around his waist and holding tight.

"Oh, thank God you're here," she sobbed into his chest

before lifting her tear-stained face to look up at him. "He's out of surgery and so far he's holding his own."

Stefan held on to his sister-in-law's slender shoulders. "What's the prognosis?"

"Better than when he first arrived," she told him, tears pooling in her red-rimmed eyes. "They didn't think he'd make it through surgery. But since he has, they are monitoring him. He has…"

She dropped her head to her chest, sobbing once again. Stefan pulled her close, and as much as he wanted to know what the hell they were up against, he also knew the most important thing—his brother was alive. Karina had been here for hours all alone, and right now she needed someone to comfort her.

"I'll go see what the doctor says," Victoria whispered behind him.

He nodded and led Karina over to the sofa. "Would you like some water?"

Easing back from him, she shook her head and toyed with the tissue she had clutched in her hand. "No."

"Have you eaten?"

Again she shook her head.

"Victoria would be happy to get you something, or you can go and we will stay here," he offered.

"I can't leave," she told him. "I can't even think of eating. I just want someone to tell me for certain that Mikos will be fine. That he'll be able to walk again, talk again and not be a vegetable."

That meant his brother obviously had a brain trauma.

Stefan took her hands in his. "Does he have swelling in his brain?"

Karina nodded. "They drilled holes to alleviate some of the pressure, but all we can do is wait. They put him in a drug-induced coma."

Stefan closed his eyes. How many times had they been rock climbing in Kalymnos? Countless. It's what they did. Anything to be reckless and adventurous.

"He'll be fine," Stefan said, squeezing her hands. "He's tough, and there's no way he won't fight to come back to you."

Karina sniffed. "I'm pregnant."

Stefan sat up straight in his seat. "Excuse me?"

"I just confirmed with the doctor while Mikos was out climbing. I was going to tell him when he got home. What if…"

Again she collapsed against him and sobbed.

Dear Lord, a baby? Stefan couldn't imagine his brother not pulling through, but even if he did, what would they all be faced with?

His baby brother was just as strong and determined as he was. So there was no way, even if he woke up and couldn't walk, that his brother wouldn't move heaven and earth to get back on his feet…especially with a baby on the way.

Victoria rounded the corner and took a seat across from them. "The nurse said the doctor would be out shortly to talk to us. He's actually in Mikos's room right now evaluating him again."

"Thank you," Stefan told her.

"Can I get you guys anything?" she offered. "I saw a lounge down the hall. Coffee, water?"

Both he and Karina declined and Victoria nodded as she eased back in her seat. In no time the doctor came down the hall.

Stefan stood and extended his hand. "I'm Stefan Alexander. How's my brother?"

The doctor shook his hand. "I know who you are, Prince Alexander. I'm happy to tell you that your brother made it through the surgery better than any of my colleagues or I thought he would. We will be keeping a close watch on him, but even in his drug-induced coma, he's responding to us being in the room."

Hearing such positive news had Stefan expelling a breath he'd been holding for quite some time.

"So where do we go from here?" he asked.

"Well, I think it's good that you're all here. He needs strength and support from his loved ones to encourage him. I can let you visit, but only one at a time and not for very long."

Stefan nodded. "I understand. When do you believe he'll wake up?"

"That really depends on the swelling, when we will back off the meds, and how his vitals are when we try to bring him back from the coma. This could be a long process, but right now all we can do is pray and hope he'll fight the rest of the way."

Stefan had no doubt his brother would do just that. "Thank you, Doctor."

"Go see him," Stefan urged Karina. "Tell him your news and give him something to fight for."

Karina smiled. "You think I should tell him before he wakes up?"

"Absolutely." He leaned in, kissed her damp cheek. "Go on. We'll be here."

She all but ran down the hall, and Stefan sank to the sofa. Scared, helpless, yet optimistic, he really had no idea how to feel or what to do next. He just wanted his vibrant brother to be up on his feet and celebrating the good news of the baby.

"She's pregnant, isn't she?" Victoria asked, sitting beside him.

"Yes."

"Bless her heart. I can't imagine how scared she must be." She rested her delicate hand, the one that held his diamond ring and wedding band, on his leg. "What can I do for you?"

Stefan wrapped an arm around her, pulling her against his side. "Be here. Don't leave me."

She tilted her head to look up into his eyes. "Stefan, even if we weren't married I would've dropped everything to be with you."

And he knew in his heart she meant that. Which made her invaluable and precious. He'd always known she was the best thing in his life, but now he knew he couldn't get through another trying time without her. Yet if he couldn't commit to loving her the way she deserved, what did that possibly mean for their future?

Fourteen

"Can you tell us about your brother, Prince Stefan?"

"Is he going to pull through?"

"Was this an accident or a suicide attempt?"

That last question from the slam of paparazzi stopped Stefan cold outside the hospital as he and Victoria were trying to make their way to his car waiting at the curb.

"Excuse me!" Victoria shouted with her hands up. "But my brother-in-law is in there fighting for his life. We request that you respect our family's privacy. There will be a formal announcement on his prognosis later, but for now you can put on record that this was in no way a suicide attempt. We would appreciate if you would get facts straight before going to print."

Victoria looped her arm through his as she led the way, plowing past the flashbulbs and reporters screaming questions. Thank God she was experienced in handling the media circus. Being one of the famous Hollywood Danes, she was no stranger to the chaos.

She held tight to his arm as she pushed through the crowd and slid into the awaiting car. Before another question could be shouted their way, his driver slammed the door to the busybodies.

"They've never known the meaning of the word privacy," Victoria muttered. "I'm sorry."

"You're apologizing after that?" he asked, turning to look at her. "I can't thank you enough for handling that mess."

"That suicide comment was uncalled for."

He shifted, staring straight ahead. "Yes, it was. But you handled it beautifully."

"I hope it was okay that I mentioned a formal announcement later. I just assumed…"

Stefan glanced over to her as she closed her eyes and rested her head against the back of the seat. She was exhausted. Only yesterday she'd put in nearly twelve hours designing, then they'd made love until well after midnight and had woken up at five in the morning to fly to Greece. He was tired, but she was exhausted. He'd had his adrenaline to keep him pumping forward, but he had no clue what she was running on.

"That was fine. The media will spin a story or make up one if the truth isn't juicy enough. Letting them know there was more to come will pacify them for a bit," Stefan told her. "Once Mikos comes to and can speak for himself, this will be easier to handle."

Eyes closed, head still back, she gave a slight nod. "Yes, it will. Just tell me how I can help."

Stefan smiled. Even when she was dragging and on her last leg, she was still putting herself out there for him and his family. She was the strongest woman he knew and perfect to be reigning as queen...if she stayed.

No, he couldn't think about that right now.

"The best thing you can do is rest," he told her, wrapping his arm around her and pulling her down to his side. "Once we get back to the palace we'll both try to get some sleep."

And then he planned on staying at the hospital until his brother showed a vast improvement. He needed to give Karina some time to eat, to sleep, but once the doctor had assured them all that Mikos wouldn't be waking or likely showing much change for the next day or so, they'd all promised to go home, rest, shower and refuel and return the following morning.

Stefan glanced at his watch. He was so confused on time. Between not getting enough sleep before arriving and the time difference, he didn't know what time he thought it should be. But his body knew it was time for sleep.

By the time they reached the palace, Victoria had a soft, steady snore going. He smiled. He'd tried telling her once when they were teens that she snored when she'd stayed for a movie and had fallen asleep. Like any young lady, she refused to believe that she could do something so rude... or normal. So he'd let the moment go, until they'd fallen asleep once while on an evening picnic. They'd stayed out late and lain beneath the stars talking when she had drifted off and started snoring. She occasionally joked that maybe she did snore, but it wasn't loud like he claimed.

And every night for the past three months, he'd been lulled to sleep by those soft purrs, as she liked to call them. She may think it was a catlike purr, but it was more like a tiger growl.

When the driver opened the door, Stefan carefully slid her into his lap and eased from the car to carry her inside.

The palace wasn't a small place and his room was at the end of the long corridor, but that didn't matter, not when he held such precious cargo.

He wasn't about to wake her to make her do the zombie walk of exhaustion up to the room. Besides, she didn't weigh much, not when he was used to pulling his own body weight up while rock climbing.

Would he ever be able to climb again? If his brother didn't make it, he honestly didn't know. But he couldn't think like that. He wasn't scared to tackle the rocks again, but he didn't want to do it alone when he'd done it for so long with his brother.

Victoria was being strong through this process; he needed to mimic her actions in order to get Karina through this tough time.

The weight of Victoria in his arms felt so…right. He didn't know how he would've gotten through this initial shock of his brother's accident without her. She may have not done much, but being by his side, refusing to leave the hospital until he did and then handling the paparazzi like that only gave further evidence that she did love him.

But did she truly love him as deeply as she thought she did? Part of him wanted that to be true, but the friend side wanted her to be mistaken. He could admit his feelings for her had deepened since their wedding, but…love? No. He couldn't—wouldn't—go that far.

For years he'd wanted to explore their friendship to see what could come of it, but he never thought love or marriage would be a step in their lives.

Maybe fate didn't want them together since the timing was always off. Or maybe fate knew just when to throw them together for maximum support and impact. Between his father's death, her scandalous breakup and now his brother's accident, he knew they needed each other now more than ever.

Not to mention the upcoming coronation. Yes, they were always there to offer support and for consoling, but that's what friends did, right? All of that did not allude to love.

Stefan entered his suite, closing the high double doors behind him, and crossed to the bed, where he laid her down.

He stood over her, looking at all that pale blond hair spread across his navy, satin sheets. She was such a beauty, such an angel to have come into his life to save him over and over again.

How could he truly ever repay her?

Love had never been on his bucket list, had never been a priority. Love was something his brother had found, Victoria's brothers had found. Love wasn't something for a man who enjoyed women as much as he did or who didn't plan on marrying and settling down.

Yet here he was married to the most precious woman in his life. And, if he were being honest with himself, he'd admit that being married to Victoria was amazing. But they'd not really been married long and they'd been jet-setting back and forth. They hadn't lived in a realistic wedded atmosphere—or as realistic as it could get with being thrown into the proverbial spotlight as royalty.

As he slid off his own shoes and stripped down to his boxers, he slid in beside her and held her against his chest.

How would he manage if she stayed? Could he give her the marriage she deserved? She'd been engaged before—she obviously believed in happily ever afters—so why had she settled knowing he couldn't offer her a bond any deeper than their friendship and sex?

There were no easy answers, and Stefan had a sickening feeling he was going to hurt her before this was over.

* * *

Victoria had been working via phone and email with her staff back in L.A. Between a few mishaps on the set of her brothers' film that her assistant had to take care of and a glitch in the Italian silk she'd ordered not arriving on time, Victoria was ready to pull her hair out.

Added to all of the work tension, she was worried for Stefan. His brother was showing remarkable progress, but Stefan was so dead set on staying at the hospital to give his sister-in-law breaks whenever she needed them. Like any loving, dedicated woman, Karina wasn't leaving Mikos's side. Victoria envied their love.

On a sigh, Victoria sent off another email to her assistant to remind her to check on the dates for the bridal expo she hoped to be ready for…if that blasted silk would arrive.

As she was looking at possible backup outlets for material, her cell rang. Grabbing it from the oversized white desk in her suite, she answered.

"Hello."

"Tori," Bronson said. "So glad I caught you."

Her stomach sank. "There's another problem with a piece of the wardrobe?"

His rich laughter resounded through the earpiece. "Not at all. Your assistant did an amazing job coming to our rescue the other day. She deserves a raise."

And she was going to give her one, for all that poor girl would probably have to take on in Victoria's absence.

"So if it's not the wardrobe, what are you calling about?" she asked.

"I've been trying to reach Stefan, but it keeps going to voice mail. Are you with him by any chance?"

"No. And he keeps his phone off while he's at the hospital."

"How's his brother doing?" Bronson asked.

Victoria sank back into her cushy chair and dug her toes into the plush white carpet. "The doctors are astonished at the progress Mikos is making only two weeks after a near-death experience."

"That's great. You guys must really feel relieved."

"Stefan is still like a mother hen," Victoria told him. "He spends his days and evenings there. I think he'll feel better once Mikos is released and a nurse is with him at home."

"I hate to bother him," Bronson said, "but when he gets a chance could you have him call me?"

Victoria drew her brows together. "Something wrong?"

"Not at all," he assured her. "I just wanted to discuss that documentary we are going to be working on."

Victoria sat up straight. "Documentary?"

"Yeah, the one on his mother's death? Anthony and I are thrilled he came to us and trusted us to take on such a project."

Stefan went to her brothers for a film? And didn't say anything to her? A sliver of betrayal and dèjà vu spread through her. Had she been used again for her family name?

"Anyway, just tell him no rush," Bronson went on, no idea of the instant turmoil flooding through her. "He can call me when he gets a chance."

Victoria hung up, laced her fingers together and settled her elbows on the desk. Her forehead rested against her hands and she refused to let her past relationship make her have doubts and fears about this one.

Stefan was not Alex. Alex had used her to gain an upper hand in Hollywood. To be part of the Danes, to be on camera whenever possible and to gain access to her famous brothers.

Alex had never loved her the way she had him—or

thought she had—he'd only been with her to see how far he could get with his goal of becoming famous.

A ball of dread filled her stomach.

Was Stefan using her? He'd technically used her to gain his title, but she knew about that and was happy to help. But was he using her as a way to get to her brothers? To make sure that he was in the family and make it that much harder for Bronson and Anthony to turn him down?

And what was this documentary about his mother's death? She had no idea he was even thinking such a thing. Oh, she'd known about the scandalous way the media had portrayed the accident, but Victoria had never believed the late King Alexander had anything to do with his wife's death. The media just wanted to make it a Princess Grace type of story and glamorize something that was so tragic.

So why hadn't he told her? And what else had he been hiding?

Had he lied about other things—like all those calls from other women? Had he not answered them because she'd been sitting right there?

Oh, God, she was going to be sick.

Before her humiliation with Alex she never would've entertained such terrible thoughts about Stefan and wouldn't be analyzing this situation so hard, but she'd been burned so badly, she was still scarred.

On a groan, she dropped her arms, headed to the desk and tried to come up with some plausible explanation for all of this. But she couldn't defend him. He'd taken her already battered heart and pressed harder on the bruise.

Victoria had to confront him, and she knew if he told her he had indeed used her, lied to her, she would not be able to stay married to a man who had humiliated her like that.

She'd thought Stefan was different. How could she have made the same mistake twice?

Fifteen

When stress overcame Victoria, she did what she knew best. She designed.

She grabbed a notepad and pencil from the drawer of Stefan's desk in the master suite and took it to the balcony overlooking the Mediterranean Sea. The tranquility, the peacefulness of the crystal-blue water ebbing and flowing to the shore should've calmed her nerves.

Unfortunately when you were lied to, even by omission, nothing could relieve the hurt and betrayal. Not even the beauty of the country she was legally the next queen over.

But the deception wouldn't have been so bad, so crippling if it hadn't come from her best friend…the one person outside her family she depended on, cared for. Loved.

Victoria dropped to a cushy white chaise and began sweeping her pencil across the paper. Soon a dress formed, but not just any dress. Her wedding dress. The dress she'd taken vows in, promising to love, honor and cherish her husband. The dress she'd designed for a princess.

Letting the pad fall to her lap, Victoria closed her eyes and leaned back against the chair. Why did life have to be so complicated, so...corrupt? Didn't anyone tell the full truth anymore? Was she naive in taking people at their word?

But she hadn't just taken anyone at their word; she'd taken Stefan at his. The rock of stability who had always been there for her. How dare he do that to her emotions, her heart? He of all people knew how she'd been battered and bruised. Why hadn't he come to her with the idea of the documentary? Why go to her brothers behind her back?

Another crippling ache spread through her, and she had no idea where to put these emotions. Did she cry, throw something, pack her bags and leave?

"There you are."

At the sound of Stefan's voice, Victoria turned her head. With a smile on his handsome face, he strode through the open patio doors. And she knew how to handle this situation. Right now she couldn't look at him as her best friend, couldn't see him as the man whom she'd confided in for years. No, she had to see him as was—a man who'd lied to her.

"Sketching another gown?" he asked, leaning down to her notepad. "That's the dress you wore for our wedding. Why are you drawing it again?"

Laying the pad aside, she came to her feet, ready to take the blow of the truth...if he revealed it.

"Just remembering the day I married my best friend," she told him, watching his eyes. "The day we promised to be faithful and honor each other. And even though I had my doubts and worries, I knew you'd never hurt me because we have something special."

He tipped his head to the side. "Everything all right, Tori?"

A sad smile spread across her face. "Not really. You see, I married you because you needed me and I wanted to get over the pain and humiliation of my last relationship. You promised to provide me with that support and stability. You promised to never hurt me, and I assumed that meant honesty, as well. Obviously I was wrong."

He reached for her, touching her arm, and she didn't step back. Because even though he'd damaged something inside, she still craved his touch. But she wasn't begging for his love. Never again would she put her heart on the line for such foolishness. And damn him for destroying that dream.

"What happened?" he asked, concern lacing his voice.

As tears threatened to clog her throat, she tamped down the pain, knowing she needed to be strong or she'd crumble at his feet and never stop crying. The inevitable emotional breakdown could and would be done in private.

"I learned the truth," she told him. "I discovered that no matter what your heart says, not even your best friend is trustworthy."

"Victoria, what the hell are you talking about?" he demanded. "I've never lied to you."

Moisture pooled in her eyes, making his face blurry. She couldn't lose it, not here, not when he'd try to console her and break her down.

"Bronson called." She stared into his eyes, wanting to see the moment he realized that she knew the truth. "He's ready to move forward with your documentary. And since you've used me for the title and your film, I guess that's my cue to exit stage left."

His eyes widened, and he took both her arms in his strong hands. "Victoria—"

"No. There's no excuse as to why you couldn't have told me. Not one. So don't even try. I'm done being hurt. I'm done being lied to. My God, if you lied about this, what else have you kept from me?"

She jerked away from his grasp, tilting her chin. "I will be leaving as soon as my jet is ready. Since your brother is doing better, you don't need me here. Actually, you shouldn't need me at all anymore. You're getting your crown in a few short months, but after the coronation I'll be divorcing you."

Sharp, piercing pain speared through her. She never imagined she'd be divorcing the one man she loved with her whole heart. Every shattered, broken piece of it.

As she moved by him, she stopped, looking into his eyes. His face was only a breath away.

"If you'd let me—"

Shaking her head, she stepped back. "I just want to hear one thing from you. Did you know you were going to ask my brothers to help you before or after we married?"

Stefan swallowed and held her gaze. "Before."

And the last of Victoria's hope died.

Head held high, shoulders back, Victoria walked inside, through their master suite where they'd made love countless times and out the door. She didn't break down until she was safely locked inside the guest bath down the hall.

Her iconic actress mother would be so proud of her departing performance.

Stefan's world was completely and utterly empty. Two days ago Victoria had gotten on her jet and left Galini Isle. Two days ago she'd stood before him, hurt swimming in her eyes, and accused him of betraying her trust, and in the next moment she was gone.

She'd known exactly how to bring him to his knees

and cause the most guilt. He hadn't been fully truthful with her and now he was being damned for it. Nothing less than he deserved.

Stefan slammed his empty glass back down on the bar in his study. Scotch wouldn't take the pain away, and to be honest, he deserved any heartbreak he had because he'd brought every bit of it on himself. He'd known she'd been lied to before. Why the hell hadn't he discussed his plans with her?

He hadn't called Bronson back. Who knew what Victoria had told her brothers when she returned home. For all Stefan knew, this project was over before it got started.

But right now he didn't give a damn about his project.

What he did care about was the fact that he'd damaged something, someone so beautiful. He didn't know if they could get past this trauma, not just for the marriage, but the friendship.

He had to get her back. He couldn't lose their friendship. Victoria was the single most important woman in his life, and living without her was incomprehensible.

Stefan gripped his glass, resting his other hand on the bar and hanging his head down between his shoulders. Hindsight was just as cruel as fate, in his opinion. He'd known he was using her, had known that he needed to in order to gain what he wanted. But fate had dangled all those opportunities in front of his face and he'd taken chances he never should've taken—the marriage, the documentary…the sex. Because all of those chances didn't just involve his life, they affected Victoria's.

He hurled the Scotch tumbler across the room, not feeling any better when the crackling of glass and shards splintering to the floor resounded in the room.

Seconds later his guard burst through the door. "Your Highness, are you all right?"

Stefan shook his head. No, he was not all right.

"Glass broke," he said. "I'll clean it."

With that, the guard backed out again, leaving Stefan alone once more. But alone wasn't good. Alone meant he had only his thoughts to keep him company, and it was those haunting thoughts that had that invisible band around his chest tightening.

Memories of Victoria washed over him—on their wedding day gliding down the aisle, swimming in the ocean, beneath him in bed, gazing up at him like he was her world.

If they were just friends, then this revelation about the movie wouldn't have hurt her so badly. He'd lost her as his wife...he refused to lose his best friend, too.

Victoria was still in her office. Her employees had left long ago, but she stood in the middle of her spacious sewing room in front of the three-way mirror trying her hardest to pin the dress without sticking herself...again. The design was finally coming along, and she wanted to get it finished tonight.

Working through a broken heart was the only way she would get past this. She had to throw all her emotions into her work because if she went home, if she had to stop and even think for a moment about her personal life, she'd crumble and may never recover.

A knot formed in her stomach. She hated regrets, and hated even more that those regrets circled around Stefan. Fury filled her, pain consumed her. But at the end of the day she only had herself to blame for falling in love with him. She should've known better. Hadn't she seen over the years how he was with women? Hadn't she witnessed firsthand how he'd discarded them when they got too close?

And Victoria had fallen into his trap, fallen for those

charms and assumed that bond they'd formed as teens would get them through anything. But even the strongest bonds could be broken with enough force.

On a sigh, she shoved a pin through the silk gathered at her waist and glanced up into the mirror. A scream caught in her throat at the sight of the man standing behind her.

"Need a hand?" Stefan asked.

She whirled around. "How did you get in here?"

"Door was unlocked."

She'd been so wrapped up in her anger, her hurt and work to check it after her last employee left.

"I've called you for days. You never answered or returned my calls."

Victoria crossed her arms over her chest, as if that could protect her from allowing any more hurt to seep in.

"I went by your house first," he told her, still remaining in the doorway as if he were afraid to come closer. Smart man. "I should've known you'd be here working."

"And as you can see, I'm busy."

She lifted the heavy skirt of her silk gown and turned back to the mirror. Reaching for another pin from the large cushion on the table beside her, she tugged at the bustline. If that didn't get pinned, she'd be spilling out, and she refused to ever let Stefan have the privilege of seeing her naked again.

"I flew all this way to talk to you, Tori. Don't shut me out."

With care, she slid the pin in, annoyed at her shaky hands. "I didn't shut you out. You did that when you chose to keep the film to yourself and use me for my brothers."

"*Na pari i eychi*, Victoria." He moved farther into the room, his eyes locking onto hers in the mirror. "You won't even listen to me? I've been up front with you about everything else other than the film, but you've already lumped me into that same jerk category as Alex and assumed the worst."

"So what if I have?" she asked him. "You took my trust and loyalty for granted. You knew going in you wanted to use my brothers for this documentary. Why not just tell me?"

Resting his hands on his denim-clad hips, he shook his head. "I knew you had enough going on in your life. This film really didn't involve you."

She was wrong. The hurt could slice deeper. She'd always heard that the people you love most could also hurt you the most. Too bad she had to experience the anguish and despair to understand the saying.

"I see." She swallowed, turning back around to face him. From up on the large pedestal where she stood, she was now eye to eye with him. "I've been your best friend, then wife and lover, but you didn't think this involved me. That pretty much says it all, doesn't it? I obviously wasn't as much a part of your life as I thought because I assumed we shared everything. My mistake and one I certainly won't make again."

"Tori, I can't change what I did, but I can't let you go, either. I need you."

"Ah, yes. The beloved crown and country," she all but mocked.

"Don't," he told her. "Don't let your anger get in the way of doing what is right."

She nearly laughed at that. *Doing what is right?* Fine, then, since she prided herself on honesty, she'd do what was right and tell him how she felt.

"I fell in love with you," she blurted out. Her eyes locked on his. "Crazy, isn't it? And I don't mean love in the way a friend loves another. I love you in the way a woman loves a man, a wife loves a husband. You don't know how I wish I could turn these emotions off."

When he remained silent, Victoria kept going, ignoring the dark circles beneath his heavy-lidded baby blues.

"I thought you loved me," she said, not caring that she was bearing her soul. This situation couldn't get any more humiliating, anyway. "I was naive enough to think that all your actions were signs that you were taking our relationship deeper, but you don't love me. If you did, I wouldn't be hurting like this right now. You only flew here because you care about yourself, not me."

Moisture filled Stefan's eyes, but Victoria refused to believe he was affected by her declaration.

"But I'm willing to give you a chance to speak for yourself. Do you love me? Is that why you're here?" she asked, searching his eyes. "Honestly?"

"As much as I ever did," he told her. "You're my best friend."

She lowered her lids over the burn, a lone tear streaking down her cheek. "Do you love me as more than a friend, Stefan?" she asked, opening her eyes.

"If I could love anyone, Tori, it would be you."

"So the answer is no."

Silence enveloped them, and she couldn't stand another minute in his sight. And since he was making no move to leave, and this was her turf, she'd have to be the one to walk away.

"You're the last man I will ever let humiliate me," she told him, damning her cracking voice. "And you're the last man I'll ever love."

He reached up and swiped away a tear with the pad of his thumb. "Can you at least work with me for the coronation?"

"I will stay married to you until then, but I cannot live

with you. This marriage will be in name only from here on out."

She stepped off the platform and started to move by him.

"But you'll you be at the coronation?" he asked.

She stopped in her tracks, her shoulders stiffened, but she did not turn around. "I would never go back on my word to a friend. I'll be there."

Countless times he'd lied. He'd lied his way through his teen years, lied when he knew the truth would only get him into trouble, but he couldn't mislead Victoria when she'd asked him if he loved her. Not even when he knew the truth would break her even more.

She'd accused him of humiliating her, which made him no better than the bastard who'd publicly destroyed her. The end result was the same. Victoria trusted and loved with her whole heart and had ended up hurt.

Stefan rested his hands against the marble rail on the edge of his master suite's balcony. Over and over during the past three months, he'd replayed his time with Victoria, looking for those moments he'd missed, trying to see exactly where he went wrong.

He knew she loved him as a friend. Friend love was something he could handle. But this deeper love he'd been afraid of coming from her was just something he couldn't grasp. He'd never loved a woman other than his mother. In his world love meant commitment and loyalty—two things he reserved for his country.

Victoria's declaration of love had speared a knife through his heart sharper and deeper than anything. Victoria Dane, the woman who'd captured his attention as a teen and quickly turned into his best friend, the woman who saved him time and time again with her selfless ways and her kind heart, and the woman who would've graciously helped him work on clearing his family's reputation, had walked out of his life. And there was no one to blame but himself.

He missed hearing her voice, missed knowing her smile would be waiting for him at the end of the day. Missed her body lying next to his. He missed everything from her friendship to their intimacy.

Every time he walked into their closet he saw her standing there in her silky lingerie trying to decide what to wear. When he lay in bed at night, his hand reached to her side as if she'd magically appear. And when he'd tried to take a stroll on the beach, he recalled the day he'd kissed her by the ocean, when he felt that something was turning in their relationship. He'd known then something was different, but he hadn't wanted to identify it.

He was going to go mad if he didn't concentrate on something else. Unfortunately, no matter what he did, all thoughts circled back to Victoria.

Stefan shoved off the rail and marched to his room. Maybe if he tried to rid their room of reminders, that would help. After all, he was still hanging on to her doodles and sketches. He yanked open the drawer on his desk and pulled out the random drawings from Victoria's late-night dress designs.

Something slid beneath his hand as he picked up the sketches. An SD card. And not just any SD card, but the one he'd taken from the intruder that day at the beach.

Obviously he felt the need to torture himself further because he found himself popping it into the computer. In actuality, he wanted to look at Victoria when she was happier, before he'd filled her life with anguish.

He rested his palms on the desk, waiting for the images to load. In no time several small pictures appeared on the screen, and Stefan sank into his office chair. He clicked on the first one, maximizing the image.

Click after click he saw the same thing over and over: Victoria smiling at him, hope and love swimming in her eyes, her hair dancing around in the ocean breeze and the sunset in the distance.

But the last image was different. The final picture was like a knife through his already damaged heart.

Victoria sat with her back to the camera, her face to the ocean as he looked at her. There was no smile on his lips, but it was the expression in his eyes. The image smacked him in the face. No man looked at a woman with such adoration, such passion, like nothing else mattered in the world, if he didn't love her. How could he not have realized that all this time, everything he'd felt, every twinge in his chest, had been love? All those times she'd smiled at him and he felt a flutter and each moment he wanted to just hold her near…damn, how could he have missed what was right in front of him?

Stefan fell against the back of his seat as the picture stared him in the face, mocking everything he'd had in his grasp and had let go.

The ache he'd felt for days intensified to a level he never knew existed. Pain consumed him, and he knew he had to take action or face a lifetime of loneliness because no woman could or would ever replace his Tori.

There was no way he would give her up without a fight. No way in hell. If he had to recruit her brothers, her mother, even God himself, Stefan had to win her back.

He would make her see that she *did* mean everything to him. She was his best friend, and he seriously didn't think he could get through life without her.

With his mind working in overtime, he started plotting how he would get his wife back.

Sixteen

Against her family's wishes and best attempts to talk her out of it, Victoria wasn't about to miss the coronation. Stefan may not have gone about their relationship the right way, but he did deserve to be king.

After all, his country was the one thing in life he actually loved. At one time she would've given anything to hear him say those words about her, too.

No matter the months that had passed, the pain was just as fresh, just as raw. Even though her bridal line had launched with great success, she couldn't enjoy the overwhelming attention and adoration her designs were getting.

Victoria smoothed a hand down the royal-blue gown she'd designed for the coronation. She'd wanted to match Stefan's bright sash that stretched from his shoulder to his hip. Though why she tried so hard was beyond her.

No, she had to be honest, at least with herself. She wanted him to shine. Wanted them to put up a united front for the public. If anyone knew about pretenses, it was her. Having come from the prestigious Dane family, she was all too aware of what could happen if the right image wasn't portrayed, and this was Stefan's final step into the role of king.

As she glanced in the mirror, she couldn't help but have a sense of déjà vu. This was the exact room she stood in six months ago when she'd married. Only this time she'd traveled alone. Her mother wasn't supportive and her brothers weren't too happy, either. Her sisters-in-law, well, they totally understood the stupid things women did for love.

And yes, after all she'd been through, she loved the man. Dammit, she couldn't help herself. Stupid female hormones. She wanted to hate him for the pain he'd caused, wanted to despise him for making her fall in love. But she only had herself to blame. How long had she known him? How many times had she seen a broken heart lying at his feet?

She smoothed her hair back and glanced from side to side to make sure her chignon was in place. A soft knock at her door had her cringing.

Showtime.

"My lady," one of the guards called through the door. "I'm ready to escort you down to the ballroom."

The ballroom would be transformed into a vibrant display of royal-blue silk draped over every stationary item. The bold color symbolized the country, and the crest would be hung from banners surrounding the room. After all, this was a celebration of the next reign.

Too bad she didn't feel like celebrating. She hadn't seen Stefan since he'd walked out of her office three months ago. She'd seen pictures of him via the internet rock climbing and surfing, always alone. All the tabloids were speculating a separation between them. Both she and Stefan had issued press releases stating they were each busy working on various projects, but they were very much still married and looking forward to the coronation ceremony.

Which wasn't a total lie. She was looking forward to it because after this day was over, she could divorce him and move on with her battered heart. But she still hadn't gotten the nerve to contact her attorney. She just couldn't. The thought of closing the door on their relationship brought on a whole new layer of pain she just wasn't ready to deal with. Because she knew there was no way in hell they could go back to being just friends.

Victoria crossed the room, her full silk skirt swishing against her legs. She opened the door with a smile on her face and looped her hand around the arm of the guard. Time to get her last duty as royalty over with.

"You look stunning, Your Highness."

She swallowed the lump of guilt over the pretense. "Thank you. I'm a bit nervous."

His soft chuckle sounded through the marble hallway. "Nothing to be nervous about. All you have to do is smile and take the crown."

The crown, the one that symbolized leadership and loyalty. And in a few short months, she'd give it up because she couldn't remain queen of this country. She couldn't stay with Stefan, no matter how she loved him or how much he claimed to care for her. Wasn't there a song about sometimes love not being enough?

Victoria descended the steps, ready to get this day over with. A day most women in her shoes would want to savor, relish, remember. Unfortunately, Victoria was too busy trying to erect a steel wall around her heart for when she saw her husband again.

* * *

Stefan stood outside the grand ballroom and watched as one of the palace guards escorted Victoria toward him. Her beauty had been in his dreams every night. That flawless elegance from her golden hair to her sweet smile to her delicate frame.

And every night he'd lain in bed alone, wishing he could have her by his side, wishing he could hear those very unladylike snores coming from the other side of the bed.

He knew he had it bad when he missed Victoria's snoring.

But it was the epiphany brought about by those images that prompted him to make the biggest decision of his life. One that was life-altering, but there was no other choice. Not if he wanted to have any type of peace and happiness. And not if he wanted to keep the woman he loved.

As she approached him, he extended his hand, eager for that first contact after being without her familiar touch for too long.

"You're the most beautiful sight I've seen in three months," he told her, bringing her hand to his lips.

Victoria bowed. "Thank you, Your Majesty."

Na pari i eychi, she was going to keep it formal and stiff. Like hell. He wasn't having any of that and in about two minutes she'd see just how serious he was about keeping things between them very, very personal.

She'd turned him down in L.A. because he'd been uncertain. Well, after three months of living without her, then finding those damning pictures from the beach and knowing he could indeed have all that was important, he was not going to end this day without getting the one thing in life he could not live without. And his revelation would no doubt shock her. Surprisingly, once he'd made the decision, he wasn't upset about it.

But for the first time in his life he was scared. A ball of nerves settled deep into his stomach. He couldn't lose her. Right now, nothing else mattered but his goal. And that was another first…this goal had absolutely nothing to do with his country.

"Are you ready?" he asked, looking into her blue eyes that never failed to captivate him.

For months he'd had a band around his chest, and seeing her in person only tightened it. The ache for her was unlike anything he'd ever known.

"Do I have a choice?" she whispered, holding his gaze.

Without a word, he wrapped her fingers around his arm and headed toward the closed set of double doors leading to the ballroom. On the other side, hundreds of very important diplomats, presidents and royalty waited to see the crowning of the next king and queen of Galini Isle.

Were they in for a surprise.

Two guards pulled open the tall, arched doors, revealing a ballroom adorned with royal silk the color of his vibrant sash and banners with the Alexander family crest suspended from the ceiling, the balcony and between the windows.

Everyone came to their feet as he and Victoria made their way down the blue satin stretched along the aisle before them, the Archbishop waiting at the end dressed in pristine white robes with a blue sash.

Even Mikos, who was still in a wheelchair but recovering nicely, waited at the end of the aisle. His brother knew exactly what was getting ready to take place. Mikos flashed a knowing smile and gave him a nod of approval.

Stefan swallowed the inkling of fear that kept trying to creep in. This was the right move to make, the only move to make. He had to take this leap and pray it paid off in the end. He wanted Victoria back and would do whatever it took.

Her fingers curled into his forearm and he knew she was nervous, angry, scared. Hopefully after today he could make her happy from here on out. He had to try, at least. What kind of man would he be if he didn't?

Once they reached the end of the aisle, the archbishop gestured for them to step up onto the stage, where two high-back thrones, centuries old, awaited them.

Stefan slid Victoria's hand from his arm and assisted her, careful not to step on the skirt of her gown. Once she was up and seated, he joined her. They faced the crowd, and Stefan knew it was go time.

He'd scaled the death defying rocks of Kalymnos, but that was nothing compared to the anxiety that slid through him, knowing his life and everything he loved was on the line. Every goal he'd ever wanted was within his reach... but he'd give it up in a flash for a lifetime with this woman.

When the archbishop opened his mouth, Stefan held up a hand, cutting the elderly man off.

"I do apologize," Stefan said. "But I have something to say before we proceed, if that's all right."

Obviously shocked, the archbishop stuttered a bit before bowing. "Of course, Your Majesty."

"What are you doing?" Victoria whispered beside him.

"Taking control of my life," he told her before coming to his feet.

Stefan glanced over the crowd, pulling up all his courage and strength. He'd need a great deal of both to get through the next several life-altering moments.

He glanced down to Mikos, who was still smiling. And Stefan knew that if Mikos could practically come back from near death, then Stefan could lay his heart on the line in front of millions of viewers.

"Sorry to interrupt the ceremony before it starts," he said to the crowd of suspicious onlookers. "But I have something important to say and this may change the outcome of today's festivities."

"Stefan," Victoria whispered from behind him. "Stop. Sit down."

Ignoring her, he moved to stand on the other side of her chair because all of this was for her benefit...not the spectators'. He looked down into her eyes and took a deep breath.

"Victoria Dane Alexander, you have been my best friend since we were teens. There's nothing I wouldn't do for you and I've come to learn there's nothing you wouldn't do for me."

Victoria bowed her head, clamping her hands tightly in her lap. He wanted to know what she was thinking, but he had to keep going, had to make her see this wasn't just about a title or a stupid movie.

"I've been using this beautiful woman," he admitted to the crowd. An audible gasp settled over the ballroom. "I needed her to keep this country in my family and become your king. She agreed to marry me, and I promised her after the coronation if she chose to end the marriage, I would step aside."

Stefan couldn't stand it anymore. He reached out, placing a hand over her shoulder and squeezed. She trembled beneath his touch.

"But I can't step aside."

Her head jerked up to meet his. Tears swam in her eyes, ready to fall down at the next blink.

"I can't step aside and let this woman out of my life," he continued. "I don't deserve her or her loyalty. I certainly don't deserve her love for the way I've treated her. But she fell in love with me."

His eyes locked on to hers. "And with no doubts of our future together, I fell in love with her."

Victoria's watery eyes searched his face and Stefan got down on one knee beside her chair. Taking her hand in his, he kissed her knuckles.

"I haven't been honest with Victoria, or all of you. This marriage was a fake, but I do love you, Victoria. And if I can't be your king, then so be it. I couldn't live with myself if I let this woman out of my life."

He took a deep breath as he continued to lay his heart on the line. "Victoria," he said, softer now because nothing else mattered except her response, "I wasn't respectful when I didn't tell you the full truth, but I swear on my life if you let me back into that loving heart of yours, I'll spend the rest of our lives making it up to you. Nothing else matters but you and us…if you'll have me."

She chewed on her bottom lip. "You don't mean this."

Stroking the back of her trembling hand, he smiled. "I've never meant anything more. I'm not sure when I fell in love with you. Maybe it was when I first met you or maybe it was when you were walking down the aisle to become my bride. Looking back, I think I've always been in love with you and I just couldn't admit it to myself. At least I didn't know the level of love I had. It's so much deeper than I ever could've imagined."

Victoria sighed, closed her eyes and let the tears fall.

"Can you say that again?" she asked, lifting her lids to meet his gaze.

Stefan searched her beautiful face. "Which part?"

"The part where you fell in love with me with no doubts of our future."

He chuckled. "I'm a fool not to have realized that I've loved you for years. All this time I wanted to get closer to you, wanted more than a friendship, but I didn't know what. Now I know that what I was searching for was love. And it was there all along."

Her head dipped to her chest as she sniffed. "I'm scared," she whispered. "What if you fall out of love?"

Tipping her chin up with his finger and thumb, he eased in for a gentle, simple kiss. "I've loved you most of my life, Tori. I just didn't have the courage to admit it to myself. There's no way I could ever fall out of love. I've been absolutely miserable without you. Nothing matters, not this title, crown or movie, if you aren't in my life. I'd give it all up for another chance."

"But if you step aside, Galini Isle will go back to Greece."

He smiled. "I found a loophole, finally. When it mattered most, I found a way out."

Her teary eyes searched his. "But how?"

"Mikos will step up if I need him to," he told her.

"I didn't think he could."

He took her hand, kissed it and smiled. "I'll explain later. Can you please put me out of my misery and tell me this marriage will be real from here on out?"

A beautiful, hopeful smile spread across her face. "I don't want you to give up your title or the documentary... though my brothers are pretty upset, but I can talk to them."

Stefan squeezed her hands. "I seriously don't care about anything but being with you. If you're in my future, I can handle whatever comes my way."

She leaned toward him and kissed his lips before whispering in his ear, "Then let's see if we can finish this coronation ceremony and we can celebrate alone wearing only our crowns."

The archbishop stepped forward. "Are the two of you certain this marriage is legitimate now?"

Victoria smiled and nodded. "I'm certain."

Stefan stared into her watery eyes. "Never been more sure of anything in my life."

"Then I approve the continuation of this coronation ceremony," the archbishop declared as the crowd began to clap and cheer.

Stefan hadn't seen Victoria for several minutes and was starting to wonder if she'd changed her mind and run out the palace doors with their last guest.

Midnight had come and gone and the coronation celebration had just calmed down. Dancing, laughing and holding Victoria in his arms nearly the entire evening had been the best moments of his life.

When she could've chosen to turn her back on him, on his title and his beloved country, she hadn't. She'd stood by his side, even when he'd hurt her.

And that gnawing ache would haunt him the rest of his life. Knowing he'd caused her even a second of grief made him ill. But the fact their love overcame his moments of idiocy proved they were meant to be.

"Your Majesty."

Stefan stopped in the corridor leading to his wing and turned to the sound of Hector's voice.

"Yes?"

His loyal assistant and guard smiled. "I'm to give you a message from your queen."

A smile spread across Stefan's face. Yes, she was his queen, his wife, the love of his life.

"And what is it?"

Hector cleared his throat. "I am to tell you, and I quote, 'Tell my king that the last part of his dream is coming true, and he'll know where to find me.'"

Stefan thought for about a half second before he

laughed. "Thank you, Hector. Please make sure the staff stays out of the east wing tonight."

With a faint redness to his wrinkled cheeks, Hector bowed. "As you wish, King Alexander."

As much as he loved hearing that title and knowing it belonged to him, he was loving even more what his sneaky wife had in store for him. He knew just where to find her.

Arousal shot through him fast and hard as his long strides ate up the hallways leading to the destination.

Through the wall of glass, he saw her—his queen wearing her jeweled crown...and nothing else. She hadn't been kidding about the celebration wearing only the crowns. He liked her style of thinking.

Stefan entered the pool area and began undoing the double-breasted buttons of his jacket.

"Queen Alexander, are you aware of the age and expense of that crown upon your head?" he asked, slipping out of the garment.

She smiled, rested her arms on the edge of the pool and peered up at him. "I have a pretty good idea, but I wanted to add a bit to this fantasy, too."

Unlike her, he left his crown sitting on the bench where she'd draped her silk gown.

"And what's your fantasy?"

"Making love while wearing my crown," she told him, a sultry grin inviting him to join her. "I added some pins, so I think we're safe from it falling off."

When he slid off the last of his clothes and turned, he waited until recognition dawned in her eyes.

"Stefan?"

Unable to stop his grin, he took a step closer. "What do you think?"

"I can't believe... When did you get it?"

He glanced down at the new ink on his chest. "A few

weeks ago. I found some of your drawings lying on the desk. I was partial to the one with the crest and our initials. Since I already had the crest, I only had to add your work."

"Come closer and let me see," she told him. "I want to get a better look."

He moved to the edge and hopped in, coming to stand directly beside her. "By all means, feel free to look all you want. Touching is allowed, too."

Her fingertip traced the design that he'd had done in her honor, imagining her face when she finally saw it.

"It's beautiful," she whispered. "I can't believe you took one of my crazy doodles and turned it into something so beautiful. Meaningful."

He grasped her bare shoulders in his hands and pulled her against him. "Everything about you is beautiful and meaningful, Tori. And I think this should be your royal wardrobe," he told her. "The tiara and nothing else."

Soft laughter spilled from her lips. "That's exactly how I want you all the time," she told him.

He nipped at her lips, tilting his hips toward hers. "I'll see about setting that into an order."

"Speaking of orders, how did you manage to find a loophole that would allow Mikos to take your place?"

Not something he wanted to talk about when he was aroused and his wife was wet and in his arms, but he did want her to know the lengths he would go to in order to keep her.

"When I told Mikos that our family would lose control of Galini Isle to Greece because I had to give up the title, he started doing some digging about the rules of divorce and taking the title for himself. Since Karina is pregnant, Mikos could act as ruler until the child became of age, and then that child would take over as ruler."

Tears shimmered in her eyes. "And you were going to step aside?"

"Without a doubt. I would've turned this country over to Satan himself to get you back." His hold tightened on her. "Mikos and I went to the head counsel and stated our case. They were more than willing to let him take the title temporarily until his baby was twenty-one if I chose to step aside."

She searched his eyes. "I didn't know I could ever love like this. Didn't know that someone could love me so unselfishly. God, Stefan, I'm so glad you fought for us."

He ran his hands up her bare, wet back then slid them down to cup her rear. "I wouldn't have let you go, Tori. I can't live without you."

As he claimed his wife, he knew there was nothing he wouldn't do for her. His life was completely perfect, and the girl with braces who'd once captured his teenage attention now held his heart until the day he died.

Epilogue

One year later...

Love surrounded her. Even with the flashbulbs going off like a strobe light outside her limo, Queen Victoria Dane Alexander knew she'd remember this monumental moment forever.

As the car pulled up to the red carpet, Victoria waited for her driver to open the door.

"Are we all ready?" she asked.

Her entire family, Bronson, Mia, Anthony, Charlotte, Olivia and Stefan, all smiled. They'd agreed to ride together to the L.A. premiere of *Legendary Icon*. So much had happened in the past few years, and they wanted to make a united front, to show they were a family first, movie moguls second.

The limo door opened; screams, cameras and the red carpet awaited them. Victoria never tired of the positive attention the media gave to her brothers and mother. They were so talented and she was thrilled to be part of this night, this movie.

The driver helped Olivia out first and the crowd grew even louder.

"She's going to shine tonight," Bronson said with a smile on his face.

Anthony nodded. "She always shines, but she's waited for this for so long. I'm glad we could give this to her."

Emotions overwhelmed Victoria. It wasn't that long ago that Bronson and Anthony were at each other's throats, but now they were family and they loved each other…all because of Olivia Dane.

Anthony and Charlotte exited the limo next, followed by Bronson and Mia. Stefan reached over and took her hand.

"Have I told you how *oraios* you look tonight?"

Victoria had learned over the past year that the Greek term meant "beautiful," but she always loved hearing it come from his lips.

"You've told me." She took a deep breath, ready to really change his life. "I have something to tell you, as well."

He glanced to the open car door. "Shouldn't we be getting out?"

Victoria shrugged. "They're all still dazzled by the rest of my family. I wanted to impress you with my own Greek I've been working on."

One dark brow rose. "Oh, really? And what is that, my love?"

She leaned in and whispered, *"Moro."*

Those dark chocolate eyes widened, dropped to her stomach and back up. "A baby?" he asked. "Tori, my God. Are you serious?"

With tears clogging her throat, she nodded. "Yes. I know we wanted to wait a bit longer, but—"

Stefan took her face in his hands and kissed her, thoroughly, deeply, passionately. Who needed lip gloss for the premiere anyway?

When he leaned back, he was still grinning like she'd never seen before. "I'm thrilled. Are you feeling okay?"

She nodded. "I haven't been sick once, and the doctor said I'm about seven weeks along and very healthy."

He kissed her again. "I love you, Victoria. I can't tell you how much."

She started easing toward the open door, toward the shouts and cameras. "After we celebrate this premiere, you can show me at home."

* * * * *

A ROYAL
TEMPTATION

CHARLENE SANDS

To Allyson Pearlman, Robin Rose, Mary Hernandez and Pam Frendian. You're my crew, my Best Friends Forever. Your friendship puts lightness in my heart and a smile on my face every day. I am surrounded by the best and I love you dearly.

One

Juan Carlos Salazar II stood at the altar in Saint Lucia's Cathedral, holding his head high as he accepted the responsibility and honor of being crowned King Montoro of Alma. In a dreamlike state he went through the motions that would bring the monarchy back to what it had once been decades ago. He'd been orphaned at a young age and taken in by his uncle. Since then, he'd lived a life filled with determination and dignity. He'd always known great things would come to him if he worked hard and kept his focus. But king? Never in his life would he have guessed his own true destiny.

With the golden orb and blessed scepter in his hands, he saw the austere ceremony in the cathedral was coming to a close. Prime Minister Rivera had given a speech full of renewed hope for the country, the small set of islands off the coast of Spain that had been ravaged by the now overthrown dictatorship of the Tantaberras. Seventy years of oppression overturned by loyal citizens, who looked to Juan Carlos for the reinstatement of a monarchy that would capture their hearts and minds.

Archbishop Santiago placed the royal robe over Juan Carlos's shoulders. As he took his seat on the throne, the archbishop set the jeweled crown of Alma upon his head. All of the tradition, ritual and protocol of the coronation had been observed, and he was now King Montoro of

Alma, the true heir to the throne. He spoke an oath and vowed to be much more than a figurehead as he promised to restore order and hope to the country.

It was a monumental time in Alma's history and he was happy to have the support of his cousins, Gabriel, Rafe and Bella. They were smiling and nodding their approval from their seats, Bella with tears in her eyes. They'd all lived and thrived in the United States before this, and forgive him, but heaven knew Rafe and Gabriel, who were once thought to be first in line to the throne but had been disqualified for separate and unique reasons, were not cut out for the rigors and sacrifice of royal life. They were only too glad to see Juan Carlos accept the position of sovereign.

A woman seated several rows behind his cousins caught his attention. Deep cerulean-blue eyes, clear and large, stood out against her porcelain face and white-blond hair. She reminded him of a snow queen from a fairy tale in his youth. And as he was ushered down the aisle after the coronation their gazes locked for an instant and her one eyelid closed in a wink. Was it for him? His lips immediately quirked up at the notion and he forced the smile from his expression. Still, his heart did a little tumble as it had been doing all day, but this time it was the woman, and not the ceremony, that had caused the commotion.

The next hour passed, again in dreamlike wonder, as he was escorted out of the cathedral by Alma's finest royal guards, to be met with unrestrained jubilation all along the parade route. He sat atop a convertible car and waved with gloved hands, as they made their way toward the palace. And there, on the top steps of Alma's regal old-world palace, Juan Carlos began his first speech as king.

"Citizens of Alma, as your new king, I promise to honor the sovereignty of our nation, to always put the country first and to work alongside our parliament to restore our democracy. It is a vow I take with an open but steady heart and a determination to see that our freedoms are never threatened again."

Cheers went up. "Viva Juan Carlos!"

Juan Carlos waited until the crowd calmed to finish a speech that was interrupted three more times by applause.

He left the palace steps energized, instilled with the very same hope he saw in the eyes of his fellow countrymen. He was a foreigner, by all rights, an American, and yet, they'd accepted him and looked to him to help establish a newer, brighter Alma.

He would not let them down.

As austere as his day was, he took a moment to reflect on the coronation and picture the beautiful woman in the light blue chiffon gown, her eyes as vibrant as deep ocean waters. He'd searched for her during the procession, the parade and the speech that followed, only to be disappointed.

She'd been a diversion from the gravity of the day.

Winking at him had brought a smile to his lips.

Who was she?

And would she have his children?

"Do I need to call you Your Highness?" his cousin Rafe asked as he pumped Juan Carlos's hand. They stood off to the side in the palace's grand ballroom. The coronation gala was well underway and the orchestra played lively tunes. An array of fresh flowers decorated the arched entryways, aisles and tables.

"You mean, as opposed to Squirt, Idiot and Bonehead like when we were kids?"

"Hey, I wasn't that bad."

"You were a year older and that gave you bullying rights."

"Okay, guilty as charged. But now you can have me hung by the neck until dead."

"I could've done that to you back then, too."

"Ha, funny."

"Call me Juan Carlos or cuz, just like you do now. Your Highness comes into play only on formal occasions or royal business."

All amusement on his cousin's face disappeared. "Seriously, Juan Carlos, congratulations. The family is proud of you. You're the only one of the lot who was cut out for this. You are honoring our aunt Isabella's final wishes by restoring the monarchy."

Juan Carlos came to the throne quite by accident, after Bella discovered a secret cache of letters that revealed Rafe, Gabriel and Bella's late grandfather, Raphael Montoro II, was illegitimate and not the true heir to the throne. As such, neither of Juan Carlos's cousins would have been the rightful king. The former queen's indiscretion had been kept hidden all these years until her great-grandchildren had uncovered it.

"Thank you, cousin. I've thought about my grandmother these past few weeks and I think she would approve. It means a great deal to me." He sighed. "I hope to make a diff—" He caught a glimpse of a woman in blue and craned his neck to get a better look.

It was her. She was attending the gala. Only dignitaries, friends and family members along with the royal photographers and journalists had been invited to the party, two hundred strong.

"Hey," Rafe asked. "What are you stretching your neck to see?"

"She's here," he muttered, without shifting his gaze. She was standing near an archway leading to the foyer, looking to make an escape.

"Juan Carlos?"

"Oh, uh, I saw a woman at the coronation and I haven't stopped thinking about her."

"This I've got to see. Any woman who can take your

mind off a day as big as this has got to be something special. Where is she?"

"I'm not going to point. Just look for the most beautiful woman in the room and you'll find her."

"Emily is right there, talking to Bella."

"Spoken like a besotted newlywed. Okay, yes, Emily is gorgeous, now find a woman in blue who is not your wife."

"If you'd agreed to a formal receiving line, you'd have met her already."

He hadn't wanted a stiff, awkward line of people congratulating him. He'd make his way over to his guests and speak with them during the course of the evening. He'd vowed to be a king *of* the people and *for* the people and that started right now. "Do you see her?"

"Ah, I do see her now. Very blonde, nice body, great eyes."

"That's her. Do you know who she is?"

"No, but apparently she knows Alex and Maria Ramon. They just walked up to her and they appear friendly."

"Well, then, I think it's time I spoke with Alma's deputy prime minister of commerce and his wife, don't you?"

Juan Carlos moved swiftly across the ballroom and as he approached, Alex spotted him and smiled. "Your Highness." Juan Carlos nodded. It would take some time getting used to that greeting.

Maria, not one to stand on ceremony, hugged his neck. She and Alex had just married and postponed their honeymoon to attend the coronation. "I'm happy to see this day, Your Highness. You are just what Alma needs."

"Thank you, Maria."

As he made eye contact with the blonde woman, it felt as if something quick and sharp had pierced his body. Her eyes were large, shaped like perfect twin almonds, the sparkle in them as bright as any star. Mesmerized, he couldn't look away.

"And please, let me introduce you to Portia Lindstrom, Princess of Samforstand."

Princess?

She *could* have his children.

Juan Carlos offered her his hand and at the touch of her delicate palm, he once again felt that quick, sharp sensation. "Nice to meet you, Princess. I'm glad you could make the coronation. It's a good day for Alma, I hope."

"I'm sure it will be, Your Majesty. And please, call me Portia."

"I will," he said. "If you call me Juan Carlos."

A pink cast tinged her porcelain skin. "I couldn't."

"Why not?"

"Because, you're the king."

"I'll let you in on a secret. Up until a few months ago, I was living in Miami and running a rather large business conglomerate. I'm afraid I still have American ties and king is not in their vocabulary, unless we're talking about Elvis."

She smiled. "I live in America, too. I'm on the west coast right now. My family was from a tiny country near Scandinavia."

"Well, then, we have a lot in common. As you can see, Alma is not a large country, either."

Maria and Alex exchanged looks and excused themselves. He'd forgotten they were there. It was rude of him. But now, he was alone with Portia.

"You are a curiosity. You won't call me Juan Carlos, but yet you wink at me just as I am crowned king."

Portia froze. Surely the king didn't believe she'd actually winked at him. It was that darn nervous twitch of hers. It would have to happen at the exact moment she'd first made eye contact with him. She should be immune to royalty—she'd met enough princes and princesses in her twenty-eight years—but Juan Carlos Salazar seemed different, strikingly handsome and down to earth. Before she could explain about the wink, the orchestra began playing a lovely Latin waltz.

He bowed in old world fashion. "Princess Portia, I'd be honored if you danced with me."

"I'm afraid I don't waltz."

"Neither do I," he replied. "We can wing it and set a new trend."

She chuckled. He didn't act like the stuffed-shirt royals she'd met in the past, and when he took her hand and led her to the unoccupied dance floor, she didn't protest. He was a better dancer than he let on, and she glided across the floor with him, fully aware every set of eyes in the room were on them.

"We're the only ones out here," she whispered.

He grinned, flashing white teeth against golden-brown skin. He was tall and dashing and at the moment, charming her silly by staring into her eyes as if she was the only person who existed in the world. It was quite flattering.

"Don't worry. Other guests will join in after the king's first dance. It's tradition."

"Then I should be honored you picked me."

"After that wink, how could I not pick you?" He held her possessively and spoke with authority, as if he'd been king all of his life.

"It was a twitch. I had something in my eye."

"I choose to believe it was a wink."

"Yes, Your Highness."

He smiled again and moved her across the dance floor as if she were light as air.

When the dance ended, he didn't release her hand. "Will you take a walk with me?"

"You want to leave your own gala?"

He shrugged and didn't appear worried. "It's been a long, monumental day. I could use a little break."

Portia couldn't very well say no. And getting some fresh air did sound good. Because of her title, she'd been invited to the gala, and to refuse such a high honor would've been unheard of. Her mother and father's greatest wish, as her grandmother told it, was for her to remain true to her royal bloodlines, even while having a career and life of her own. So she juggled her time accordingly, to honor her deceased parents' wishes. She hadn't had enough time with them, but she'd hoped to make them proud. "Well, then, yes. I'll walk with you."

They strode off the dance floor in silence. His hand pressed to her back, he guided her toward a small back door and they ducked out to a deserted foyer. "There are private gardens just outside where we can sit."

He opened a door she was sure only royals were privy to, and a gust of cool autumn air hit her. Without a second's hesitation, Juan Carlos removed his tuxedo jacket and placed it around her shoulders. "Better?"

"Yes, thank you." She tugged the lapels closed and kept her hands there, away from the king's tempting grasp. His dark eyes were on her every move, and when he touched her, her pulse raced in a way it hadn't in a very long time.

He led her to grounds surrounded by lattices covered with vines. "Would you like to sit down?"

"Okay."

She sat on a delicately woven rattan love seat and he lowered down beside her, his six-foot presence looming large next to her. Aware of the solid breadth of his shoulders and the scent of his skin, she found the new king of Alma a little too appealing. "It's nice here. Quiet," she said. "You must be exhausted."

"Yes, but invigorated, too. If that makes any sense to you."

"It does. When I'm researching a piece of art for a client, I might work sixteen-hour days, but I always get excited when I locate it." His brows came together as if he were puzzled. "I'm an art advisor," she explained. "I help collectors build their collections."

"Impressive. And do you work in your country?"

"I'm based out of Los Angeles and New York. I don't spend any time in Samforstand."

"That's how it was for me. I worked out of Miami and New York, but now, Alma will be my permanent home. My duty is here and I will adjust. The country is beautiful, so it won't be a hardship."

"Excuse me, Your Highness," said a voice from behind the bench.

"Yes?" Juan Carlos turned around.

"I'm sorry to interrupt, but Chancellor Benoit has been called away and insists on saying his farewells to you personally. He is waiting in the antechamber."

"All right, thank you. Please tell the chancellor I will be in to see him shortly."

The man gave a curt nod and walked off.

"Well, looks like duty calls. I'm sorry." He rose and extended his hand. "Please save another dance for me tonight, Portia. There's more I want to learn about...*art advising*." He smiled.

Her heart hammered. She didn't know what to make of the cocoon-like hold he had on her. She'd only just met him and already he was wrapping himself around her thoughts with his silent compliments and easy ways. "I will."

She rose and he walked her back to the ballroom, depositing her exactly where he'd found her, beside Maria and Alex.

"I will be back," he said.

Portia's throat hitched and she nodded.

"Looks like the king is smitten." Maria kept her voice

low enough for only Portia's ears. She was sure Maria, a public relations expert and friend, had been instrumental in her receiving an invitation to the coronation and gala.

"He's being gracious, Maria."

Maria seemed to ignore her comment. "He's a good man."

"Perfect for Alma. But not for me." She was attracted to Juan Carlos. Any woman with blood running through her veins would be, but talk about high profile. You couldn't get much higher, and that's the last thing Portia needed in her life. It had taken her three years to climb out of the hole she'd dug for herself by getting involved with the Duke of Discourse, Travis Miles, LA's favorite talk show host.

Charming, debonair and controversial, he'd dragged her into his limelight from the start of their love affair to the bitter, heartbreaking end. Her career had suffered as the details of his neglect and wandering eye came into play. She'd almost lost all credibility with her clients. Luckily, she'd managed her way out of that situation, vowing to keep a low profile, stay in the small circle of the art world and not allow another high-profile charmer to get to her. And that included the king of Alma.

"I don't know about that," Maria said, matter-of-factly.

"I do," she said, convincing herself of that very thing. "I have an important meeting in Los Angeles with a client in a few days."

"A lot could happen in a few days, Portia."

But the conversation ended when a nice-looking gentleman approached, introduced himself as Alma's secretary of defense, and asked her to dance.

Portia accepted, and as she was being led to the dance floor, shot an over-the-shoulder glance at Maria.

Only to find Juan Carlos standing there, his gaze following her every movement.

He had indeed come back for her.

* * *

Gnashing his teeth, Juan Carlos ran a hand down his face to cover the tightness in his jaw. Princess Portia had danced nonstop with three men since he'd returned from seeing Chancellor Benoit off. Every time Juan Carlos thought to approach, he was interrupted or summoned into a conversation with a group of dignitaries. He couldn't fall short of his duties on his coronation day, yet the beautiful snow queen consumed his thoughts, and as he spoke with others, he kept one eye on Portia.

Finally free from conversations, he had an aide approach the orchestra and suggest that they take a five-minute break. The music died instantly and Juan Carlos strode over to the table where Portia had just taken a seat. "Hello again."

Those startling blue eyes lifted to him. "Hello."

"I'm happy to see you having a good time."

"I am," she said. "Would you like to sit down?"

"I have a better idea."

Her eyes twinkled. "Really? What would that be?"

He offered his hand again, hoping she'd take it. "Come with me and find out."

Her hesitation rattled his nerves. "Where?"

"Trust me and I'll show you."

She rose then, and as they walked out of the ballroom again with her hand in his, she watched him carefully. She had no reason not to trust him. He would never steer her wrong.

"In here," he said.

He tugged her into a spacious office and shut the door. It was black as coal at first, but the light of the full moon streamed in and his eyes adjusted so that he could make out Portia's silhouette. He took her gently into his arms and overwhelming sensations rushed through his body. Silently, with a look, she questioned his actions, but with his eyes he assured her she had nothing to fear. Then the orchestra began playing and as music piped into the room through the air ducts, he began to move her along to the beat. She tossed her head back and laughed. "You aren't serious."

He grinned. "It's the only way I can assure us not being interrupted again."

"You are resourceful, Your Highness. We have an entire dance floor all to ourselves."

"What would make it perfect would be if you'd call me Juan Carlos."

"But you've earned the right to be called king."

"Tonight, for now, think of me as a man, and not a king."

"I'll try, but you have to understand, after all the adoration, the photos and parades and galas in your honor, it's not easy for me."

He did understand, but pressed his reasoning a little further. "Think of it this way. How would you like it if everyone you knew called you Princess Portia?"

She gave it some thought and nodded. "I see your point."

He drew her inches closer, so that her sweet breaths touched his face, but he didn't dare do more. Though he wanted to crush her against him, feel her body sway with his, he couldn't rush her or scare her off. These feelings pulsed through him with near desperation. He'd never been so…besotted. Such an old-world word, but that's exactly how he felt.

"How long will you be in Alma?" he asked.

"I leave for the States in two days. I'm due back at work."

News he didn't want to hear. "Are you working with a client?"

"Yes, he's someone very influential and I'm thrilled to have the chance to meet with him for the first time. He's new to collecting, and I have an interview with him to see where his tastes lie."

"I see. It's a good opportunity for you. I would imagine being Princess Portia of Samforstand carries some weight in your line of work."

"I'll admit, using my royal heritage has helped me attain clients, but it's my expertise that has earned their trust."

"Trust is important," he said.

"You have the trust of the entire country right now."

"Yes," he said, sighing. "It's a big responsibility. I'm sure you take your responsibility seriously."

"I do. My reputation earns me that trust and I guard it like a mother would her child."

He smiled at the image gathering in his mind, of Portia, mother of his child.

Dios. He was in deep. How was it possible? He had known her less than a day.

And already, he was naming their first-born child.

Two

Stately and grand, Portia's hotel in Del Sol was just a short distance from the palace. The big bed in her room was cushy and comfy. The morning sunlight streamed in to warm her and the air was sweetened by a bouquet of roses, compliments of the hotel manager. It was all fit for a princess. Yet she hadn't slept well.

Last night, as Juan Carlos bid her farewell, he'd almost kissed her. She was sure he would have if they hadn't been surrounded by his guests. She'd thought about that non-kiss during the night. How would his lips feel against hers? Heavens, she hadn't had so much as a date with a man in almost a year, and it had been even longer since she was ravaged by a kiss. Which, she was sure, would have happened had they been alone.

She was thankful that he hadn't locked lips with her in front of the attendees at the gala. Yet, lightbulbs had flashed and pictures had been snapped of the two of them. It was last thing she needed and she'd dashed out as rapidly as Cinderella racing against the midnight hour.

When he'd asked her to join him for brunch this morning, she'd quickly agreed, despite her tingling nerves and fuzzy brain.

Her brunch "date" with the King of Montoro would happen precisely at ten o'clock and he'd promised they wouldn't be interrupted.

She heard the familiar Bruno Mars ringtone of her cell phone and grabbed it from the nightstand. Her assistant's name popped up on the screen and she smiled. From the very beginning, her assistant had been her closest friend. "Hello, Jasmine."

"Hi, Portia. I hope I didn't wake you?"

"No, not at all. I'm getting ready to have brunch. It's good to hear your voice."

"Did you survive the coronation?" Jasmine Farr never minced words. "I know you weren't thrilled about attending."

"Actually, it wasn't so bad." The newly named king was quite a man. "And it's my lot in life to attend these functions every so often."

"That's what you get for being a princess." She chuckled. "I saw some of the coronation on YouTube."

"That was fast."

"It always is. Anyway, I'm calling to tell you that Mr. Greenboro had to cancel your meeting this week. He's flying out of the country and won't be back for three months. He sends his apologies, of course, and he did reschedule. I hope it's okay that I took the liberty of making that appointment. I didn't think you'd want to let him get away."

"Oh, I'm disappointed. I'd set the entire week aside to work with him, but I'm glad you're on the ball and rescheduled with him. Text me that date and I'll mark it on my calendar."

"Will do. So, now you don't have to rush back. There's really nothing else going on this week."

"Right."

"You've worked hard these past few months and you've been meaning to pencil in a vacation. Seems like a perfect opportunity."

"It is beautiful here."

"From the pictures I'm seeing, the beaches are to die for. I wish I could join you. I'd come in an instant."

"Why don't you come? We could have spa days together."

"I can't. I'm flying to Maryland for my cousin's wedding at the end of the week. "

"I'd forgotten about that. Darn."

"But that doesn't mean you can't stay on. I can book you a villa suite in Playa del Onda. The beach resort is top notch. You'll get lots of R&R."

"Let me think about it. I'll get back to you later on today."

After she ended the call, she stripped off her pajamas and entered the shower. The pounding water rained down and woke her up to the possibility of an actual vacation: away from phones, away from the hectic pace of gallery openings, away from the pressures of making art selections for her obscenely rich or drastically eccentric clients. Her schedule was a busy one, and this did seem like a perfect opportunity to unwind.

When she was finished with her shower, she slipped into a white dress with red polka dots that belted at the waist, slid on navy patent leather shoes and tossed her hair up into a ponytail. She applied light makeup, including eyeliner and soft pink lip gloss.

The jewelry she chose was delicate: a thin strand of pearls around her neck and wrist. She fastened her watch on her left arm and noted the time. Juan Carlos was sending a car for her in ten minutes. She grabbed her purse and left the hotel room.

In the lobby, she was greeted by a uniformed driver who escorted her to an ink-black limousine. She played the role of princess well, but she would rather be wearing a pair of jeans and going to the local café for a bite of breakfast.

"Your Highness," the driver said, as he opened the door for her, "allow me."

She slid into the backseat and bumped legs with Juan Carlos. Her breath hitched in her throat. He took in her wide-eyed surprise and grinned. "Good morning, Portia."

"Excuse me, but I didn't expect you to come to pick me up."

Should she worry about the implications? This wasn't a date. At least, not in any real sense.

"It's a nice morning for a drive. After yesterday's events, I thought you might like to join me to see some of the city. I hope you don't mind, but I've changed our brunch plans for today."

He wore dark slacks and a casual white silk shirt, opened slightly at the collar. She glimpsed his tanned chest and gulped for air.

"Of course not."

"Great. You look very pretty this morning."

"Thank you." *And you look dynamic, powerful and gorgeous.*

He issued directions to the driver and they took off.

"How were your first twenty-four hours as king?" she asked.

He rubbed his chin, thinking for a second. "It's strange that I don't feel any different. I keep expecting a big transformation, but I'm just me."

She smiled at his earnest answer. "I thought it would be an adjustment for you. Every move you make now will be documented somehow." She glanced out the window, expecting to see photographers following the limo, snapping pictures. She'd had experience with her ex-boyfriend's fame and it had gotten old very fast. No one should be followed and photographed at every turn for entertainment's sake. "How did you escape the palace?"

He chuckled. "You make it seem like prison."

"No, no. I'm sorry. That's not what I meant."

"I know what you meant, Portia." Her name slid effortlessly from his lips. "There are some advantages to being king."

"Such as?" she probed.

"Such as, I didn't make my intentions known. No one expected me to take a drive this morning. No one questioned me. I had the car ready to pick you up, and then I merely slipped into the backseat before anyone at the palace got wind of it."

"You snuck out."

He laughed again and she joined in. "Okay, yes. I snuck out."

Speaking to him put her at ease and she settled back in her seat. "Do you have bodyguards?"

"Yes, they are following behind somewhere."

"You're not worried?"

He shook his head. "No. I'm not worried. And neither should you be."

"Okay, I'll trust you." She'd never traveled with bodyguards, but her situation was quite different. As an exiled princess, she'd grown up in America and never had what Juan Carlos now had: a citizenry eager to reinstate their monarchy. "But you must have dozens of dignitaries and family members waiting to speak with you at the palace."

"Which I will do later. But for now," he said, reaching for her hand, "I find being with you more important."

Juan Carlos held her hand during the tour of the city. He showed her sites of great historical significance and some trendy new hot spots that were cropping up. The rise of democracy was good for enterprise, he explained.

As he spoke, the tone of his deep and sincere voice brought a smile to her lips more times than she could count. It was intimate in a way, hearing the love he had for a country that was almost as new to him as it was to her. He kept her hand locked in his as if it was precious. As if he needed the connection. To hear him say that being with her was important did wonders for her ego.

Yet she only indulged him because nothing could possibly come of it. And because it had been a long time since she'd enjoyed a man's company so much.

Tomorrow, she would leave Del Sol.

The limo stopped at a tiny café off the main street of town. "I hear Matteo's is fantastic."

"You've never eaten here before?" she asked.

"No, I haven't. We'll experience it together. Do you mind?"

"I love adventure."

He nodded, a satisfied glimmer in his eyes. "I thought you might."

They exited the limo, which looked out of place on the backstreets of the royal city. Once inside, they were escorted to their table by the owner. He was sweating, nervous and fidgety. Juan Carlos clapped him on the back gently to reassure him. "Bring us your specials, Matteo. I hear they are the best in all of Del Sol."

"*Si, si.* I will be glad to serve you myself, Your Majesty."

Juan Carlos nodded. "Thank you."

Though the café walls showed signs of age, it was a clean, modest place. "Are you sure the food is good here?" she asked.

His brows gathered. "It comes highly recommended. Why?"

"We're the only ones seated."

Juan Carlos looked around the empty café. "My bodyguards. They called ahead to announce my arrival. I'll make it up to Matteo. I can't have him losing business on my account."

"I'm sure he'll be boasting that King Montoro of Alma dined in his café. His business will double by next week."

Juan Carlos sharpened his gaze on her. "I hadn't thought of that."

"You're new to this royal thing."

"Yes, I guess I am."

Just wait, she wanted to say. He was an intelligent man, from all she'd read about him. He managed the sizable personal accounts of the Montoros and had helped build a fortune for the family. He had wits and smarts, but nothing would prepare him for the limelight he'd just entered. He'd have to experience it himself, the good, the bad, the ugly. His life would be under a microscope now.

And she didn't want to be the amoeba next to him.

Coffee was served, along with fresh handmade tortillas, butter and a bowl of cut fruit. "Looks delicious," Juan Carlos said to Matteo.

"Please, is there anything else I can bring you while the meal is cooking?"

"This is perfect. Don't you agree, Portia?"

She nodded and smiled at the owner.

When Matteo left the room she continued to smile. "You're kind. He will always remember this day because you put him at ease."

Travis Miles had been kind, too, in the beginning.

"Now who is being kind?" he asked.

"I'm just speaking the truth. You'll impact a great many lives."

"In a positive way, I hope and pray."

"Kind," she repeated. "You care about the people in the country."

"Thank you." His incredibly warm brown eyes softened and her stomach did a little flip.

She buttered a tortilla, rolled it up and took a few bites. She sipped coffee and asked Juan Carlos a few pointed questions about his life to keep the conversation flowing and her mind off the fact that King Montoro was a hunk.

The meal was delivered with fanfare. Matteo and his staff put out the dishes in sweeping motions and finally left them to dine privately. The food was delicious. The main dish consisted of bits of sautéed pork topped with eggs and lathered with a creamy, mildly spicy sauce. There was also some type of sweet corn soufflé served inside the husks, as well as caramelized plantains. Every bite she took rewarded her taste buds. "Mmm…this is heavenly."

Juan Carlos nodded, his mouth full.

As he chewed, his gaze remained on her. He had warm, luxurious, intense eyes that didn't stray. Goose bumps rode up and down her arms. As far as men went, Juan Carlos had it all, except for one thing. His fatal flaw. He was king. And that meant after today, she couldn't see him again.

"So what are your plans for the rest of the day?" he asked.

"Oh, I'm, uh, going to…" She really didn't have any plans. Maybe do a little shopping. Check out the only art museum in the city. "I'll be packing."

"That can't take all day."

"I wouldn't think so."

"Would you consider having dinner with me?"

No. No. No. "I really shouldn't."

Juan Carlos leaned back in his seat, studying her. "Do you have a man in your life, Portia?"

Slowly, she shook her head. She felt a trap coming.

"No one? I find that hard to believe. Do you date?"

"Rarely. My career is demanding. And it's very important to me. I've worked hard to get where I am."

"Admirable. Are you working tonight?"

"No, but I…"

He grinned. "I'm only asking for a dinner date, Portia."

Her shoulders sagged an inch. A barely noticeable move,

but she felt the defeat all the way down to her toes. She couldn't insult the king. "Then, yes, I'll have dinner with you."

After the meal, Juan Carlos escorted her to the limo. She took a seat at the far window and he climbed in after her. To his credit, he didn't crowd her, leaving a modest amount of space between them. But as the car took off, he placed his hand over hers on the empty seat, and wild pings of awareness shot through her body.

Don't let him get to you, Portia.

He's not the man for you.

As the limo pulled up to the hotel, Juan Carlos spoke to the driver. "Give us a minute please, Roberto."

The driver's door opened and closed quietly. Silence filled the air and suddenly she did feel crowded, though Juan Carlos hadn't made a move toward her. "I cannot walk you to your door, Princess."

"I understand."

"Do you? Do you know how much I want to?" His eyes were down, gazing at her hand as his thumb worked circles over her fingers. Her nerves jumped, like kernels of corn popping in a fry pan, one right after the other. "I don't want to cause you any inconvenience."

"I...know."

He tugged her hand gently and she fell forward, closing the gap between them. His dark-fringed eyelids lifted; she was struck by all-consuming heat. He wasn't moving a muscle, but leaving it up to her. As if she had a choice now. As if she could deny him. His mesmerizing hunger was contagious; years of abstinence made her hungry, as well. Her gaze lowered to his mouth. Lord in heaven, she wanted his kiss.

She moistened her lips and his eyes drew down immediately. "You leave me no choice, Princess."

He used a finger to tilt her chin, and then bent his head

toward her. Anticipation pulsed through her veins. Every single second was an unnerving kind of torture. And finally, his mouth was on hers, his hand coming to wrap more firmly around her jaw, as if he couldn't get enough, as if he would devour her.

Long live the king!

Her tummy ached from goodness and she indulged like a miser finding a hidden supply of cash. She touched his face, his jaw steel under her fingertips, and a groan erupted from his throat.

A whimpering mewling sound came from hers. Mortification would have set in, if the king wasn't equally as needy. But there was no shame, just honesty, and it was, after all, the kiss to end all kisses. Juan Carlos didn't let up, not for a moment. His lips worked hers hard, then soft, then hard again. Under her dress, her nipples ached. She was pretty sure the king was experiencing the same agony, but farther south on his body.

She didn't know whose mouth opened first, or whether it was at the exact same instant, but suddenly she was being swept up and hollowed out, his tongue doing a thorough job of ravaging her. Any second now, she'd be out of her head with lust. But Juan Carlos placed his hands on her shoulders and, she sensed, with great reluctance, moved her away from him.

He leaned back against the seat, breathing hard. "I've never made love to a woman in a limo before, Princess. It wouldn't take much to change that," he said. He tried for amusement, tried to chuckle, but a serious tone had given away his innermost thoughts.

"It would be a first for me, too," she said, coming up for air.

A rumpled mess, she tried her best to straighten herself out before she exited the limo.

He pressed a button and the window rolled down. Ro-

berto appeared by the car door. "See Princess Portia to
her hotel room," Juan Carlos said calmly. He'd gotten his
emotions in check already, while she was still a ravaged
jumble of nerves.

Again, those warm brown eyes lit upon her. "I'll send
a car to pick you up for dinner at seven."

She swallowed. "Maybe...we shouldn't," she squeaked.

"Are you afraid of me?" he asked, though his confident
tone indicated that it wasn't even a concern.

She shook her head. "I'm leaving in the morning."

"And you love your job. Your career means a lot to you.
Yes, that's clear."

He'd made her refusal seem silly. And it was. Nothing
would happen unless she wanted it to happen. She already
knew Juan Carlos was that type of man.

"I'll see you tonight," she said finally. When the driver
opened the car door, she rushed out.

She hadn't exactly lied to him, had she?

She said she'd be gone, and he thought she meant back
to the States. But she'd made up her mind to vacation on
the shores of Alma, at least until the end of the week.

But he didn't need to know that.

After a late lunch, Juan Carlos had a meeting in the city
with the prime minister and few of Alma's most trusted
and prominent business leaders. He struggled to keep his
mind on the topics at hand. The restoration of the entire
country was a tall order. But every so often, his mind traveled to that place where Portia was in his arms. The image
of her lips locked on his, their bodies pulsing to the same
lusty rhythms, knocked him for a loop and sent his brain
waves scrambling. She was, in his estimation, perfect. For
him. For the country.

Wow. Where had that come from? Why was he thinking of her in terms of permanence? As a queen for Alma, for goodness' sake.

Because aside from the fact that his sensual response was like the national flag being hoisted to full mast every time he looked at her, there was no doubt in his mind that she could take a place by his side at the throne.

As a public figure, he was never alone much anymore, but that didn't mean he wasn't lonely. He hadn't had a serious relationship for years. His ambition had gotten in the way and sure, he'd had a few women in his life, but nothing serious. No one who'd made him feel like this.

Portia's face flashed in his mind, that porcelain skin, those ice-blue eyes, that haughty chin, that mouth that tasted like sweet sin. The snow queen had become important to him in a short time, and…

"Your Majesty? Juan Carlos, are you all right?"

"Huh? Oh, yeah, I'm fine." Prime Minister Rivera was giving him a strange look. "Just deep in thought."

They'd been talking about how to bring new enterprise to Alma and how the rise of the monarchy would bring in tourism. They needed to brand themselves as a free country and show the world that democracy reigned, that new visitors and new businesses were welcome to their stunning Atlantic shores.

"Actually, I have an idea as to how to draw more tourists," Juan Carlos said.

"Really?"

Alex Ramon's ears perked up. As the deputy prime minister of commerce, he was fully immersed in the issue. "Tell us your thoughts."

"It's been rumored in our family for years that our ancestors had stashed a considerable amount of artwork, sculptures and paintings on land that had fallen to ruin. Land that Tantaberra overlooked. Right before the family was deposed, they'd thought to hide the art so it wouldn't fall into the dictator's greedy hands."

Juan Carlos's mind was clicking fast. He didn't know how true those rumors were. He'd only heard the tales while growing up; Uncle Rafael had spoken of hidden treasures the way a master storyteller would about a pirate's bounty. It had all been exciting, the sort of thing that captured a little boy's imagination. But the rumors had held fast and true during his adulthood, and only recently, his cousin Bella had found a hidden cache of letters at one of the family's abandoned farms, letters that proved that he, a Salazar and not a Montoro, was the rightful heir to the throne.

"I have plans to visit the area myself and see what I can find. If it's true, and artwork is indeed on the property, think of the story. The art could be restored, and we could have a special showing or a series of showings to bring awareness to Alma."

"It's genius, Your Highness," Prime Minister Rivera said.

Others around the board table agreed.

The meeting ran long and Juan Carlos didn't get back to the palace until six. He had just enough time to shower and dress for dinner. His pulse sped up as he thought of Portia again, of her sweetly exotic scent and the way she'd filled his body with pleasure when he was near her. She caused him to gasp and sweat and breathe hard. It wasn't ideal. She was a hard case. She didn't seem interested in him. And that worried him, because as far as he was concerned, she was The One.

He came down at precisely six forty-five and bumped into his new secretary at the base of the winding staircase, nearly knocking the clipboard out of her hands. "Oh, sorry, Your Highness." She was out of breath, as if she'd been running a marathon.

"My apologies," he said. "I've been preoccupied and didn't see you."

Alicia was redheaded, shapely and quite efficient. She wore glasses, but under those glasses were pretty, light green eyes. She'd taken on a lot, being a first hire, as there was much ground to cover. "Your seven o'clock appointment is here."

Warmth spread through his body at the mention of his dinner date. "Princess Portia?"

"Oh, uh. No, Your Highness. I'm sorry. I don't see Princess Portia on the books." She studied her clipboard, going over the names. "No, you have appointments every half hour for the next few hours. I penciled in a dinner break for you at nine."

"I thought those were on tomorrow night's schedule." Surely, he hadn't been mistaken, had he? Yet he had to take Alicia at her word. He'd already come to find that she rarely if ever made mistakes. He, on the other hand, had been hypnotized by a pair of deep ocean-blue eyes and was more than distracted.

"I can't possibly make all of those appointments." High-ranking officials and the heads of businesses along with their wives or husbands wanted to meet the new king. It was as simple as that. It was good for commerce to know the pillars of trade in Alma, so he'd agreed to a few evening appointments. Under normal circumstances, he'd rather cut off his right arm than cancel them, but he couldn't break a date with Portia. "See what you can do about cancelling them. Who was first on the schedule?"

"Mr. and Mrs. Rubino. The Rubinos are in the royal study. And your next appointment after that is already here, I'm afraid. They are notoriously early for every occasion, I'm told. They are waiting in the throne room."

He ran his hands through his hair. "Fine. I'll see them. But see what you can do about cancelling the rest."

"Yes, Your Highness. I'll do my best." She bit her lower lip, her eyes downcast. "Sorry for the confusion."

"Alicia?"

"Yes?"

"It's not your doing. I forgot about these appointments. We're all learning here. It's new to all of us."

She had ten years of experience running a duke's household in London, coordinating parties and events with dignitaries and the royal family. She hadn't much to learn. He was the one who had screwed up.

"Yes, Your Highness. I'll get on those cancellations right away."

Juan Carlos rubbed the back of his neck and headed to the study.

With luck, he could salvage the evening.

Portia had been stood up. She'd been delivered to the palace minutes before seven, only to be informed that the king had visitors and to please be patient and wait. She was shown to the dining room and shortly after, the palace chef himself had set dishes of appetizers on the table before her.

Candles were lit and soft music filtered into the room.

The only problem? Her date wasn't here. And she wasn't about to eat a thing until he showed. Call her stubborn.

It was after eight. She knew because her stomach refused to stop growling and finally, she'd glanced at her watch.

She'd already taken in the paintings on the walls, assessing them and noting that they weren't up to par with usual palatial art. Oh, they were lovely pieces, but from contemporary artists. Many of them were replicas of the real thing. It was a curiosity. The monarchy stretched way beyond the years of the dictatorship. There should be older, more authentic works on the walls. But this was only one room. Maybe for security reasons, the gallery held the most valuable pieces.

After wandering the dining hall, she picked a particular patch of space near the fireplace and began pacing.

She couldn't fault Juan Carlos. His secretary had taken the blame, explaining that she'd failed to remind the king of his visitors. She'd tried her best to cancel the meetings, but she was afraid she wasn't as successful as she'd hoped.

But the more Portia thought about it, the more pangs of anger replaced her patience.

How long would he keep her waiting?

Travis is in a meeting. He won't be available for hours. He'd like you to wait, though.

This isn't the same thing, she reminded herself. Her ex-boyfriend wasn't a king. Well, maybe the king of late-night television. And she'd fallen for him. He was funny and charming and kind. It was like a regular Cinderella story, the poor broke comedian hooks up with a real live princess. Travis was far from poor now, although he'd come from humble beginnings and the press loved their story and ate it up.

A new American fairy tale, they'd called it.

Travis had been on top of the world when they were together. Everyone loved him and thought he was worthy of a princess from an obscure little country. Only dating a supermodel would have given him more credibility.

And here she was, doing the same thing. Another American fairy tale, only this time with a real king.

Stupid of her.

Her nerves were jumpy and by the time eight-thirty rolled around, she was royally pissed.

Juan Carlos had twisted her arm to accept this dinner date, the way charming men did. He'd trapped her and then kissed her until every brain cell was lulled into capitulation. God, she'd been looking forward to being alone with him again. That kiss was good. Better than good. It was the best kiss she'd ever had. Not even Travis could kiss like that, and he'd been plenty experienced in that department.

"Sorry, so sorry, Portia."

She jumped. "Oh!" Juan Carlos entered the room, looking dashing in a dark buttoned-up suit but no tie. Another growl emitted from her stomach, this time not due to hunger.

"Did Alicia explain what happened? It was my fault. This is the first chance I've had to—"

"It's been over ninety minutes," was all she could think to say.

"I would've cancelled with you and sent you home, but this is your last night in Alma. Selfishly, I wanted to see you again."

Guilt rose like bile in her throat. She remained silent.

He glanced at the feast of food that had been put before her. "You didn't touch anything Chef prepared. You must be famished."

"I'm not hungry anymore, Your Majesty."

His lips pursed in disapproval.

She still couldn't bring herself to call him by his given name.

"You've been so patient. There's just one more meeting I have to get through. Will you wait?"

She shook her head. "Actually, I think I'd like to go."

"You're angry."

"No, I'm tired and, and…"

"Angry."

She didn't respond. "Will you have your driver take me back to the hotel?"

Juan Carlos closed his eyes briefly. "Yes, of course. I just assumed after we kissed, you'd… Never mind. You're right. I shouldn't have made you wait."

A man who admitted when he was wrong? How rare.

"Duty called. I'm afraid it always will."

That's how it had worked with Travis. The difference? Travis had been building his own personal dynasty, while Juan Carlos was trying to build one for his country. But that still left Portia with the same end result. She'd never be a top priority and while she liked Juan Carlos, she had vowed, after many disappointments with Travis, to never get herself in that situation again.

With that, she wished Juan Carlos a good evening, assured him she wasn't angry and put enough distance between them that he couldn't touch her, couldn't plant his delicious lips on hers again and make her change her mind.

Three

The beach at Playa del Onda was one of the most stunning Portia had ever visited. Warm sand squeezed between her toes as she sat on a lounge chair, reading a book. This morning she'd gotten up early and taken a long jog along the shoreline, the October sun warming her through and through. She'd met a lovely family of tourists and had breakfast with them at a terrace café that overlooked the Atlantic. But their two little children, aged five and three, reminded her that it would probably be a long time before she was blessed with motherhood.

Often, she thought of having a family. She'd been orphaned at a young age. Aside from her great-aunt Margreta, she had no other family. Her grandmother Joanna had died during Portia's sophomore year in college. But she had her work and it fulfilled her, and she had good friends. She wasn't complaining. Yet being here on this beautiful beach was not only relaxing, it was…lonely.

Face it, Portia. How many books can you read this week? How many hot stone spa treatments can you indulge in? How many solo dinners in your room can you enjoy?

It had been three days of torturous relaxation. And it didn't compute. How odd for her to realize while on a vacation in a beautiful locale that she wasn't made for inactivity. She liked to keep active, to busy herself with things that mattered. Yesterday, she'd given herself a mental slap.

You deserve this vacation, so shut up, sit back and enjoy yourself.

Today, the mental slaps weren't working. Her relaxation was even more forced. She fidgeted in her chair; the book in her hands no longer held her interest. Sunglasses shading her eyes, she watched others frolicking on the sand, tossing a Frisbee, their laughter drifting over to her, reminding her how lonely she was. How bored.

She wished Jasmine was here. They would've had a good time with shopping, spa dates and maybe a nightclub or two.

The Frisbee landed at her feet and a teenage boy trotted over and stopped abruptly, blasting sand onto her legs. "Excuse me," he said. He reached for the Frisbee slowly, eyeing her legs, then her bikini-clad body. "Want to play with us?" he asked.

He had Spanish good looks, dark hair, bronzed skin and a charming smile. He was sixteen tops, and she would've actually considered tossing the Frisbee around with him, if he hadn't been so blatant about ogling her breasts.

She was saved from refusing, when the concierge from the Villa Delgado approached. "Excuse me, Princess."

The boy blinked at her title, turned a lovely shade of cherry-blossom pink and bowed, before dashing off. She chuckled under her breath. Her royal status did have some advantages. "Yes," she said to the concierge, removing her sunglasses.

"You have a phone call at the desk. A woman named Jasmine. She says she works for you. Apparently, she hasn't been able to reach you on your cell phone."

"I left my cell in my room," she replied. She didn't want to be interrupted in her state of lonely boredom. Now she realized how silly that seemed. "Sorry you had to track me down."

"Not a problem, Princess Portia."

"Will you tell her that I'll call her as soon as I get to my room?"

"My pleasure," he said.

When he walked off, she gathered up her beach bag, hat and sunglasses and promptly made her way toward the villa. Her suite with its second-floor terrace came into view. It was really quite picturesque, the columns and archways suggesting old-world grace and style. Why couldn't she like being here more? Why wasn't she okay with being idle? Maybe things had changed with Jasmine. Maybe her friend would come join her, after all. Her hope in her throat, Portia hiked a little faster to reach her suite of rooms.

Once inside, she set her things down on the dining table and headed for the bedroom, where she was sure she'd left her phone. It was charging on her nightstand. She unhooked the charger, just as she heard a knock at the door.

She belted her cover-up a little tighter and moved to the door. With a gentle tug on the knob, the door opened and she came face to face with Juan Carlos Salazar. The king.

She blinked and a rush of heat rose up her neck. She trembled at the sight of him, *the gorgeous, unexpected, surprising* sight of him. The phone slipped slightly in her hand and she grabbed at it before it crashed onto the floor.

His eyes were on her, and those dark raised brows made her flush even hotter. With guilt. Piercing disappointment flickered in his eyes. She hadn't told him the absolute truth when she'd left Del Sol.

"Princess," he said.

"Your Majesty," she responded.

His lips twitched. "I see you've decided to stay on in Alma, after all."

"I, uh, yes." She didn't owe him an explanation. One heart-robbing kiss didn't give him that right. "My plans changed."

"Quite unexpectedly, I assume."

"Yes, that's right." The movement of two bodyguards caught her attention. They stayed back, at least five feet away, but she was certain they could hear every word. "Would you like to come in?"

His gaze dipped down to her bikini-clad body, covered only by a soft robe of silk that reached her thighs. "Yes."

She backed up a few steps and he nodded to his bodyguards and then entered. They stood face-to-face again, alone in her suite.

Despite her guilt and a sense of being caught red-handed, this was the most exciting thing that had happened to her in three days. But how did he find out where she was and what did he want from her?

Her cell phone buzzed and she looked down at the screen. A text was coming through from Jasmine. She hadn't had time to call her back yet. Quickly, she scanned the message.

Heads up. I might've made a mistake by giving King Montoro your location. He was charming and said it was a business thing. Apologizing in advance. Love you!

She lifted her lids to him. Okay, so he wasn't psychic. But he was thorough.

"It's good to see you again," he said.

Warmth swelled inside her like an overflowing river. He had too much of an effect on her.

"It's nice to see you, but I do admit, it's quite a surprise."

On this warm day, he was wearing dark trousers and a tan shirt, sleeves rolled up with his hands in his pockets, looking as casual and delicious as any man she'd ever met. Man, *not king*. But she couldn't forget who he was. "I have to admit, I was also surprised to learn you hadn't left the country."

"You were looking for me?"

"Yes, I spoke with your assistant. She's very nice, by the way, and she's loyal to you. But the fact is, I have something of a business venture for you. And after I told her a little about it, she was willing to let me get in touch with you."

His eyes skimmed over Portia's body. Another wave of heat shimmied down to her belly and she turned away from his hot, assessing stare. Man or king, he was dangerous. "Would you like to sit down?" She waved him over to a latte-colored leather chair by the window that faced the Atlantic. "Please give me a minute to change my clothes."

"Only if you have to."

There was a wicked twinkle in his eyes that tweaked something lusty and recently unleashed in her body. It made her run, not walk toward her bedroom. "I'll be a minute, Your Majesty," she called over her shoulder.

His chuckle followed her into her room.

She scrubbed her face clean of sunscreen and removed her hair fastener, combing the tangles away and then gathering the strands back up into a long ponytail. She put on a pair of white capris and an off-the-shoulder cornflower-blue blouse.

A hint of lip gloss, some shading to her eyelids and she was ready. And more than mildly curious as to what was so important that King Juan Carlos had come all the way here to seek her out. She gave a last glance in the mirror and nodded. She felt a little less vulnerable to the king's hungry eyes now.

Juan Carlos stood when Portia entered the room. His heart hammered in his chest at the sight of her. She didn't know it yet, but he was determined to possess her. Aside from his newfound reign over Alma and his duties here, she'd become the most important thing in his life.

In such a short time.

It wasn't rational. He had no explanation for it. He'd never experienced anything quite like this. When she'd left the palace the other night, remorse had plagued him and lingered for days. Was he pathetic? Or simply a man who knows what he wants.

She was perfect, his ideal woman. She was royal, beautiful, smart, but at the moment…quite unattainable.

"Princess," he said.

"Would you like something cold to drink?" she asked.

"No, thank you."

"Okay, then maybe we should sit down and you can tell me what this is all about."

She took a seat, her eyes widening as she waited for him to explain.

"It seems I might have need for your services."

"My services? As an art advisor?"

"Well, yes. In a way. It would be something quite adventurous. You did say you liked adventure, didn't you?"

"I do."

"Well, then, let me explain. I don't know how much you know about the history of Alma, but it's been rumored that right before my family fled the country, they hid artwork dating back before World War II on the grounds of their abandoned farm. It's very run-down and Tantaberra never went there, so it was the perfect hiding place. Now that I'm king, I want to find those treasured pieces belonging to the royal family. It would go a long way in helping the country heal and bring new hope to our people. Imagine what a find that would be."

"It would be monumental," she agreed. Fireworks lit in her eyes at the mention of hidden art.

Good. He had her attention.

"But I see that you're vacationing here, so maybe you'd be too busy to help me locate the treasure."

"You want my help in locating the artwork?"

"Yes, I would need someone to help me hunt for it, and then assess its value. You'd be able to look at something and determine if it's authentic, I would imagine."

"Yes, for the most part. It's what I do. But you plan on doing this by yourself?"

"I can donate a few days of my time, yes. I wouldn't want word to leak out about what I was doing. If I come up empty, or if there are other issues regarding the artwork we find, I would rather it not become public knowledge immediately. Bella and her husband had already begun renovations on the property but given the site's historical significance, they've agreed to allow me to take over and devote the full resources of the crown to the project. As we speak, there is a team working on the grounds, getting it ready for my arrival. So Princess Portia, would you consider helping me? Of course, you'd be paid for your time."

"So, this is a job offer?"

"Yes, I'm offering you a job and an adventure."

She smiled, leaning forward and placing her hands on her crossed knee. "Who else will be there?"

He gathered his brows. "No one but my bodyguards. As I said, I plan to do this discreetly."

"It's intriguing, Your Majesty. But the two us alone, all that time?"

"Is that a problem for you?" God only knew, it was a problem for him. How could he keep his hands off her? It would be a living hell, but not worse than having her living a continent away. A few days was all he was asking of her.

"Maybe. Answer one thing for me, please."

He extended his arms, palms up. "Anything."

"Do you have an ulterior motive in offering me this opportunity? And please don't make me spell it out."

He smiled. She'd made her point and he wouldn't do her a disservice by lying to her. "If you mean, do I value a few more days in your company, then yes. I suppose. But I do honestly have good reason to be asking this of you. You are an expert, are you not?"

"I am."

The sparkle in her eyes evaporated.

"What is it?"

She rose from her seat, and good manners had him rising, too. She walked behind the chair, putting distance between them, and leaned her elbows on the back, a battle raging in her eyes, on her face. "I'm not presuming anything here, but I do have to tell you where I stand. It's… it's complicated. Because I do like you."

Encouraging. He nodded.

"And that kiss we shared…well, it bordered on amazing."

He nodded again. She had something to say and he wanted to hear it.

Or maybe not.

"But the truth is, you're King Montoro of Alma. You're new to this king thing, but you'll find out how demanding a job it will be. And you'll be in the spotlight. All. The. Time."

"Does that worry you?"

"Yes. You see, I'm not one to share heartbreak stories, but in this case, I should probably share with you, why I've been—"

"Playing hard to get?" He couldn't hold back a smile.

"Yes. Only I'm not playing. I'm seriously not interested in getting involved with a man with so much…glitter."

"Glitter?" He laughed. "What's that?"

"You're always going to shine. No matter what." His smile faded. She was dead serious. "And any woman who gets involved with you, will be giving up her identity, her dreams, her heart, to someone who has pledged his life to his country."

"Who was he, Portia? Surely, someone has broken your heart."

"Yes, my heart was broken. I don't like talking about it, but since it's important to our conversation, I'll tell you about Travis Miles. He's like a king in America, a big time Hollywood celebrity."

Juan Carlos nodded. "Of course I know of him. I don't go in much for entertainment news, but he sure has quite a résumé."

"Travis knows everyone of substance in the country from sports figures and superstars to high-ranking politicians. We ran hot for a short time, and then…I became old news to him. He didn't have time for me and we began seeing less and less of each other. Shortly after, I found out he'd been cheating on me with a woman on the staff of his TV show for a long time. Seems that everyone knew about it but poor little gullible me. He'd made me out to be a fool and my career and credibility suffered. It's taken me three years to get my reputation back. Princess or not, I wasn't immune to the blonde-bimbo stigma and so now, I'm cautious. Which is why your royal status isn't a plus in my book."

He stood with hands on hips, silent, taking it all in. He understood her caution. The pain in her eyes, the tremor in her voice were telling, and his heart hurt hearing her confession. He should leave and let her resume her vacation. He shouldn't press her. But his feet were planted and they weren't moving. He couldn't face not seeing her again.

"If things were different, would you accept my offer?"

"Yes," she said, her eyes clear now. "I wouldn't hesitate. It sounds far too exciting to pass up."

"Then let's pretend that we've just met. There was no amazing kiss from before. We haven't danced and spent time together. This is a business meeting. And I promise to keep things completely professional between us."

"Why is it so important to you?" she asked.

"Because, I…I see how much you want to say yes. I see that you'd love to locate the secret artworks."

"And you promise that after we discover this wonderful treasure, we'll just be friends?"

He let a split second go by. He was a man of his word.

If he promised, he'd have to adhere to his vow, regardless of how much he wanted things to be different.

"I promise, Princess."

She nodded. "I know you mean what you say. So yes, I accept your offer."

The next morning, Portia informed the concierge that she'd be checking out earlier than expected from Villa Delgado and offered her thanks for his accommodations. He'd questioned her, hoping she hadn't been disappointed in her stay, and she assured him that was not the case. She'd been called away unexpectedly, she explained. And his brows arched as if he'd suspected King Montoro had something to do with her sudden departure.

And so, her adventure was beginning. Dressed for the search, wearing a pair of Gucci jeans and a red plaid shirt tucked in and belted at the waist, she swopped out her Bruno Magli shoes for tall leather boots and stood outside the villa at precisely eight o'clock. Sunglasses shielding her eyes, her bags packed and ready to go, she gave one last glance to the Atlantic shoreline and the clear azure waters lapping the sands. There would be no five-star accommodations where she was going. She was told to expect rustic and that was fine with her. She'd gone camping before; she knew how to rough it.

Sort of. Jasmine had convinced her once to rent a motor home and they'd trekked as far as Pismo Beach, California. They'd parked the giant thing facing the ocean, and then had gone out for lunch and dinner every night. They'd hit a few clubs, too, dancing until dawn. So maybe that wasn't roughing it per se.

But they had cooked their own breakfasts and hiked the beach in the mornings. Did that count?

One of Juan Carlos's bodyguards drove up in a black SUV, right on time. Poker-faced, he promptly opened the door for her and she got into the backseat as he hoisted her luggage into the cargo space.

As they drove off, she sat quietly in the car, enjoying the sounds of morning, excitement flowing through her veins.

She'd taken Juan Carlos at his word. He would treat her as a professional and so she had nothing to fear and everything to look forward to. Her little heartfelt speech seemed to convince him that she wasn't looking for romantic involvement. Surprisingly, it hadn't been hard admitting her failings to him. He'd put her at ease and that was saying something, since she didn't go around revealing her innermost feelings to anyone but her best friend.

They drove away from the shore, through the streets of Playa del Onda and onto a highway that led inland. "Excuse me. When will we be picking up King Montoro?" she asked Eduardo, the driver-slash-bodyguard.

"His Majesty will be meeting you there," he said.

Ah…discretion.

"Is it a long drive?"

"Not overly so. We should arrive in less than an hour. Is there anything you need, Princess?"

"No, no. I'm perfectly comfortable."

She gazed out the window taking in the scenery, where residential streets were soon replaced by more rural-looking spaces. As the minutes ticked by, the groomed vegetation bordering the road gave way to untamed brush and wildflowers. There was a certain neglected beauty to the land that inspired her. The road though was becoming less and less car friendly. The tires spit broken gravel as they traveled along a bumpy country road.

"Sorry, Princess," Eduardo said. "The road is washed out from here on."

"Is it much longer?"

"No, just another mile or two."

And shortly, he turned onto a path and drove through

wrought-iron gates clawed by fingers of dead branches and vines. Weeds and overgrown scrub led to a two-story house in desperate need of a good solid paint job. Banging sounds reached her ears and she searched for the source as the car came to a stop in front of the house. Juan Carlos appeared on the porch holding a hammer, his shirt slung open and sweat glistening on his beautiful bronzed chest. His dark hair gleaming under the October sunshine, he gave her a wide welcoming smile.

She sucked oxygen in. If she could slither away in a trembling mass, she would. She could order Eduardo to turn the car around, drive and keep on driving until she forgot the exact chestnut color of Juan Carlos's eyes, the deep dark shine of his hair and the powerful rock-solid muscle of his body.

She bit her lower lip until it pained her.

As he made his approach, she bucked up and remembered why she was here, and the promise Juan Carlos had made to her. Now, if she could get her heart to stop racing…

"Welcome," he said, opening the door wide for her. He offered her his hand and helped her out of the car. Eyes shining, his smile broadened. "I hope your trip wasn't too uncomfortable."

"No, no. It was fine," she said, looking beyond him to the house.

"Sorry about my appearance."

She nearly choked on her own saliva. Was he kidding?

"I found some loose planks on the porch. They could be dangerous."

"You're handy with a hammer?"

"You sound surprised. Actually, I had a lot of odd jobs in my younger days. My uncle believed in hard work and I was always employed during my college years."

"Doing?"

"All sorts of things. Remind me to tell you about the time I worked at a strip club in Miami."

"You were a stripper?"

The image of him shedding his clothes made her mouth water.

"I didn't say that. But I sure got a quick education." Her eye fluttered and he squeezed her hand. "There's that wink again. I'm very happy you're here, Portia."

"It's not a wink," she assured him.

He smiled again and released her hand. Breath quietly swooshed out of her mouth.

"Let me assure you, the inside of the house is in better shape than the outside. Bella and James had two bedrooms renovated upstairs and my crew made sure the kitchen and living space are clean and functioning."

She flinched at the mention of the bedrooms and slid a glimpse at Eduardo, who was removing her luggage, appearing stoic as ever. "That's…fine."

She only wished that Juan Carlos would button his shirt so that she could breathe freely again.

Eduardo stopped at the steps with her two suitcases. "Just leave them. I'll take it from here," Juan Carlos said. "Thanks, Eduardo."

The man nodded, but it looked more like a bow. "Your Highness."

Juan Carlos rolled his eyes.

She chuckled. It would take him a while to get used to being royalty.

"Stop laughing," he whispered out of earshot of his bodyguard.

"I'll try," she whispered back. "Not promising anything."

He shook his head but grinned like a schoolboy.

She was up against massive charm and a killer body.

"Let me show you around." Juan Carlos took her arm and guided her inside.

The living room was cozy with a large brick fireplace and old wood floors that looked as though they'd been scoured and polished. A new patterned rug was laid down between two sofas covered with floral tapestry pillows. The smell of fresh drying paint filled the room.

"Come see the kitchen," he said, taking her hand. "It's rustic, but I didn't have the heart to replace everything. I'm assured the oven is in working order." The oven was indeed, quaint and lovely. She could tell it, too, had been scoured to a new brilliance, but it must date back to the 1940s. The refrigerator had been replaced, and the counters were chipped in places but the sink had passed the test of time. A kitchen table sat in front of windows overlooking the backyard grounds. Someone had recently plowed the area and planted a garden of fresh flowers and herbs so the immediate view was quite picturesque.

"It's charming the way it is."

"The refrigerator is stocked. Would you like a cold drink?"

"Sure."

He opened the door and peeked inside. "Lemonade, soda, orange juice and sparkling water."

"Lemonade sounds good. I'll get the glasses." She flipped open a few cupboards and found them. It was obvious the dinnerware and glassware were all new, or imported from the palace. "Here we go." She set two glasses in front of him on the counter and he filled them.

A cool, refreshing swallow quenched her thirst and as she sipped, she strolled through the kitchen, exploring. She passed a utility room and then entered a large bathroom. Juan Carlos was just steps behind her and prickles of awareness climbed up her spine. She felt his eyes on her and as she turned slowly, he didn't even try to look away. He was in the doorway, his arms braced on the doorjamb, his shirt hanging open loosely from his shoulders. All that pure masculinity in one man didn't seem fair.

He stared at her for long seconds, until regret seemed to dull the gleam in his eyes. She had the same regret. If only she was just a woman and he was just a man and they were here together, sharing a grand adventure.

She swiveled around, pretending interest in a claw-foot tub, running a finger along the porcelain edge. "Makes you wonder about what life was like here when the farm was active." She turned to him again. "Do you know if there were animals?"

"Hmm. I think so. There are many outer buildings on the acreage. Supply sheds, barns and feed shacks. They owned livestock. Probably sheep, maybe cattle, but definitely horses. Do you ride?"

"Horses? Yes, I do. I'm no expert but I know how to plant my butt in the saddle."

He smiled.

"Will we be riding?"

"Possibly. There's five thousand acres here to investigate. Between the Jeep and the horses, we should be able to scour the entire grounds. The horses will be here this afternoon."

"Did your family ever live here?"

"I don't think a Salazar ever lived here. But a Montoro must have at some point. This land is all part of the Montoro holdings."

"Do you have any idea where to start looking?"

"I'm thinking we should stick close to the house today and if we come up empty, we can venture out tomorrow."

"Sounds good. I have to admit, I'm eager to start."

"Okay, then I'll get your luggage. Your room is upstairs at the end of the hallway. It's been painted and furniture was brought in yesterday. Take some time to relax. I think you'll like the room, but if there's anything you need, just let me know."

"I'm sure it's fine." She'd roughed it with Jasmine, after

all. She really could handle her own luggage, but His Majesty would never allow that. His sense of gentlemanly duty would become tarnished. And darn, if she didn't find that amazingly appealing. "Thank you."

As she headed upstairs, a sigh escaped from her lips.

Juan Carlos was a big juicy ripe apple, dangling his unabashed charm and beautiful body in front of her.

And the wicked serpent in her head was daring her to take a bite.

Four

Portia's room was more than adequate. A queen-size bed, adorned with Egyptian cotton sheets, a snowy comforter and pale pink pillows took up most of the space. Southern light streamed into the room through twin windows with ruffled curtains and an exquisitely crafted armoire made of inlaid mahogany and cherrywood held the bulk of her clothes.

She glanced out one window to the unkempt grounds below. The Montoros owned all the land as far as her eyes could see. Would they find the hidden artwork somewhere out there? Her belly warmed to the idea. She was grateful for the opportunity to search for it.

And ready.

As she headed for the stairs, movement caught her eye from a room at the opposite end of the landing. Juan Carlos was in his bedroom, changing his shirt. Twenty feet separated them, and she immediately glanced away, but not before she caught sight of bare broad shoulders tapering down to a trim waist. She gulped and scurried down the stairs before she got caught ogling him.

She wandered outside into the yard. Birds flitted between tree branches and flew away. She knew the bodyguards were out here somewhere, watching over the place, but she'd yet to see anyone else since Eduardo had deposited her here this morning.

She heard the door open and close behind her and foot-steps crunching the fallen leaves as Juan Carlos approached. "Where are they? I know they are out there somewhere," she said.

He chuckled. "Luis and Eduardo have orders not to disturb us unless there's danger. They're here, trust me."

"I'm not worried." She put on a pair of sunglasses.

"That's good. How do you like your room?" He sidled up next to her. Dressed in jeans and a chambray shirt, with a black felt hat shading his eyes, he looked like a modern-day Spanish vaquero.

"It's better than I imagined, considering the state of the grounds around us. I'm sure you had a hand in making it comfortable for me."

He shrugged. "If you're comfortable, that's all that matters. Let's check out what we can on foot. There's a stable and a few broken-down buildings nearby." He reached into his back pocket and came up with a pair of work gloves. "Here, put these on."

She slipped them on. "I'm ready." And off they went.

The stable was in ruins, like pretty much everything else on the property. As they entered, she spied a wagon wheel, some rusted harnesses and a stack of rotted grain bags. It didn't seem as though anything could be hidden in here, but Juan Carlos touched every wall, kicked clean every stall and scoured the entire area with assessing eyes.

She took his cue, and searched the outside perimeter of the building, looking for anything that could be used as a hiding place.

He met her outside. "Nothing here. I didn't think we'd find anything this close to the house, but we need to be thorough."

"Okay, where next?"

"There's some feed shacks farther out we should check. Are you up for a long walk?"

She stared into his eyes. "You know that pea under my mattress didn't ruin my sleep last night."

He gave her a look of mock concern. "There was a pea under your mattress, Princess? Twenty lashes for the chambermaid who made up your bed last night."

She grinned. "More like fifty lashes for the king who thinks I can't keep up with him."

"Okay, I get your point. You're not frail."

"Not one little bit. But I think your concern is sweet."

"And antiquated."

"That, too. But what woman doesn't dream of a knight in shining armor once in a while?"

He peered directly into her eyes. "Do you?"

"I'm...not going to tell."

With that, she dashed ahead of him and hoped she was heading in the right direction.

Juan Carlos's laughter reached her ears, but he hung back a little, watching her.

She came upon three outer buildings, each one fifty feet or so from the others. She was just about to enter one when Juan Carlos called out, "Portia, wait!"

She whirled around. He came marching toward her, making up their distance in long strides. "Let's do this together."

He was being overprotective again. "I don't see why I can't—"

"Humor me," he said, sweeping up her hand and tugging her inside with him.

The small shed was in better shape than the stable had been. Juan Carlos remarked on how it was a newer building, perhaps added on later as the farm prospered. The open door allowed a sliver of light inside the windowless and otherwise dark space. Juan Carlos released her hand and the tingles streaming down her arm finally eased.

He got down on his knees and scoured the floorboards, looking for a trap door while she tapped at the walls. She tugged at a splintered hoe leaning against the far wall, moving it out of her way. A deafening hiss broke the silence. She looked down and saw a snake coiling around her boot. Panicking, she gasped quietly.

Juan Carlos jumped up. "Don't move!"

She froze. Oh, God, no. "What should I do? What should I do?" The thing was moving up her leg.

"Hold still, sweetheart. Trust me."

Juan Carlos reached into his boot and a glint of silver caught her eye. A knife?

There was a flash of movement as he lunged forward, and she squeezed her eyes shut. He ripped the thing off her in seconds flat. When she opened her eyes, she saw that he'd slashed the snake's neck all the way through. Juan Carlos tossed the dead reptile, head and all, across the shed. It landed with a smack and her stomach recoiled.

She shook uncontrollably and Juan Carlos took her into his arms. "You're okay, Portia. You're okay, sweetheart."

Tears spilled from her eyes and she nodded.

"Let's get outside," he said softly.

"I don't know if I can move."

"You can. I'll help you."

She nodded. "Okay." She clung to him as he guided her into the daylight. Fresh air filled her lungs and helped with her shaking.

"I'm sorry," he said, over and over, kissing her forehead.

She held his neck tight. She'd never been so frightened in her life. It all happened so fast, but the thought of that thing crawling up her body would surely give her nightmares for days to come.

"No, she'll be fine. I've got this," he was saying to someone, shaking his head. Then he turned his attention back to her. "Sweetheart, we'll go back to the house now."

"Who were you talking to?" She glanced past his shoulders and caught Eduardo gazing at her for a second before he lowered his eyes.

"We can walk, unless you want Eduardo to drive us back to the house?"

"No." She clung to Juan Carlos tighter, still shocked. She wasn't ready to let go. "No, we have more to do."

He ran his hand over her ponytail, like a father would a child. "But not today, Portia." His voice was gentle. "Not if you're not up to it."

She glanced to where Eduardo had been standing. He'd disappeared.

"Just hold me a little longer, please."

"Of course." One hand ran comforting circles on her back.

"I…I guess you have your answer." She spoke into his shirt, still too freaked out to back away.

"What do you mean?"

"You're my knight in shining armor today."

"Just today?" There was amusement in his voice and Portia couldn't deny how safe she felt being in his protective arms.

"Hmm." To say more would be too revealing. She was vulnerable right now and had let her guard down with him. She didn't want to let go of him. She needed his strength. He bolstered her courage.

"I guess, I'll settle for that," he said.

She tipped her chin up and gazed into his eyes. It would be so easy to kiss him now, to thank him for saving her from that creature.

"Portia," he whispered. His gaze tumbled down to her lips and the longing in his voice tortured her.

Debating with herself, she closed her eyes.

She heard him sigh deeply as one hand gripped her shoulders. He gave a little shove and she stumbled back and then blinked. He'd set her away deliberately. She focused on the blade he still held in his other hand and the image of that snake's split body flashed again in her mind.

A tick worked at his jaw, beating an erratic rhythm. "You test my honor, Portia. I made you a promise."

"I...know."

He put his head down, not meeting her eyes, and then bent to wipe the blade clean on the grass. One, two, three slashes were all that he needed. Then he stood and sheathed the knife, placing it in his waistband. "Come," he said, reaching for her gloved hand. "We should go."

"Yes. I can make it to the other shacks now."

He nodded and led the way.

"Here." Juan Carlos set a glass of whiskey into her hand. "Take a few sips and drink slowly." She sat on the sofa near the fireplace and kept her eyes focused on the jumping blue-orange flames. They sizzled and popped and brought warmth to the cool evening. "You'll need it to calm down."

"I'm calm." She wasn't really. Her body still quaked inside even as she sipped the numbing whiskey. The thought of that snake wrapped around her made her stomach curl. Yuck, it was disgusting. And frightening. Juan Carlos had been wonderful. He'd stayed by her side and comforted her, and hadn't balked when she'd insisted on continuing on their search. Though he'd made a thorough check of the next two buildings for creatures before he allowed her to step foot inside. He'd told her he was proud of her. It hadn't been courage on her part, but rather sheer stubborn determination that made her put one foot in front of the other and kept her from running back to the house for refuge. They hadn't found a thing in those other sheds, not one clue as to the whereabouts of the treasure, and she'd been ridiculously happy to return to the house after they'd exhausted their foot search.

"How's that going down?" he asked.

"Smooth. I'm not usually a hard drinker."

"But you needed something tonight."

"I'm not usually such a wimp, either," she said, smiling awkwardly. She'd felt like an idiot for panicking after Juan Carlos explained that the snake probably wasn't poisonous or deadly, but her fear was real, and he'd understood that. Rather than take a chance, he'd done the manly thing. He'd killed the culprit. Her knight.

"You were very brave. You kept your cool."

"You mean I froze in panic?"

He stared at her from his perch atop the sofa arm. "I'm sorry you had to go through that. I promise nothing like that will ever happen to you again. I'm very cautious. I'll take care to secure the site before you go pouncing."

"I don't *pounce*," she said.

"Don't you?" He smiled over his glass and sipped whiskey. "I had to stop you from going inside by yourself."

"I didn't know there would be snakes."

He arched his brows. "All the more reason for us to stick closer together."

"Can't get much closer than this," she said, chuckling. Oh, but yes, they could, and Juan Carlos's arched brow, the amusement in his eyes, said he was thinking the same thing. The thought of sleeping just down the hall from him tonight killed her laughter. The alcohol was already affecting her brain, and her rational thinking. She set her glass down, looking into the amber liquid that remained. She needed her wits about her. It would be too easy to fall into lust with the king. "I think I'll be okay now. What's the plan for tomorrow?"

He thought about it a few seconds. "Tomorrow, we go out on horseback. There's some terrain I want to explore that we can't get to with the Jeep."

"Are the horses here?"

He nodded. "They arrived this afternoon. Eduardo and Luis have stabled them."

"You've thought of everything, Your Highness."

"Juan Carlos."

She grinned. "I'm sorry. Still can't get there."

He shrugged, and it dawned on her that she needed that wall of separation in order to remind herself who he was. She'd do better to think of him as a monarch, rather than a man.

"Are you getting hungry?" he asked, and she was glad he didn't press the issue.

"A little." It was after six and up until now, she hadn't thought about food.

"Wait here, I'll be right back."

He rose and entered the kitchen. She heard him rustling around in there, opening the refrigerator door and banging shut the cupboards. The dance of lights in the fireplace mesmerized her for the few minutes he was gone.

Juan Carlos returned with a plate of delicacy cheeses, a bunch of deep red grapes and a loaf of bread. "I hope this will satisfy your hunger. If not, I can cook a few steaks and bake some potatoes."

"No, this is perfect. I don't think I could eat much more."

"Want to sit in front of the fire?"

"Sure." She grabbed a fringy knit throw blanket hanging over the sofa and fanned it out in front of the fireplace. Juan Carlos waited for her to sit, and then handed her the plates before taking his seat facing her.

"This is nice, thank you." She arranged the plates in front of them.

The flickering flames cocooned them in a warm halo of light. She nibbled on the cheese and bread. Miles away from the city, she was at peace in this farmhouse.

She reached for a grape, and met with Juan Carlos's hand as he did the same. Their fingers touched and she lifted her eyes to him. He was staring at her, as if memorizing the way she looked right now. Her heart began to beat faster. Their gazes remained locked for a second, and then she tore a bunch of grapes off and popped one into her mouth.

Outside, breezes blew, making the windows rattle. The distant sound of horses whinnying carried on the wind and she pictured them in their stalls. How long had it been since there was life in those stalls? She hoped the winds wouldn't frighten the animals.

"What is it?" he asked.

"I'm just wondering if the horses are okay out there. The stable walls aren't solid anymore."

"I was going to check on them after you went to bed."

"I'd like to see them."

He pulled air into his lungs and nodded, as if convincing himself of his suggestion. "Then you'll join me."

Juan Carlos held a battery-powered lantern in one hand and Portia's hand in the other. He hadn't planned on spending more time with her tonight. Holding her shaking body and consoling her after the snake incident had stirred a possessive streak in him. He'd wanted to protect her from harm and keep her safe, but having her melt into him, her heartbreaking tears soaking his shirt, had sliced him up inside. He could have held her for hours and not tired of it, yet they'd continued on their search and he'd cursed that damn promise he'd made to her. He'd been desperate to get her to stay on in Alma. And he'd had to agree to her terms with a promise he hoped like hell he could uphold.

Tonight, he'd thought to escape her. Maybe he would have had a drink with Eduardo and Luis or taken a late-night ride, or simply waited until Portia was safely ensconced in her bedroom before making it up to his room. Yet he couldn't refuse Portia her request to join him in the stables.

So here he was, gritting his teeth as she walked beside him under the stars. The stables weren't far and he'd given the bodyguards strict orders to watch without being seen. They were out there somewhere.

The night air had grown cooler, and Portia wrapped both of her arms around herself despite her coat. She might've shivered once or twice.

"Cold?"

"Yes, but I'm okay. I have Scandinavian blood flowing through my veins. Cold weather doesn't bother me."

Juan Carlos hunkered down into his jacket. He'd lived in Miami most of his life. Neither Florida nor Alma got down into freezing temperatures very often. He could tolerate cold weather, but it wasn't his favorite thing. "This is about as cold as it gets here," he said. "At least that's what I'm told."

"It's mostly the wind I don't like."

Right on cue, a howling gust blew from the north. She shivered again and on impulse, he wrapped his free arm over her shoulder and drew her close.

She looked up at him.

"Thanks for keeping me warm," he said.

"Yes, Your Majesty. Anything for the king." A teasing smile played at her lips.

He laughed.

Before long they reached the stables.

"Want me to go in and check for snakes?"

She drew a breath and glanced around the property completely encased in darkness. "I have a feeling it's safer inside than out."

She had a point. There could be all manner of animals roaming the land. Wolves, wild boars and lynx were indigenous to the area. "Okay, then stick close to me."

"You still have your knife?"

"Of course."

"Then you won't be able to shake me."

"I wouldn't even try," he said, quite honestly.

A hum ran through her body. His subtle compliments did crazy things for her ego. After what she'd been through with Miles, that part of her brain had needed nourishment and was now being fed day in and day out by His Hunkiness the King.

She gasped.

"What is it?"

"Oh, nothing. I was just thinking." Jasmine would have a good laugh over this one. Portia was resorting to using terms from a romance novel to describe the handsome, honorable Juan Carlos Salazar II, King of Montoro.

He gripped her hand and led her into the stables. The protective way he held her was another turn-on.

The lantern lit up about five feet of the path in front of them. The place was dank and colder than she'd hoped for the animals. Juan Carlos lifted the lantern to his shoulder and illuminated the stalls. There were shuffling sounds, whinnies and snorts as all four horses came into view. Beauties.

They were curious enough to approach their individual gates. Though she'd been here earlier, Portia could see hints of work done today to make the stable more secure for the horses. The stalls had been shored up, and beds of straw had been laid down. Holes in the walls letting in cold air had been hastily boarded up. Juan Carlos knew how to get things done.

Her eyes darted to the animals' backs. "They're wearing blankets."

"To keep warm. I put Luis on it tonight. They seem comfortable enough, don't they?"

She smiled, relieved. "Yes, I feel better now. They are amazing creatures. Are they yours? I mean do they belong to the palace?"

"We haven't had time to build a remuda of horses for the palace. The transition takes time, but we will have a royal guard on horseback one day soon. These horses belong to me personally, as of two days ago. I have it on good authority they are gentle and trustworthy. I've yet to ride any of them. Tomorrow will be a good test."

"For them or for you?"

His brow arched. "Maybe for all of us."

"Maybe," she agreed. "I've never claimed to be an expert, but I do love animals. What are their names?"

"Come. Let me introduce you." Straw crunched underfoot as they made their way to the first stall. "This is Julio. He's a two-year-old gelding," Juan Carlos said. The sleek charcoal-colored horse had a thick black mane and tail. "He's an Andalusian."

"The horse of kings," she said.

"Yes, I've heard them referred to that way."

"Because they're powerful and sturdy?"

"Because they're intelligent and docile."

She eyed the commanding animal in front of her. He was gorgeous. "Docile?"

"Not as hot-blooded as a thoroughbred. He'll be my mount."

Julio was tall and grand. His curious ink-black eyes watched her. She lifted her hand to him cautiously and he edged closer. She took that as an invitation to stroke the side of his face. "That's it, boy. You and I are going to be good friends," she crooned. Back in Los Angeles, she volunteered at an animal rescue when she wasn't working. Her lifestyle and schedule didn't allow having a pet of her own and she enjoyed donating her time to animals in need.

"You're good with him."

She touched her cheek to Julio's cold nose and he nuzzled her throat eagerly. The force pushed her back a step and she righted herself and giggled. "Oh, he is sweet."

Juan Carlos's gaze touched upon her. Something flickered in his eyes. He swallowed and stroked his hand over his chin. He hadn't shaved today, and his stubble only added to his good looks.

With an inward sigh, she focused back on Julio, giving his mane a solid but loving stroke. She sensed that she had indeed made a new friend today.

Juan Carlos tugged her along to the next stall. "This is Sugar. She's an Arabian. Quick, sharp and good-natured. You'll ride her tomorrow."

"Hello, Sugar. You're a pretty one."

Sugar wasn't as tall or commanding as Julio, but was equally as stately. She had sensitive eyes and seemed friendly. Her chestnut coat glistened under the lantern light. "I'll see you in the morning, girl."

Juan Carlos showed her the other two horses, Arabians named Estrella and Manzana, who were presumably for Eduardo and Luis. Were the king's bodyguards good riders? Was that part of their job description?

New feedbags hung from nails in the walls, replacing the shredded ones from this morning, and a bag of carrots sat on a splintered bench. "Can we give them a treat?"

"Good idea." Juan Carlos went to retrieve the carrots. He dipped his hand inside the bag and came up with four. "One for each."

"Only one?"

"We don't want to spoil them."

"I bet you'd be a tough disciplinarian with your children."

At the mention of children his eyes twinkled and somehow the mischief seemed aimed directly at her. "I'm ready to find out."

Her blood warmed. She hadn't thought along those lines for herself. Parenthood was a long way off for her. But Juan Carlos seemed to know exactly what he wanted. He was resolute, an action taker and at times, he intimated her with his decisiveness. "You want a family one day?"

"Of course...I've lived my life without my parents. I have

no brothers or sisters, although I have my cousins and we have been on good terms. But to have a child of my own, to share that bond with someone I love…it's a dream of mine."

He handed her all four carrots and she walked the stalls, allowing Sugar to nibble at hers first.

"I would think being king would be your dream."

"It's my duty and a role I'm proud to uphold. But a man can have more than one dream, can't he?"

His eyes darkened, his gaze boring into her like a nail being hammered into the wall. He was too close, his expression telling her too much. She couldn't look at him and not see his life all planned out…with her beside him. Were the limited lighting and her silly imagination playing tricks on her?

She turned away from him, taking interest in the horses again. "I suppose." Three beggars were vying for her attention, shuffling their feet, bobbing their heads back and forth. She walked over to Julio next. "Here you go, boy."

Juan Carlos shadowed her to the next two stalls and watched her feed the other Arabians. "Do I make you nervous, Princess?"

Her eyes crinkled as she squeezed them closed. Why did he have to ask her that? She took a breath to steady her nerves and pivoted around. Her back to the stall door, the lie was ready to fall from her lips. Her one eye fluttered, like a wink, but certainly *not* a wink. Oh, boy. She wanted to sink into a black hole. "Y-yes." Damn her honesty. So much for pretending disinterest in him.

Juan Carlos gave her an approving smile as if he'd expected her answer. As if he was pleased with her honesty. "I promised not to pursue you, Portia. But I didn't say I would back off if you came to me. If you decided you wanted me, craved my body as I do yours, I would claim you in an instant and not feel I'd betrayed my vow to you."

He took her hand then, and led her out of the stable. "Come, it's time for bed."

Five

Sugar kept an even pace with Julio as they ambled farther out onto the property. The horse was gentle, took commands well and her sure-footed gait put Portia at ease. She gazed at the cloudless blue sky above. The warmth of the rising sun removed the bite of coolness in the morning air and made the ride pleasant.

Juan Carlos's felt hat shaded his eyes. Portia had put her hat on, too, one that Juan Carlos, who planned for everything, had given her to wear.

"How are you doing?" Juan Carlos asked after five minutes of silence.

"I have no complaints, Your Highness."

He paused. Gosh, why did she goad him? Oh, yeah, to put distance between them. "We've been riding a while now. Is your rear end sore?"

She chuckled. "A little, but I'll survive."

"You just let me know when you want to take a break."

Things had been a little weird between them since last night. Juan Carlos had put a bug in her ear. He'd given her an out. Up until then, her idea to keep their relationship strictly platonic had rested solely on Juan Carlos's shoulders. She'd made him promise to keep his distance. But now he'd tossed the ball into her court. And it had gotten her thinking. But it wasn't a good thing for a woman desperately attracted to a man who was all wrong for her to be given those options.

If you decided you wanted me, craved my body as I do yours...

Those hot words had thrown her. She'd thought of them, of him, all through the night. What would it be like to have Juan Carlos make love to her? What if, here, in this remote, private place, she gave in to temptation and spent the night touching him and being touched. Kissing his perfect mouth, running her cheek along that sexy stubble and nibbling on his throat? What would it be like to have him inside her, the steely velvet of his erection impaling her body?

She squirmed in the saddle, suddenly uncomfortable. Mentally, she forbade Juan Carlos to look over, to see her struggling with thoughts he'd planted inside her head. *Don't look at me. Don't see the expression on my face. Don't see me...wanting you.*

"Portia?"

Darn it. "I'm fine." She stared straight ahead. "Everything's good and dandy."

She sensed him studying her as they rode the length of five football fields until they came upon a graveyard surrounded by a run-down picket fence. The square of ground was full of weeds, unkempt. The neglect was almost sacrilegious. It was out in the middle of nowhere, a place long forgotten.

Juan Carlos slowed his gelding and she did the same. "We'll stop here," he said.

Her rear end rejoiced. She spotted trees that offered perfect shade just yards away. The horses moved toward an oak, massive in size, its roots splayed in all directions.

Juan Carlos dismounted quickly and strode to her. Sugar wasn't as tall as Julio, but Portia still needed help with her dismount. Either that, or run the risk of breaking an ankle when she tried to slide down the horse's left flank.

Juan Carlos's arms were up, reaching for her. She swung her leg over the saddle and his hands found her waist, securing her with a firm grip and guiding her down until her boots hit the ground. He held her for a few beats of time, with her back to his chest, his nose tickling her neck, breathing in her hair. "You smell delicious," he whispered, and then released her.

She sighed. If only she didn't miss his hold on her. Didn't enjoy having him touch her.

I would claim you in an instant and not feel I'd betrayed my vow to you.

He stood beside Julio, gazing at the graveyard as he unlatched a saddlebag and came up with a bottle of water. He walked over to her. "Here," he said. "Take a drink, you must be thirsty."

The water, cool and refreshing, slid down her throat. "That's good." She handed it back to him. His mouth clamped around the lip of the bottle and he tipped it back. He swallowed a big gulp, then another. A trickle of sweat ran down his forehead and he wiped it away.

Simple gestures. Yet her heart raced being near him, sharing water, doing natural things that seemed to bind them together.

"I'd like to check out the graveyard. You can stay here and rest. I'll put a blanket down. You'll be in the shade."

She shook her head. She was curious about the graveyard, too. "I'll come with you."

He nodded and began walking. She followed behind. Wind kicked up and almost blew her hat off. She grabbed it just in time and held it to her head as she approached a wooden gate. Overhead, tree branches made a makeshift archway, and scrolled in wood a sign read: Montoro Family Cemetery.

"So this is where the farm families ended up," she said.

Juan Carlos nodded. "They were probably distant cousins, relatives of my uncles. I'd bet Tantaberra made sure no one has ever come to honor their graves."

They walked through the battered gate. There were many headstones, maybe twenty-five in all. Portia stopped beside Juan Carlos as he bent his head in prayer over one after another. She sent up her own prayers for the lives forgotten here, stepping from one grave site to the next. "Do you know any of these names?" she asked.

"Some sound familiar," he said. The first and middle initials were etched on the headstones along with the last names. "Montoro, of course, and Olivio I've heard mentioned, but many I don't know. I will have this cemetery restored to honor their graves."

Juan Carlos insisted on clearing away the larger of the weeds that had overgrown the area. She bent to help him. "No, please. Your hands will be cut," he said.

"I'll be careful. I want to help." Her chin up, she was ready to do him battle.

He stared at her. "I forgot to bring you gloves." And then he warned, "See that you are careful, Princess."

She smiled and something tugged at her heart. He was angry with himself for the oversight. "I promise to be careful."

He began to pull away tumbleweeds clustered around the graves, staring at the names embedded on the stones as if embedding them into his brain. She, too, had little family. She could see the sadness and the loss in the contoured planes of his face, in the shadows of his dark eyes. The dictatorship had taken so much from his family.

"Let me see your hands," he said when they were all through. They'd cleared away as much as they possibly could. The wind was howling; breezes that had cooled the day's heat were swirling more rapidly now.

She turned her palms up.

Juan Carlos inspected her hands carefully, turning them one way then another.

"See. I'm not a wimpy princess."

He laughed, the shine returning to his eyes. "I'd never describe you that way. I'm grateful for your help."

"You're welcome. But there's one more thing to do."

His right eyebrow shot up. "What would that be?"

"I'll be right back. Don't follow me. I'll only be ten minutes."

She left him in the graveyard. This was something she wanted to do by herself. For his family. He leaned against the post outside the cemetery and watched her march into the fields. Every time she turned, his gaze was glued to her. He wouldn't let her out of his sight. She got that. He was a protector by nature. Gallant. He didn't interfere with her independence though and she appreciated that.

Ten minutes later, she returned to the Montoro family cemetery. Juan Carlos smiled broadly as he gazed at the large bunch of wildflowers she'd gathered in her hands. Some were probably classified as weeds, but they were indisputably pretty anyway. Bluebonnet blues, pale yellows, creamy whites and carnation pinks.

"Would you like to help me lay these down?"

He nodded, a play of deep emotion on his face.

They walked through the cemetery one last time, offering up the flowers to grave sites and headstones to tell the deceased that someone remembered them. Someone cared.

They left the place quietly, Juan Carlos taking her hand. It was a solemn moment, but a sweet one, too. Portia was moved by the care he'd taken with his distant relatives, the honor he'd bestowed upon them.

How many would have just ridden past? How many wouldn't have bothered to stop and clear up the neglect and mess?

This feeling she had for Juan Carlos wasn't going away. It grew stronger each moment she spent in his company.

The horses whinnied upon their return, huffing breaths and stomping hooves. Juan Carlos dipped into the saddlebag again, this time to offer the animals a handful of oats to keep them satisfied. "There, now. You two be quiet. No more complaining." He stroked Julio's head a few times and then turned to Portia. "Let's sit a minute. Take a rest."

"All right."

He grabbed a blanket and spread it out under the tree. The shade was no longer an issue; the weather had cooled and gray clouds were gathering in the skies. She shivered and walked to her saddlebag, picking out a jacket from the things she'd brought along.

"Cold?"

"A little bit."

"We can head back."

It was too early to return to the house. They had more ground to cover and she didn't want to delay their mission because of a little cold weather. Her family hailed from Scandinavia, where food was put out on windowsills to freeze quickly, where the elderly lived over one hundred years because germs couldn't survive the environment. She refused to slow Juan Carlos down.

"Ten minutes is all I need," she said.

She put on the jacket and sat down. He sat next to her and roped his arm around her. It seemed only natural to put her head on his shoulder.

"There is a giant rock formation about half an hour from here. The terrain is rough but these horses can make it up there. I found it on a GPS map of the area." His voice soothed her even as he spoke of a tough task. She closed her eyes. "I think it's a good hiding place for the artwork. I suspect caves have formed between the interlocking rocks. At least, that's what I'm hoping."

"Sounds reasonable. We'll check it out."

"Are you up for it? We can return tomorrow if you're not."

"I'm up for it," she said. "We're already halfway there, aren't we?"

"Yes, but the weather might be a problem."

"It won't be, Juan Carlos. I'm not a wimpy princess, remember?"

Laughter rumbled from his chest. "How can I forget? You keep reminding me."

"Good," she said, snuggling deeper into his arms.

The solid beats of his heart were like the revving of a powerful engine. It was dangerous and thrilling and though she hated to move, it was time to break this cozy moment with him. She slid away from his grip and rose to her feet. "I'm ready when you are."

He bounded up, regret in his eyes, as if she'd taken something precious from him.

From both of them.

The rocks were adobe-red, huge and intimidating. They were also beautiful against the landscape of gray skies and brown earth. The horses treaded with agility through the gravelly terrain, their sure-footed gait assuring her she would not fall to her death as they climbed a plateau that led to the face of the mountain. "This is amazing. It reminds me of Sedona back in the States. Have you ever been there?"

"In Arizona?" Juan Carlos gave his head a shake. "No, but I've seen pictures. It's an artist colony, isn't it?"

"Yes, among other things. There are some wonderful galleries and art exhibits in the area. I studied there one summer."

"Did you ever climb the rocks?"

She nibbled her lower lip. "I'd been tempted a few times, but no, I didn't climb the rocks. I was there for the art. Are we climbing rocks today?" she asked pointedly.

Juan Carlos spread his gaze over the entire mountainside, studying the terrain. "Just like back then, you came here for the art. So no. We don't have to climb the rocks.

The openings seem to be on the lower levels. We can reach them without climbing."

She released a tight breath. She didn't like heights and they didn't like her, so no rock climbing was a good thing. "I'm excited. I have a good feeling about this," she said. "I'm imagining the artwork tucked inside the mountain somewhere, deep inside a cave."

"Then let's go find it," he said.

He dismounted and strode over, lifting his hands to her waist again. Dust kicked up by the strong wind mingled with the potent scent of horseflesh and earth. More threatening clouds gathered above, and a shiver shook her shoulders as she slid into his arms. His hands steadied her until her boots hit the ground. Then he took the reins of both horses and they began walking toward a row of rocks, stacked neatly like building blocks five stories high.

He stopped at the base of a formation where two giant boulders separated and an opening appeared. It wasn't much wider than a double-door refrigerator, but large enough to allow a man to enter. "Wait here," he said. "Stay with the horses. I'll go inside and see if it goes anywhere. It might be a dead end. I'll be back in a minute." He pulled out a flashlight and turned to her. "Okay?"

She took the reins with one hand and stroked Sugar's nose with the other. Eyeing him, Portia confessed, "I'm not very patient."

A grin crossed his features, that gorgeous mouth of his lifting crookedly. "Good to know."

For real? The man had a one-track mind. "Come and get me, if you find anything."

"Will do. We're in this together," he said, and then disappeared into the gap.

Just then, the wind knocked her back against the rocks. It was fierce today. She huddled behind the horses, allowing them to block the sharp bite of cold. Her teeth chattered anyway. Goodness, it seemed as if Juan Carlos had already been gone for hours but it was more like a minute or two.

Then she heard his approach, his footfalls scraping the ground of the cave. Thank God. A thrill shimmied through her belly. She really wasn't patient, not when it came to this. If only they could find the artwork today.

When he emerged from the opening, she took one look at Juan Carlos's expression and her shoulders slumped. "You didn't find it?"

He shook his head. "Not in there." His eyes were solemn as they toured over her face and body. "You're freezing."

"I'm…not."

His lips twisted at her denial. Then he turned away from her and grappled with both of their saddlebags, freeing them from their fasteners and tossing them over his shoulder. "Come," he said, handing her their blankets. "It's warmer inside. Besides, there is something I want to show you."

"Really? What is it?"

"You'll see." He took her frigid hand and immediately the blood began pulsing more warmly through her veins. One would think he was a flaming hot furnace with how easily his touch could heat her up through and through.

He led her into the darkness. The flashlight illuminated the way and she squinted as her eyes adjusted. Around her, stone walls made up a cavelike space, tall enough for them to stand in and wide enough for an entire hunting party to take refuge. The air inside was cool, but without the outside wind gusts it was warmer by a dozen degrees. "You're right, it is warmer in here."

"Take a look at this," he said, aiming his flashlight at a far corner.

Eyes appeared first, round and frightened, and then the light followed the length of the animal, stretched out on the ground nursing her young. "Kittens!"

Five tiny bodies fought for a place at mama's table, eager for their meal. The mother cat, striped in reds, browns and grays, eyed both Juan Carlos and Portia warily. "She's scared," Portia said. "Poor mama." She'd had lots of experience with birthing pups and kittens at the rescue where she volunteered. "She might be feral, though I doubt it. She would've been hissing and scratching her way out of here by now. The babies look to be only a few weeks old."

"You think she's domestic?" he asked.

Portia crouched down, studying the cat from five feet away. "I think she's somewhere in between. She might've been abandoned. She's doing what comes natural and found this place to have her kittens. Cats like dark cool isolated places to give birth."

"Well, she found that," Juan Carlos said, keeping his voice soft. Both of them whispered now, so as not to startle the wary cat.

"I wonder if she's hungry. She looks pretty scrawny."

"About all we've got is water and sandwiches."

"Water, for sure. She'll need that. And we can pull out cheese and bits of meat from our sandwiches. If she's hungry enough, she'll eat it."

"Good idea. I'm getting hungry. Maybe we should stay inside and eat, too."

Portia kept her eyes fixed on the new little family. "I'd like that."

Outside the wind howled. The refuge they'd found would do for now until the weather let up. Portia worked with Juan Carlos to fix the mama cat a meal of beef and cheese, and laid it out on a cloth napkin. She was at a loss as to where to put the water. They had narrow-necked bottles and not much else that would work for a bowl.

"Here," Juan Carlos said, handing her his hat, tipped upside down in his palm. "She needs it more than I do."

Under the dim flashlight rays, his eyes were full of

compassion. He was a problem solver, but it was more than that. He was doing this as much for Portia's sake as he was for the sweet cat family. "You'll freeze your head off when we go back out there."

"Not if we stay here overnight."

Her heart skipped. To be alone with Juan Carlos all night? She couldn't possibly. He didn't mean it. It was hard enough knowing he was sleeping down the hallway at the farmhouse. "Surely, we can't."

His eyes twinkled. "It was a nice thought, though. Being trapped in here with you all night...*to watch over the kittens.*"

Blood rushed to her cheeks. Suddenly, the cold dank cave sizzled with heat. She coughed, to cover errant thoughts of spending the night with Juan Carlos, of wearing nothing but a blanket to keep each other warm. His arms would wrap around her, and then their bare bodies would conform, mesh and he would nudge himself inside her.

"Are you okay, sweetheart?"

He knew. The sparkle in his eyes lit up even brighter.

"I'm fine."

"Are you sure?"

"Perfectly," she snapped. Goodness, she sounded like a witch.

He shrugged a shoulder, a smile teasing his lips as he handed her the cat's meal. "Do you want to take it to her?"

She nodded, recovering from the image that had sprung up in her head. "I'll try. I hope she doesn't run."

Portia took pained steps toward the cat, catching her eye and hoping her slow movements would show her she wasn't a threat. The cat's tail tensed and arched, her head came up and those tigerlike eyes watched her every move. Then she meowed.

"It's okay, sweet mama. I don't want to hurt you. Look, I have food. I hope you'll eat it."

The cat hissed, but she was just protecting her young. "This is as far as I'll go," Portia said softly. "See." She set down the napkin two feet from her and as soon as she backed away, the cat sniffed at it. "Put the hat down carefully," she said to Juan Carlos. He was only half a step behind and he set the water down next to the food. Then his hand clamped over her arm as he guided her several feet back, the beam of light dimming on the mama cat.

"Chances are, she won't eat or drink anything until she gives everything a complete smell test."

"We've done what we could for them," Juan Carlos said. "They are cute."

"Adorable," Portia said. The fuzzy fur babies were nestled against mama cat's underside, many of them satisfied and ready to nap.

Juan Carlos spread the blanket out and they began eating their sandwiches. Nibbling on her sliced steak sandwich sitting cross-legged, her eyes kept darting over to the cats.

"She'll eat eventually," Juan Carlos said.

"She's starving, but she won't make a move until we leave."

"Then we'll go as soon as we finish up here."

She nodded and within a few minutes, Portia was back atop Sugar, waiting for Juan Carlos to take his mount. She was torn about leaving the kittens in there, hoping the mama would survive the cold and be able to care for her young babes. How would she feed herself after the food they left behind was gone?

"Where to next?" Portia asked, blinking away tears, trying to distract herself from the sick feeling in her gut. She was a softie when it came to animals.

He stared into her eyes and smiled. "They'll survive. Don't worry."

He'd read her mind, but unlike most people, Portia didn't believe cats had nine lives. Sometimes, they couldn't beat the odds. If only this wasn't one of those times. She mustered a smile, but her heart wasn't in it.

"Since the wind has died down, I'd like to check out two of the nearby dwellings while we're here. If you stay put, I'll go in and be out quickly." He pointed north. "They aren't far. We'll get home before we lose light."

"I'm fine with that." She really was, though part of her wanted to stay behind and nurture the kittens. But that was impossible. Mama cat wanted no part of them right now. "I like the plan."

He nodded. "Let's go."

After showering and getting dressed, Portia marched downstairs in new jeans and a beige ribbed sweater to start dinner. She wasn't going to have Juan Carlos waiting on her. She planned to do her part. As she reached the bottom stair, she saw the fire crackling in the hearth and warmth settled around her. It was after seven; the darkened sky was lit with a scant few stars tonight. Her stomach grumbled, protesting over only having a light afternoon lunch. Thank God Juan Carlos wasn't around to hear the commotion her belly made.

The blaze in the front room beckoned. She could just as easily plop in a chair and watch the flickering fire, but she moved on and headed for the kitchen.

She found fresh tomatoes, whole garlic cloves, cans of tomato paste and packaged pasta in the cupboard. "Spaghetti it is." She wasn't a bad cook. She could crush tomatoes with the best of them.

Inside the fridge, she also found a covered dish of already cooked meatballs.

It seemed as though Juan Carlos had kitchen minions. She wasn't complaining.

She turned the stove on, grabbed a cast-iron pan, peeled and mashed two garlic cloves with a butcher knife and poured a little oil in the pan. Garlicky steam billowed up and pungent scents filled the room.

The back door opened and Juan Carlos walked in. "Mmm. Smells great in here."

"I hope you like spaghetti and meatballs."

"Who doesn't?" he said, coming to stand beside her.

"Hand me those tomatoes," she said, fully aware of his freshly groomed presence beside her.

Instead of walking to get them, he grabbed her waist with one hand from behind and stretched the other hand out as far as he could, snapping up three ripe tomatoes from the counter without leaving her side. "Here you go."

His touch sent heat spiraling through her body. "Into the pot with them, please."

"Like this?" He lowered them down gently, his face brushing against her hair.

He was a tease.

"Thank you."

"Don't you have to peel them?"

She shook her head. "The skin will peel off easily later from the heat. And then, you'll get to crush them."

"Me?"

"Yes, you. They need a manly crush."

"Well then, I'm your man."

She stopped and gazed into his eyes. Those words. They could be true. If she allowed it. Juan Carlos had owned up to his deal. He hadn't really come on to her, but every single second of every single minute of the day, he told her in his own silent, heart-melting way that he wanted her.

"Yes, well, uh…just let me get the meatballs."

How was that for a change of subject?

"I can crush those, too," he said.

She laughed. "I'm sure you can."

Dinner was half an hour later. They decided to eat in the kitchen this time, at a wooden table with inlaid painted tiles. One of the nearby windows faced the backyard garden, now bathed in starlight, and if she squinted she could see the plants. It was cozy and nice, and she'd put out a mason jar candle that cast a pretty glow over the room. Juan Carlos kept glancing at his watch as they forked spaghetti into their mouths and spoke of easy simple things. She refused to think any more about the snake with the severed head lying in that shack. Or the cemetery with so many families who'd lived here before.

After his eyes shifted to his watch once again, her curiosity got the better of her. "Am I keeping you from something?"

There was no television in the house. No important soccer games to watch. No distractions. Maybe he couldn't wait to get upstairs to finish the book he'd been reading.

He shook his head. "There's no place I'd rather be than right here."

Oh, she'd stepped into that one.

"The meal is delicious," he said.

"It was all that manly crushing," she remarked, and he put his fork down to grin at her.

She jingled in places that normally jangled. He turned her life upside down. She'd miss him when this adventure was over and she went back to LA.

She rose and grabbed up their empty plates. "Would you like another helping?"

He patted his flat, washboard stomach. "No, I'd better stop here."

"Then no cherry cobbler? It seems the kitchen minions made a trip to the bakery."

"Maybe later, Princess."

She washed dishes and he dried. It was all so domestic. Well, as domestic as she'd seen on the Hallmark Channel. Her life was hardly a typical American tale. What did one do after the dishes were cleaned and the night loomed ahead?

Her gaze slid to Juan Carlos, wiping his hands on a kitchen towel. He folded the towel neatly, set it on the counter and smoothed it out. With a slight tilt of his head, he sought her out, a question on his lips.

Before he could voice his thoughts, the purr of an engine reached her ears. Juan Carlos strode to the kitchen window that faced the side yard. "It's Eduardo. He ran an errand for me. Wait here, I'll be right back."

"Why?"

But he dashed out the door before giving her an answer.

She heard their voices and strained to hear what they were saying, but she couldn't make it out.

The back door opened with the slight kick of Juan Carlos's boot and he strode in holding a wire cage in both hands.

Meeeow.

The cats! Juan Carlos had the mama cat and her kittens.

Eduardo followed behind him, his hair rumpled, drops of blood staining his scratched hands. He looked almost as frazzled as the cat.

"Eduardo, you're bleeding!"

"Hazard of the job," he mumbled.

It took only a second for her to figure out what he'd done. What they'd both done. Juan Carlos had sent Eduardo on a mission to rescue mama cat and her babies.

"He wouldn't let me go," Juan Carlos was saying.

"My job is to protect you, Your Majesty."

"Not from cats." The king appeared annoyed at himself for allowing Eduardo to do the job he'd wanted to do. "I should've gone. Now look at you."

"Better me than you. They're nothing but a few scrapes. She put up a good fight." Eduardo grinned. "She is a feisty one."

Juan Carlos gritted his teeth. "Those injuries should've been on my hands."

"Stop arguing, you two," Portia said. "What you both did was very kind. Juan Carlos, take the cats in the living area. The room is dark and cozy. It might put mama at ease. Eduardo, come with me. I'll take care of your hands." She marched into the bathroom and heard footsteps behind her. Grateful that Eduardo had obeyed her order, she grabbed a washrag, filled a bowl of warm water and pointed for him to sit on the edge of the bathtub.

Goodness.

She sat, too, and took his big hands in hers, scouring over half a dozen scratch marks. "She must've been very frightened."

"That made two of us."

"Oh, Eduardo." She began dabbing at the wounds. He flinched, but took the pain. She dabbed a little more gently, cleansing and dressing his wounds. "There."

"The king is very angry with me. Luis and I both, we convinced him not to go. He wanted to do this thing... for you."

Portia closed her eyes. "I...know."

Her chest tightened. It was the sweetest gesture anyone had ever done for her. Or tried to do.

"He is a proud man. But don't worry, he won't be angry for long."

"He won't?"

"No. I think not. And thank you, Eduardo, for rescuing the animals."

She placed a chaste kiss on his cheek. He was large, built like a block of stone, but his expression softened and as he rose, he bowed to her with his eyes twinkling.

And she felt as though she'd made a new friend.

Six

"Do you think she'll try to escape if we open the cage?" Portia asked as she sat facing Juan Carlos on the floor beside the fire. The cage was between them. The leery mama cat's eyes were guarded and wide. Portia made a move to get a better look at the babies, and a mewling hiss, one born of fear more than anything else, pressed through the feline's tight lips.

Juan Carlos shrugged. "She has nowhere to go. The house is locked up and the doors to this room are closed. Right now, I think she needs to see us and know we won't harm her."

"I think you're right." Portia tilted her head to one side. "You're intuitive when it comes to animals."

While she had been bandaging up Eduardo, Juan Carlos had set out a bowl of water and a plate of leftover cheese bits for when they let the cat out later.

"At least she won't starve tonight," he said.

Outside the wind was howling again, even pushing through the flue of the fireplace. The flames scattered momentarily in the hearth, blazing wildly before returning to a normal easy burn again. "No, she won't starve and the kittens will thrive. Thanks to you."

He kept his eyes on the fire, not commenting, refusing to take any credit for the deed. It didn't matter. He couldn't hide his intentions from her.

"They're the cutest little things," she said, her voice squeaking. She couldn't help it. Babies in all forms brought her voice to a higher pitch. Who in the world didn't love furry new kittens? "I'm glad they're here."

She had a view of his profile, so sharp and defined. Firelight played across his face and when he turned to her, his expression softened. "Me, too."

"Why didn't you tell me your plan to rescue her?" It was what all his watch-glancing had been about. It made sense to her now and she was incredibly relieved to learn the reason for his impatience. "Was it a surprise?"

He nodded. "I didn't want you to be disappointed if Eduardo couldn't bring her back."

And there it was. On his face. Concern. Caring. Almost love.

Something shifted inside her. It wasn't a blunt move, but something that had been tilting and leaning gradually, like dominoes toppling in super slow motion. She could feel each one fall, until every shred of her defenses was being taken down by this good, kind, *sexy* man.

"It's late," he said.

No, it wasn't.

"We should unlatch the cage now and leave her, so she can eat."

"Okay," Portia said, sorely disappointed. She knew that meant saying good night to Juan Carlos and parting ways at the top of the stairs once again.

He sighed as he rose to his feet and strode to the fireplace to take up a metal poker. He slashed at the logs, until only simmering embers heated the brick floor inside.

Portia carefully unlatched the hook on the cage and flipped it away. The wire door swung open but the cat stayed put. "Here you go, Duchess. You're free now."

"Duchess?" Juan Carlos turned to her.

"She needs a name." She shrugged. "It seems fitting somehow."

He smiled, but his eyes remained hooded. "Duchess it is. What's one more royal around here, anyway? Well, I'll say good-night now. We have an early call tomorrow."

They did. They were going even farther out on the grounds in the Jeep.

"Are you coming up?" he asked. He had almost reached the hallway door.

She rose to her feet and stared at him from across the room. Words wouldn't come. Her heart was thumping, drowning out everything else in her world.

"Portia?"

"What if…?" A swallow stole her next words.

He waited, his face in the shadows so she couldn't see his expression.

"What if I said I was a w-wimpy princess, after all?"

He paused. "Would you rather not go out in the Jeep tomorrow?"

"No." She shook her head, her hair falling like a sheet around her shoulders. "Juan Carlos, it means I don't want you to go to bed…"

He stepped out of the shadows, his eyes dark, intense. Waiting.

She froze. Oh, God, she was breaking every rule she'd ever committed to.

"Say it."

The force of his command sent thrills careening through her body.

"Say it, Portia."

He wouldn't break his vow to her. She had to do it. He'd told her as much just the other day. His honor meant that much to him and he wouldn't have it any other way.

"Without me." She nodded, convincing herself. "I don't want you to go to bed without—"

And suddenly, he was there in front her, gazing into her eyes, cupping her head in his hands and brushing his lips over hers. Once. Twice. His hungry mouth devoured her over and over again. His arms wrapped around her, his hand brushing away her hair tenderly, his body trembling as he took her in kiss after kiss.

She was lost in the goodness of him, the thrill of his hands finally on her. The scent of his skin. The power of his body. Tears spilled down her cheeks at the clarity of this moment. She was his. He was hers. It was so easy, so simple. How had she managed to keep this amazing man at bay? How had she not realized earlier how perfect they would be for each other?

"Portia, don't cry," he was murmuring between kisses.

"I'm…happy, Juan Carlos."

"Oh, God. How I've waited for this. For *you*. Say my name again."

"Juan Carlos. Juan Carlos. Juan Carlos."

He grinned, a flash of white teeth in a broad happy smile that branded her heart. His gaze roved over her face and traveled the length of her body, his smile fading into something delicious. Something dangerous. And something she no longer feared. His eyes burned with want, the heat in them back full force. The man knew how to smolder.

"Portia." He breathed her name as if his life depended on it. "I need you."

"I need you, too," she admitted softly. She reached for the hem of his shirt, pushing the material up his torso.

"No," he said, taking her hands in his. "We'll do this right."

And in the next instant, he swooped her up into his arms. She wound her arms around his neck and as he headed upstairs, she pressed her lips to his, kissing him until they reached the threshold to his room.

"Here we are," he said, his voice reverent, as if the next step he took would be monumental. He carried her over the threshold with great ceremony and smiled at her. "I've wanted you since the moment I laid eyes on you."

"You have me," she said softly.

"God. I cannot wait much longer, but I will not rush with you." He lowered her down onto the bed. The mattress cushioned her body and then his hands were there, removing her sweater and unbuttoning her blouse, spreading it out so he could see her breasts. "You are beautiful," he said, planting both hands on the mattress beside her head, trapping her. She may never want to escape. His kiss was rough and hungry, and when she looked up, the sharp lines of his face tightened, a passionate preamble of what was to come. Her skin prickled in anticipation.

His fingertips grazed over her breasts lightly, hovering, teasing the sensitive tips. Hot liquid warmth pooled between her thighs. Then he wound his hands behind her back and she lifted herself up enough for him to unfasten her bra. With his help, she shrugged out of it and then lay back down.

"Fair is fair," he said, rising to grab the hem of his shirt. He pulled it up and over his head. Her mouth gaped open and she took a hard swallow, gazing at the tempting sculpted bronze chest.

"That is totally *unfair*," she whispered.

A smile spread across his face as he bent on his knees to remove her boots, her belt and then slowly, achingly moved the zipper of her pants down. Cool air hit her thighs, but she was too swamped already, too raggedly consumed by heat for that to have any lasting effect. He tugged at one pant leg and then the other, until she was free of them. All that was left on her body was a pair of teeny hot pink panties. "I like your style, Princess," he murmured, sliding up her thighs to hook the hem with his fingers.

"I like yours." She gulped.

He smiled again and dragged her panties down her legs.

Then the mattress dipped as he lowered down next to her. Immediately, his scent wafted to her nose: fresh soap and a hint of lime. She squeezed her eyes closed, breathing him in. He cupped her head and kissed her lips, her chin, her throat. "Let me explore you, Portia," he whispered.

She nodded. "If I can explore you."

"Be my guest," he said, his tone once again reverent. He fell back against the bed.

She rose up part of the way to lay a hand on his chest. Heat sizzled under her palm as she slid her fingers over tight skin and muscle. His chest was a work of art and as she continued to explore, he took sharp gasps of breath. Empowered now, she moved more confidently, her fingers flat over his nipples, weaving them through tiny chest hairs and reaching his broad shoulders. She nibbled on him there, nipping his hot skin and breathing the scent of raw sex emanating from his pores. "You are amazing, Juan Carlos," she said. And suddenly she was eager for him to explore her, to touch her in ways she'd secretly dreamed about. "Your turn."

She lay back on the bed and he rose over her to take a leisurely tour of her naked body, his eyes a beacon of light flowing over every inch of her. Then his hands began to trace the contours of her body, caressing her curves and moving effortlessly over her skin. He was thorough, leaving no part of her untouched. Goose bumps rose on her arms and legs, his precision and utmost sensitivity leaving her trembling in his wake.

Next, he covered her trembling body with his, wrapping her in his heat and claiming her with his presence. She bore his weight and peered up at him. He was amazing, so handsome, so incredibly virile. His hands cushioned her breasts, massaging them until the peaks were two sensitive tips. The pads of his thumbs flicked at them gently, and something powerful began to build and throb below her waist.

She had not been with a man in a long time. It felt so good. So right. Being with him.

He pressed her a little harder and she cried out. "Juan Carlos."

It seemed to satisfy him. He took her in an earth-shattering kiss, pressing her mouth open and sweeping into her. She moved under him, arching her hips, that feeling below her waist becoming stronger and stronger the longer the kiss went on.

His hand was moving again, leaving her full breasts and moving down her torso, past her navel and below her waist, where she ached and ached for him. "Trust me," he said.

All she could do was nod.

And his hands and mouth worked magic on her, shredding her into tiny pieces, squeezing tortured moans from her lips and making her squirm until she finally reached a fantastic, bone-melting orgasm.

"Juan Carlos," she breathed, lifting her head to find his eyes on her as he unbuckled his belt. He shucked out of his clothes quickly and sheathed himself, in all his naked glory, with a condom.

He touched her where she was most sensitive, lending her comfort and warmth in the aftermath of her pulsing release. She relaxed and eased back slowly, as another fire began to build. "I've waited for you all of my life, Portia. And now, you're mine."

She was ready for him when he entered her, wanting him this way, taking his weight and watching a fiery veil of passion burn in his eyes. He began to rock back and forth, each thrust a love note, a daring caress and sugary candy for her hungry body. "You are all I will ever need," he murmured.

She smiled as he pressed farther and farther inside her body. She was his. *He* was all she would ever need and as she met his driving rhythm, arching up and down, her breaths heavy, her body primed, she found solace and peace in his arms and lust and desire in his bed.

Juan Carlos drew a deep breath into his lungs. He'd often dreamed of waking up next to Portia, and now his very fantasy had come true. He turned his head and watched her chest rise and fall slowly. Her hair fanned across the pillow. He ached to touch it and sift the strands through his fingers. He wanted to kiss her awake and then make love to her again. But the sun had barely risen and the day would prove a long one. She needed her sleep. He'd worn her out last night. He shook his head at the thoughts running through his mind. He couldn't touch her again this morning and have her think he was lecherous, waking her with only one thing on his mind.

He smiled. He would come to her again sometime today. It would be hard to keep to the task at hand, but they were on a mission. Though a wicked part of him wanted to play hooky today. Why couldn't they just stay in bed all day? The States had snow days. Why couldn't he declare a Royal Day?

A little noise pressed through her lips, a moan that he'd come to know. Last night, she'd moaned plenty and turned his world on end.

She shifted toward him and one hand—warm, delicate and soft—flopped onto his cheek. He moved his head enough to press his lips there and kiss her.

"Hi," she said, smiling, though her eyes were still closed.

"Good morning, sweetheart."

"Is it time to get up?"

"You can stay in bed as long as you'd like."

"With you?"

"Yes, only with me."

Her eyes opened and he gazed into their sleep-hooded amazing blue depths. He could fall into those eyes and never want to return.

"Juan Carlos," she said, "last night was…"

"I know."

"I didn't know it could be that good."

He leaned in and kissed her tenderly. "I'm humbled to hear you say that."

"Humbled? Not over-the-moon, cocky and feeling proud of yourself?"

He chuckled. "Maybe that, too."

"I had…uh, you know. Three times. That's never happened before."

"Keep telling me things like that and we'll never get out of this bed."

She grinned and reached over to move a tendril of hair off his forehead, her delicate fingertips sliding down his cheek. He loved it when she touched him. "You know, that doesn't sound like a bad idea."

He caught her wrist and kissed her pulse point. "We can make that happen, sweetheart."

"If only," she said, sighing, her head falling back against the pillow. "But we need to finish what we started."

She would be leaving soon. She didn't have to say the words. He had only a few more days with her, before she would head back to the States. How quickly reality reared its ugly head. "We will finish it, one way or another."

"I hope we find something today," she said.

"We'll give it a good shot."

"I should get dressed. I'm anxious to see how our little family is doing."

She meant the cats. Juan Carlos had almost forgotten about them. "Right. Let's go check on them together."

She rose from the bed and turned away. As she fitted

her arms through the sleeves of his shirt, he glimpsed her lush blond hair falling down her back, the creamy texture of her skin, her rounded backside and the coltlike legs that had wrapped around him last night.

He sighed, enjoying the view and ignoring his body's immediate reaction to her. He threw on a pair of jeans and a T-shirt. Hand in hand, they strolled out of the bedroom and into the living area.

"Shhh," she said, spying the cat nursing her kittens outside the cage on a loop rug in front of the fireplace. "We don't want to startle her."

Duchess was resting with her head down, her eyes closed, allowing her five offspring to take their morning meal. Juan Carlos was moved by the sweet look on Portia's face as she silently watched mama and babies. He wrapped his arm around her shoulder and drew her closer, kissing the top of her head. How could he ever let this woman go? The answer was simple: he couldn't. It wouldn't be easy but he would convince her to stay. And marry him.

"Do you think Duchess will eat eggs?" she asked Juan Carlos as she scrambled four eggs in a cast-iron skillet. Morning sunshine brightened the kitchen, filling it with warmth. Bacon sizzled on the griddle and toast was cooking under the broiler. "I'll put a little cheese on them."

"You can try," he said, pouring two mugs of coffee. "She'll eat when she gets hungry enough. I'll send Eduardo out this morning for cat food."

She'd managed to get fresh water over to the cat without her running for cover. Duchess was still wary, but the kittens slowed her down or else she probably would've bolted when Portia set the bowl down. In time, Duchess would come to trust her. Sadly, she wouldn't be around long enough to see it.

She had work waiting for her in Los Angeles.

It was for the best that she leave Alma. She couldn't fall in love with Juan Carlos. He didn't fit into her plans for a quiet, unassuming life. Yet spending time with him had been magnificent.

He came up behind her, kissed the side of her throat and ran a hand up her thigh. She tensed in all the good places. He'd asked her not to dress yet, and now she knew why. She was only wearing his shirt, which gave him easy access to her body. Not that she minded. Heavens, no. She loved him touching her. "I'll be right back," he said. "Coffee's ready and on the table."

"Where are you going?" she asked.

"Don't be so nosy. I'll be back before you know it."

She smiled and turned, and his arms automatically wound around her. "See that you are. Breakfast is almost ready."

"Bossy, Princess," he said, staring at her mouth.

Her heart skipped a beat and a moment passed between them before he kissed the tip of her nose.

She shrugged a shoulder. "Kings."

He laughed and exited the back door.

Juan Carlos may have originally been a reluctant king, but there was no doubt in her mind that he was good for Alma and that he would put the country's welfare above all else. As it should be. Alma had been through tough times under a ruthless dictatorship. The country needed a strong man.

So do you.

No, she couldn't go there. The map was already drawn up for both of them, and after this little interlude, their paths wouldn't cross again.

After she set the table, Juan Carlos returned holding a bouquet of tall azure flowers. "For you," he said, handing her all but one stem. "Scilla hispanica."

"They're beautiful." She lifted them to her nose. "Are these from the garden?"

He nodded. "Spanish bluebells. They're almost a perfect match to your eyes, sweetheart." He pinched off the end of the one he still held and fitted it behind her right ear. "There. Now you're perfect."

"Hardly," she said.

"I think so."

"You think I'm bossy."

"Dressed like that, cooking my breakfast and wearing flowers in your hair? I can deal with a little bossiness."

She shook her head. "You're wicked." And so very thoughtful.

"So I'm told."

He took the flowers from her hands, snapped off the tips of the stems and arranged the bouquet in an old thick green glass bottle. After he filled it with water, he placed it on the table. "Have a seat, Princess," he said, pulling out a chair. "I'll serve you."

She had a protest on her lips, but Juan Carlos's expression wouldn't allow arguing. "Yes, Your Highness."

He smiled. "Good. I'm glad you know who the real boss is around here."

Portia's heart swelled. And as they sat down and ate, easy conversation flowed between them. Juan Carlos touched her hand often, as if needing the connection. She leaned over to brush hair from his forehead and he'd steal a kiss or two. They were in sync with each other; nothing had ever been as perfect as it was now, with the two of them doing ordinary everyday things, like cooking breakfast, sharing a meal and worrying over the cat family.

"So what will happen to Duchess and her babies when we have to leave here?" she asked.

"She'll become the official palace cat, of course."

"And the kittens?"

"We'll find them good homes, Portia. Don't worry."

Her eye twitched. "I know you're doing this for me." She covered his hand with hers. "Thank you."

The feelings between them were getting too heavy, too fast. She had no way of stopping it, short of leaving him right here and now. But she couldn't do that. Not only did she not want to, but she'd promised to spend a few days here helping with the search, and with the exception of a snake decapitation, she was having a wonderful time.

"You're welcome. Now, if you'll excuse me, I have to speak with Luis about a few matters."

Juan Carlos rose and began clearing the dishes. What a guy. She bounded up quickly and took the plates from his hands. "I'll take care of that," she said with enough authority to keep prison inmates in line.

"Okay," he said. "Thanks."

He bent his head and took her in a long amazing kiss. When their lips parted and he was through, her head spun. "That was…promising."

He grinned, shaking his head at her understatement. "Get ready. We'll be leaving in a little while. Unless you've changed your mind and want to play hooky today."

He was reaching inside her shirt. She slapped his hand away and pointed. "Go."

He went.

And Portia cleared the dishes and cleaned up the kitchen. She checked on Duchess and her brood; they were all sleeping. What a pretty serene picture they made, a mass of calico colors and balls of fluff all nestled together. She was grateful they'd have a home after they left the farmhouse. Her heart had never been so full.

Thirty minutes later, Portia climbed into the passenger side of the Jeep and Juan Carlos got behind the wheel. They said goodbye to Luis, though that didn't mean anything. He was sure to follow. Eduardo had gone into the local town on a cat food mission.

"All set?" Juan Carlos said, gunning the motor. "Strapped in?"

She nodded. The weather was glorious, the temperature in the mid-seventies with clear blue skies. She wore a lightweight white jacket that billowed in the breeze as Juan Carlos drove off and picked up speed.

"We're going out about five miles," he shouted over the engine's roar.

She sat back and relaxed, enjoying the scenery, excitement stirring her bones. Maybe today they'd find the art treasures.

For four hours they traveled at a snail's pace over lush lands, where wildflowers and lantana grew in abundance, the vista opening up to a prairie as they scoured the grounds looking for possible hiding places. They came upon another shack but after a thorough inspection, with Juan Carlos insisting on going inside first, they found absolutely nothing. Not even a snake.

"We have a little more land to cover before we head back," Juan Carlos said, and she heard the disappointment in his voice. She, too, was disappointed.

"Let's stop for lunch by that little lake we passed a few minutes ago." Maybe regrouping would give them a fresh perspective.

"It wasn't much of a lake," Juan Carlos said. "More like an oversize pond."

She entwined their fingers. "But it's pretty there and I'm getting hungry."

He smiled and gave her hand a squeeze. That was all it took for her heart to do a little flip. "Okay, we'll have a picnic." And he maneuvered the Jeep around, heading for the lake.

Warm breezes ruffled her hair and sweat beaded her

forehead as the sun climbed high overhead. She loved being outdoors. Much of her time in the States was spent indoors at art exhibits, galleries or simply poring over books and surfing the internet. She took a full breath of Alma air and vowed not to let disappointment ruin their day.

They'd packed a lunch and had a blanket. That was all they would need.

Juan Carlos braked the Jeep several yards from the water's edge. There were no shade trees so they used the vehicle to provide a bit of cover. From Luis. They were always being watched, but Portia was starting to get used to the idea and it wasn't as creepy as she'd once thought. Juan Carlos jumped down first as she gathered up the blanket. Then he reached for her and helped her down, crushing her body against his and taking her in a long, slow, deliberate kiss.

When he released her, her breathing sped up, coming in short clips. The blanket between them was her only salvation from being ravaged on the spot. She clung to it and backed away. "I should spread this out."

He backed off, too. "You do that," he said, his voice tight. "I'll get the cooler."

Once everything was in place, they sat down facing the water, their backs propped against the side of the Jeep. "The kitchen minions make great sandwiches," she said, taking a bite of chicken salad.

"I'll remember to thank them."

At some point during the day, either Luis or Eduardo would fill the refrigerator and cupboards with food, much of it readymade. She wasn't entirely sure it didn't come from the palace itself. The King of Montoro had a wonderful cook staff. But she decided the mystery was exciting and she didn't want to know how it magically appeared. She liked that it just did.

"What do we do now?" she asked, taking another bite.

Juan Carlos's throat worked, as he tipped a water bottle back and took a sip. He wiped the back of his hand across his mouth and turned to her, his eyes dark and searching. "I don't know. I think we've exhausted all possibilities. Where else is there to look?"

She had to agree. They'd searched the entire grounds—the prairies, the hills, the outer buildings—and found nothing. "The art could be anywhere and we'd never know it. There are no clues and sadly those secrets have been buried along with your family members."

He nodded. "At least the artwork didn't fall into the hands of the dictator, which was their main intent. I can't say I'm not disappointed. I thought we'd find something, a clue, some hint that would lead us to it. I can only hope it is found one day."

"I'm sorry, Juan Carlos." She set her sandwich down and brought her lips to his mouth. It was a chaste kiss, one of commiseration.

Instantly, his arms wound around her shoulders and he tugged, pulling her practically on top of him, deepening the kiss. "You're the only woman who can make me feel better," he murmured.

A pulse throbbed in her neck. She loved hearing his sweet words, even though they might be some of the last she'd hear from him. Soon, when the search was finally concluded, she'd have to say goodbye to him and all that they'd meant to each other in this short span of time. Yet, right now, she wanted to make him feel better—but she couldn't do it here. Out in the open. "We should go," she said. "Luis is watching."

He kissed her again, and then lifted himself up, pulling his phone out of his pocket. He spent a few seconds texting someone and then returned to her. "He's not watching anymore."

"Juan Carlos! What did you say to him?"

His lips twitched. "I told him to retreat one hundred yards and turn his head away from the Jeep for twenty minutes."

"You didn't!" Her face instantly burned. Her pride was stung. "He's going to know."

Juan Carlos touched her face gently, his fingertips on her cheeks, calming her. "Sweetheart, any man who sees how I look at you *knows*. Luis won't say a word."

"But I'll know he knows."

"It's beautiful here, Portia. And I need you. Do you not need me, too?"

His words worked magic on her. Yes, she needed him, too. She nodded. "But—"

He kissed away her doubts and then lowered her onto the blanket. His mouth was brutally tender, claiming her with each stroke of the tongue as soul-wrenching groans escaped his throat.

Thrills ran up and down her body as he exposed her to the sun's rays. The scent of fresh water and clear skies combined made her forget her inhibitions. She'd never made love outdoors and she only wanted to experience it with this one exciting man.

Firelight created jumping shadows across the living room walls. Juan Carlos sat with Portia beside him on the sofa as they watched Duchess bathe a kitten, her tongue taking long swipes across its furry body. The kitten took a playful swing or two at mama cat, but Duchess didn't relent. She used one paw to hold her charge down, determined to finish the job and lick away the grime of the day before moving on to her next one. She cleansed and fed her young diligently. Duchess, for all her wildness, was a good mama cat.

"You're quiet tonight," Portia said. "Still thinking about the missing art treasure?"

That was part of it. His failure to find it bothered him. He'd been so certain that there were clues here on the property and yet, he felt as if he was missing something important. He couldn't say what, but deep down in his bones he still believed the answers were here.

Yet most of his thoughts concerned Portia. They'd exhausted their search and there was nothing to keep them on the farm any longer. Tomorrow they would head back to Del Sol and then Portia would return to the States. Eventually. Unless he could convince her to stay.

"I'm thinking about us," he answered honestly.

Portia put her head on his shoulder. "What about us?" she asked, her smooth-as-velvet voice tapping into his heart. At least she didn't say, *there is no us*. She recognized that they were edging toward a precarious cliff.

Three sharp raps at the door interrupted their conversation. He gave it a glance and waited for the next two knocks, which would signal him that all was well. Those two knocks came and Juan Carlos rose, striding to the door. "It's either Luis or Eduardo," he said over his shoulder to reassure Portia, and then opened the door. "Eduardo. I trust everything is all right?"

"Yes. But I have something of interest I thought you would want to hear right now."

Eduardo glanced at Portia, who was now sitting on the edge of the sofa, her eyes round with curiosity. "Regarding?"

"Your search, Your Majesty."

Juan Carlos swung the door open wider. "Come in."

"Your Highness," he said to Portia as he made his way inside the room.

"Eduardo." She granted him a beautiful smile, most likely grateful it wasn't his counterpart, Luis, seeking them out. He could see the relief in her eyes. This afternoon, making love under blue skies behind the Jeep, Portia had let go her inhibitions and made a memory that would live forever in his mind. But afterward his Portia had gone on and on about Luis, asking how she could ever face him again.

Juan Carlos had succeeded in kissing away her worries.

"Would you like to sit down?" Portia asked.

"No, thank you. I didn't mean to interrupt." Eduardo regarded the kittens, his expression softening.

"Duchess is coming around," Portia said, her eyes glittering.

One look at Eduardo and the cat's back arched, and a low mewling hiss sprang from her mouth.

Portia rolled her eyes. "*Slowly* she's coming along. She should know better than to bite the hand that feeds her. Sorry, Eduardo. And how are your hands?"

He waved them in the air. "They are fine, Princess. No need to worry."

"What did you find out of interest, Eduardo?" he asked. "Something about the search?"

"Yes, Your Highness. You gave me the list of names on the graves at the Montoro family cemetery."

"Yes, I committed many of them to memory." He'd tasked Eduardo with contacting his uncle Rafe and alerting him about the cemetery. Juan Carlos wanted those family plots cleaned up and the headstones that were damaged beyond repair to be replaced as soon as possible.

"Yes, well, I spoke with your uncle, as you asked. He has no knowledge of those family members or that there even was a Montoro cemetery on the grounds. Not one name seemed to jar his memory."

"We didn't have first names. We only found initials on the headstones. It doesn't matter if he remembered the names or not. We will have that cemetery restored."

"There's more."

Juan Carlos nodded. "I'm listening."

"Your uncle claims that as a rite of passage, every Montoro had the privilege of being buried in the family mausoleum in Alma, whether rich or poor. If they were related to Montoro and had bloodlines, it was an honor to be buried there."

"Yes, I know that. But surely during Tantaberra's reign, that wouldn't hold true anymore. After the war, everything changed. I assumed those graves were there because Tantaberra controlled even where a person would lay to rest."

Portia walked up to take his hand. "But Juan Carlos, think about some of the dates on the headstones. Many were pre-Tantaberra."

He gave it a moment of thought, his mind clicking back to the headstones. "You're right. There were at least four that I remember that dated back to the 1920s and '30s. Before the war, before Tantaberra."

"Yes," Portia said, her voice reaching a higher pitch. "And those initials might've been used to throw people off. They'd have no real way of investigating who was laid to rest there."

"Hold on a second," Juan Carlos said, pulling out his phone. He clicked over to the list he'd brought with him of the known art pieces missing from the palace. His heart racing, he located the titles.

"*Joven Amelia.* J.A. were the initials on one of the headstones," he said. "It means Young Amelia. *Almas Iguales.* A.I. was another set of initials. The sculpture is called *Equal Souls* in English. And then there is *Dos Rios.*"

"D.R. I remember that one," Portia said. "I thought he was a doctor."

"There's a painting called *Dos Rios* that's missing," he said. "Portia, you said it yourself this afternoon, the secrets have been buried along with my family members.

But I don't think there are any family members buried in the cemetery."

"You think the artwork is buried there." Portia's voice was breathless and eager.

"It's a long shot, Princess. I think the cemetery is bogus. It was the family's way of protecting the art from Tanta-berra. We have to find out. Eduardo, get in touch with Luis. We'll need a bulldozer, but for now, round up shovels and some high-powered lights. I'm going tonight."

"Oh, Juan Carlos, do you really think you've found it?"

"*We* found it, Portia. You're as much a part of this as I am."

Portia nodded, an excited smile teasing her lips. "I'll go change my clothes."

"Portia," he said, "are you sure you want to go? If I'm wrong, it will be pretty gruesome."

"If you really want to see *gruesome* try and stop me, Your Highness."

He grinned. "That's right. You're not a wimpy princess."

He was glad. It wouldn't feel right going on this search without her by his side.

Whatever they found.

Seven

"I really know how to show a lady a good time, don't I?" With shovel in hand, Juan Carlos dug at the foot of a grave alongside Eduardo and Luis as the high beams of two cars cast the cemetery in an unearthly glow.

Dirt flew through the air and landed at the toes of her boots. If she weren't so excited, she'd be totally creeped out. "I can't think of anywhere else I'd rather be," she countered honestly.

Even her embarrassment with Luis had been forgotten.

"I can help out," she said, "when anyone wants to take a break."

Eduardo covered his laughter with a grunt.

Juan Carlos slanted her a be-serious look. "I'll keep that in mind, Princess."

Luis was too busy digging to look up.

She wrapped her arms around her sides as the night air became chillier. She'd refused Juan Carlos's suggestion to sit it out in the car and so she stood watching, waiting.

They were digging up the grave of J. A. Molina. The headstone dated the death to 1938.

After ten minutes of silent digging, she heard a thump. Eduardo's shovel smacked against something solid. Thump, thump. "I hit something, Your Highness," Eduardo said.

"Let's keep digging," Juan Carlos said. There was a

boyish tone to his excitement. "It shouldn't be long now before we know."

The men worked twice as fast now, focusing their efforts. The scraping sounds of shovels against wood filled the quiet night.

"Portia, will you get the flashlight and shine it down here."

The men were five feet below ground level now and working furiously.

She grabbed the biggest flashlight she could find and stood as close as possible over the grave site, sending beams of light down. Portia's heart sank. "It's a coffin, isn't it?"

"Maybe," Juan Carlos said. Under her flashlight, his eager eyes had lost some of their gleam. A layer of dirt remained on top of the box, and he used his gloved hands to swipe it off, searching for any hint of what lay inside. He found nothing written. "Let's bring it up."

It took some doing, but the three men hoisted the box up and set it on a patch of flat ground.

"Hand me the ax," Juan Carlos ordered. He made the sign of the cross over his chest. "And may God forgive us."

Luis handed Juan Carlos the tool and he carefully began to hack at the very edges of the coffin. Each blow of the ax brought the mystery closer and closer to an end. Eduardo used his shovel to help pry the lid of the box open.

It was time. Their work was nearly over. Juan Carlos hesitated a moment, drew breath into his lungs and then glanced at her. "Ready?"

She nodded.

"You might want to look away," he said.

"No, I will be fine with whatever we find." Her eye twitched, closing in a wink.

Juan Carlos stared at her. Perhaps he was equally as nervous as she was. With his gloved hands, he lifted the

hacked lid. She beamed the flashlight on the contents, her
heart thumping hard.

"There's no corpse." His voice elevated, he continued,
"But there's something in here."

She held her breath, her pulse jumping in her veins.
He unfolded a sheath, and found another box, no more
than two by three feet, this one carved and quite ornate.
He lifted it out and she shined the flashlight on it. *Joven
Amelia* was etched in golden lettering on top.

Juan Carlos's hand shook. "It's here. Thank God," he
said. Setting the box down on the ground, he kneeled,
and she took a place beside him. He took great care to
remove his filthy gloves and then opened the latch and
lifted the lid.

Inside, surrounded by lush black velvet, there was a
painting of a little girl, no more than ten years old, playing near the seashore with a much younger sister. The can-
vas was secured, not rolled up as one might expect, but
mounted to a frame as if taken from the palace in a hurry.
Portia would have to inspect it thoroughly and do some
research, but she was almost certain that it was genuine,
given the great pains the royal family had taken to hide
the painting decades ago.

"It's beautiful," she said. "She is Young Amelia."

Tears welled in Juan Carlos's eyes. "We did it, Portia.
We found the missing treasures."

"Yes," she breathed, her heart swelling. "Yes."

"Eduardo, Luis, come see."

Taking her hand, Juan Carlos rose and tugged her up
with him. Once standing, he wrapped his arms around
her waist and drew her close, so they were hip to hip. Joy
beamed in her heart. It was a monumental occasion and she
found no reason for pretense. As Juan Carlos had said, the
way he looked at her left little room for doubt of his feelings, anyway. They were lovers. It was hard to disguise.

The bodyguards peered at the painting in its casing. Both seemed awed and a little surprised to be looking at a royal masterpiece lost for generations.

"Congratulations, Your Majesty," Eduardo said.

"Alma's precious treasures have been restored," Luis said.

The two men shook the king's hand. There was pride and resolve in all of their eyes.

Eduardo turned to her. "Princess Portia, congratulations to you, as well. It is a great find."

"Thank you, Eduardo. That's very kind of you to say." She stepped forward and placed a kiss on his cheek. "I'm thrilled to have helped in a small way."

Eduardo blushed, but gave no indication he was alarmed by her affectionate display. A smile tugged at his lips, bringing her a rush of friendly warmth inside.

Juan Carlos got right down to business again. "I would like you to secure the grounds tonight. When the bulldozers arrive, we will resume digging in the morning. Assemble a team. I would like to have all the art secured by the end of the day tomorrow, if possible."

"Yes, Your Highness," Luis said. "It will be done."

The men turned to do their tasks, and Juan Carlos took her hand and began dragging her away from the stream of lights. "Come with me, sweetheart," he said.

"Where are we going?"

"To bed, as soon as I can arrange it," he said. "But for now, this will have to do."

He pulled her behind the cars, out into the darkness under the stars. And the next thing she knew, Juan Carlos's hands were about her and she was flying, sailing through the air, spinning around and around. "We did it, Princess. We did it."

"Yes, yes, we did." Laughter spilled from her lips and a lightness of spirit filled her.

"This is an amazing moment. I'm glad to be sharing it with you," he said.

Her smile broadened. "I feel the same way, Juan Carlos. I'm bursting inside."

He brought her down to earth gently, her boots gracing the sacred grounds. And his lips sought hers instantly, kissing her mouth, chin, cheeks and forehead. His hands sifted through her hair and his dark, luscious eyes bored into her. "Do you have any idea how much I love you, Portia? I do. I love you, Princess. With all my heart."

"Oh, Juan Carlos, I love you, too." And there it was. Her truth. Her honest feelings poured out of her in this instant of happiness and joy. She could no longer hide away from the sensations rocking her from head to toe. The words she spoke were not damning, but blissful and joyous. She loved Juan Carlos Salazar II, King Montoro of Alma.

"You do? You love me?" His grin spoke to her heart in a language all its own. His was the sweetest of tones, as if he was in total awe of her love.

She nodded eagerly. "I love you."

He lifted her up and twirled her around once more before he set her down. His kiss this time made her dizzier than a dozen spins in his arms. His mouth claimed her, his lips demanding, his tongue penetrating through to sweep in and conquer. Her knees wobbled and she sought his sturdy shoulders for balance, her monumental declaration swaying both of them.

"Oh, Portia, my love. I cannot think of a life without you. Marry me. Be my wife. Be with me forever."

The words rang in her ears. It wasn't as if she hadn't expected them to come, but the surprise came only in her answer. "Yes, Juan Carlos. I will marry you."

The next morning, Portia woke in Juan Carlos's arms, opening her eyes to a face she had come to love. Handsome, breathtaking and dynamic. He was a man who got things done. He'd certainly pursued her to the point of her complete compliance. How could she not fall in love with this man?

"Good morning, fiancée," he said, kissing the tip of her nose.

"Hello, my love," she said.

They'd celebrated in this very bed well into the night. There was champagne and candles and bone-melting caresses.

As she plopped her head against the pillow, the sheets pulled away, exposing her bare shoulders. Her eyes lifted to the ceiling, focusing on tiles that were chipping away. The farmhouse, old and neglected as it was, had undeniable charm. She sighed. "Is this real?"

"So real," Juan Carlos said. "Here, feel my heart."

He grasped her hand and placed it on his chest. Under her fingertips, life-sustaining beats pulsed through his veins. "I am real. A man who loves a woman."

"But you are the king of Alma."

"And you are the princess of Samforstand...we are meant to be, sweetheart. Can you not see how perfect this is? Fate has stepped in and brought the two of us together. I can only marry a woman of royal blood. And that's you." He brought her hand to his lips and tenderly kissed one finger, then another and another. "When I became king, marrying was the last thing on my mind. But then I saw you at the coronation and all bets were off."

"And what if I weren't a princess? Then what would you have done?"

"I would have..." He hesitated and sighed, bringing her up and over his body so that she straddled his thighs. He nipped at her lips and wove his fingers through her hair, eyeing the locks as if they were made of gold. "Luckily, I don't have that burden."

"No, you don't," she said, taking his hand and placing it on her chest. The heat of his palm warmed her breast and she squeezed her hand over his. "Feel my heart."

His eyes filled with hunger and every cell in her body reacted to his sensual touch. "You are wicked, Princess."

She chuckled. "You bring it out in me."

"You see, we *are* a perfect match."

"Are we?" She nibbled on her lip. She'd disobeyed her hard and fast rule of not falling for a high-profile man. You couldn't get much higher than king. Was she destined to fame through association even though it's the last thing she wanted?

"Let me show you again, so that you will never doubt it."

His hands on her hips, he gently guided her over him and they welcomed the dawn with their bodies and hearts joined as one.

But her doubts remained, locked and hidden away, even as she agreed to marry him. Even as she claimed her love for him. Half an hour later, she was showered and dressed. She and Juan Carlos ate a quick breakfast of cereal and fruit, both anxious to get back to the cemetery site this morning. But Portia couldn't forget her six charges. She walked into the living area with bowls of water and cat food in her hands and set them down by the fireplace hearth, where Duchess had taken up residence. "Here you go, girl."

Duchess no longer looked at her with frightened eyes. She had at one time been domesticated, and she was beginning to remember her life before hunger and fear had changed her. Portia kneeled and watched the cat rise, stretch her neck and shake out her limbs, and then walk over to the water. She lapped furiously as five balls of fluff scrambled to be near her, one kitten losing his balance and plopping half his body into the bowl. He jumped back, as if hit by a jolt, and gave himself a few shakes. Tiny drops of water sprinkled Portia's clothes.

She giggled and pressed her hand to the top of the little one's head. Silky fur tickled her palm. "You are a feisty one."

Juan Carlos strode into the room. "Are you ready to go, sweetheart?"

She stood. "Yes. I can't wait to see what else we uncover."

According to Eduardo, two bulldozers and a full crew were working furiously this morning. In the middle of the night, he'd called upon and assembled a team of men he could trust with this secret. Soon, the entire country would know about the hidden artwork. What a story to tell.

Last night, Juan Carlos had shared his hopes of putting many of these treasures on display for Alma citizens as well as tourists who would come to view the find. It would be nothing short of a boon for the country. The restoration of the artwork would instill pride and honor in a country once diminished and downtrodden by a dictator. First, though, Portia, along with a Latin art specialist, would have to verify that the pieces were not fakes.

By the time they reached the site, half the graveyard was dug up. Dust swirled through the air from the many mounds of dirt dotting the cemetery. Ten men with shovels and axes were hoisting boxes up from the graves. Luis, with pen and pad in hand, was making an inventory list. As ordered, none of the boxes had been opened.

Juan Carlos helped her down from the Jeep. He took her hand and they walked to where Luis stood next to a gravestone marked with the initials P.P. Tasked with documenting and photographing each headstone before the box was brought up, Luis lifted his head to greet them.

"Your Highness, Princess," he said. "We have twelve boxes already accounted for. As you can see, we have more to do. We've placed them inside the tent over there," he said, pointing to a room-size tent set up outside the cemetery under guard by two men, "and they are ready for you to open."

"Thank you, Luis," Juan Carlos said. "Your men are working faster than I thought. Now, if you'll come with me, I'll need you to document what we find as I open the boxes."

"I'll take the photos," Portia said.

Luis handed over his digital camera and nodded. "Thank you, Your Highness."

Excitement stirred in her belly. To be a part of this find was a dream come true. How many dreams was one person allowed in a lifetime? All this joy in such a short span of time? She'd found adventure and love where she'd least expected it, in the arms of a king.

Inside the tent, Juan Carlos opened box after box, carefully removing the pieces for documentation. Oil paintings, sculptures, bronzed statues and the famed ancient Alma tiara had been locked away and hidden from the world for decades. Portia photographed everything, carefully making mental notes of the pieces she would research for authentication.

They worked alongside the men, until all the pieces were uncovered and the mock cemetery was emptied out. By late afternoon, they'd unearthed twenty-two boxes in all, the grave sites now nothing but pockmarks in the earth.

Juan Carlos climbed to the top of a pile of dirt in the center of the graveyard, his boots spread out, his voice booming to the loyal men who had labored here. As he spoke, shovels were held still, conversations died down. "The Montoro family cemetery has done its job to preserve what is sovereign to our country. You are all a part of Alma history now and I thank you for your hard work today. Until these items are authenticated, I would ask for your silence. Luis and Eduardo have assured me all of you can be trusted. The next step is to transport these pieces back to the palace in the trucks you arrived in. Again, thank you all for your diligence."

Juan Carlos jumped down from the dirt hill and once again, Portia was reminded of how well he fit the position of king. He was a true diplomat and leader. A man to be admired. Staunch in his beliefs and fair-minded…she was sure if the clocks were turned back in time to when Alma was last ruled by a king, he would have reigned over his people justly.

"What are you staring at?" he asked, approaching her.

She shook off her thoughts and smiled. "How handsome you are with dirt on your face."

He grinned. "I could say the same about you, Princess. The smudges on your face only make you more beautiful." He touched her nose, right cheek and forehead.

Goodness, she'd never considered what the hours of dust and grime had done to her fair complexion. "I must be a mess."

"Nothing a hot bubble bath wouldn't cure, and I'm volunteering to scrub your back," he whispered.

"I'll take you up on that, Your Highness."

And shortly after, they left the graveyard and returned to the farmhouse.

They had one night left to share here. And Portia was sure, Juan Carlos would make it memorable, bubble bath and all.

Portia was too much in love to think about her future and how marrying Juan Carlos would affect her life and her career. She had no details to cling to, only love, and it would have to see her through the tough decisions she would have to make. Now, as she sat at a long dressed table in the palace's elegant dining room, she gazed first at her secret fiancé seated at the helm. Dressed in a charcoal-black suit, he was beaming and full of determination. He appeared ready to make the announcement to his family. Rafe and Emily sat across from her with her friend Maria and Alex Ramon.

Gabriel and his wife, Serafia, sat to her left, along with Bella and James. James's little girl, Maisey, was holding tight to her chest a princess doll dressed in aqua-blue with hair the color of glistening snow.

"It's a lovely doll, Maisey," Portia commented, smiling at the child.

"She looks a lot like you, Portia," Bella commented. "I'm just noticing the likeness."

Maisey's curious eyes shifted to Portia and the girl giggled. It was true that she shared a resemblance with a famous cartoon character that all young girls seemed to love.

Juan Carlos covered Portia's hand, entwining their fingers. "Ah, but Portia is a one-of-a-kind princess."

All those close to Juan Carlos were here. He'd invited them for dinner tonight under the pretense of disclosing the facts around the graveyard find. Only he and Portia knew the truth.

"Before the meal is served, a toast is in order," he said. "We have much to celebrate tonight."

Waiters poured champagne into crystal flutes.

Once all the bubbles settled, Juan Carlos rose. "Thank you, cousins and friends, for joining me tonight. We all have much to be thankful for. As you know, with Portia's help, we have found the missing pieces of art at the Montoro family farm. Yes, it's true, we dug up mock graves to unearth the treasures. The finds are yet to be authenticated, but we are fairly certain our ancestors wouldn't have gone to such extreme measures to hide fake artwork. Portia will do the preliminary research on the items we've found and under her advisement we will also hire an expert to verify each piece.

"But that is not why I've called you here today. I have

something more personal to share with you." He turned to Portia, offering his hand. She took it and rose, warmth traveling up her cheeks. All eyes were on her and the king.

Juan Carlos went down on one knee, and gasps erupted from the diners at the table. She had no idea he would go traditional on her in front of his family. But how silly of her not to think it. Juan Carlos was a man of tradition and so as she gazed into his gleaming dark eyes, she began to tremble.

"Princess Portia, you know I love you with all of my heart. I have since the moment I laid eyes on you."

Tears wet her eyes.

"I have one precious thing left of my childhood and now, I am offering it to you." He reached into his jacket pocket and came up with a diamond ring, the stone so brilliant, it caught the chandelier light and virtually illuminated the room. "This was my mother's wedding ring," he said, his voice tight. "And here before our family and close friends, I ask you to wear it and become my wife. Portia, Princess of Samforstand, will you marry me?"

Not even a breath could be heard in the roomful of people.

Her cheeks were moist with tears as she nodded. "Yes, yes. Of course I'll marry you, Juan Carlos. I am honored to wear your mother's ring."

Her hand shook as he slid the ring that once belonged to his mother onto her finger. He stared at the ring, his eyes deeply reverent, and then grinned wide, looking foolishly happy. With the pads of his thumbs, he wiped at her tears and then took her in a kiss that nearly muffled the screams of delight and applause coming from behind her.

After the kiss, they were both swarmed with handshakes and hugs.

She was beside herself with happiness. The love and acceptance she experienced from his family and friends was more than she'd ever expected. There were no, *Are you sures?* or *This has happened so fasts*, but rather, "Congratulations" and "You two are perfect for each other."

After everyone returned to their seats, Juan Carlos lifted his glass of champagne. "Please join me in welcoming my fiancée, Portia, to our family. Today, she has made me the happiest man on earth."

Glasses clinked and sips were taken.

Portia's heart swelled. All doubts about her future were laid to rest. She and Juan Carlos would work things out. They would find a way to keep each other happy and not lose their own identity. She would be his wife in all ways. She would one day bear his child, an heir to the throne of Alma.

She locked the thought deep inside her heart and it filled her with joy.

"Jasmine, yes. It's true, it's true. I'm engaged to Juan Carlos. I wanted to tell you before news of our engagement reached the States. The king's assistant will be speaking to the media tomorrow to share our engagement news." Portia held the cell phone to her ear as she looked out the window of Juan Carlos's master suite in the palace. The king's room had a view of the gardens below, with its expertly groomed fall flowers.

"Congratulations, Portia. Wow. It's hard to believe. The king moves fast, doesn't he?" Jasmine asked, a little bit in awe.

"Yes, he does," she said softly, focusing on a row of red carnations growing in the garden. They were hardy this time of year. "He's quite persuasive when he wants something. That's why he'll be a great king and not just a figurehead. After news of our find comes out, the country will see how much Alma means to him. They'll rally behind him, and he'll be… Jas, forgive me, I'm rambling, aren't I?"

"Oh, my gosh, Portia. I hear it in your voice. You're really in love, aren't you?"

"He's amazing, Jas. And I resisted him as long as I could, but Juan Carlos…well, when you meet him, you'll see what I mean."

"I'm going to meet him?" She pictured her friend's eyes snapping to attention.

"Of course, silly. At the wedding. Jasmine, I want you by my side. I know it's a lot to ask, since the wedding will be held in Alma, but I'd be thrilled if you'd be my maid of honor."

"Portia…this is… Of course I'll be your maid of honor! I wish you could see me jumping up and down right now."

She chuckled. "I've got the image in my head. Just be careful. The last time you jumped for joy, you crashed into my dining table and nearly broke your leg."

"Okay, I've stopped jumping now," she said, out of breath. "This is all so very exciting."

"I can hardly believe it myself. Juan Carlos wants to be married, like, yesterday, so I think it's going to happen as soon as we can put all the pieces together."

"Count on me to help."

"Thank you. I was hoping you'd say that and I'm glad you're going to be in my wedding. Right now, I'm working on an art authentication project that will take me until the end of the week to finish. I should be home in three days. Then it'll be full steam ahead with wedding plans."

"I can't wait to see you. I have a million questions for you."

"And I don't have a million answers. But it'll work out," Portia said, taking a deep breath. "It has to. Have to run now. Love you, Jas."

"Love you, too," her assistant said, and then hung up.

"What don't you have a million answers to?" Juan Carlos was suddenly beside Portia at the window. His arms around her waist, he took the cell phone from her hand and turned her to face him. She looked into curious, warm dark eyes.

"All of this?" she said. She couldn't lie. The roller coaster was going fast and she was holding on for dear life. "I don't know how this will all work out. I have a career, a life and a job on both US coasts. As it is, I'm not home much."

He lifted her chin and tilted his head. She braced herself for the onslaught of his kiss. When he held her this way and gazed at her, she turned into a puddle of mush. The kiss was long and leisurely. He took his time with her and every bone in her body melted. Yes, her fiancé knew how to devastate.

"As long as we love each other," he said, "the obstacles won't be too great. I don't expect you to give up your work, Princess. I won't demand anything of you but your love."

When he spoke so sincerely, she believed him. She saw her future bright and clear. Nothing was more powerful than their shared love. "You have that, Your Highness."

His fingertips traced the outline of her lips. "I heard you say you'll be going in three days."

"Yes," she said. "When I'm through researching and authenticating what I can of the Montoro art collection, I'll head back to the States. I have appointments to keep."

"And you'll look into wedding protocols from your native Samforstand?"

"Yes, I know that's important to you. It is to me, too."

"Our union should reflect both of our heritages and royal traditions. The wedding must be a melding of both of our countries. The sooner, the better, my love. I can hardly stand the thought of you leaving." He sent her head swirling with another earth-shattering kiss.

"Well," she said, licking her lips. "We do have three

more days together. And nights." She arched her brows and slanted her head, playing coy.

Juan Carlos took the bait. With a growl, he lifted her up and carried her to the bed, unceremoniously dropping her so that she bounced on the mattress. A chuckle ripped from her lips. "Your Highness," she said, staring at the bulge growing in his pants. "It's half past eleven in the morning."

"Princess, I don't see a problem with that, do you?"

She shook her head, giggling. It didn't take much to tempt her new fiancé and she loved that about him.

He climbed onto the bed and Portia spent the next hour making up for the time she and Juan Carlos would be apart.

Eight

"Wow, Portia, you look beautiful in this dress. I think it's the one," Jasmine said, nodding her head in approval. Her friend was having a grand time getting her in and out of wedding dresses, much to the dismay of the shop owner who stood just outside the dressing room, hoping to be called in to aid and assist in the fitting.

Portia stood on a pedestal platform gazing at her reflection in the three-way mirror in the tiny wedding shop in Santa Monica. "You said that about the last three gowns I've tried on."

"I can't help it. They all look amazing on you. But this one with the ivory tulle and Swarovski crystals." Jasmine sighed. "It's heavenly."

"It is lovely," Portia said, admiring the lines of the dress. "It's such a big decision."

"I'll say. It's not every day a friend of mine marries a king. Princess or not."

Portia chuckled.

Once word of the new king of Alma's American fiancée had hit the Los Angeles newsstands, Portia had been inundated with offers of gown fittings, hair and makeup, photographers and wedding planners. She'd had requests for radio and television talk shows. She'd refused them all, trying to scale down the hoopla. She hadn't expected to be crowded at the airport by the paparazzi, or followed home for that matter. Once again, her personal life was under the spotlight.

None of it mattered, though. She was so deeply in love with Juan Carlos, the unwanted attention was manageable. On some level, she understood the public's desire for a fairy-tale love story. Ghastly news reports of wars, poverty and chilling murders needed some balance. The country craved something positive and lovely to grasp onto, and a newly crowned king marrying a princess, both of whom had lived in America, fit the bill.

Portia stepped out of the gown and redressed in her own clothes before letting Amelia of Amelia's Elegance into the dressing room. "Thank you for your time," Portia said to the shop owner. "I will keep this gown in mind. It's certainly beautiful."

Jasmine was careful handing the wedding dress over to Amelia. "This is my favorite, with the chapel length veil."

"I agree. It's certainly fitting for a princess," the shop owner said, nodding her head. "It's from a most talented designer. I shall put it on hold for you, if you'd like?"

Jasmine nodded. "Yes, the princess would like that."

Portia did a mental eye roll. Jasmine loved using the princess card for special favors.

"Your Highness, thank you for considering my shop for your wedding needs."

"You're welcome. I appreciate your time. You do have some stunning things here."

Amelia beamed with pride. "Thank you. We try to accommodate our clients with only the highest quality material and design."

"We have a few other stops to make, but I will personally call you when the princess makes up her mind," Jasmine said.

Amelia thanked them and walked them out the door.

"Did you love the dress?" Jasmine asked. "A bride has

to fall in love with her dress. They say as soon as she puts the right one on, she knows. Did you know?"

"Well, I did like it."

"But you didn't love it?"

Portia got into the front seat of Jasmine's car. "No, I didn't *love* it."

Luckily, no one had followed her to the dress shop. Jasmine got into the driver's seat and glanced around. "Did you hear? Rick Manning just got engaged to the daughter of a United States senator. It's all over the news. They claim to be crazy about each other."

Rick Manning, an A-list movie star, was dubbed the man least likely to ever marry. Handsome and charming and very much a ladies' man. "Yes, it was all over the news this morning. I've met Eliza Bennington. She's a nice person."

"Well, you can thank them both. Luckily, the tabloids have dropped you like a hot potato. At least, until more royal wedding news is announced. The dogs are on a different scent right now."

"I don't envy them. It's no fun having your every move analyzed."

"I hear you," Jasmine said, and pulled out of the parking spot. "Are you hungry?"

"Starving. Let's have lunch."

"Okay, but afterward, the great wedding dress search goes on."

Portia agreed to that plan and looked out the window. Jasmine was taking her maid of honor duties seriously. The truth was, Portia had a hundred loose ends to tie up before the wedding, and she missed Juan Carlos like crazy. They spoke at least twice a day since she'd left him at the airport in Alma.

"You are perfect for me, Princess. Always remember

that," were his last words to her as she boarded his private airplane.

It was after six in the evening when Jasmine dropped her off at home. She climbed the few steps of her one-level Brentwood condo, knowing she had another hunt on her hands. She'd promised Juan Carlos she'd look up royal wedding protocols from Samforstand. She'd been too busy with rescheduling her work appointments and dress shopping to dig into her old files until now.

She dropped her purse on the couch and then strode to the fridge and grabbed a Coke. Sipping from the can, she walked into her bedroom and pulled out the old cedar trunk from the back of her walk-in closet. The trunk held the few remaining things she had left of her parents.

Unlatching the lid, she found a massive amount of papers, deeds, bank account records and folders upon folders of news clippings about her parents when they were a young royal couple in exile. She lifted out an article written about them from the *New York Times*, just days before the tragic car accident that claimed their lives. Her eyes misted as she looked at a picture of the loving couple that accompanied the article. Her father was decked out in royal regalia with her mother by his side. They were young and happy and it hurt her heart still to look at them and think about all they had lost.

Her mother's wedding ring was in its original sapphire-blue velvet box, her father's tie clips and a gold wedding band were stored in a polished walnut case. She assumed most of their other possessions were sold to keep her comfortable and pay for her expenses. She'd been raised by her grandmother Joanna. But now all she had was her great-aunt, Margreta, who was a little senile. Portia paid for her care in a nursing home and visited her whenever she could.

As the evening wore on, she pored over every piece of paper in the trunk. She read every article and viewed every picture taken. Yet nowhere could she find any research that dated back to her great-grandparents' era of rule before they'd migrated to the United States after World War II. Surely, there had to be something? Having lost her parents early in life, she had only a fragmentary account of her heritage from her grandmother. Grandma Joanna hadn't liked to talk about the old days. It was too painful, a past wrought with the loss of her only son. Portia's questions about her parents were met with hushed tones and sadness and she'd never really learned much about them. She did remember her mother's bright smile and her father's light blue eyes. But even now, she wondered if those were true memories, or just recollections of the pictures she'd seen.

Her cell phone rang and a name popped up on the screen. She answered before the second ring. "Juan Carlos." She sighed.

His baritone voice drifted to her over thousands of miles. "Hello, Princess. I had to hear your voice once more before I started my day. I hope I didn't wake you."

She glanced at the clock. It was 8:00 a.m. in Alma. "No, not at all. I'm doing some research right now. I'm glad you called. How are you?"

"Besides missing you, I'm doing well. I'm scheduled to do a television interview later this morning. All of Alma is rejoicing over our art find, sweetheart. But I have a feeling the interviewer is more interested in our engagement. I'm sure I will be barraged with questions about our wedding."

"I'm sure you can handle it, Your Highness."

"What I can't handle is not being with my perfect princess. When will you be returning to me?"

"Give me a week, Juan Carlos," she said. "I need the time to get some things in order."

"Sounds like an eternity."

"For me, too, but I have a lot to accomplish. Jasmine

has been persistent. We are very close to choosing a wedding gown."

"I can't wait to see you in it. No matter which you choose you'll be beautiful. But what have you decided about your work?"

"I've managed to take a three months' leave of absence. I'm thinking of relocating to Europe. There are many American art collectors living abroad who might need my services. I...I don't have it all figured out yet."

"Take your time, sweetheart. I want you to be happy with whatever you choose."

"Okay. Thank you."

"I've been thinking. How does a Christmas wedding sound?"

"A Christmas wedding?" She pictured lush holly wreaths, bright red poinsettias and twinkling lights decorating the palace. "Sounds heavenly. But it's less than two months away."

Her fiancé was eager to make her his wife. She couldn't complain, yet her mind spun. She had so very much to do.

"We can make it work, Portia."

"Yes, yes. Okay," she said, smiling. The idea was too tempting to pass up. "Let's have a Christmas wedding."

There was a pause, and she pictured him smiling. "I love you, Portia."

"I love you, too, Juan Carlos."

The nursing home smelled of lye soap and disinfectant. Yet somehow the word *sterile* didn't come to mind as Portia walked the halls toward her great-aunt Margreta's room. Her aunt had once told her, "The odors of old age are too strong to conceal." Sharp old bird, Aunt Margreta was, back in the day. But Portia never knew what she'd find when she visited. Some days, her great-aunt was lucid, her wits about her. And some days, it was as if she'd fallen into a dark hole and didn't know how to get out.

This kind of aging was a slow, eternally sad process. Yet, as Portia popped her head into her aunt's room, she was greeted with cheery buttercup-colored walls and fresh flowers. Aunt Margreta sat in a chair, reading a crime thriller. A good sign.

"Hello, Auntie," Portia said. "It's me, Portia."

Her aunt looked over her thick eyeglasses and hesitated a moment. "Portia?"

Her voice was weak, her body frail and thin. "Yes, it's me."

The old woman smiled. "Come in, dear." She put the book down on her lap. "Nice of you to visit."

Thank heaven. Her aunt was having a good day. Maybe now, she could gather information about the Lindstrom monarchy that Portia hadn't been able to find anywhere else. She'd used up every one of her massive tools of research, including going through newspaper archives searching for an inkling about her family's rule and traditions carried out in Samforstand. She found nothing, which was very odd, and that lack of information brought her here today. Maybe Aunt Margreta could shed some light. She was her grandmother's sister and had lived in the homeland before the war.

Portia pulled up a chair and sat down beside her. "How are you, Auntie?"

"I can't complain. Well, I could, but it would do no good. I'm old, Portia. And you," she said, gazing over her glasses again. "You are as beautiful as I remember."

Portia took her hand and smiled. Aunt Margreta's hands were always soft, the skin loose and smooth over the aging bones. At ninety-three years old, she was as physically fit as one could expect, but for daily bouts of arthritis. But her mind wasn't holding up as well as her body and that worried Portia. "So are you, Aunt Margreta. You're a beautiful lady."

She'd always been a sweet woman, though as Portia remembered, she'd also been feisty in her day and not always in agreement with her sister, Joanna. The two would argue when they thought Portia couldn't hear. She never knew what they argued about, but as soon as Portia would step into the room, they'd shoot each other a glare and stop arguing, pretending things were all fine and dandy. Which they were, most of the time. Portia missed her parents, but she'd never discount the love Grandma Joanna and Great-Aunt Margreta bestowed upon her. It was the least she could do for her aunt to see to her care here at Somerset Village.

"Auntie, are they treating you well here?"

She nodded. "I'm fine, dear. The food's better now. We have a new chef and he doesn't cut corners. You'll see. You'll stay for lunch?"

"Of course I will. I'm looking forward to it."

"Then I'll get dressed up and we'll go to the dining room later."

"Okay. Auntie, I have good news." She lifted her left hand and wiggled her fingers. "I'm engaged."

Margreta squeezed her eyes closed. "Is it to Johnny Valente? That boy wouldn't leave you alone when you were younger. I never liked him. "

Johnny Valente? Portia used to play with him in grade school, two decades ago. He was a bully who'd called her Polar Bear Portia, because of her light hair and skin tone. "Gosh no, Auntie. I never liked him, either." She hoped her aunt wasn't digressing. "I'm engaged to…" How should she say this? "I met this wonderful man when I was visiting Alma."

"What's Alma?"

"It's this beautiful island country just off the coast of

Spain. I met him at his coronation. Auntie, he was just crowned king. His name is Juan Carlos Salazar, King Montoro of Alma."

Aunt Margreta put her head down. "I see."

Her aunt's odd reaction surprised her. "Do you like my ring?"

She gave Portia's left hand a glance. "It sparkles."

"Yes, it does."

"But it looks old."

"Yes, I suppose it's at least fifty years old. It was his mother's ring. He...lost his family at a young age also."

"In a car accident, just like your mother and father?"

"Yes, the same way. We have a lot in common."

Pain entered her aunt's eyes. "That's terribly sad, isn't it?" Her aunt made a move to get up from the chair. "Is it time for lunch yet, dear?"

Portia's eye twitched. "Not yet, Auntie."

Her aunt relaxed back into her seat.

"Auntie, I have a question to ask you. It's very important to me, so please try to concentrate. I will be marrying a king and, well, since I also have royal bloodlines, my fiancé wants very much for me to carry out the protocols of my homeland during our wedding. Do you know where I might find that information? I can't seem to find anything about our family's rule before World War II."

Aunt Margreta put her head down again.

"Auntie, please. Try to remember."

"There are no protocols from the family," she said stoically.

"But surely...there have to be. Have you forgotten?"

"No, my dear. I have not forgotten. Your grandmother and I never saw eye to eye about this."

"About what, Auntie?"

Margreta stilled. "Tell no one. Tell no one. Tell no one," she repeated.

"Not even me, Auntie? What is it you're not supposed to tell?"

Margreta looked straight ahead, as if Portia wasn't there. As if she was going back in time, remembering. "Don't tell Portia. She must never know the truth."

"What?" Portia absorbed her words, but they didn't make any sense. "What do you mean, I must never know the truth? What truth?" Portia grabbed her aunt's hand, gently squeezing. "Auntie, please. You have to tell me."

Her aunt turned to stare at her. "You are not a princess," she said. Her voice was sorrowful, etched in pain and Portia's heart sunk at her earnest tone. "Our family never ruled in Samforstand. Your mother wasn't royalty and neither was my sister, Joanna. It's all a lie."

Surely, the old woman was having a senile episode. "But, Auntie, of course Grandmother was queen. She raised me. I would know if she wasn't."

Silence.

"Aunt Margreta, please?"

"Yes, you're right, dear. You would know. Never mind."

Her aunt's quick compliance confused her even more. And she started thinking back about her life and how she'd never really seen any official documents regarding the Lindstrom monarchy. They'd been figureheads, holding no great power, yet she'd never known much about her homeland. It wasn't talked about. It seemed from her recent research the monarchy started to take shape in the United States, just after World War II.

"Oh, my God," she murmured. Her body began to tremble as tears stung her eyes. "You're telling the truth, aren't you? I'm not a princess."

Her aunt's eyes softened, dimmed by sorrow. "I'm sorry, Portia dear."

"But how can I believe that? How can that possibly be true?"

Could she take the word of an elderly senile woman who went in and out of coherency?

"There's a diary," her aunt said. "Joanna kept a secret diary."

"Where?" Now Portia would get to the truth. "Where's the diary?"

Aunt Margreta pointed to the bookshelf against the far wall overflowing with books. "Behind Agatha Christie."

Portia strode over to the bookshelf. Her hands were shaking as she parted half a dozen mystery novels. She lifted a weathered, navy blue soft-covered book from the shelf and brought it close to her chest. It had no title on the cover. Her heart racing, she took her seat next to Aunt Margreta and began reading the words that made a lie out of her entire life.

Portia lay quietly on her sofa, a cool towel on her forehead. She'd cried a river full of tears and every cell in her body was now drained. Princess Portia Lindstrom of Samforstand no longer existed. She never had. She was a fraud, a fake. An imposter. How could her family do this to her? How could they have perpetrated a lie that would affect her entire life?

How cruel.

How unjust.

Damn the circumstances behind their decisions right now. Their bold blatant betrayal was all that mattered to her. How dare they mislead her and let her believe in the fairy tale? She wasn't the snow queen. Hell, once the truth got out, she'd be deemed the black witch.

She'd been involved in one scandal already and it had taken years to live that down. But this? This was too much. The press would devour her. They'd make her out to be the villain, a lying deceiving bitch out to ensnare a wealthy king.

The humiliation alone would destroy all the positive good Juan Carlos had done for his country.

She muffled another sob. She didn't have it in her to shed more tears.

Feeling empty, she closed her swollen eyes, unable to rid herself of the thoughts plaguing her. The lies she'd been told, the deceptions perpetrated by her family. What of her career? Most importantly, what would she do about Juan Carlos? He was king, and as king he was pledged to only marry a woman of royal heritage. It was his destiny. It was what the citizens of Alma expected. Juan Carlos was the most dutiful man she'd ever known. This would destroy their relationship.

The towel was removed from her head. "Feeling better yet? Want to get up?" Jasmine asked.

"Nooooo. I don't want to ever get up."

Jas sat down on the floor beside the sofa. "Hey, that doesn't sound like the Portia I know. You've been wallowing for two hours."

"I'm not the Portia you know. I'm not… I don't know who I am. And I have a right to wallow."

"Yes, it sucks. But Portia, you are you, no matter if you have the title of princess or not."

"It's just…it's just so darn humiliating. I feel like a fool. I feel, well, I feel like everything's a lie. My childhood, my upbringing, my friends."

"Hey, watch it there."

"You know I don't mean you."

Jasmine reached for her hand and squeezed. "I know."

"All the doors that have opened for me because of my title, Jas… Those people will think the worst of me. They'll think I deliberately deceived them to get ahead in my career."

"When in truth, we know, they were using you. They

wanted to be associated with a princess. So it was a trade-off. You have nothing to be ashamed of."

"I'm ashamed of everything."

"And angry."

"Yes, of course. I'm spitting mad at my family."

"I'm not justifying what they've done, honey. But they came to the States after the war destitute, and like so many immigrant families, they didn't know how they'd survive here. And, well, pretending to be royalty from a tiny country…"

"It's far-fetched. Yet they got away with it."

"Yes, your grandmother speaks of it in the diary. How scared they were and how confused things were in Europe and Scandinavia after the war. There was a lot of rebuilding and restructuring and things just fell into place for them. Surprisingly, they weren't questioned. After all, we didn't have close ties to the monarchy of Samforstand the way we did England. Your grandmother speaks of Americans having much to deal with after the war. Hundreds of thousands of soldiers were coming home. Work and housing in our country was scarce. Things were chaotic."

"But others found a way to survive without deception. They worked hard and built honest, decent lives for themselves." Portia hinged her body up from her prone position and swiveled to plant her feet on the floor. Sitting upright, her head spun a little. "I don't know what I'd do without you, Jasmine. Honestly, you're the only person I can trust with this."

Jasmine rose from the floor and the sofa cushions dipped as she came to sit next to her. Her friend hung her arm around Portia's shoulder and they sat there like that for long minutes, quiet.

"I'm scared, Jas."

"I know."

"I don't know who I am. I can't expect you to understand fully how I'm feeling, but suddenly, I'm confused about everything. My heart is aching so badly right now."

"That's why I'm here, Portia. You're not alone."

She rested her head on Jasmine's shoulder. "Thank you."

The house telephone rang. "Want me to get it?"

"No," she said to Jasmine. "I can't talk to anyone right now."

Jas nodded.

Shortly after that, her cell phone began ringing and she knew both calls were from Juan Carlos.

They spoke every evening before she went to bed. Never fail.

Until tonight.

She couldn't speak to him and pretend everything was all right. She couldn't pretend that she was still a princess. She had a lot of thinking to do and she couldn't burden Jasmine any further in the decisions she'd have to make about her future.

Thoughts of Juan Carlos always squeezed her heart tight in a loving embrace.

This time, though, it was as if her heart was being strangled.

And the pain of losing Juan Carlos wouldn't go away anytime soon.

Portia sat in the throne room at the palace in Del Sol, her eyes closed, her heart pumping hard. Yesterday, she'd texted and emailed Juan Carlos one excuse after another as to why she wasn't answering his calls until she'd realized the only way to break it off with him was to face him in person. She'd flown half the night to get here. To see him one last time.

His family had been through a great deal to once and for all return the true and rightful heir to the Alma throne.

There'd been one debacle after another with his cousins, as they attempted to reinstate the monarchy, and the entire process had come under great scrutiny. All eyes were on Juan Carlos now and he'd made promises, staunch, determined promises to the citizenry that he would take his role seriously. By royal decree from decades ago, he was obligated to marry a woman of royal stature. The last thing he needed was to be made a fool of by marrying an imposter, a woman who hadn't a drop of royal blood flowing through her veins.

She wasn't his perfect princess any longer.

A tear dripped down her cheek. She wiped it away and steadied her shaky breathing. She glanced down at the engagement ring she wore. It was magnificent and maybe someday would belong to a woman worthy of wearing it and claiming a place beside Juan Carlos.

Her stomach ached at the notion of Juan Carlos living with and loving another woman. But it would happen one day. Rightfully so. She could only hope getting over him wouldn't destroy her.

She heard footsteps approaching along the corridor. She rose from her seat and mustered her courage. She'd never been much of an actress, but today she needed to provide an award-winning performance.

The door opened and there he stood, dressed in a crisp white shirt, sleeves rolled up—as if he'd been busy at work—and tucked into well-fitting black trousers. A lock of his neatly combed hair swept across his forehead and his tanned face showed a hint of stubble. Some days, when he wasn't going out in public, he didn't shave. She preferred him that way…a little rough around the edges. Tall, elegant, gorgeous.

Juan Carlos's gaze lit upon her and her heart tumbled. Oh, how she'd missed him.

"Portia, sweetheart. You're here." His warm winning

smile devastated her as he strode across the room. Genuine love entered his eyes. "I'm so glad to see you. You've come back to me early."

"Yes."

"I was worried when I couldn't reach you. But now I see, you wanted to surprise me."

He took her into his arms and heaven help her, she allowed him to kiss her.

His lips were warm, welcoming, filled with passion and beautifully familiar. She'd never been kissed the way Juan Carlos kissed her. She held her back stiff and didn't partake, but he was too caught up in the moment to notice her reluctance.

"We have much to talk about," he murmured, brushing his lips over hers again.

She stepped back and gazed into his dark gleaming eyes. "Yes, Juan Carlos. It's the reason I've come back to Del Sol so quickly."

He took her hand, covering it with his. "Come, let's sit then and catch up."

He began walking, tugging her along to the king and queen's thrones, two ornate tall chairs of plush red velvet and gilded carvings.

The irony of sitting upon that chair was too much. "I'd rather stand," she said.

"Okay." He looked at her oddly, but then nodded. "Would you like to take a walk? It might feel good to stretch your legs after the long plane ride. We can talk of the progress you've made with our wedding."

"No," she said. "No, Juan Carlos. I didn't come here early to discuss our wedding. I came to say that I can't go through with it."

"With what, sweetheart?" He blinked and appeared totally confused.

"The wedding. I can't marry you, Juan Carlos. I went home and really gave our situation some thought."

"Our situation?" He frowned. "You love me, I love you. That's our situation. We're engaged, Portia."

"No, as of today, we are not."

She inhaled and twisted the diamond ring off her finger. He was shaking his head, baffled. The gleam in his eyes dimmed. He almost appeared frightened. It killed her to wipe the joy from his face. "I'm terribly sorry."

"What is all this, Portia?"

She took his hand, spread open his palm and dropped his mother's wedding ring inside. "It's too much, Juan Carlos. We…we got caught up in the moment. Finding the art treasures put us both on a crazy romantic high and we took the little fling we had too far."

"Little fling?" he repeated, his voice hitching.

Oh, God, she'd hurt him. She knew she would, but she almost couldn't bear seeing that expression on his face. Better a small lie to save him, than the truth, which would make him look the fool in the eyes of his family and country. She loved him enough to suffer his anger and wrath. But the pain she'd inflicted would stay with her a long, long time.

"It happened so fast. You and I, we're different people. I love my job, Juan Carlos."

"You wouldn't have to give it up."

"Please understand," she said softly. "It isn't going to work out. I don't want to live here. I don't want to get married or have children right now."

His eyes snapped to hers. "I never rushed you about children, Portia."

"You'd expect it one day. And…and I'm afraid I'd disappoint you. I—I… It was a mistake to get engaged."

She backed up a step, putting distance between them. God should strike her dead for the lies she was telling. But it had to be done. Her sacrifice would make it easier on Juan Carlos in the long run. Yet her heart burned at the thought of leaving him forever.

"You're having cold feet. I hear it's common before a wedding."

"No, being away from here, from you, made it all clear to me, Juan Carlos. It's not cold feet, it's reality. I hope you'll understand and not make this harder on me than it already is."

He opened his palm to stare at the diamond ring. Then the sound of his deep wobbly sigh reached her ears. He was in pain. God, she hated this. "I love you, Portia," he said, searching her eyes.

Tears blurred her vision. Her throat constricted. She couldn't return his love. For his sake, she said nothing.

He gripped her forearms, gently shaking her. As if the impact would somehow clear her head of this nonsense. "Portia, you told me you loved me. You agreed to be my wife."

"I'm...I'm..." She took a swallow. Could she do this? Could she tell the biggest lie of all? She forced the words out. "I'm fond of you, Juan Carlos."

He dropped her arms. "Fond?"

She nodded.

"Then why are you crying, sweetheart?"

Her tears now were soaking her dress. She hated herself at the moment. "I don't like hurting you."

"Then don't. Stay and we'll talk this over. Give us time, Portia."

"I can't, Juan Carlos. It won't do any good. We're... over." She sobbed now, unable to hold back any longer. "I'm s-sorry."

He didn't reach for her. Thank goodness. If he touched her again, she'd melt into his arms. But he watched her carefully, as if trying to figure her out. Skepticism lingered in his eyes. He didn't believe her, but there was also resignation there and definite injury. She must have baffled him. He didn't know what to say to convince her she was wrong.

There wasn't anything he could say to her to change her mind. This was the hardest thing she'd ever had to do. She had to leave, to muster her strength and walk out the door. "I'll never forget the time I had with you… It was… *amazing*," she whispered.

He closed his eyes, shaking his head.

And that was her way out.

She turned her back on him and dashed away, leaving the palace and Juan Carlos and the love they'd shared behind.

Nine

"If you don't mind me saying so, Your Highness, you could use some sleep. Why not close your eyes while we travel," Eduardo said.

Juan Carlos sat facing his bodyguard in the reclining lounge chair on the palace's private plane. Under normal circumstances, Juan Carlos wouldn't travel so extravagantly; he wanted to be known as the king who flew coach. But it was imperative that this journey be kept secret and away from curious eyes. "Are you saying I look less than kingly, Eduardo?"

His bodyguard straightened in his seat. "No, I, uh, I know how hard this week has been on you, Your Highness."

"Eduardo, I'm in total agreement with you." Juan Carlos sighed. "I know I look like hell. I will fix that before we arrive in Los Angeles. The best I can, that is."

Eduardo's eyes softened. "Yes, Your Majesty."

Eduardo was quickly becoming his good friend and confidant. "Do you have a girl, Eduardo?"

"Yes, I do."

"Is it serious?"

Eduardo shook his head. "No, not really."

"Because of what you do for a living?"

"Yes. I cannot get serious with anyone while I'm away so much of the time. She understands."

"Ah, an understanding woman. It's lucky for me, not so fortunate for your girl."

"*Si*, that is true. But I am twenty-eight and not ready to settle down."

"I used to think that way. But sometimes fate steps in and knocks you over the head when a beautiful snow queen enters your path."

Eduardo chuckled. "Princess Portia."

"Yes, Princess Portia. And now I'm chasing her all over the globe."

"She is worth it, I would say, Your Majesty."

"*Si*, she is worth it."

He lifted the tumbler of bourbon he held in his hand and stared into the golden liquid. "I wish you could share a drink with me, Eduardo. We'll be in the air for five more hours. Surely the effects will have worn off by then."

"Thank you, Your Majesty, but no. I cannot drink while on duty."

Juan Carlos nodded. "Coffee then and a pastry?"

"I'd never refuse a pastry from Chef Andre, Your Highness. He showed me his creations before packing them up for this trip."

Juan Carlos pressed the button on the arm of his chair and ordered up coffee and pastries from his personal flight attendant. Then he rested back in his seat and sipped bourbon. Sleep was elusive lately and eating had become a chore. But he could tolerate a shot or two of bourbon when his mind wouldn't shut down. It helped blur the pain of losing Portia.

It had been one solid week since she'd left Alma and he hadn't heard from her since. What was she doing? Had she gone back to her work routine as if *they* hadn't happened? As if the time they'd shared together was nothing more than a passing fling?

He couldn't believe that. Something was up with her.

He felt it deep down in his soul that something had happened to Portia to make her deny their love and break off their engagement. Juan Carlos had waited patiently all week to hear from her, anticipating a call that had never come, and his patience was at an end. Now he was taking matters into his own hands. He knew enough about relationships to know women liked to be pursued. They liked to have men come after them. Maybe Portia was testing him? Maybe she'd expected him to come running and convince her she'd been wrong?

If only it would be that easy.

But he had to try.

Outside of his bodyguards, he hadn't told a soul of their breakup. He couldn't bring himself to share the news so soon after publicly announcing their happy engagement. He had hopes of winning Portia back, hopes of restoring their love. He'd vowed to bring honor and credibility back to the monarchy of Alma as well as to carry out his grandmother Isabella's dying wishes for the country. He wanted, needed Portia by his side. He and Portia belonged together. She was the love of his life.

Living without her would only be half a life.

Hours later, the plane touched down in Los Angeles, a place Juan Carlos had visited often. But this time, he had more than business to attend to—he had come to retrieve his woman. He'd managed to get a few winks of sleep, shaved and changed his crumpled clothes while they were in the air. Now he felt human again and more like himself, rather than the shell of the man he'd been this past week. Dressed in a slate-gray suit and neatly groomed, he planned on sweeping his princess off her feet again.

Returning home without her wasn't an option.

"Are you ready, Your Highness?" Eduardo asked, rising from his seat.

"Yes, and you have our little surprise all set?" he asked.

"I do. If it doesn't help your cause," Eduardo said, grinning, "nothing will."

Juan Carlos nodded. He couldn't disagree.

A frozen waffle popped up out of the toaster and Portia set it next to the scrambled eggs on her plate. She doused the waffle with maple syrup, grabbed a fork and took the plate over to the kitchen table. Breakfast for dinner was always an option when one didn't have the stomach to really cook. Or eat for that matter. Her belly squeezed tight as she looked at the food. She'd promised Jasmine she would eat something tonight.

Her friend had apologized profusely for breaking their dinner date. Jas had planned to cook a roast prime rib tonight, her specialty. They were going to do it up right with champagne and soufflé, and have a fun girls' night watching Turner Classic Movies on television. It was the only reason Portia had put on a dress, instead of wearing her usual comfy gray sweats. She didn't want to disappoint her friend.

"Poor Jas." She'd come down with a bug. Hopefully it wasn't the flu. Portia felt a little guilty about it, having dominated a lot of her time lately. Jasmine had been the best friend she could ever hope to have. Every day she'd come over to help Portia clean out her closets or rearrange furniture or cook a meal. Jasmine would bring in Mexican food on Taco Tuesdays and play card games with her until very late at night. She understood Portia needed to kill time so she didn't have to think too hard.

Now her friend was sick.

"For you, Jas, I'm going to eat this." She took a bite of her eggs and chewed and chewed. The eggs went down like rubber. She'd overcooked them again.

The waffle wasn't much better. It was still frozen in the center. Two bites later, she figured she'd fulfilled her promise and took her dish to the sink, dumping the contents down the garbage disposal.

Now what? She glanced around the condo. It was spotless. She'd been cleaning all week long. She had no official work to do. She hadn't been back to the office yet—they weren't expecting her anyway since she'd taken a three-month leave to deal with wedding plans and her new life as wife to a king.

She'd truly questioned whether to go back to her job. Could she continue with the pretense? How could she go back, when her friends and associates still believed her to be Princess Portia of Samforstand? Could she go about her life, living the lie? And what if she decided it was impossible to resume her life as usual? What if she revealed all the lies about herself and her family? What would that mean for Juan Carlos? His humiliation would be monumental. He would hate her. And appear a fool, a man easily duped.

She was at a crossroads in her life, and didn't know which way to proceed.

No one could possibly know how she felt right now. She was a phony, a fraud and an imposter. Jasmine kept telling her it wasn't her fault and no one would blame her if the truth got out. But Portia didn't know who she was anymore. Her life had been ripped out from under her. She felt at odds, lonely and bereft. Her emotions were all over the place. Anger took up residence, but sympathy crept in sometimes, as she imagined her family's plight after the war. Still, those emotions didn't come close to the emptiness she felt deep inside her heart. Because of something that had happened decades ago, she had had to give up the man she loved. The price was high, costing her her happiness.

The doorbell chimed and she jumped. "Who could that be?" she whispered. Surely, Jasmine wouldn't come out tonight. She was in bed with a fever.

Portia had a mind not to open the door, but the bell chimed once again and her curiosity had her heading to the front door.

She stuck her face up to the peephole and gazed out. "Eduardo?" What on earth was he doing here?

"*Si*, Princess, it's me."

She cringed at his reverent greeting. She didn't deserve to be called Princess. The chain lock allowed her to open the door three inches. She peered out and he smiled wide. "Hello."

Eduardo had become her friend. Seeing this solid block of a man on her doorstep was a welcome sight.

"Hi."

"Will you open the door for me?"

"Oh...of course." She undid the chain and opened the door.

Eduardo stood rooted to the spot. "Are you alone, Princess?"

"Yes, I am alone. Why?"

"I had to ask as it is my duty to protect the king. It's good to see you, but I am here on official bus—"

Juan Carlos stepped into her line of vision from a place on the porch that had concealed him. "Thank you, Eduardo. I'll take it from here."

Portia's mouth dropped open. She blinked and started trembling. "Juan Carlos."

He held a cat carrier in his hand. "Before you say anything, I brought you a gift. Well, two gifts. May I come in?"

With a lump in her throat, she looked away from Juan Carlos's face to the two kittens from Duchess's litter she'd appropriately named Mischief and Mallow. The kittens—one black and gray and mostly all trouble and the other almost all white with spots of caramel color here and there looking like a toasted marshmallow—were sleeping, curled up into little balls of fluff. Mallow's head rested on Mischief's body. Their sweetness brought a tear to her eye.

"Juan Carlos, you…you brought them," she said, touched by the thoughtful gesture. Words she wanted to say tightened in her throat and wouldn't come out. Initially, her heart had lurched when she spotted Juan Carlos, though he looked worn out. His eyes were rimmed with red—from sleepless nights? His handsome face looked haggard, as if he'd been through a war and his hair, while combed, needed a cut. She should have known he wouldn't take no very easily. He wasn't a man easily dissuaded. It was one of the qualities she loved most about him. "You didn't need to do that," she said, finally realizing she wasn't up to caring for pets. She'd barely been able to care for herself lately.

"I figured you might like the company. They are yours as much as they are mine."

She gazed into his solemn eyes. "Come in," she said.

She'd been engaged to a man who had never stepped foot into her home. How telling was that? An impetuous engagement, even though love was involved, wasn't an ideal way to start a relationship. She understood that now. During the coronation and then while living at the farmhouse searching for hidden treasures, they'd lived in a fantasy world, untouched by outside influences. It wasn't reality.

Juan Carlos stepped inside and glanced around, taking in the details of her home. "It's as beautiful as you are, Portia. I wouldn't expect any less."

"Thank you," she said. Her heart thumped hard in her chest. Thankfully, Eduardo's presence helped defuse the situation at the moment. She peered over Juan Carlos's shoulder. "Eduardo, would you like to come inside?"

She'd spent enough time with Juan Carlos and his bodyguards to know what Eduardo's answer had to be. He would be securing the premises and standing watch outside. "I wish I could, Your Highness," he said. "Thank you, but I will be right out here."

It was just as she'd suspected. "Okay, I understand." She turned to Juan Carlos and pasted on a false smile. "Surely, you and I both know that bringing me the kittens wasn't the reason you've come."

"But you're glad I did?"

She glanced at the sleeping kittens. "I'm glad to see them. They are sweet and I did…miss them." She cleared her throat. She couldn't admit she'd missed Juan Carlos also. "They've been weaned from Duchess, I'm assuming?"

He nodded. "Early this week. Where shall I put them?"

"A good question. If you'd called and asked me I would've told you not to bring them, Juan Carlos," she said softly. "I'm not equipped to care for them."

"I'll take them back to Alma with me, if you prefer." His back stiffened a little.

"No, no. Now that they're here, I can't turn them away. I… They're special to me."

Juan Carlos set the cat carrier down on the floor of the foyer. When he returned his gaze to hers, his eyes bored into her. "I had hoped you would say the same of me, sweetheart."

Her eyes closed at his hopeful plea. "You shouldn't have come, Juan Carlos."

"I couldn't stay away. It's not finished between us."

She sighed. "It has to be. We're not right for each other."

He approached her and heaven save her, her pulse accelerated as he laid his palm on her cheek. She lifted her eyes to his. His heavy expression softened, as if touching her made all the difference. As if a light inside him was turned back on. "Not true. We're good together. We're meant for each other. I am here. Don't turn me away, Portia. I would hope I am special to you, as well."

His gaze dipped to her mouth. She swallowed. Oh, God, the pull, the magnetic force of his love surrounded her like a protective shield. She didn't know where she found the will to back up a step, and then another. She couldn't hide her emotions or the passion he instilled and as she moved, he moved with her, thrusting his body against hers until her backside met with the wall.

"I've come a long way for you, Portia." His hands braced the wall, trapping her, so that she could only stare into his face and see his truth. "I've waited my entire life."

His sweet, sincere words stymied any defenses she could muster. She put her hands on his chest but instead of shoving him away as she'd planned, her fingertips clung onto his shirt and her palms flattened against him. His breath hitched from her touch, and his immediate reaction to her nearly buckled her knees. How could she not love this man? How could she turn him away now?

"I came here to talk to you, sweetheart."

She whispered, "Is that what you're doing to me? Talking?"

He flashed a charming, inescapable smile. "Maybe showing is better than telling, after all."

Then his mouth swooped over hers and claimed her in a breath-stealing kiss. His lips were rough but not unkind, wild but not crazy, sexy but not demanding. Caught up in the kiss, she couldn't think beyond the pleasure he evoked. The love she'd tried to bury was resurrected and she fell deeper in love with this man, this honorable king who had come for her.

She'd missed him and didn't know how much until this very second.

His tongue played over her lips and she opened for him. Sweeping inside her mouth, he kissed her again and again. A fire was building in her belly. She was past the point of refusal.

She was putty. He could do with her what he liked.

And she would enjoy every second.

She was lifted, floating on air now, held by two strong arms. She wrapped herself around his body, nestling her head into his chest. "Where's your bed, Portia?"

She pointed to the doorway down the hall.

His strides were long and determined and steady.

He continued to kiss her without missing a step.

Juan Carlos set Portia down on a ruffled lavender bedspread. Matching pillows, some big, some small, surrounded her head. He did a quick scan of her room decorated in soft whimsical colors. Wispy white curtains covered the windows and modern pieces of art, mostly pastels and some oils, adorned the walls. It was so Portia: soft, delicate, sweet.

God, he loved her.

And he wasn't going to leave here without her.

She was his prize, his love, the treasure he couldn't live without.

He unbuttoned his shirt, spread it wide across his chest and then gave it a toss. He kicked off his shoes and socks and gazed into her eyes as he unfastened his belt.

Her brows lifted, her lips parted slightly and a sharp breathy gasp escaped her lips. Her hungry expression softened his heart, but made every other part of his body hard. He had one night to change her mind. He wouldn't waste a minute. He took her hand and lifted her to her knees. "Come here, sweetheart," he demanded. "Touch me. Put your hands on my body."

Another gasp ripped from her lips and she moved to him. She wore a simple black dress with thin straps and short hemline. It adorned her breasts with just enough material to tempt him beyond belief. He ached to touch her, to shed her clothes and join their bodies, but first, he had to make her see how much she needed him, too. How perfect he was for her.

Her hands came to his torso and he gritted his teeth. She explored the breadth of him, tracing her fingertips over his chest, and then kissed everywhere her fingers had just touched. His body flamed; it was almost too much to bear. She was proving to him that they belonged together.

"Your touch is like no other, Portia. You know that. See what you do to me."

"We are good here, in bed, Juan Carlos," she whispered.

"We are good everywhere, sweetheart. Why do you fight me on this?"

She turned her face from him and disengaged, and he knew he'd pushed her too far. Something was eating at her. Something was making her hold back from him. "Don't retreat," he whispered. He couldn't let her think. Couldn't let whatever notions she had in her head continue to separate them.

He sank down on the bed beside her and unleashed his love for her, stripping down her defenses, loving her with everything he had inside. Holding her steady with one hand, he eased her dress off with the other, baring her upper body. He cupped her breasts, made love to them with his mouth and tongue and was rewarded with sighs of pleasure, little throaty moans of delight. Her throat, her chin, her lips. He devoured them all while covering her body with his. She arched her hips and they moved in the same unique rhythm, thrusting, aching, groaning until he couldn't take another second. He joined their bodies, pushing through her mental defenses and bringing them skin to skin.

Her eyes closed to the pleasure, her face beautifully masked in satisfaction. He thrust into her deep and long. It was hot and damp and sweaty and when he sensed her readiness, he called her name. "Portia." Her eyes snapped open. He stared into them and announced, "This is our place."

Connected by more than their bodies, she sighed and nodded her head.

Then he brought her home.

* * *

Early dawn broke through the curtains and Juan Carlos smiled in his drowsy state, his eyes still closed as images of making love to Portia flashed in his head. God, how he'd missed her. And now she was where she belonged. With him. After the night they'd shared, he hoped he'd convinced her that she loved him, he loved her and whatever was bothering her could be worked out and put to rest. It wasn't rocket science. Perhaps he'd pushed her too far early in their relationship. They'd only known each other for weeks. Not the months or years some take to cement their connection. She'd gotten cold feet. Any problems that arose could be dealt with. He couldn't see a reason why they shouldn't live their lives together. They'd made love twice during the night, and the second time had been even more thrilling and revelatory than the first. No one could tell him that Portia didn't love him. She'd displayed that in the way she'd taken the initiative, kissed him, touched him and made love to his body.

It was good, so good, between them. In all ways.

Juan Carlos rolled over to cradle her in his arms. They'd welcome the day together. But his hands hit upon cold sheets. He squeezed his eyes open. Portia was gone, her half of the bed empty. Was she always an early riser? He didn't know. They'd spent time together at the farmhouse in Alma on his schedule, not hers. There were still things they needed to learn about each other.

He hinged his body up, eager to see her. Eager to kiss her. Rising from the bed, he dressed in his trousers and shirt, ran a hand through his hair to comb down the spiky ends and then padded out of the room.

Halfway down the hallway of her modest three-bedroom condo, he halted, hearing mewling sounds coming from the living room. Of course, the kittens. Portia must have been anxious to see them this morning and tend to them the way she always had. Their carrier came equipped with kitty food, and water was their drink of choice. He grinned. He could almost picture her playing with them on the carpeted floor. Bringing them here had been a good plan to get his foot in the door and soften Portia's heart, but ultimately he'd done it to bring a smile to her face.

As he approached the sounds grew louder and no, they didn't appear to be coming from the kittens. It was a human sound, the heartbreaking echo of quiet crying. He stood on the threshold of the living room to find Portia, sitting up on the sofa, her arms around her legs, rocking back and forth with tears soaking her face.

The kittens were happily swatting at her feet, but it was as if they weren't there. Her sorrow was so deep she didn't hear him stride into the room. "Portia, sweetheart. What's wrong?"

She wiped her cheeks with the back of her hand, shaking her head. "You shouldn't have come, Juan Carlos," she whispered.

He narrowed his eyes. What on earth? Last night, they'd settled things. Maybe not verbally, but after the night they'd shared she had to recognize what they meant to each other. He'd come to retrieve her and bring her back to her rightful place, beside him on the throne of Alma. But now she was crying, looking so achingly sad. His gut clenched seeing her that way. "I don't understand."

He sat beside her and she unraveled her legs to face him, her eyes swollen from tears. "I can't be with you. I can't..."

"Sweetheart, my perfect princess, of course you belong with me. We don't have to rush into a wedding, if that's your concern. Whatever it is, we'll work it out. Just tell me. It kills me to see you in so much pain."

She rose then, yet her body slumped in defeat, her long hair falling onto her face. "That's just it, Juan Carlos," she said, shoving her hair aside. "I'm not your perfect princess.

I'm nobody's princess. I'm a fraud. I don't have an ounce of royal blood in my body. I cannot marry you. Ever."

Juan Carlos blinked several times, absorbing her words. He rose slowly, his heart pounding, his body shaking. "What you do mean you're not a princess?"

"I'm not. I never was. It's all a lie my family told after they migrated to the United States after World War II."

Portia spent the next few minutes explaining her family's duplicity to him. She gave him very little to hold on to as she presented the cold cruel facts that tore his life into shreds. Everything she told him made sense, yet nothing made sense. This couldn't be happening. Suddenly, he looked at Portia Lindstrom differently. She'd lied to him. Why? "How long have you known this?"

"I found out a little more than a week ago while researching our…my wedding rituals."

Juan Carlos stood ramrod stiff, his shoulders back and his heart breaking. "Yet you came to me and lied about the reasons for breaking it off between us. You told me you weren't ready to marry. You gave me excuses about your career and your love of the States. You knew, and yet you lied. How many other lies have you told me, Portia?"

"I didn't know what to do when I found out. Who to turn to. I'd just found out I'm…I'm an *imposter*." She spit the word out as if saying it stung her tongue. "I had trouble facing it, Juan Carlos."

His voice rose. "You should have trusted me with the truth. Or maybe you didn't want anyone to know the real truth? Maybe you wanted to keep on with the deception? Being of royal blood has its privileges. If I hadn't shown up here, what were you going to do? Live the lie forever?"

Her words from last week rang in his ears. *I'm fond of you. This isn't going to work. I don't want to get married. I don't want children.*

Had the woman he loved been nothing but a gold dig-

ger? Had her hard-to-get act been a ploy? All the warmth
he had nestled inside evaporated. Last night had meant
nothing to her. She'd deceived him over and over during
the past few weeks. She'd broken off her engagement to
him, but she hadn't revealed the truth to anyone. Of course,
her precious career would suffer. She'd hidden the truth because she couldn't afford another scandal. She needed the
art world to believe that she was a princess. So, of course,
she had to come to him with lies about why she was breaking off their engagement in order to keep her secret.

"I took the bait and you reeled me in, didn't you, Portia? Then what happened? You ran scared when I offered
marriage? Did you have a bout of conscience? Or did you
finally realize you'd get caught if you didn't break it off
with me? You couldn't marry me and risk being found out.
Just think what would happen to your career if you were
discovered to be a fraud. You'd never survive another scandal. Not professionally. No one in their right mind would
hire you so you lied your way out of our engagement."

Her tears gone now, she squeezed her eyes closed for a
second. As he waited, her breathing steadied and when she
opened her eyes again, they were twin pinpoints of blue,
focused on him. "You see things in black-and-white, Juan
Carlos. There is no room for grays in your narrow line of
vision. You only wanted me when I fit into your plans,
but now you know the truth. I'm not royal. I'm flawed and
can't be a part of your unblemished world."

His lips tightened. "You should've told me the truth,
Portia."

"Another point against me. I'm human. I make mistakes." She folded her arms across her stomach. "Now
that you have the truth, what are you going to do with it?"

He stared at her, wondering what had happened to the
woman he'd fallen in love with. Thoughts clogged his head.
She wasn't a princess. She had no royal blood flowing

through her veins. She was an imposter. A fraud, as she put it. His shoulders dropped as he shook his head. He had no answer for her.

"You only loved the idea of me, Juan Carlos. You said it just a little while ago. You think of me as your perfect princess. But now you know I'm not perfect. Hardly that. And how can a man who demands perfection in everything and everyone want me? I was only good to you when I was Princess Portia of Samforstand."

He let that sink in. He loved her, wanted her as his wife. Now, nothing made sense, and blackness from deep in his soul overwhelmed him. His Portia, the woman he'd thought she was, was gone. She wasn't a princess, but a fraud. He couldn't marry Portia Lindstrom. According to royal decree he was obligated to marry royalty. She was once a part of everything good that had happened to him and now there was nothing left between them.

"We had a fling, and it's over," she whispered. "Let's let it go at that. I think you should leave. Go back to Del Sol, be the king you were meant to be. Give me some time, I'll make sure…no blame will come to you about this."

"Portia," he said. He couldn't bring himself to move.

"Go, please." Her quiet plea broke his heart. "You shouldn't have come back. Goodbye, Juan Carlos."

She picked up the kittens playing at her feet, hugged them to her chest and walked out of the room.

She was right. He should leave.

There wasn't anything left for him here.

"Mr. Tanaka, it was a pleasure seeing you again. I'll be in touch once I've found the right prints and antique paneled floor screens to separate your work spaces. You've given me a good idea what you are looking for. I promise you, you'll be happy with the collection I come up with for your magnificent new corporate offices."

"Thank you, Princess. I have faith in your abilities. Your recommendations for my home have worked out nicely. I'm grateful you would take time from your leave of absence to do this for me."

Portia shook hands with her client outside his private office, her belly squeezing tight every time he called her princess. The title she'd grown up with no longer rang true and his respectful use of it during their meeting reminded her constantly that she was a fraud. "Goodbye."

Mr. Tanaka, founder and president of a highly successful Japanese food chain, hadn't wanted to work with anyone else. He'd called her personally to request her expertise, offering a big bonus if she would consider advising him on the artwork for his new offices. She'd agreed without hesitation. Pining for Juan Carlos and what would never be had grown old. She couldn't cry herself to sleep any longer. Three days' worth of tears had exhausted her. But she was glad her secret was out. At least to him. Admitting the truth to Juan Carlos had been difficult, but it had also been liberating. There would be no more lies between them now.

He'd been angry with her when he'd left her condo the other day. She'd seen the pain in his eyes, too, and she'd shivered when he'd looked at her as if she were a stranger. It had been so very hard to hear him berate her. He hadn't believed her, and even thought so little of her that he'd accused her of putting her career above her love for him. His accusations had slashed through her body like a dagger. But ultimately, it was better to allow him to believe the worst about her. It was a clean break.

Still, the love she had for him would never die. It would be hard, if not impossible, to get over him. Even if he had believed her claims, he couldn't marry her. They would have no future. He lived by a stringent set of rules. He did everything by the book. It was a no-win situation. So she'd made the supreme sacrifice for his benefit. She'd dismissed him without defending herself. As if her life wouldn't be forever altered after knowing and loving him.

He would get over her. He had to. He had to go about his life as if they had never met. In the near future, she didn't know exactly when, she would quietly make an announcement that they'd broken off their engagement. Their whirlwind romance was over. And then at some later point, when it had all died down, she would admit to the world, or anyone who cared, that she wasn't of royal heritage.

She would not go on living a lie.

But for now her goal was to protect Juan Carlos from a scandal. She would not have him looked upon as a fool.

As she headed to the parking garage, her eyes clouded with tears. She was broken inside and there was no way to repair her. Taking on Mr. Tanaka's account would be a good distraction. She'd focus on work for the next few weeks and the terrible ache in the pit of her stomach would eventually go away.

She got in her car and glanced in the mirror. She looked a wreck. With the tips of her index fingers, she smoothed away moisture under her eyes. "No more," she whispered. She had to put on a happy face. It was Jasmine's birthday today and she was taking her to dinner to celebrate the big three-oh.

Ten

Juan Carlos ran a hand down his face. He stood at the bar in the study of his living quarters in the palace and poured himself a double whiskey, straight up. "It's impossible." He lifted the glass to his mouth and took a sip.

"What's impossible?"

He turned, a little shocked to find Maria standing beside him. He'd been so deep in thought, he'd almost forgotten about his dinner date with the Ramons tonight. Normally his senses were keen and no one could sneak up on him. Especially not a woman wearing a pretty dress and heels and smelling like something exotic. It served to show him how off he'd been lately.

"Sorry if I startled you. Your staff assured me I was expected."

"No, it's okay. You are." It was good to see a friendly face.

"Alex is running late. He's meeting me here."

Juan Carlos nodded. "That'll give us a chance to talk. Let me get you a drink. What would you like?"

"Just a soda, please."

He dropped two ice cubes into a tall glass and poured her a cola. "Here you go."

She took the offered glass and sipped. "So what were you mumbling about when I came in?"

The corner of his mouth crooked up. It was the best he could do. He didn't have a smile for anyone these days. "My life."

"Your life?" Maria's aqua eyes opened wider. "Your perfect, kingly, marrying-a-beautiful-princess life?"

He lifted his whiskey glass and pointed with his index finger to the bone leather sofa. "Have a seat. I have something to... I need some advice."

Maria arched an eyebrow. "Advice? About your wedding?"

He waited for her to sit and then planted himself on the other end of the sofa. "Maria, uh, there isn't going to be a wedding."

It was hard getting the words out, and seeing Maria's mouth drop open only added to his discomfort. "That's why I asked you here. I haven't told a soul yet. I can hardly believe it myself."

"But you and Portia seemed so perfect together. What happened?"

Perfect. He was beginning to really hate that word. Portia had accused him of demanding that everyone and everything around him be perfect. Was he guilty of that? Did he expect too much?

"We're not perfect. Far from it. We've broken up and I don't know what to think about it."

"Why? What happened, Your Majesty?"

"She came back to Del Sol almost two weeks ago to break it off. She claimed she didn't want to get married and move to Alma. She loved her career and didn't want it to end. She claimed all we had was a fling, and that she, we, were high on romance. Finding the hidden artwork and being on the adventure together made it all seem possible but when she got back home, she was hit with reality."

"Do you think she was running scared?"

He hung his head, staring at the ground. "Initially, that's what I thought. I believed I could convince her that we could work out logistics and that we belonged together."

He met with Maria's eyes. "I was fool enough to go after her. I was in love."

"Was?"

He shrugged. "From the day I met her, something inside me told me she was the one. I pursued her like crazy. She didn't make it easy and now that I'm home, putting the pieces together, I think I know why."

There was a beat of silence. Maria was waiting for him to continue. It was difficult to admit to anyone how wrong he'd been. "When I went to Los Angeles, we…connected again. And it was as it had always been—amazing. I thought I'd relieved her of her cold feet. But in the morning, I found her quietly crying. She said she wished that I hadn't come for her. I was confused and didn't know why she'd had a change of heart."

"Why did she?" Maria asked.

He shrugged and shook his head. "I think she was cornered and didn't see a way out, so she finally told me the truth. Portia is not who she says she is. She's not a princess. She never was. She claims she found out while trying to dig up protocols for our wedding. Her family fled to the United States right after World War II and assumed the role of royalty. They were impoverished and used their phony status to gain a leg up. Supposedly, Portia's great-aunt has a diary that confirms all this."

"Wow, this is…big. Poor Portia. She must've been devastated when she found out. I can only imagine how she feels right now."

He stared at her. "You mean you believe that she didn't know about this all along?"

"Why wouldn't I? More importantly, why wouldn't you?"

"I'll tell you why. When she came back to Del Sol a couple weeks ago she lied about her reasons for breaking it off. She made up one excuse after another and if I hadn't gone to LA, I would still believe those lies she'd told. Only when she couldn't get rid of me any other way, she was forced to reveal the truth."

"Oh, I don't know about that." Maria began shaking her head. "That doesn't sound like Portia. What did you say to her when you found out?"

"In the beginning I was shell-shocked. And then my methodical mind started working and I said some things out of anger. I practically accused her of being a gold digger. Now that I think back on it, she looked so…lost. She kept saying she was an imposter, and I couldn't sympathize with her. I wasn't in the frame of mind. I felt betrayed. She should have come to me with the truth from the beginning."

"It must've been a hard thing for her to admit. To herself, much less to the man she loved. Just think, everything she believed about herself and her life is a lie. If that were me, I wouldn't know what to do, who to turn to. I don't know if I'd have the courage to do what she did. It was a hard day for both of you."

He drew oxygen into his lungs. "I suppose. I still don't know what to think."

"What else did she say? How did you part?"

"She pretty much told me off. She said that I expected perfection in everything and that I only loved the idea of her." He stared into his tumbler at the last gulp of whiskey left. "That's not true."

"No?"

He gave Maria a glance. "No," he assured her. "I loved her."

"You still love her, Your Majesty. You can't shut down those emotions so quickly. And what if she still is that woman you fell in love with, without the title of princess in front of her name? What if Portia Lindstrom is the woman for you?"

"How can I believe that when she doesn't believe it? She

didn't try to defend herself against my accusations. She didn't try to convince me that I'd been wrong about her."

"Well, since you asked me for my advice, I'm going to give it to you. I know Portia a little bit, and I'm a pretty good judge of character. I have seen the way she looks at you. The eyes don't lie. She was deeply in love and happy."

A lump formed in his throat. In the short weeks that he and Portia had been together, they'd gotten to know each other pretty well. They'd shared an adventure or two, but it went deeper than that and he'd felt they were meant for each other from the very beginning. It was a sense he had, a feeling that clamped onto him and never let go. It wasn't an overreaction to her beauty or the fact that she was a princess. But that factored into the equation, at least a little bit, because her status meant he was free to seriously pursue her.

"I thought so, too," he said. "We were good together."

"Did you ever stop to think that she wasn't thinking about herself when she broke up with you? Maybe she loved you so much she didn't want you portrayed in a bad light. A hasty then broken engagement wouldn't instill much faith in the monarchy you are trying to reestablish. After the big splash announcing your engagement, how would King Juan Carlos appear to the country that trusted his honor? Wouldn't it make you seem frivolous? Or duped? Or worse yet, impetuous? Seems to me, if I was in that situation, I would do everything in my power to protect the man I loved from scorn and speculation."

He scrubbed his jaw and sighed. "The last thing she told me was that she would make sure no blame came to rest on my shoulders."

Maria smiled. "There, you see. Only a woman still in love would say that. She was shielding you from harm. I would bet on it."

"You would?"

"Yes, and you should, too, if you still love her."

"To what end? I can't change the future…"

"Who says you can't? You're the king."

"I'm not that kind of king. I don't want to break with tradition."

"No, you'd rather have your heart broken."

Juan Carlos sighed. She was right. He would never love another the way he loved Portia. Right now, he physically ached for her.

Maria continued, "Think of it this way. You'll rule with more clarity and fairness having Portia by your side. You won't be stung by bitterness and regret and live an empty life without her."

"But the people expect—"

"A ruler they can admire and look up to. If you make it clear to them that this is for the best, they will rally behind you, my friend. And as the newly reigning king of a lost monarchy you have the luxury of not needing a parliament to vote on changes you might want to make in your dynasty."

A slow smile spread across his face. "I hadn't thought of that." And just as the notion elevated his hope, another thought brought him down again. "No…it's too late after the way I walked out on Portia, without believing in her. She may not forgive me."

Maria scooted closer to him, the sparkle in her eyes grabbing his attention. "But she may. And I think she will. She sacrificed herself for you. Don't you think you owe your relationship one more chance? If you don't try, you'll always wonder and you'll live to regret it."

Did he still love Portia? Yes, very much, and the more he thought about Maria's argument, the more he began to believe she could be right. He couldn't throw away something so precious to him without giving it one more try.

A light flashed in his head as he began to formulate a

plan. Finally, after these past few days of living in a depressed stupor, he was waking up alert and seeing things much more clearly. He had the power of the throne behind him. He hoped it would be enough.

"Maria, I'm going to need your help."

"I'll give it gladly, Your Highness."

A knot formed in the pit of his stomach. "A lot will be riding on this," he warned.

"I know. But I have enough faith in love for both of us. Alex says I've taught him something about that."

Juan Carlos nodded. If only he had that same faith. He leaned forward to kiss Maria's cheek. "Thank you."

"What is it exactly that you've taught me, sweetheart?" Alex stood at the threshold of the study, catching Juan Carlos's lips leaving Maria's cheek.

"How important *trust* is, Alex," Maria said slowly, straightening her position on the sofa, "when it comes to matters of the heart."

Alex gave them a nod as he entered the room. "It's true…once upon a time my fist might've met with His Majesty's jaw seeing him kiss you. But now, I only see love shining in your eyes for me."

A chuckle rumbled from Juan Carlos's chest. It was a good sound. One he hoped to make more often, after Portia was back where she belonged.

The sound of her Nikes pounding against the treadmill echoed off the gym walls. Sweat beaded up on Portia's forehead as she gazed out the window of the high-rise. She was offered a view of distant mountains and below, a city waking just after dawn. It was a good time of day to work out, before the world came alive. She had about thirty minutes before the gym would crowd with businessmen and women coming for their daily fix. She'd be gone by then, away from any nosy members who'd try to talk to her, get to know her. Many people recognized her, but thankfully she was old news as the other royal couple— the Brits—were in town for a charity event and all eyes had turned to them.

It was a lucky break and she valued the bit of anonymity it afforded her.

"Oh…kay, Portia," Jasmine said, shutting down her machine. "I've had enough."

Portia continued running at a six-mile-per-hour pace. She had one more mile to go. "You've barely broken a sweat."

"You're insane this morning." Jas used her towel to wipe her face as droplets rained down from her eyebrows.

Portia slowed her pace, allowing her body to cool down. "I know. But this is the only time I have to work off my…"

"Sexual frustration."

Portia swiped at her friend's butt with her workout towel. "Shh…no. Stop that! Just frustration in general."

Jasmine reached over and pushed the Off button on Portia's machine. "You're done."

The treadmill's thrumming quieted as it shut down and Portia finally stood stationary facing Jas. "I know I am. So done." She sopped up her face and neck and allowed herself a moment of accomplishment. It had been a hearty workout.

"I meant on the machine, girl. You're being cryptic today. What's really bothering you?"

Aside from her broken heart? It was hard to put into words exactly but she tried to explain. "I'm almost finished with the Tanaka account, Jas. You've helped me so much this past week and we've been working at breakneck speed for long hours. When I'm through… I don't know how it will play out. I'm still officially on leave. I don't know what to do after this. I'm living a lie, but I can't do anything about it at the moment. I feel weird in my own skin right now."

"Wow, Portia, I'm sorry. Juan Carlos doesn't deserve you. You're hurting because of him."

"You got that backward. I don't deserve him."

"Oh, brother. Listen, I know it's going to take time getting over him, but you will, honey. I hate to stand by and see you beat yourself up over something out of your control."

"Thanks, Jas. It means a lot to know you have my back."

"I do."

They left the workout area and headed to the showers. After a quick rinse off, Portia dressed in her casual street clothes and combed her hair.

"Too bad we can't grab breakfast," Jas said, exchanging a look with Portia in the dressing room mirror as she slipped her long mane into a ponytail.

"Wish we could, but we've both got busy mornings. Sorry if I'm overworking you on this account."

"You're not at all. I was only looking for an excuse to have waffles and bacon this morning."

"And you wanted an accomplice, right?"

Jas nodded. "No fun eating alone."

"Another day, I promise."

"Okay, then I'll talk to you later. Oh, and thanks," she said, wrinkling her nose, "for dragging my butt in this morning." She pouted. "I ache all over and my legs feel like Jell-O."

"You'll thank me in twenty years when you're still hot and gorgeous."

"So I guess I'll have to be your friend forever now."

"BFFs. That's us."

"Yeah, that's us," Jas said, waving goodbye.

Portia rode the elevator down to the parking garage. Just as she was getting into her Volvo, her phone beeped. She glanced at the screen. Odd, she'd gotten a text from Maria Ramon.

I'm in town and would love to see you. Can you make time for me today?

"No," she whispered. Any reminder of Juan Carlos right now was hard to take. Seeing Maria would only bring back memories of her time in Alma. She did have a terribly busy day. Hadn't she just turned down a breakfast date with her best friend?

Another text came in. It's important that I see you.

Portia's breath caught in her throat. Her heart began to pound. She couldn't refuse Maria. She was a friend and more than that, Portia was curious as to what she wanted. But that didn't stop her hands from trembling as she typed her answer. Sure, would love to see you. Stop by this morning. She gave her the address and sighed, starting the car. She planned on working from home this morning, anyway.

As it turned out, Portia couldn't concentrate when she returned home. Those phone conversations could wait another day, she decided. She changed into a powder-blue silk blouse and white slacks, and brushed her hair back and clipped it on one side with a gemstone barrette à la Gwen Stefani. She finished with a few flips of mascara to her lashes and some pink lip gloss.

In the kitchen, she prepared coffee, arranged fresh pastries on a plate, and then brought it all to the dining table. Mischief and Mallow played at her feet, swatting none too gently at her toes. Before they destroyed her sandals, she scooped them both up and carried them to the sofa. "Here, let's cuddle," she said, laying them across her chest. They obeyed, burrowing into the warmth of her body. The sound of their purring brought a smile to her face. She stroked the top of their soft downy heads. She loved the two fur balls with all of her heart.

A few minutes later, the doorbell chimed and Portia jerked up straight. The quick move sent the kittens tumbling to the floor. The little guys landed on their feet. Oh, to be a cat.

Portia rose and glanced at herself in the foyer mirror, checking hair and makeup. She approached the door, but her hand shook on the knob. She paused, took a deep breath. *Stay calm, Portia. Maria is a friend.*

She opened the door to find Maria smiling warmly, her pretty aqua eyes bright. A sharp twinge tightened Portia's belly. "Hi, Maria."

"Portia, it's good to see you."

She stepped forward to give Maria a hug. "I'm happy to see you, too. Please come in," she said, retreating as Maria made her way into the foyer.

She glanced around, noting the high-vaulted ceilings and the living and dining rooms. "It's a lovely place, Portia."

She shrugged. "Thanks. It's a rental. I travel back and forth from coast to coast a lot, so I have a small apartment in New York City, too. I haven't really made this place my own yet." She'd never felt settled enough in either place to put too much of herself into them. Aside from her treasured artwork on the walls, the rest of her furniture was simply… there. She had no emotional attachment to it, which had never really dawned on her before now. "It's not a big place. Would you like a tour?"

"Sure." Portia walked her through the condo, showing her the home office, the guest bedroom, her master suite and the kitchen. They stopped in the dining room. "Would you like coffee and a pastry?"

Maria's eyes darted to the dish of fresh pastries. They were impressive. Portia knew the pastry chef at the Beverly Hills Hotel and she'd made a call this morning to have them delivered. "I'd love some. Thank you. It's good seeing you in your own element here. This is very nice."

"Let's have a seat," Portia said. "Everything's ready." Maria sat down across the table and Portia poured them each a cup of coffee. "I was surprised, in a good way, to hear from you this morning. What brings you to California?"

Maria cradled the cup in her hands. "I, uh, I had no real business here, Portia. I came specifically to see you."

"Me?" Portia halted before the cup touched her lips. "Why?"

"Maybe because I'm a hopeless romantic. Maybe because I found the love of my life in Alex and want my friends to find that same kind of happiness. Don't get me wrong, Portia, I'm not here to meddle, but I do think Juan Carlos made a mistake with you."

"He told you?" Portia wasn't sure how she felt about that.

"Yes, I know you've broken the engagement."

"Who else knows?"

"No one. I don't think he's told his cousins yet."

Portia nodded. Her belly began to ache. "Do you know everything?"

Maria's expression softened. "I know you're not a princess, Portia. Juan Carlos told me the entire story. I'm so sorry you were misled all those years. It must have been extremely difficult finding out the way that you did."

Portia's eyes squeezed shut at the truth of those words. "Yes." Oh, God. This was so hard. If only she could blink this entire ordeal away. Too bad life wasn't that easy. Soon everyone would know her dirty little secret and they probably wouldn't be as kind as Maria. "It's been an adjustment. My whole life is a lie."

"Not all of it, Portia."

She snapped her eyes open, just as Maria's hand came to touch hers. She welcomed the warmth of her friend's gentle touch. "I can't possibly know exactly how you feel, but I do know you. Portia Lindstrom is a wonderful, sweet, caring woman. She's smart and funny and she's terribly in love with a good man."

Portia shook her head. "No. Juan Carlos...there's nothing left between us."

"There's love, Portia. Don't discount it. It makes the world go round, you know."

"Well, I'm spinning fast, Maria. And I'm about to fall off."

"No, you don't have to fall off. I know Juan Carlos still loves you. He's made a terrible mistake. He was in shock, I think, hearing the news about your identity, and he regrets how you two left off. He's sorry for how he treated you, Portia."

"I accept his apology. If that's what you came for, you can tell him not to worry about me. I'm...fine."

"That's not why I came. You love him very much, don't you?"

Portia sat silent.

"I know you're protecting him, Portia. I know, because if I were in your shoes, I'd do the same thing."

"You would?"

"Yes. Isn't it why you initially lied about the reason you broke off your engagement?"

"Maybe."

"Maybe yes?"

"Okay, yes. That's why I lied. It was inevitable that we had to break up, so why should both of us go down with the ship? I was to blame. It was my family's illicit behavior that put us in this position. Juan Carlos didn't need to suffer, too."

"I thought so." Maria selected a pastry and eased it onto her plate. "Juan Carlos is very lucky."

Portia scoffed. "Hardly. I'm a fraud."

"No, you're not, Portia. You may not be a princess, but that's not all you are. Juan Carlos believes in your love."

"Then why isn't he here? Never mind. I'm glad he's not. It was hard enough breaking it off with him the first and second time."

Maria chewed her raspberry cheese tart with a thoughtful expression on her face. "The third time's the charm, they say. And he's not here, because well, he wants to see you again. In fact, it's urgent that he see you. But he wants you to come to Alma. What he has to say must be said in Del Sol."

"Me? Go back to Alma? I couldn't possibly."

"I was afraid you'd say that. I'm not to leave here without you, but…I think I have something that will change your mind."

"Nothing much could change my mind."

"Wait right here. I have something in my car. I'll only be thirty seconds," Maria said, rising. "Don't you think about putting those pastries away."

Portia smiled despite the mystery unfolding. What on earth was Maria up to?

Just seconds later, Maria walked back into the dining room holding a large package wrapped in brown paper. The box was the size of a small television or a microwave. Ridiculous.

"What do you have there?"

"Oh, no, I'm not telling. You have to open it. First read the note."

"I don't see a note?"

"It's inside."

Portia stared at Maria and shook her head. Nothing would get her to change her mind. But she had to admit, she was intrigued. Her eye began to twitch. *Damn. Stop it.* Okay, she was nervous.

"Go on," Maria said.

Portia dug her fingers into the wrapping and tore it away. Paper flew in all directions. An envelope with her name on it taped to the box popped into her line of vision. She lifted it off, pulled the note out and read it silently.

Portia, sweetheart,
Give me another chance to prove my love.
This was to be my wedding gift to you.
I hope you will accept it and me back into your life.
It speaks for itself.
Juan Carlos

Tears trickled down her face. The note was short, but held the words that could make all things possible. She loved Juan Carlos. Would always love him. And now, dare she take a chance? What could he have possibly sent that would impact her more than those loving words?

"Open the box, Portia."

"I'm afraid to," she said, eyeing the lid, her body shaking so badly she could hardly move. "What if it isn't..."

"It is. Trust me," Maria said.

Portia pulled open the lid and found yet another box. She lifted it out and set it on the table, staring at the ornate workmanship on the box, the beautiful wood carvings of intricate design.

She undid the latch and slowly eased the lid open. She eyed her gift and a soft gasp rose up from the depths of her throat. This was amazing. Sweet. The gesture meant more to her than anything else she could imagine. Her lips began to quiver, her heart pounded and her tears fell like heavy rain.

"It's the s-statue. My favorite p-piece of the artwork we..." She gulped and whispered, "It's from the hidden treasure we uncovered." A man reaching his hand out for the woman he loves. *"Almas Iguales. Equal Souls."*

A royal chauffeur met her at the Del Sol airport terminal, grabbing up her suitcases and guiding her toward the limousine parked just outside the entrance. She was taking a giant leap of faith coming here, offering up her heart once again. But Juan Carlos had done the one thing, given her the one gift that could change her mind. His generous gesture told her he understood her, believed in her and wanted her back in his life. She didn't see how it was possible. She didn't know what terms Juan Carlos would dictate to her when she arrived. Could she bank on his integrity? Could she trust in him enough to believe there was a solution to their dilemma?

His gift had jarred her into believing the best was yet to come. But as the hours had worn on, she'd started to doubt again. It had taken Maria and Jasmine both to convince her that if she didn't travel to Del Sol and give it one last try, she would live to regret it.

"He's been solely devoted to you since the minute he set eyes on you," Maria had said.

"Think of your time at the farmhouse," Jasmine had prodded. "How many other men would rescue feral cats and give them a good home, much less a royal palace, to make you happy? And don't forget how he battled a snake to keep you safe. He's been there for you, Portia. And he'll be there for you again."

"Go, give your love another chance," they'd both chorused.

So here she was back in Del Sol where in less than an hour, Juan Carlos would address the citizens of his country in a speech that would set the tone for his rule.

The driver opened the limo door. "Thank you." She slid inside and immediately turned, startled to find Juan Carlos in the seat beside her.

"Hello, sweetheart."

The richness in his voice seeped into her soul. She faced the most handsome man she'd ever known. His eyes were deep dark shades of coffee and cocoa, flecked with hints of gold, and he was gazing at her in that intense way that made her heart soar. His smile was warm, welcoming and filled with the confidence she lacked at the moment. Oh, how she'd missed him. A whisper broke from her lips. "Juan Carlos."

"I am glad you came."

He didn't reach for her, didn't try to touch her, and she was glad. She had to catch her breath just from seeing him. Anything more would send her into a tailspin. "I, uh, I don't know why I'm here."

He sighed. "It's because you love me."

She couldn't deny it. "Yes."

"And I love you, above all else. I have misjudged you and I am truly sorry, my love. I hope your being here means you have forgiven me."

A lump formed in her throat. How could she explain the complexities of her feelings? "I do forgive you. Though it hurt, I realized you reacted as anyone might."

"But I am not just anyone, Portia. I am the man who loves you unconditionally. And I should have recognized that sooner. I should have believed in you."

"Yes. But that wouldn't have changed the outcome. Our situation is impossible, Juan Carlos."

He only smiled. "Did you like my gift?"

Tears welled in her eyes. "It's magnificent. I was truly surprised by the gesture."

"Not a gesture, sweetheart. It's a gift from my heart to yours. And I have another gift for you. One that will make all things possible. I am only asking for your trust. Do I have it?"

She hesitated for only a moment. And in that moment, she realized that yes, she trusted him with her life. She trusted him to make the right decision. She trusted him. With. Her. Heart. She nodded.

"Good."

He took her hand and lifted it to his lips, pressing the

softest, most reverent kiss there. The sweetness of the gesture left her floating on air. "I have missed you."

Their eyes met then. His were unflappable, determined, loving. She saw everything she needed in their brown depths. Then his hands were on her, cupping her face, his thumbs stroking her cheeks as his gaze flowed over her face. She was out of her depths now, living in the moment, heat crawling up from her belly to lick at her. When his lips rained down on hers, devouring her mouth in a kiss to beat all kisses, tremendous hunger swept her up and carried her away.

His groans matched her unbridled sighs. "I cannot live without you in my life," he murmured between kisses.

"I feel the same," she whispered, as he dragged her farther into his embrace. She was nearly atop him now. His hands were in her hair, his tongue sweeping through her mouth, their bodies trembling, aching.

"We have arrived, Your Highness," the driver announced through the speaker. They'd arrived? She didn't remember them taking off.

Juan Carlos stilled. "All right," he said to the chauffeur.

They had indeed arrived at a secluded private entrance in the west wing of the palace.

Juan Carlos sighed heavily and pulled away from her. "One day, we will finish this in the limo."

"I'll look forward to that." Her eyelid fluttered. Heavens, another unintended wink? She was hopeless.

Intense heat entered his eyes and a savage groan rumbled from his chest. "You are a temptation, Portia," he said. He took a second to smooth the hair he'd just mussed. The care with which he touched her and gently pulled tendrils away from her face sent shivers down her spine. Then he smiled wide and destroyed her for good. "You will attend my speech?"

"Yes." That was why she had come. His only request

was that she be in attendance when he spoke to the press and his fellow countrymen. Her flight had been delayed and there was a moment when she'd thought it an omen. A moment when she almost turned back. But Portia wasn't going to run from the truth any longer. No matter how bad. No matter that her life would be forever altered. She had gotten on the plane ready to hear what Juan Carlos seemed eager to say. He would be giving the speech very shortly. "I will be there."

He nodded, satisfied, and the door on his side of the car opened. The driver stood at attention waiting. "You'll be driven to the palace lawn now," he said to her. "I will see you very soon."

Then he climbed out of the car and was gone.

Juan Carlos stood tall and erect at the podium looking out at the crowd that had gathered on the palace lawn. Dressed regally in a dark suit and tie, he scanned his audience. Luis and Eduardo flanked him on either side, on the lookout for signs of danger. News crews from Del Sol's three television stations were in attendance, as well as reporters and journalists from far and wide. Portia saw Juan Carlos now, as the king surrounded by people who banked on his every word. He was a model citizen, handsome, refined, a man to be admired. He was the king of his people. The press loved him. Even more, they loved the idea of him *with Portia*. Who didn't love a good fairy tale?

Her stomach ached. She had no idea what he was going to say, but it was important to him that she hear him say it. There was no doubt she loved him. And she was fairly certain of his love for her. So she stood in the front row, but off to the side somewhat with Maria and Alex Ramon. Maria slid her hand over hers and squeezed gently. God, how Portia needed that show of support right now. Her legs were two rubber posts, holding her up only by sheer stubborn will. She swallowed as Juan Carlos tapped the mike, ready to begin his speech.

And when he spoke, his voice came across clear, strong and confident. Tears of pride pooled in her eyes. He addressed the crowd, garnering cheers as he began his speech. Then he graciously spoke of the future, of how he planned to work alongside the parliament to better the country. He spoke of helping the needy, working with charities and letting the people of Alma have a voice.

He seemed to seek her out of the crowd and as those gorgeous dark eyes landed on her, her breath caught in her throat. He trained that killer smile on her once again. How unfair of him to have such power over her, to stop her breathing with a look, a smile.

All eyes in the crowd seemed to turn her way. She was no stranger to the press, to having people recognize her, but today, she wanted no such attention. She'd rather be invisible.

Maria squeezed her hand again, giving her silent support. Portia inhaled and began breathing again.

"I have one more announcement to make," he continued to his audience. "Actually it is the reason I have called you here. I have made a decision that will change the ways of the monarchy for the better, I hope. For decades past, those in power, the honorable men and women who held the highest rule of the land, often did so out of duty. But with their duty often came great sacrifice." Juan Carlos glanced at Portia again briefly and then went on. "Many true loves went unheeded. Many of those loves were lost to baseless marriages, unions that held no great affection. The sacrifice was thought to keep the bloodlines pure. I have called you here today to say that my rule, this monarchy, is one that looks forward to the future, not backward at the past. It is time to bring the monarchy into the twenty-first century.

"As you know, Portia Lindstrom and I are to be married. Our engagement was swift, yes, but when it's right, you know it deep in your heart." His fist covered his heart and he awarded the crowd his beautiful smile. "And I am here to tell you it is right."

His eyes sparkled and he sent her a look filled with so much love, Portia's heart did somersaults. "Recently, it's come to light that Portia is not the true princess of Samforstand. In fact, she has no royal bloodlines at all. She came to me when she learned this news from an elder in her family. It seems there was much confusion about the legal heirs to the throne after the chaos and hardships of World War II.

"My family went through great hardships at that time, as well. Many of you here today know all about the recent trials and tribulations my family went through to find the true heir to the throne. Our great-grandmother's recently discovered letters proved to all of us the high price that was paid to keep to the letter of law when it came to royal protocol. In those letters we learned that her son, king Raphael Montoro II, and his direct descendants were not the rightful heirs to the throne, and thus am I standing before you today, a Salazar, as your king.

"Similarly, Portia has discovered the truth of her family's past and now needs to move forward with her life. But I will not allow mere decorum to once again steer the Montoros' destiny toward a tragic outcome. We will not let history repeat itself. We will not sacrifice our love in the name of an outdated custom. Portia Lindstrom is here today, as my fiancée, and princess or not, she is the love of my life and will become my wife."

Juan Carlos put out his hand. "Portia? Will you join me here? Be by my side."

The crowd was stunned into silence. Cameras angled her way, shots were snapped off by the dozens.

"Go," Maria whispered. "He is changing a centuries-old tradition for you. Don't leave him waiting."

She blinked, coming to grips with what had just happened. The depth of his commitment astonished her, delighted her and sent her hormones into a tizzy. She caught Eduardo giving her a smile and an encouraging nod from behind Juan Carlos. She smiled back.

Maria was right; she couldn't leave the king waiting. Not for another second. If he could do this for her, then she wouldn't hesitate to show him her love. With him by her side, she could conquer anything. She wasn't a wimpy princess. Well, she *wasn't* a princess at all, but she wasn't wimpy, either.

Her head held high, she stepped forward and made her way to the podium. As she reached it, she took Juan Carlos's outstretched hand and gazed into his eyes. In them, she saw her life, her future. The details were negotiable, but the love, that never wavered. She loved him. She would always love him. Thank God, King Montoro of Alma was a determined man.

Juan Carlos pulled her close and there before the world, bruised her lips in a kiss that left no one doubting their king's commitment. "Juan Carlos," she murmured. "Everyone's watching."

"Are they?"

Cameras clicked like crazy and she had no doubt this epic scene would go viral.

When Juan Carlos broke off the kiss, he nudged her tight to his side to present a united front and turned to the crowd. "Portia is a wonderful, bright, talented woman and in the days and years to come, you will all see in her what I see. I ask only that you welcome her today. Give her the same chance you gave me."

The crowd was silent and Portia's heart plummeted. And then a sole cheer rang out from a man shouting his support. And then another cheer went up and another, in a show of loyalty. And soon, the entire gathering displayed their acceptance as boisterous cheers and booming applause echoed against the palace walls, the citizens of Alma giving the king their allegiance.

They had accepted her.

Portia couldn't keep a wide, teary-eyed smile from spreading across her face. She was grateful for their support, but she was certain that even if the crowd had turned hostile, nothing would have deterred Juan Carlos. He had her back, and that was the best feeling in the world.

The speech over, Portia walked off with Juan Carlos. "I love you, you know," she said, winding her arm around his waist and leaning her head on his shoulder.

"I do know, but I think I'll need to hear you say it about a thousand times. Tonight?"

She nodded. "Tonight." She lifted her lips to his. "Do you think you can make me say it a thousand times?"

He laughed. "Oh, I know I can. Just let me alert the chauffeur we'll be needing the limo soon."

Her eyes went wide. "Juan Carlos, you don't play fair!"

"Sweetheart, I play for keeps. Princess or not, you're a royal temptation that I can't live without."

"So you're keeping me?"

"For as long as you'll have me."

"Forever, then. It's settled."

"Settled," he said, grinning as he picked her up and twirled her around and around.

She floated on air.

And her feet never did touch the ground again.

Epilogue

One month later

Juan Carlos couldn't stop grinning as he held Portia in his arms and danced to the royal orchestra's rendition of "Unforgettable" under hundreds of strung lights and a moonlit sky on the grounds of the newly restored farmhouse. This place that Bella and James would someday call home was where Juan Carlos and Portia had found love, too, and it seemed fitting to have a small intimate exchange of promised vows here in front of their close friends and family. His new bride dressed in satin and ivory lace, with his mother's diamond wedding ring sparkling on her finger, was the most beautiful woman on the planet.

"Are you happy?" he asked, fairly certain his answer was found in the sky-blue gleam in her eyes.

"I don't think I've ever been happier."

"That's how I want to keep it, sweetheart." He pressed her close and kissed her forehead, brushing his lips over her cheeks and nose and finally landing on her sweet mouth.

"I loved our sunset wedding," Portia said. "This is a special place."

Their first dance ended and Juan Carlos swung Portia to a stop in the center of the circle of their guests, who applauded them, their dance and their marriage. Portia's elegant grace, her help in discovering the hidden artworks and her work with local charities had endeared her to the country. Even the doubters had begun to come around as she constantly proved to them that she belonged at his side. It was a good thing, too, because Juan Carlos would rather give up the throne than live without Portia.

His cousins approached. "Welcome to the family, Portia," Rafe said, his very pregnant wife on his arm. "We couldn't be happier for you both."

"It was a lovely ceremony," Emily said.

"Thank you. I've heard all about your special ceremony, as well," Portia offered, glancing at Emily, Rafe, Gabe and Serafia. "I've never attended a double wedding before."

"We wish we would've known you then," Serafia added.

"Might've been a triple wedding, who knows?" Gabe said with a teasing smile.

Juan Carlos found it all amusing. His cousins had met their wives in uncanny ways and now every one of them was married. Rafe had resumed his position as head of Montoro Enterprises and the company was thriving. Good thing, too, because Rafe's father had decided to retire in Alma. After the ceremony he'd been the first to offer his congratulations, giving Portia a kiss on the cheek and wrapping Juan Carlos in a tight embrace. Juan Carlos owed a great deal to the man who had raised him from early childhood.

Gabe, the younger of his male cousins, had finally shed his bad boy ways and settled down with his lifelong friend and love, Serafia.

"I think I just felt something," Bella announced. She took James's hand and placed it on her small rounded belly. "Here, see if you can feel the baby."

James kept his hand there several seconds. "I'm not sure," he said softly, diplomatically. "It's early yet, isn't it, honey?"

"Maybe for you, but I think I felt it." Bella's eyes were two bright beams of light. She was carrying James's child.

James kissed her lips. "I can't wait to feel our baby, too."

Portia slipped her hand in Juan Carlos's and they watched the scene play out. James had one child already and Bella was proving to be a fantastic stepmother to one-year-old Maisey. And now, their family was expanding. Juan Carlos was glad that Bella and James had settled in Alma and James was back playing professional soccer—football as they called it here—and winning games for the home team. Things had been rough there for a while between James and his father, oil tycoon Patrick Rowling. Patrick had picked James's twin brother, Will, to marry Bella. The arranged marriage was an antiquated notion to say the least, and Bella was having none of it. James was the man for her. And then Will had also found love with Catalina Ibarra, his father's maid. The whole thing had sent Patrick into a nosedive but he was finally coming around and softening to the idea that perhaps his sons could make up their own minds about their love life and beyond.

"Now that we're all here together, I have good news to share with all of you," Juan Carlos said. He couldn't help his ever-present smile from intensifying. He had his family's attention now. "I'm told by Alex and the prime minister that Alma has never seen a better year. The country is well on its way to being financially solvent again. Thanks in part to our efforts here, I might add. With the discovery of the lost art treasure, tourism will climb, especially once we put those pieces on public display. We are working to that end. Since the state of Alma is now finally secure once again, a sizable portion of the Montoro fortune has been repatriated. It has been decided that the money will fund a new public school system named for my grandmother Isabella Salazar."

"That's wonderful," Bella said.

Rafe and Gabe slapped him on the back with congratulations.

"If it wasn't for Tia Isabella's determination to see the Montoros return to Alma in her lifetime—and those letters I discovered—none of this would even be possible," Bella said.

It was true. Juan Carlos wouldn't be king, he would never have met Portia and who knew what would have happened among his other family members. "We owe my grandmother quite a bit."

They took a solemn moment to give thanks to Isabella. And then the orchestra music started up again.

Couples paired off and moved onto the dance floor.

Little Maisey Rowling had woken up from her nap. Wearing pink from head to toe, she was sitting on the front porch playing with the palace kittens alongside Portia's maids in attendance, Jasmine and Maria Ramon.

"I owe those two women a dance," Juan Carlos said to Portia. "If not for them, you may never have come back to Alma. Actually, I owe them much more than that."

"Yes, but first, my love, I have a wedding gift for you. I hope it will match the one you gave me. I cannot wait another second to give it to you."

"Okay," he said, eager to please her. "I'm yours."

She tugged him to the back of the house, to the garden area that was in full bloom, despite the late fall climate. Oh, the miracle of royalty that made all things possible. She sat him down on the white iron bench and then took a seat beside him.

"Juan Carlos," she began, taking his hands and holding them in her lap. "You have given me your love, a new family and a beautiful palace to live in."

"You deserve all those things, sweetheart."

"But there's one thing missing. One thing I want and hope you want, too."

He had no clue where she was going with this. He had everything he wanted. "Have you found another brood of cats to adopt?"

She shook her head and grinned, her eyes beaming with the same glow he'd seen in Bella's. His heart stopped beating. He gathered his thoughts and came to the only conclusion he could.

"You're not?"

She nodded now, bobbing her head up and down rapidly. "I am."

"We're going to have a baby?"

"Yes!"

A glance at her belly gave him no indication. "When?"

"Seven months from now."

Carefully, he pulled her onto his lap. "I'm…I'm…going to be a father."

"Yes, you are."

He curved his hand around her nape and brought his lips close to hers. "You're going to be a mother."

"Yes."

The idea filled him with pride. His Portia would give him a child. It was the best gift in the world. His mouth touched hers reverently and he tasted the sweetness of her lips. "I couldn't be happier, sweetheart."

"I'm glad. Our baby will grow up in a home filled with love. Neither one of us knew our parents for very long. But now, we will have a family of our own. It's quite unexpected…"

"It's all I've ever wanted, Portia. For us to be a family."

"Really?"

He nodded. His throat constricted. His emotions had finally caught up to him today. His life had come full circle—the orphaned boy who would be king, married to his heart's desire, was to have a family all his own now.

There was no better kingdom on earth than for a man to share his life with the woman he loved.

He and Portia were two of a kind.

Almas Iguales.

Equal souls.

* * * * *

LESSONS IN SEDUCTION

SANDRA HYATT

To Gaynor and Allan.

One

Keep calm and carry on. Danni St. Claire had seen the slogan somewhere and it seemed apt. She flexed her gloved fingers before tightening them again around the steering wheel.

Her passengers, one in particular, behind the privacy partition, would pay her no attention. They so seldom did. Especially if she just did her job and did it well. In this case, that job entailed getting Adam Marconi, heir to the throne of the European principality of San Philippe, and his glamorous date for the evening, back to their respective destinations.

Without incident.

And most importantly without Adam realizing that she was driving for him. She could do that. Especially if she kept her mouth shut. Occasionally she had trouble in that department, speaking when either her timing

or her words weren't appropriate or required. But she
could do it tonight. How hard could it be? She'd have
no cause to speak. Someone else would be responsible
for opening and closing the door for him. All she had
to do was drive. Which, if she did it well meant without calling attention to herself. She would be invisible.
A shadow. At a stop light she pulled her father's chauffeur's cap a little lower on her forehead.

A job of a sensitive nature, the palace had said. And
so she'd known her father, although he'd never admit it,
would rather the job didn't go to Wrightson, the man he
saw as a rival for his position as head driver. Danni still
had clearance from when she'd driven for the palace
before, back when she was putting herself through college. She hadn't seen Adam since that last time.

All the same she hadn't known it would be Adam
she'd be driving for tonight. When she'd intercepted
the call, she'd thought all she'd have to do was pick
up Adam's date for the evening, a beautiful, elegant
Fulbright scholar, and take her to the restaurant. But
then, and she should have realized there'd be a "then"
because such instructions usually came on a need-to-
know basis, she had to drive them both home. It was
obvious, with hindsight, that there would be something
that justified the sensitivity required.

Her stomach growled. She hadn't had time for her
own dinner. And her father never saw the need to keep
a wee stash of food in the glove compartment. There'd
be all sorts of gourmet delicacies in the discreet fridge
in the back but she could hardly ask them to pass her
something over. Not appropriate at the best of times.
Even less so tonight. She'd had to make do with crunch-

ing her way through the roll of breath mints she kept in her pocket.

At a set of lights she glanced in the rearview mirror and rolled her eyes. If the palace had thought that sensitivity was required because there might be shenanigans in the backseat, they needn't have worried. Adam and his date were deep in conversation; both looked utterly serious, as though they were solving the problems of the world. Maybe they were. Maybe that was what princes and scholars did on dates. And Danni should probably be grateful that someone had more on their mind than what they were going to be able to unearth for dinner from the shelves of the fridge.

Still, she would have thought the point of the date was to get to know one another. Not to solve the problems of the world, not to discuss topics with such utter earnestness that they looked like two members of the supreme court about to hand down a judgment. Danni sighed. Who was she to know about royal protocol? Things were different in Adam's world. They always had been. Even as a teen he'd seemed to carry the weight of the world on his shoulders. Had taken his responsibilities and his duties seriously. Too seriously, she'd thought.

What she did know was that Adam was on the lookout for a suitable wife.

And one of the prospective candidates was in the backseat with him.

At thirty-one years old, he was expected—by his father and by the country, if the media were to be believed—to do the right thing. The right thing meant getting married, settling down and providing heirs, preferably male, to continue the Marconi line and to ensure succession.

If anyone had cared to ask Danni, she'd have happily shared her opinion that what the prince needed was to shake things up a little, not to settle down. She'd always thought the narrow focus of his life stopped him from seeing what was really there—the variety and opportunities. And for as long as he kept that narrow focus, it stopped anyone else from seeing who he could be, if he only let himself.

For Adam, finding the right woman meant dating. Romantic dinners like the one she'd just picked him up from in the revolving restaurant that towered above the new part of the city.

Maybe, instead of dwelling on Adam, Danni should be trying to pick up a few pointers on how a real woman comported herself on a date. She glanced in the back. Obviously sitting up straight was important, manicured hands folded demurely in the lap, polite smiles, what looked like polite laughter, occasional fluttering of long dark eyelashes, a slight tilt to the head exposing a pale slender neck.

Who was she kidding? Danni didn't do fluttering. And manicuring with the life she led—working in the motor-racing industry—was a waste of time and money.

She might sometimes wish she wasn't seen quite so much as one of the boys by all her male colleagues, but she knew she couldn't go so far as to look and behave like a Barbie clone. Scratch that, even Barbie had more personality than the woman in the backseat seemed to. Didn't they make a Pilot Barbie and NASCAR Barbie? Although she'd never heard of a Speak-Your-Mind Barbie or a Put-Your-Foot-In-Your-Mouth Barbie. Danni mentally pulled herself up. She was taking out her insecurities and inadequacies on a woman she didn't even know.

She glanced up, again determined to think better of the couple in the backseat. No. Surely not? But yes, a second glance confirmed that Adam did indeed have his laptop out, and that both he and his date were pointing at something on the screen.

"Way to romance a woman, Adam," she muttered.

He couldn't possibly have heard, not with the privacy screen up and her speaker off, but Adam glanced up, and for a fraction of a second his gaze brushed over hers in the mirror. Danni bit her tongue. Hard. Fortunately there was no flicker of recognition in his dark eyes. His gaze didn't pause; it swept over hers as if she was invisible, or of no more importance than the back of her headrest. That was good. If only she could trust in it.

Because she wasn't supposed to be driving for him.

Because he'd banned her. Actually, it wasn't an official ban. He'd only intimated that he no longer wanted her to drive for him. But in palace circles an intimation by Adam was as good as a ban. Nothing official was necessary.

Though, honestly, no reasonable person would blame her for the coffee incident. The pothole had been unavoidable. She sighed. It wasn't like she needed the job then or now. Then she'd had her studies to pursue and now she had her career as part of the team bringing a Grand Prix to San Philippe.

But, she reminded herself, her father did need the job. For his sense of self and his purpose in life, if not for the money. Close to retirement age, he'd begun to live in fear of being replaced in the job that gave his life meaning. The job that his father and his father's father before him had held.

Danni didn't look in the mirror again, not into the backseat anyway. She consoled herself with the fact that her unofficial banning had been five years ago while driving on her summer break, and surely Adam, with far more important things to think about, would have forgotten it. And definitely have forgiven her. In those intervening years he'd become a stranger to her. So she drove, taking no shortcuts, to San Philippe's premier hotel and eased to a stop beneath the portico.

"Wait here." Adam's deep voice, so used to command, sounded through the speaker system.

A hotel valet opened the rear door, and Adam and the perfectly elegant Ms. Fulbright Scholar with the endless legs exited. Clara. That was her name.

Wait here could mean anything from thirty seconds to thirty minutes, to hours—she'd had it happen before with other passengers. He was seeing a woman home from a date; Danni had no idea if it was their first or second or something more. Maybe Clara would invite him in. Maybe she'd slide his tie undone and tear that stuffy suit jacket off his broad shoulders and drag him into her hotel room, her lips locked on his, making him stop thinking and start feeling, her fingers threading into his dark hair, dropping to explore his perfectly honed chest. Whoa. Danni put the brakes on her thought processes hearing the mental screech that was in part a protest at just how quickly her mind had gone down that track and just how vividly it had provided the images of a shirtless Adam.

Danni had grown up on the palace estates, so yes,

despite their five-year age difference they'd sometimes played together, as had all the children living on the palace grounds. There was a time when she'd thought of him as almost a friend. Certainly as her ally and some-time protector. So she couldn't entirely see him as just a royal, but he would be Crown Prince one day. And she *knew* she wasn't supposed to imagine the Crown Prince shirtless. She also knew that she could too easily have gone further still with her imaginings.

Besides, Danni hadn't picked up any of those types of signals from the couple in the back, but then again, what did she know. Maybe well brought up, cultured people did things differently. Maybe they were better at hiding their simmering passions.

She eased lower in her seat, cranked up the stereo and pulled down the brim of her cap over her eyes to block out all the light from the hotel. The good thing about driving for the royal family was that at least she wouldn't be told to move on.

She leapt up again when she felt and heard the rear door open. "Holy—"

Minutes. He'd only been minutes. She jabbed at the stereo's off button. The sound faded as Adam slid back into the car.

Utterly unruffled. Not so much as a mismatched button, a hair out of place, or even a lipstick smudge. No flush to his skin. He looked every bit as serious as before as he leaned back in his seat. Nothing soft or softened about him. Even the bump on his nose that should have detracted from the perfection of his face somehow added to it. Or maybe that was just wishful thinking.

Had they even kissed?

Danni shook her head and eased away from the hotel. She shouldn't care. She didn't care.

Normally, with any other passenger she'd say something. Just a "Pleasant evening, sir?" At times a chauffeur served as a sort of butler on wheels. But Adam wasn't any other passenger, and with his head tipped back and his eyes closed, he clearly wasn't needing conversation from her. Long may the silence last. She'd have him back to the palace in fifteen minutes. Then she'd be free. She'd have pulled it off. Without incident. Her father would be back tomorrow. No one would be any the wiser.

Finally, a quarter of an hour later, she flexed her fingers as the second set of palace gates eased open. Minutes later, she drew to a sedate stop in front of the entrance to Adam's wing, the wheels crunching quietly on the gravel. Nobody knew what it cost her, the restraint she exercised, in never once skidding to a stop or better yet finishing with a perfectly executed handbrake slide, lining up the rear door precisely with the entrance. But she could imagine it. The advanced security and high-performance modules of her training had been her favorite parts.

Her smile dimmed when the valet who ought to be opening the door failed to materialize. Too late, Danni remembered her father complaining about Adam dispensing with that tradition at his private residence. Her father had been as appalled as if Adam had decided to stop wearing shoes in public. Danni didn't have a problem with it. Except for now. Now, Adam could hardly open his own door while he was asleep.

There was nothing else for it. She got out, walked around the back of the car and after a quick scan of the surroundings opened Adam's door then stood to the side, facing away from him. She'd hoped the fact that the car had stopped and the noise and motion, albeit slight, of the door being opened would wake him. When he didn't appear after a few seconds she turned and bent to look into the car.

Her heart gave a peculiar flip. Adam's eyes were still closed and finally his face and his mouth had softened, looking not at all serious and unreachable. Looking instead lush and sensuous. And really, he had unfairly gorgeous eyelashes—thick and dark. And he smelled divine. She almost wanted to lean in closer, to inhale more deeply.

"Adam," she said quietly. Right now she'd have been more comfortable with "sir" or "your highness" because she suddenly felt the need for the appropriate distance and formality, to stop her from thinking inappropriate and way too informal thoughts of the heir apparent. To stop her from wanting to touch that small bump on the bridge of his nose. But one of the things Adam had always insisted on was that the personal staff, particularly the ones who'd effectively grown up with him in the palace circles, use his name.

He was trying to be a prince of the times. Secretly she thought he might have been happier and more comfortable a century or two ago.

"Adam." She tried to speak a little louder but her voice came out as a hoarse whisper. Danni swallowed. All she had to do was wake him and then back out of the car. She leaned closer, steeling herself to try again. Ordering her voice to be normal. It was only Adam after all. She'd known him most of her life though five years and infinite degrees in rank separated them.

His eyes flew open. His gaze locked on hers and for a second, darkened. Not a hint of lethargy there. Danni's mouth ran suddenly dry. "Can I help you?" he asked, his voice low and silky with a hint of mockery as though he knew she'd been staring. Fascinated.

Disconcerted by the intimacy she'd imagined in his gaze, she responded with an unfamiliar heat quivering through her. "Yes. You can help me by waking up and getting out of my car."

"Your car, Danielle?" He lifted one eyebrow.

"Your car. But I'm the one who still needs to drive it round to the garage," she snapped. Oops. Definitely not supposed to snap at the prince, no matter how shocked at herself she was. Definitely not appropriate. But her curt response seemed almost to please him because the corners of his lips twitched. And then, too soon, flattened again.

Danni swallowed. She needed to backpedal. Fast. "We've reached the palace. I trust you had a pleasant evening." She used her blandest voice as she backed out of the car. Stick to the script. That was all she had to do.

Adam followed her and stood, towering over her, his gaze contemplative. "Very. Thank you."

"Really?" She winced. That so was not in the script. What had happened to her resolve to be a shadow?

His gaze narrowed, changing from contemplative to enquiring with a hint of accusation. "You doubt me, Danielle?" A cold breeze wrapped around her.

Well, yes. But she could hardly say that and she oughtn't to lie. She searched for a way around it. "No one would know other than yourself."

"No, they wouldn't."

She willed him to just step away from the car. Go on into the palace. Get on with saving the nation and the world. Then she could close the door and drive away and get something to eat. And it would be as if tonight had never happened. There would be no repercussions. Not for her and not for her father.

But he didn't move. He stood absolutely still. Her stomach rumbled into the silence.

"You haven't eaten?"

"I'm fine."

Again the silence. Awkward and strained. If he would just go.

He stood still. Watching her. "I didn't realize you were driving for us again. I thought you were in the States."

"I was for a while. I came back." Three-and-a-half years ago she had moved back for good. "But this is temporary, just for tonight in fact. I'm staying with Dad and he had something come up." Danni held her breath. Did he remember the ban? Would it matter now?

He nodded and she let out her breath. "Everything's all right with him?"

"Absolutely. A sick friend. He'll be back tomorrow."

"Good." Adam turned to go into the palace and then just when she thought she was free, turned back. "What was it you said?"

"He'll be back tomorrow."

"Not then. Earlier. When you were driving."

All manner of desperate, inappropriate words raced through her mind. No, no, no. He couldn't have heard.

"I can't remember." So much for her principles. She was lying through her teeth.

"It was around the time I got the laptop out to show

Clara the geographic distribution of lava from the 1300 eruption of Ducal Island."

She did roll her eyes then; she couldn't help it. He was too much. "My point exactly," she said, throwing her hand up in surrender. "I said, 'Way to romance a woman, Adam.' Really. The geographic distribution of lava?"

His expression went cold.

There was a line somewhere in the receding distance, one she'd long since stepped over. Her only hope was to make him see the truth of her assertions. "Come on, Adam. You weren't always this stuffy." She'd known him when he was still a boy becoming a man. And later she'd occasionally seen glimpses of an altogether different man beneath the surface when he'd forgotten, however briefly, who he was supposed to be and just allowed himself to act naturally.

Now wasn't that time.

His brows shot up. But Danni couldn't stop herself.

"What woman wants to talk about lava and rock formations on a date?" Too late, Danni remembered the saying about how when you found yourself in a hole the best course of action was to stop digging.

The brows, dark and heavy, drew together. "Clara is a Fulbright scholar. She studied geology. She was interested."

"Maybe she was. But surely she can read a textbook for that kind of thing. It's great if you're planning a lecture tour together but it's hardly romantic. Where's the poetry, the magic, in that? You weren't even looking into her eyes, you were looking at the screen. And did you even kiss her when you escorted her to her door?"

"I'm not sure that's any of your business, but yes."
Somehow he'd made himself taller.

She wasn't going to be intimidated. "Some kiss,
huh?"

"And you'd be an expert on kissing and on romance?
What would you suggest? Discussing the specifications
of the Bentley perhaps?"

Danni took a little step back as though that could
distance her from the stab of hurt. She liked cars. She
couldn't help that. Wouldn't want to, even if Adam, who
she knew for a fact also liked cars, considered it a failing in a woman. "No. I'm not an expert on romance.
But I am a woman."

"You're sure about that?"

This time she didn't even try to hide her mortification. She took a much bigger step back. Her heart
thumped, seeming to echo in her chest. She clamped
shut the jaw that had fallen open.

Her uniform—a dark jacket and pants—had been
designed for men and adapted for her, the only female
driver. It was well tailored but it wasn't exactly feminine. It wasn't supposed to be. And it was nothing like
Clara's soft pink dress that had revealed expanses of
skin and floated over her lush curves. Danni had always
been something of a tomboy and preferred practicality
along with comfort but she still had feelings and she
had pride and Adam had just dented both. Adam, whose
opinion shouldn't matter to her. But apparently did.

Shock spread over his face. Shock and remorse. He
reached for her then dropped his hand. "Danni, I didn't
mean it like that. I meant I still see you as a kid. It still
surprises me that you're even old enough to have your
license."

She shoved the hurt down, tried to replace it with defiance. "I got my license over a decade ago. And you're not that much older than me."

"I know I'm not. It just feels like it sometimes."

"True." It had always felt that way. Adam had always seemed older. Distant. Unreachable.

He sighed and closed his eyes. When he opened them again he said, "I'm sure you're a fine woman, but it hardly qualifies you to give me dating advice. I've known enough women."

"I'm sure you have," she said quietly. Of late there had been quite the string of them. All of them beautiful, intelligent and worldly, with much to recommend them for the position of future princess. But despite those apparent recommendations, he'd seldom dated the same woman twice. And never, to her knowledge, a third time. She didn't mean to keep track, but a glance at the papers on any given day, even if only when lighting the fire in her father's gatehouse, kept track for her. But it certainly wasn't her place to comment and the implied criticism would centuries ago have cost her her head.

She was thankful for the fact that beheadings hadn't been legal for several centuries because judging by the displeasure in Adam's eyes, he just might have been in favor of the practice right about now. For a moment she actually thought he might lose his legendary cool. She couldn't even feel triumph. There had been a time when, egged on by Adam's younger brother Rafe, flapping the unflappable Adam had been a pastime for the small group of children raised on the palace estate. But she was still too preoccupied with covering her own hurt to feel anything akin to satisfaction.

Adam drew himself taller. The barrier of remoteness shuttered his face, hardened his jaw. "I apologize, Danielle. Unreservedly. Thank you for your services tonight. They won't be required in future."

Sacked. He'd sacked her again.

Danni was still stung by her run-in with Adam the next night as she and her father ate their minestrone in front of the fire. Soup and a movie was their Sunday night tradition.

They finished the first half of the tradition and settled in for the movie. A big bowl of buttery popcorn sat on the coffee table and an action adventure comedy was ready to go in the DVD player, just waiting for her press of the button.

Usually, when she was in San Philippe she came round from her apartment for the evening. But her place was being redecorated so she'd been staying with her father for the last week. She had yet to tell him about the fiasco last night. Tonight would be the perfect opportunity.

But she hadn't fully recovered from the experience.

Although she pretended to herself that she was indifferent, at odd moments the latter part of the evening resurfaced and replayed itself in her head. She should have done everything so differently. Starting with keeping her mouth shut in the first place.

As head driver, her father had a right to know what had happened. Would expect to know. But she hadn't been able to tell him. Because more than head driver, he was her father and he'd be so disappointed in her. And she hated disappointing the man who'd done so much for her and who asked so little of her.

It had occurred to her that if she just kept quiet, he

need never know. It's not as if she'd ever be driving for Adam again.

Besides, her silence was justified because her father was still so saddened by the visit to his friend. She wanted to alleviate, not add, to that sorrow. At least that was her excuse. The movie they were about to watch would be the perfect tonic. The fact that it featured an awesome and realistic car chase scene would be an added bonus. And they'd both once met the main stunt driver.

It didn't matter, she told herself, if she never drove for Adam again. It was such a rare occurrence in the first place it was hardly going to make any difference. And she knew Adam wouldn't let it have any bearing on her father's position within the palace staff. No. Their exchange had been personal. He'd keep it so. That was part of his code.

She'd just found the television remote when three sharp knocks sounded at the door. Her father looked at her, his curiosity matching hers. He moved to stand but Danni held up her hand. "Stay there. I'll get it."

Visitors were rare, particularly without notice. Because her father lived on the palace grounds, in what had once been the gatehouse, friends couldn't just drop by on a whim.

Danni opened the door.

This was no friend.

Two

"Adam." Danni couldn't quite keep the shock from her voice. Was this about last night or was there some further trouble she had gotten into?

"Danielle." His face was unreadable. "I'd like to talk to you. May I come in?"

After the briefest hesitation she stepped back, giving him access. Much as instinct and pride screamed to do otherwise, you didn't refuse the heir to the throne when he asked to come in. But to her knowledge, the last time Adam had been on this doorstep looking for her was fifteen years ago when he and Rafe had turned up to invite her to join in the game of baseball they were organizing. She couldn't quite remember the reason for the game—something to do with a leadership project Rafe had been doing for school. What she remembered with absolute clarity was how badly that endeavor had ended.

Adam stepped into the small entranceway, dominating the space. He smelled good. Reminding her of last night. By rights she should loathe the scent linked with her mortification rather than want to savor it. She heard her father standing up from the couch in the living room behind her.

"St. Claire." Adam smiled at her father. "Nothing important. I wanted a word with Danielle if I may."

"Of course. I'll just pop out to the workshop."

Danni didn't want her father to hear whatever it was Adam was about to say because despite his apparent efforts at geniality it couldn't possibly be good. Nor did she want her father to go because while he was here Adam might actually have to refrain from saying whatever it was that had brought him here.

"Working on another project?" Adam asked.

A smile lit her father's face as he came to join them in the foyer. "A model airplane. Tiger Moth. I should have it finished in a few more months. A nice manageable project." Both men smiled.

Not long after Danni and her father's return to San Philippe when she was five, he'd inherited the almost unrecognizable remnants of a Type 49 Bugatti.

For years the Bugatti had been an ongoing project occupying all of his spare time. It had been therapy for him following the end of his marriage to Danni's mother.

There had been nothing awful about her parents' marriage, aside from the fact that their love for each other wasn't enough to overcome their love for their respective home countries. Her father was miserable in America and her mother was miserable in San Philippe.

And for a few years, after his mother's death, Adam

had helped her father on the car. Danni too had joined them, her primary role being to sit on the workbench and watch and pass tools. And to remind them when it was time to stop and eat. Building the car had been therapy, and a distraction for all of them. She had an early memory of sitting in the car with Adam after her father had finished for the evening. Adam, probably no more than eleven, had entertained her by pretending to drive her, complete with sound effects, to imaginary destinations.

By the time Danni was fifteen none of them needed the therapy so much anymore. Adam, busy with schooling and life, had long since stopped calling around. Her father sold the still unfinished car to a collector. Parts had been a nightmare to either source or make and time had been scarce. Though Danni had later come to suspect, guiltily, that the timing of the sale may have had something to do with the fact that her mother had been lobbying for her to go to college in the States. And fees weren't cheap.

Her father shut the door behind him and she and Adam turned to face one another. Adam's gaze swept over her, a frown creasing his brow. She looked down at her jeans and sweater, her normal casual wear. Definitely not palace standard but she wasn't at the palace.

Silence loomed.

"Sit down." Danni gestured through to the living room and the couch recently vacated by her father.

"No, that's...okay." The uncertainty was uncharacteristic. Seeming to change his mind, Adam walked through to the living room and sat.

Danni followed and sat on the armchair, watching, wary.

"I have to apologize."

Not this again. "You did that."

Adam suddenly stood and crossed to the fireplace. "Not for…that. Though I am still sorry. And I do still maintain that I didn't mean it the way you took it. You're obviously—"

"Then what for?" She cut him off before he could damn her femininity with faint praise.

"For sacking you."

She almost laughed. "It's not my real job, Adam. I have the Grand Prix work. I was covering for Dad as a favor. The loss is no hardship."

"But I need to apologize because I want you to drive for me again."

This time the silence was all hers as she stared at him.

Finally she found her voice. "Thanks, but no thanks. Like I said, the loss was no hardship. I think I demonstrated why I'm the last person you want as your driver."

"Yes, you are the last person I want as my driver because you're so perceptive and so blunt you make me uncomfortable. But unfortunately I think I need you."

She made *him* uncomfortable? And he *needed* her? Curious as she was she wasn't going to ask. His statements, designed to draw her in, to lower her defenses, had all the makings of a trap. Warning bells clamored. She just wanted Adam to leave. "I don't know what you're playing at." She stood up and crossed to him, looking into his face, trying to read the thoughts he kept hidden behind indecipherable eyes. "You don't need me. There are any number of palace drivers, and I don't need the job. Seems pretty clear-cut to me."

"I could ask Wrightson," he said with obvious reluctance.

The younger man her father saw as his chief rival. "Or Dad," she suggested.

He shook his head. "I try not to use your father for the nighttime work."

She knew he did that in deference to her father's age and seniority. But her father wouldn't necessarily see it as a favor. He didn't like to think he was getting older.

"Besides, it's not just driving that I need." Adam studied her for several seconds longer and she could see him fighting some kind of internal battle. Finally he spoke again. "I called Clara this morning to ask her out again."

"You don't think that was too soon?"

"Maybe that's what it was. But I don't have time, or the inclination, for games."

"Oh." Danni's stomach sank in sympathy. This wasn't going to be good. She just knew it.

Adam rested his elbow on the mantel and stared into the fire. "She said she valued my friendship."

"Ouch."

"But that there had been no romance." A frown creased his brow. "No spark."

"Ahh." Danni didn't dare say anything more.

"That I hadn't even looked into her eyes when I was speaking to her. Not properly. That I was too uptight." He looked into Danni's eyes now, as though probing for answers.

"Mmm." She tried desperately to shield her thoughts—that he just had to look at someone with a portion of the intensity he was directing at her, and if that intensity was transformed into something like, oh say, desire, the woman at the receiving end would have only two choices, melt into a puddle or jump his bones. Danni glanced away.

"So—" he took a deep breath and blew it out "—you were right. Everything you said."

"Anyone could have seen it," she said gently.

"Sadly, you're probably right about that, too. The thing is, not anyone would have pointed it out to me. I don't know who else I can trust to be that honest with me and I can't think who else I'd trust enough to let as close as I'm going to have to let you. I can admit my weaknesses to you and you alone because you already seem to know them."

She knew being who he was had to be lonely and undoubtedly more so since Rafe, his closest confidante, had married. The fact that Rafe had married the woman intended as Adam's bride might not have helped either. But he brought much of his isolation on himself. He didn't let people close. And she shouldn't let his problems be hers. But somewhere in there, in the fact that he had a level of trust for her, was a compliment. Or maybe not. Maybe she was the next best thing to another brother.

She didn't know what to say. Her head warned her to just say no.

He was staring at the fire again. "It's imperative that I marry a woman who'll make a good princess, someone who can lead the country with me. And I know what I'm looking for in that regard. I know my requirements."

"Your requirements?" Wasn't that just like him. "Please don't tell me you have a prioritized list somewhere on your laptop."

He looked sharply at her, but spoke slowly. "All right, I won't tell you that."

Danni slapped her head. "You do, don't you?"

"I said I wouldn't tell you."

"For pity's sake, Adam."

A wry smile touched his lips.

"You do need help."

"Not with my list or what's on it. That's nonnegotiable. I just need help with being a better me and a much better date."

She shook her head. "You don't need help being a better you. You just have to let people see the real you, not the *you* that you think you have to be."

He hesitated. "So you'll help me?"

Had she just put her foot into a trap that was starting to close? "I haven't said that. I'd like to, Adam, really I would. But I don't have time. I'm only staying with Dad for a couple more weeks while I'm on leave and my apartment's being redecorated."

He raised his eyebrows. "It's that big a job? Making me into a better date? It's going to require more than a couple weeks?"

"No. I'm sure it's not."

"Then it won't take up much of your time, will it?"

She chewed her lip as she shook her head. When she was ten, Adam, who'd had a broken leg at the time, had taught her to play chess. Over the next few years when he came back on summer vacation he always made time to play her at least once or twice. But no matter how much she'd studied and practiced he'd always been able to maneuver her unawares into a corner and into checkmate.

"For so long I haven't really had to try with women

and…after Michelle I didn't really want to. I've almost forgotten how."

Michelle, whom he'd dated several years ago, well before the advent of Rafe's wife Lexie, was the last woman he'd been linked seriously with. They'd looked like the perfect couple, well matched in so many respects. An engagement had been widely expected. Then suddenly they'd broken up, and Michelle was now engaged to another member of Adam's polo team.

"What about your mystery woman?"

He frowned. Not annoyed, but perplexed. "What mystery woman?"

"Palace gossip has it that…"

"Go on." The frown deepened.

"It doesn't matter."

"Danni? What palace gossip?"

She took a deep breath. "Rumor has it that whenever you get free time, you disappear for an hour or two. When you come back you're generally in a good mood and you've often showered."

The frown cleared from his face and he threw back his head and laughed like she hadn't heard him laugh in years. The sound pleased and warmed her inordinately. "Does this mean there's no mystery woman?" she asked when he stopped laughing.

He was still doing his best to quell his amusement. "There's no woman, mysterious or otherwise."

"Then where—"

"Let's get back on track. Because there does need to be a woman, the right one, and I think you can help. This is important, Danni. All I really want is your insight and a few pointers. It won't take a lot of your time."

Danni hesitated.

"Is there something or…someone you need that time for?"

She didn't want to admit there wasn't. There had been no someone since the rally driver she'd been dating dropped her as soon as he started winning and realized that with success came women—beautiful, glamorous women.

"You'll be compensated."

He correctly interpreted her silence as admission that there wasn't anyone. But the offer of remuneration was insulting. "I wouldn't want that. You wouldn't have to pay me."

"So you'll do it?"

"But you think finding the right woman is about lists and boxes you can check off, and it's not."

"That's why I need you. Lists and tickable boxes are part of it and you'll have to accept that, but I know there's more. I want more." He paused. "I want what Rafe has."

Danni stifled a gasp. "You want Lexie?"

"No." The word was vehement and a look of disbelief and disappointment crossed his face. "I just meant he found someone to marry. Someone he could be happy with."

"She was supposed to be yours," Danni said quietly, daring to voice the suspicion she'd harbored.

"Only according to my father. We, Lexie and I, never had anything." As far as Danni could tell, Adam seemed to be telling the truth and she wanted to believe him. But it was common knowledge that Crown Prince Henri had at one point intended that the American heiress with a distant claim to the throne herself would be the perfect partner, politically, for Adam. "And to be honest," Adam continued, "I'm inclined to believe my father's later assertion that he'd always intended for Lexie and Rafe to be together. He wanted Rafe to settle down and rein in his ways, but he knew Rafe would rebel against any overt matchmaking."

Rafe had been charged with escorting Lexie to San Philippe to meet Adam. By all accounts the two had fought falling in love almost from the time they laid eyes on one another. When Rafe and Lexie finally gave in to their feelings, they utterly derailed the Crown Prince's perceived plans and Rafe's carefree bachelor existence. They'd since married and now had a beautiful baby girl. Rafe had never looked happier. And while to all outward appearances Adam had also seemed more than happy with the arrangement, Danni had always wondered. A little.

He shook his head as he watched her. "You don't believe it?"

She shrugged.

"I like Lexie." He sighed heavily as though this wasn't the first time he'd had to explain himself. "In fact, I love her. But as a sister. It was obvious from the start that it was never going to work for us. We just didn't connect."

"She's beautiful. And vivacious."

"She's both those things. But she wasn't for me. And I wasn't for her."

Danni nodded, almost, but not quite, buying it.

He must have read that shred of doubt in her eyes. "I'll tell you something on pain of death and only because it will help you believe me."

"You don't have to."

"I think I do." Adam glanced away looking almost embarrassed. "On our first date…"

A log shifted and settled in the fire as she waited for him to continue.

"I fell asleep."

She covered her mouth. "No."

"I'd been working hard, putting in some long hours. The timing was off. Dad never should have had her brought out then." He reeled off his excuses. "But anyway, we went to dinner at the same place I went with Clara, we had a lovely meal and on the drive home…" He shrugged. "It was inexcusable. But it happened."

"Was my father driving?"

Adam nodded.

"That explains why he's always been adamant that you were okay with Rafe and Lexie."

"I'm more than okay with it. But I've seen how happy they are, and Rebecca and Logan, as well."

Hard on the heels of his brother finding love his sister, Rebecca, had, as well. Her wedding to Logan, a self-made millionaire from Chicago, would be in two months. "And I wonder…"

"If you can have it, too?" Probably every single person in country had wondered the same thing, the fairy tale come true. Danni certainly had.

He sighed. "It's not realistic though. Not with the life I lead. The constraints on it, constraints that whoever marries me will have to put up with."

He'd deny himself love? Deny himself even the chance at it? And for someone as smart as he was, his reasoning was screwy. "Don't you see? That's why it's more important than ever that there's love. That she knows, whatever the constraints, that you, the real you—" She touched her fingertips just above his heart and the room seemed to shrink. She snatched her hand away. "—are worth it."

Adam's gaze followed her hand. "So, you'll help me?"

Danni hesitated.

A fatal mistake.

"I have a date on Friday." He spoke into the silence of her hesitation. "If you could drive for me then you'll be doing me and my father and the country a favor."

"So it's my patriotic duty?"

"I wouldn't quite put it like that but…" He shrugged. "I don't know if you've heard, but the doctors have told Dad to ease up on work and watch his stress levels. This is one way I can help. So, I need to expedite this process. I want a date for Rebecca and Logan's wedding, and I can't take just anyone. It has to be someone I'm seeing seriously. So that means I need to be working on it now. We've only got two months."

Danni sighed heavily. "See? Your whole approach is wrong. It's not a *transaction* that you can *expedite*. You can't put time limits on things like this."

"This is why I need your help. As a friend."

"You might think you want my help, but I remember you well enough to know that you don't take advice or criticism well. Especially not from me."

"No," he agreed. "But I'm not looking for criticism as such, just pointers."

"You might see my pointers as criticism."

"I'll try not to." Sincere, with the merest hint of a smile.

There was a time when she practically hero-worshipped Adam and would have done anything he asked of her. So she had to fight the unquestioning instinct to agree to his request. Just because it wasn't a big job and she had a little time on her hands didn't mean it was a good idea. She hadn't been this hesitant about anything since her skydiving course last year. She needed to know what she'd be getting into and she needed Adam to know she wasn't that blindly devoted girl anymore. "Normal rules would have to not apply. Because if I agree to do this, there could well be things I want to say to you that usually I absolutely wouldn't."

"This is sounding ominous."

"It won't work if I don't have the freedom to speak my mind."

He hesitated. "If you do this for me, then I'll accept that much." His dark eyes were earnest. "I'd appreciate it, Danni." When she was younger he'd called her Danni. But somewhere along the way as they'd both gotten older, and he'd gone away to school and become even more serious, formality had crept into their relationship and he'd switched to calling her Danielle with rare exceptions. Calling her Danni now brought back recollections of those easier times. He touched a finger to the small bump on his nose. Just briefly. The gesture looked almost unconscious, and she'd seen him make it before. But it never failed to make her feel guilty. Did he know that? Was it part of persuading her that she owed him?

Whether he knew it or not, it worked. "I don't know how much help I can be."

He recognized her capitulation. She could see the guarded triumph in his eyes, the almost imperceptible easing to his shoulders.

"I can't guarantee anything. Like you pointed out, I'm no expert on romance."

"But as *you* pointed out, you are a woman. And I trust you."

She sucked in a deep breath, about to make a last-minute attempt at getting out of this.

"I'll be seeing Anna DuPont. She fits all my criteria. I've met her a couple times socially and I think there's potential for us. Drive for us. Please."

He could, if he chose, all but order her to do it, make it uncomfortable for her or her father if she refused, but his request felt so sincere and so personal—just between the two of them—that the hero worship she'd once felt kicked in and she was nodding almost before she realized it. "One date," she said, trying to claim back some control. "I'll drive you for one date."

Three

On Friday, Danni pulled up to Adam's wing of the palace in the Bentley. The sandstone building towered above her, the shadows seeming to hide secrets and to mock her for how little she knew. What had she gotten herself into? There was no protocol for this situation, for being part driver, part honest adviser, part friend. She took a fortifying breath. All she could do was to stick with what she knew and maybe trust her instincts. At least she wouldn't be expected to guard her tongue quite as closely as normal.

She got out and waited by the passenger door while he was notified of her arrival. On those occasions she had driven for him in the past, he'd been scrupulously punctual. Tonight was no different. As the clock on the distant tower chimed seven, he appeared, stepping out into a pool of light.

Danni looked at him and couldn't figure out whether this was going to be ridiculously easy or ridiculously difficult.

She was still shaking her head as he stopped in front of her. "You have something to say? Already?"

"Yes. You're wearing a suit and tie."

"Yes."

"You're going to have dinner at the riverside jazz festival?"

"Yes." He managed to make that single word of agreement intimidating.

But it was clearly time for some of the honesty he'd said he trusted her to voice. "Nobody wears a suit and tie to a jazz festival."

"I do."

"Not tonight. This is not a state dinner." She held out her upturned palm. "Hand over the tie." For a moment Danni thought he might refuse. "You want my help?"

Gritting his teeth, he loosened his tie and slid it from around his neck. He dropped the strip of fabric into her hand. "Satisfied?"

She closed her fingers around the warm silk. "No."

"No?"

"The top button." She nodded at the neck of his shirt.

His lips pressed together but he reached up, undid the button then dropped his hand and looked at her patiently. Obviously waiting for her approval. But he still didn't look quite right. He still looked tense and formal. A little fierce almost.

"And the next one."

He opened his mouth, about to protest, she was certain, then closed it again and slowly undid the second button.

"Much better," she said. "Just that extra button makes you look far more relaxed, almost casual. In a good way," she added before he could object. She wanted to tousle his hair, mess it up just a little but knew that tousled hair would be a step too far for Adam. Tonight anyway. Maybe they could work on that. She settled for reaching up and spreading his collar a little wider. "See, this vee of chest?" She pointed at what she meant, at what riveted her gaze. "Women like that. It's very appealing."

"It is?"

"Definitely. And you smell really good. That's always a bonus." She was close enough to know. Without thinking she closed her eyes and inhaled. And the image of a shirtless Adam—branded in her memory—came back. The image had lurked there since the incident that had gotten her banned from driving. Her shortcut, the potholes, the spilling of his coffee that had required him to change his shirt in the back of the limo. Oh, yes. She'd seen him shirtless then. An unthinking glimpse in the rearview mirror of a broad contoured torso and sculpted abs. More than appealing. A fleeting moment of stunned and heated eye contact. It was a sight that had left her breathless and slightly dazed and slipped into her dreams. His banning her after that episode had almost been a relief.

She opened her eyes now to find him studying her, curiosity in his gaze and something like confusion. Despite the cool night Danni felt suddenly warmer. This new role was an adjustment for both of them. The normal boundaries of protocol and etiquette had blurred—they had to—but it left her floundering. Maybe she ought not to have admitted with such enthusiasm that his chest was appealing or that he smelled good. But surely if she was going to criticize and point out where she thought he went wrong, then she also needed to point out where she thought he went right.

She reached for his door, opened it wide.

She slipped his tie into her pocket, stepped back and gestured to the open door. "Let's go find your princess."

An hour later boredom was setting in. Just another reason, she reminded herself, why she'd never have made a good chauffeur. No matter how much her father would have liked it for her.

Danni fiddled with the radio again, adjusted her seat and her mirrors, and then leaned over and opened the glove compartment. A white card stood propped up inside. Definitely not regulation. Frowning, she pulled out the card. Across the front in strong sloping letters it read, "Just in case." Behind the card sat a white card-board box. Curious, Danni pulled it out and opened it. Neatly arranged inside was a selection of gourmet snacks.

The thoughtfulness of the gesture had her grinning and taking back any uncharitable thoughts she'd ever had about Adam.

Another hour passed, during which Danni snacked and read, before Adam and his date walked out of the restaurant. Was that a hint of a stagger to the fashion-model-slender Anna's gait as she laughed and leaned against Adam? Perhaps having so little body fat meant she was just cold and needed to absorb some of his heat.

But the impression Danni got was that there had been no shortage of the champagne that they'd started—at her suggestion—on the way to the restaurant.

Anna somehow managed to stay plastered to Adam as they got into the backseat. At a nod from him—and a brief moment of eye contact, Danni drove off.

At the first set of traffic lights, she glanced in the mirror. And then just as quickly looked away.

Anna apparently had no need for eye contact or poetry. Maybe there had been enough of that in the riverside restaurant. She had undone more of Adam's buttons and had slid her hand into the opening. It certainly didn't appear that anyone was cold anymore. The screen between them blocked out most sound but Danni could hear Anna's laughter, throaty and, Danni supposed, sexy. Some men might like it. Some men apparently being Adam.

She thought of the tie still in her pocket and knew that there was something wrong with her because she wanted to pass it back to him and tell him to put it on. But really, carrying on like that, it was undignified. Then again, it was the sort of thing she'd once expected from Rafe, and never thought it was undignified in his case. But the two brothers were different. They always had been. Adam was all about barriers. And the way the woman in the back had bypassed them didn't seem right.

Danni's only consolation was that it looked like her work here was done. He'd been deluding himself if he'd thought he needed her help and she'd been deluding herself if she'd thought she had any to offer. He didn't need help at all. Anna was doing all the work. And they were both clearly enjoying themselves while she did it. Danni would be able to go home and forget all about Adam Marconi and his search for the right woman.

Her grip on the wheel tight and her jaw even tighter,

Danni pulled to a stop in front of Anna's apartment building. And maybe, just maybe, her stop wasn't quite as gentle as it ought to have been.

The couple in the backseat drew apart. Anna trailed her long red fingernails down the front of Adam's shirt. The green-and-gold-uniformed doorman stepped forward to open the car door and the couple got out, Anna still managing to drape herself over Adam. Danni wasn't sure if she was whispering into Adam's ear or trying to eat it. It looked like the latter. Danni rubbed at her own ear in sympathy.

Not wanting to watch her passengers walk to the doorway of Anna's building—public displays of affection held no appeal—she retrieved her book and reclined her seat. She hadn't even found her page when Adam reappeared and slid into the backseat.

"The palace," he said, the words terse. He lowered the privacy screen but said nothing more as she drove through the city and out toward the palace estates. She chanced the occasional glance at him in the mirror. He hadn't fallen asleep though there was a definite weariness about his eyes as he watched the city slide by.

She knew something of his schedule and so she knew that the days and evenings of the previous week had been hectic and full, meetings after functions after openings and launches.

She eased to a careful stop in front of his wing of the palace and met his gaze in the mirror.

"Better," he said.

"Better? Your date?"

"No. The date was decidedly worse. I meant your stopping. Compared to the one in front of Anna's apartment."

Ahh. "I apologize for that. My foot slipped."

"Thank you."

For apologizing or for her foot slipping in the first place? She wasn't going to ask. By the time she'd walked around the back of the car, he'd opened his door and stood. His gaze slid over her from head to toe.

Usually she was good at the whole calm, stoic thing but Danni fought the urge to squirm under his scrutiny, having no idea what he thought when he looked at her. Or maybe it was just the cold making her want to fidget. It was freezing out here tonight. Cold enough for snow.

Her gaze flicked to Adam's shirtfront, still largely unbuttoned. Frowning, as though only just remembering that they were undone, he reached for the lower buttons and slowly did them up. The movement of his fingers held her mesmerized.

It wasn't till he was finished that she remembered what she needed to say. "Thank you, too," she said. "For the food."

"It was no trouble."

And it wouldn't have been. Someone else would have prepared the food and another person would have put it in the car. But it was Adam who'd had the idea and she was still oddly touched by it.

He slid his hands into his pockets and tilted his head toward the palace. "Come in."

"To the palace?"

"Where else? I don't want to talk about the date out here."

Danni looked around. Assorted staff members stood discreet distances away, always at the ready. If she insisted on staying out here she'd only make everyone colder. Besides, she'd been into the palace before. Many times in fact, though not in the last few years. This should be no different. So she shrugged and walked with Adam, went through the door held open by a staff member she didn't recognize. As Adam led her up a flight of stairs and along a corridor hung with gilt-framed portraits, she realized where they were going.

He opened the door to the library. The room, with its floor-to-ceiling shelves of leather-bound books, and armchairs big enough to curl up in, had been her favorite when she was younger. The chess set they used to play on was still here too, nestled in a corner by a window.

Despite the fact that the room had been designed to be restful, Danni was far from relaxed. It had been years since she was last here and in that time her ease in Adam's company and her confidence in their simple friendship had vanished.

In the car she was in charge, of the car at least. Her father's gatehouse was her territory, too, and outside was…outside. A place of freedom. But here, inside the palace, where everything was governed by rules not of her making and many of them outside of her awareness, standing with the heir apparent, she was out of her depth and well out of her comfort zone.

She walked to a side table and set her cap on it then slowly peeled off her gloves, feeling oddly vulnerable without the protection her uniform afforded her. A protection that said *this is who I am and this is who you are.* We're people defined by our roles. But now, as she raked a hand through her hair, she was just Danni and he was Adam. There could never be a *just* in front of his name unless it was used in its opposite meaning.

He was *just* gorgeous. Serious, but gorgeous with those dark eyes that seemed always to be watching and thinking.

Even without the props of her uniform, she knew she had to keep focused on her reason for being here—which had nothing to do with Adam's eyes. Although maybe the eyes had helped sway her, subliminally at least. "So, your date?"

"Let's wait till after dessert."

"Dessert?"

She turned at the sound of a tap on the door. A footman walked in carrying a tray, set it on the low table between two armchairs and then left.

Danni glanced from the tray to Adam.

"I thought you might be hungry."

"Not that hungry!" She looked at the twin slices of cheesecake and the two mugs of cream-topped hot chocolate.

He smiled his first smile of the evening. "It's not all for you."

"But you've just eaten."

He shook his head. "Anna was a salad-only type of woman. No carbohydrates. No dressing. I was hardly going to eat dessert while she'd scarcely touched a thing. As it was, her pushing her lettuce around her plate all evening almost put me off my linguine. And I love linguine. So aside from it being bad manners, I was in no hurry to prolong the evening. By the time the waiter asked if we wanted to order dessert, the future chances for a relationship were crystal clear."

"You've already fed me once tonight." Her mouth watered even as she pretended that she wasn't hungry.

"It was a long evening and that was just a snack. And

unless things have changed drastically from when you were younger, you have—let's call it a healthy appetite and a sweet tooth. And cheesecake was a particular favorite." He watched her. "Have things changed?"

A grin tugged at her lips and her gaze strayed back to the cheesecake. "Apparently not all that much."

He picked up the two bowls. "Sit down then."

Once she was settled in an armchair he passed her a bowl and took the opposite chair.

Danni bit into the tart velvety cheesecake and her eyes almost rolled back in her head in ecstasy while she savored the delight. "Charlebury's still chef?" she asked once she'd opened her eyes again.

Adam laughed. "Yes."

For the next few minutes they ate in appreciative silence. Finally, sated and the dessert finished, Danni set down her bowl.

"Not licking it?" Adam asked, teasing in his tone.

"Trust me, I thought about it. I have only one complaint."

He asked the question with his eyes.

"I don't think I'm going to be able to do the hot chocolate justice now."

"You'll give it your best shot, though?"

"It would be cowardly of me not to at least try. But I think I have to stand and give it a few minutes before I make the attempt." She crossed to one of the long vertical windows. A single snowflake drifted past the narrow pane of glass, lonely and aimless.

The grounds close to the palace were well lit but farther out, the light faded to shadows illuminated only sporadically by pools of brightness for either security or decoration or both. Occasional statues and trees stood spotlighted. And in the distance a building… "I think I can see the gatehouse."

"Beyond the stand of trees to the west?"

"Yes. I don't remember being able to see it from the library."

He lifted a shoulder. "It's been a while since you were here. You're taller."

"I guess. The lights are still on," she said turning her gaze back to the window. "That probably means Dad's fallen asleep watching TV again."

"Do you remember the first time I saw you in here?"

"I try not to." Ever since he mentioned the word *taller* she'd wanted to steer the conversation in a different direction. She watched his reflection in the glass. He frowned. "I'm still a little embarrassed. I remember what I said."

His frown eased to a smile. "That just because I was taller and could reach the higher books and just because I was a prince, didn't make me any better than you."

"Yeah, that. Thanks for the reminder."

He was still smiling, with his eyes at least. "You're welcome."

"I had a little chip on my shoulder."

"No kidding."

"I was new here. Feeling out of place, and a little, no, a lot, intimidated and insecure."

"I knew that."

Danni turned back to him. "You were good to me, telling me that you were glad I didn't think of you as any different because you were a prince, because so many people did treat you differently." Danni laughed. "And then you said that maybe being taller made you a little bit better though." She pointed to a shelf. "Look.

The atlas is still up there. You helped me find America on it. Asked about where I'd come from." He had the people skills even then that made him such a good prince today, made him so well loved by his countrymen.

"I don't want to tarnish my image, but I was supposed to be studying and didn't want to. You were my excuse not to."

She remembered him sitting at the desk, books spread all over it. To her, at five years old, his ten years had made him look almost grown up. Ultimately, the fact that he became her protector and champion till she found her feet had indebted her to him.

For a long time after that she'd worshipped him, refusing to hear a hint of a bad word spoken, even in jest, about him by any of the other palace children.

"So, your date?" Danni prompted, looking back at him. That was why she was here. To help him find the right woman. Not to reminisce. She could return that favor he'd done her all those years ago.

Tension crept back into his shoulders. She ought not to be thinking about smoothing her hand over his brow, or massaging those broad shoulders. "You said the date was worse? I have to say, from where I sat, it looked to be going remarkably well."

Adam shook his head. "Appearances can be deceiving. It turned out we weren't all that compatible. I realized I'd left an important criterion off my list."

"Being?"

"A certain restraint in the consumption of alcohol."

Adam picked up the hot chocolates and carried them over to her. Danni reached for one, wrapping her fingers around the mug. "Anna could just have been nervous. She might actually be shy and reserved and conservative. Maybe she was so nervous she drank more than she would have normally. You can be intimidating."

"Not on a date. At least I try not to be," he added, forestalling her argument.

"There wasn't a lot to her, it wouldn't take much alcohol. And if she was shy…"

"That occurred to me," Adam said, standing shoulder to shoulder with her and looking out into the night. "But the suggestions she made as to how we might carry on with our date didn't seem entirely consistent with someone shy and reserved, or the least bit conservative."

Danni didn't want to imagine. "You didn't take her up on them? Because from what I saw you didn't seem entirely unhappy with the situation."

Adam turned his head and his grin had an endearing boyishness to it. "I had a beautiful woman in my lap wanting to take advantage of me. Of course I wasn't unhappy. And I didn't want to be rude."

"Of course not. Always the gentleman. But?"

The smile dimmed, turned serious. "There was no real chemistry. Not when we talked. Not even when we kissed. So, aside from the fact that she was well on her way to being drunk, there was never going to be a second date. Although she claimed that didn't bother her, it wouldn't have been…right."

Danni didn't analyze her relief or why his sense of honor pleased her quite so much. "She might not have been such a good look in a future crown princess, either."

"No."

"And your father wouldn't have approved."

"Ahh, no."

"So it worked out for the best."

"Yes."

"And clearly you don't actually need my services. Anna certainly found you attractive at least."

"Anna was drunk."

"I don't think that's necessary for a woman to find you attractive." In fact she knew it wasn't. Not a drop of alcohol had passed Danni's lips and she had no trouble finding him attractive. Too much so. His eyes, his lips, his chest—so much about him fascinated her. Which was why it might be best if they ended this arrangement.

"I know it's not. But being serious about the process certainly takes the fun out of it."

"Well of course it does if you approach it with the determination and precision of a military exercise. What was the last fun date you went on?"

"I'm not discussing past dates with you, Danni."

"You wanted my help."

"With future dates not past ones."

"But maybe if you told me about the ones that worked. Or about Michelle."

"No."

And maybe she didn't really want to know about past successful dates. She just needed to help him find a solution to his current dilemma. "So find a woman who enjoys the same things as you and do some of them together. That way you know you'll both at least have fun even if it doesn't turn into anything more."

Adam nodded as though considering her suggestion but said nothing.

"So what do you enjoy doing?" she prompted.

"I hardly remember," he said with a frown and a shake of his head that implied he didn't think it was all that important. "It's been so long since I did anything just for the fun of it. That's not what my life is about now."

"And it shows."

"Care to explain?"

Did she imagine that hint of tightness in his voice? "You don't need me to explain. And it wasn't a criticism."

"Much."

"It was a statement. You carry the weight of the world on your shoulders, you do everything you can for your family and the country, and you don't seem to do anything just for you. Just for the pure enjoyment of it. A little impulsiveness every now and then wouldn't kill you. All work and no play…"

"I play polo," he said triumphantly. "When my schedule allows," he added.

"I've seen you and the way you play—" she shook her head "—that's not anyone's definition of fun. You play as intensely as you work."

"But I enjoy it."

"It still doesn't make for much of a date for anyone else. And it's too structured. What about doing things on impulse? For laughs, for fun. Read my lips. Fun. F.U.N. Fun."

His gaze seemed to fix on her mouth as she spoke, and his frown returned. Why did he so often frown when he looked at her? She got the feeling he wasn't even listening to her.

There had been something else she was going to

add, but words and thought evaporated, replaced by an awareness she couldn't repress. Awareness of standing here with Adam. Close enough to touch. Awareness of the fact that although he'd fastened some of his buttons, he still had too many undone for her comfort, some of which he'd undone at her insistence. Awareness of that glimpse of chest, which was even more appealing than it had been earlier in the evening. And of the way he smelled—divine.

Four

Adam looked at Danni and felt himself leaning closer. He knew all about impulse—and about fighting it. Impulse told him to kiss her, to pull her into his arms and silence her with his lips on hers.

That would be pure enjoyment.

Far more even than watching her devour the cheesecake. He'd wanted some way of showing he appreciated what she was doing for him; feeding her had seemed like the perfect solution. But she ate with such uncensored sensual pleasure that he'd quickly come to regret the gesture.

The urge to kiss her now shocked him but he wouldn't let it overly concern him. His life was all about *not* acting on impulse. It was about always considering options and consequences before taking action.

But in a perverse way, it was as though since he'd

become serious about finding a wife, his subconscious was trying to thwart him, like a man looking to buy a nice safe Volvo who suddenly sees the perfect tempting Ferrari for sale.

He reminded himself that he'd known Danni since they were kids. It sent a jolt of surprise through him every time he looked at her and realized anew that she was most definitely no longer a kid.

After the evening with Anna, Danni's sparkle, her directness, her innocence were tempting him in ways that she could have no idea about. She wore no lipstick but even without her prompting to read her lips, he was most definitely thinking about them. Soft and mobile. About how the tiny smear of hot chocolate above her top lip would taste, laced with her freshness.

Her green eyes widened as he watched her and he could only hope his thoughts didn't show. Because he couldn't have thoughts like that about her. Because she was Danni.

But if she'd been any other woman, he would have reached for her and kissed that hot chocolate away.

He shook his head to clear it and stepped back, fighting the compulsion to step forward instead. Could her skin possibly feel as soft as it looked? "Danni."

Her gaze was steady on him, a measure of the confusion he felt seemed to shimmer there. She cleared her throat. "Yes."

"You have hot chocolate on your lip."

"Oh." Her quick burst of laughter held uncertainty and she glanced away. Adam passed her a napkin from the tray. "Thank you." She dabbed away the hot chocolate. He almost regretted its loss. But if it stopped him thinking about Danni's lips in ways he had no right to be thinking, then it could only be a good thing.

When he'd woken in the car the first time she drove for him the other night, with her leaning in close, smelling of mint and the cool night, he'd been swamped by an instinctive reaction of purely primal desire. The sort that had been blatantly missing from his date with Clara. It had kicked in before he'd thought to stop it.

And then, before he'd had time to rationalize it, he'd covered his unwanted response with cool civility. He'd tried to create distance and barriers. But he'd been so disconcerted that he spoke without realizing how she might interpret his words. And he'd hurt her. She was one hundred percent the woman he'd claimed he didn't see her as. No matter how desperately he wanted that claim to be true.

She watched him now, waiting for him to speak. "As for fun." That had been what they'd been talking about, hadn't it? "I don't think there's time for that right now."

She took a few steps away, putting a distance he simultaneously regretted and welcomed between them. That distance helped him think a little more clearly, and if he kept his gaze from her petite curves, it helped even more. The uniform she wore did her no favors but he'd seen those curves lovingly revealed by nothing more elegant than jeans and a soft sweater when he'd called at the gatehouse.

"You're kidding. Right?" Her eyes danced with everpresent intelligence and passion and a hint of mockery. Fortunately some things about her hadn't changed—the way she spoke her mind and the way she challenged him. Mostly he appreciated her frankness. Mostly. Other times it drove him nuts.

"This is a serious business."

"I get that," she said with a condescension he hadn't heard anybody use on him in a long time.

"Of course the woman and I need to enjoy each other's company. I want to like her, a lot, and to eventually love her, but I haven't got time to dither and get sidetracked. I'd like to be seeing someone by the time Rebecca and Logan get married. Whoever I take to that wedding will immediately come under public scrutiny. And just because I can have fun with a woman doesn't mean she's going to be suitable as a partner." If only it was that easy.

Danni sighed. "So, *fun to be with* isn't anywhere on your list of criteria."

He heard and ignored the criticism in her tone. "No."

"That explains Clara I guess."

"Clara was very nice."

"You have to admit, even if she didn't want fun, she wanted romance."

"Apparently. And I take the blame for that." He hadn't seen that one coming. "In my defense, Clara had seemed more than happy to discuss weighty issues. She was the one who introduced most of the more serious topics throughout our evening."

"Mmm-hmm." Two syllables laden with cynicism and reproof.

He sighed. Her skepticism was warranted. "The thing is, in political situations I'm good at interpreting mixed messages and subtext. I look for it. I just hadn't realized the extent to which I'd need those skills for dating. I don't *want* to have to use those skills while dating."

"It's just about listening, Adam, about not being totally fixated on your own agenda." She set down her hot chocolate. "If your work is all seriousness, then doesn't that make it more important than ever for you to have someone who can remind you to have fun occasionally, someone who's fun to be with?"

"I can see your point but you're missing mine. Besides, my list of criteria is my decision."

"You're not interviewing job candidates."

Adam said nothing.

"You're not!"

He cleared his throat. "It doesn't seem like an unreasonable way to approach it."

He could see that she wanted to argue but she bit her lip and long seconds later limited herself to a patient, "What else is on your list?"

"Just the usual."

She laughed. The sound, light and almost infectious, broke the tension. How did she make what a moment ago had seemed perfectly reasonable suddenly seem ludicrous? "There is no usual, Adam. People have preferences but they don't *usually* have such rigidly official lists of criteria in the first place."

"How on earth do they expect to find the right person?" His days and weeks were so full that he lived them by lists. They'd served him well so far.

She shrugged. "They just know. Like Rafe and Lexie just knew and Rebecca and Logan just knew. Without lists."

"It seems unreliable. I can't trust in anything as nebulous as *just knowing*."

She shook her head in reluctant defeat. "So spill—what's on your list?"

He hesitated.

"Maybe I know someone suitable."

His list made sense but he knew that Danni would somehow make it seem to not make sense. But it was his list and it didn't matter what Danni St. Claire, pest from his childhood, thought of it, so long as she helped him.

"She'll need to speak multiple languages." How had it come to this? He was sharing his dating woes with Danni. His driver. Next he'd be asking the head gardener how to manage diplomatic appointments.

"I guess I can see why you'd want that," she said.

Despite her words he didn't believe her; there was a light in her eyes he couldn't quite trust.

"You can argue and make love in a range of languages. That'll give variety, that's important. It'll keep things fresh."

He'd known she wasn't taking this seriously. "It's not for the purposes of arguing or making love. I attend endless diplomatic functions with dignitaries from around the world."

Danni was grinning at him.

"You're winding me up, aren't you?"

"You do leave yourself wide open for it. Anyway, like I said, you clearly don't need me driving for you, or giving you advice. You're managing and I don't think we're going to agree on anything important."

"No," he said slowly.

"So, I'll get going." She turned away and headed for the table to get her hat and gloves.

"I wasn't agreeing with you, I was disagreeing."

Slowly, she turned back and a smile quirked her lips. "You usually are."

Which was exactly the kind of comment he expected from her. "Anna was clearly a mistake."

"That might be one area where we agree."

"But she's not the type of woman I expect to be dating in future. I don't think there's going to be anyone else quite as…forward as her on the list. At least I hope not." If Danni didn't stop grinning at him he really was going to have to kiss her. He turned back to the window. "And I'll admit you were right about the tie." The tie she'd made him take off, practically ordering him to undress.

He shook his head sharply, disallowing the sudden image that wanted to insinuate itself there. He rested his fists on the window ledge and stared into the night. "A college education." Focus. He had to stay focused. "Preferably post graduate. Preferably international."

"Go on," he heard her say and could discern nothing of her thoughts from her voice. That was probably a good thing.

"A good conversationalist, a good hostess, diplomatic."

"Of course. Anything else?"

"She'll need to be good with the press and the public, especially children."

"What about looks?"

"Tall, slim, attractive, graceful."

"Hair color?" There was something different about her voice, something controlled. Which wasn't like Danni at all.

"It makes no difference."

"Big of you." That had definitely been a hint of anger in her voice.

He turned to see her standing with her hands on

her hips, her gaze narrowed on him and her lips thin. "What have I done now?" he asked.

She dropped her hands to her sides and shook her head. "You honestly have no idea, do you."

"I have no idea why you're suddenly so angry, like a vengeful pixie, when all I did was answer the questions you asked. You were worried about me not taking criticism well but it seems to be you who's not handling the honesty."

"I'm outraged on behalf of all women."

"Why? Because I have criteria? You can't tell me women don't do that. Must be tall, must be good-looking, must not have a beard, must drive a luxury car and be able to support the lifestyle I'd like to have."

"It's not what was on it that I objected to, it's what you left off. What about kindness, Adam? A sense of humor? What about love and someone you can just be with in the quiet moments of your life? All these criteria you have, they're just more of your barriers."

"I don't have barriers."

She laughed. At him. "You have more barriers than we'll need for the Grand Prix."

"I do not."

"You do. And they're all designed to stop people seeing the real you. You only want them to see the prince, a leader. But, trust me, you don't want to marry someone who sees you like that. You want a companion for life, not a subject. You don't want someone who's going to jump to do your bidding, who says only what you want to hear."

"Actually, that might be pleasant. Surely it would be better than living with someone who constantly challenged and provoked me."

SANDRA HYATT   **61**

"I give up. There's no point in me doing this, I can't help you if you won't even try."

She headed for the door. But the Danni he remembered from the days they'd played chess and the times they'd played baseball never gave up. Ever. She wasn't bluffing, she was mad. He thought quickly. "Skiing."

She stopped and looked back at him, her eyes narrowed in suspicion.

"I enjoy skiing. It's...fun." Even the word sounded frivolous and insubstantial.

Her smile reappeared and felt like a reward. "See, that wasn't difficult, was it?"

It hadn't been as easy as it should have been. Maybe she was right and he'd become a complete bore. "I'm not a frivolous person."

She crossed back toward him. "Nobody wants you to be. It's part of your appeal. But all work and no play..."

She'd used the word *appeal* or *appealing* in conjunction with him before. And she looked at him now as though there was something there that intrigued her. There was most definitely something in her that intrigued him.

And he had to quash it.

"So, you'll drive me and a date of my choice to the mountains next weekend?" Focus on the task at hand. That was all he had to do.

She shook her head. "I only agreed to drive for you once."

"I'll make it worth your while."

Her gaze narrowed on him as though she was affronted. "I'm not that mercenary."

"You used to be," he said evenly, not buying the mock offense.

Her grin slipped out. "When I was *ten* and only because my Dad never gave me pocket money and you and Rafe always had some. You'd pay for anything that you didn't want to do yourselves." She smiled, perhaps remembering the same things he was, the errands she'd run for them.

"I have more pocket money now." He winked at her.

She seemed as surprised by the gesture as he was. He hadn't winked at anyone in a very long time. But somehow Danni made the years slip away. He touched the bridge of his nose.

She sighed heavily. "I'll drive for you if you promise never to touch your nose again."

"Pardon?"

"You do it deliberately to make me feel guilty. So that I'll do what you want."

"How on earth does my touching my nose make you feel guilty?"

She rolled her eyes. "Because every time you touch that little bump, I remember how you got it in the first place."

"Really? And it makes you feel guilty? But it was an accident. As much my fault as yours." He'd been sixteen and she'd only been eleven. But she'd had a hell of a swing with the baseball bat. And he'd been distracted. He'd been arguing with Rafe instead of paying attention to a game he hadn't even really wanted to be a part of. The ball had come out of nowhere. That was the only time he'd ever seen Danni cry. Not because she'd been hurt but because she'd hurt him. And then she got mad at him for making her cry.

"I know that. But I still feel guilty about it."

"So, if I do this—" he touched the bump "—and

ask nicely, will you drive for me this weekend? Please, Danni."

"Don't. That's not fair."

He touched the bump again. "It's actually hardly noticeable. I don't see it when I look in the mirror, I can scarcely feel it."

"Adam. You're playing dirty."

"No, seriously. Touch it. It's nothing. I think you're imagining it." He reached for her, circling his fingers around her wrist—she had such delicate wrists, like the rest of her—and he lifted her hand.

Curiosity lit her eyes and she bit her bottom lip as she ever-so-tentatively touched the bridge of his nose. Her fingers were so close that he couldn't focus on them but he could see her eyes, could see a certain longing in them. Her lips were softly parted and she smelled as sweet as the promise of spring.

And, damn, there was that urge again. The one that would have him pull her into his arms. He shifted his grip from her wrist and grasped her hand instead and pressed a kiss to the back of it. That was as much as he could allow himself.

And apparently more than she wanted. She pulled her hand free. Hid it behind her back. A fierce blush heated her cheeks.

"You know, maybe it is a little sore still, you could kiss it and make it better." Where had the words come from, the teasing?

"Don't play games with me, Adam." Sudden anger tinged her voice, taking him aback. "I know I'm not sophisticated. But you know it, too. So do not make fun of me. You're better than that."

"Make fun of you? Danni, I'd never. The one time I

tried it, when you were about seven, you kicked me in the shins."

"You just did," she said. The anger had gone, only to be replaced by suspicion.

Usually he communicated well, allowing for no mis-understanding. He'd soothed ruffled diplomatic feathers on many occasions. How was he making such a mess of this when it should be so simple? "No." Making fun of her had been the very last thing on his mind. He'd wanted to kiss her and had settled, at great cost, for her hand instead. Because kissing her, when she was effectively a member of his staff, when he was on the lookout for a wife, and when she was…Danni, would be all kinds of wrong. But he could still feel the cool imprint of her skin on his lips. And that chaste, courtly gesture had stirred far more than the kiss he'd shared with Anna earlier this evening.

"I've offended you and I'm sorry." He needed time to make it better. To get their relationship back to where it ought to be, amiable and respectful.

"You haven't offended me. I'm not that soft."

He liked her indignation, the stubborn tilt to her chin.

"I have offended you, I can see it."

"You haven't. Believe me."

"Prove it. Drive for me next weekend."

She gave a little gasp and her eyes narrowed. "You've done it again, haven't you? You've manipu-lated me halfway to saying yes and I'm not even sure how you did it."

"I wouldn't try to manipulate you."

"I know. You do it without trying."

Had he? He hadn't meant to. "You're free to drive

for me or not. But I'd really like it if you would." She'd been right about Clara, she'd been right about the tie.

She opened her mouth.

"It'll be the last time, I promise," he said before she could deny him, because suddenly this seemed important. "You see things differently from me. In a good way. So, I'm taking your advice seriously. I'm going to go skiing and I'm going to have fun."

"Whether you like it or not?"

"Exactly." He tried to keep a straight face.

She laughed, breaking the tension he'd caused when he'd kissed her hand. The familiar sparkle returned to her eyes. "This will definitely be the last time. After that, you're on your own and you can take your fun as seriously as you like."

"You'll be able to pick me up next Friday at two?" He had to get her final commitment while he could.

"Okay."

A frown pleated her brow and she imbued that small word with a world of reluctance, but she'd agreed. That was all that mattered.

"Who are you taking?"

"I haven't decided yet. There are a number of prospective candidates."

"Hmmph. Who meet all your criteria?"

"Yes."

"Are their names in a list?"

He said nothing.

"Can I see it?"

He folded his arms.

"Why not leave earlier than two? Let the fun start sooner?"

"I have meetings in the morning."

She didn't roll her eyes, but he thought it might have taken effort on her part not to. She headed for the table and picked up her cap and gloves.

"And don't worry about the uniform. This is definitely outside of regular palace business. We'll be friends."

"That's what worries me. It feels like the ground is shifting and I don't know where I stand."

He held the door for her. "Since when did you ever *not* like a challenge?"

"Since you started using them to work against me."

She reached into her pocket and pulled out the tie he'd forgotten about. He reached for it, and for a second they were connected by that strip of silk. The fabric had been subtly warmed by her body. Her gaze flicked to his and then quickly away as she released the tie. "See you Friday."

"Thank you, Danni. You won't regret it."

She shook her head. "I already do."

Five

"There's a café up ahead." Adam's voice broke through Danni's concentration, snapping her awareness to him.

"Yes," she said warily. They'd been on the road for a little more than an hour and those were almost the first words he had spoken to her since informing her that they'd meet his date there later this evening. And the statement gave her an ominous sinking feeling sapping the pleasure she'd found in the drive. So far, he'd used the time sitting in the back making and taking calls and working on his laptop. It was an arrangement that suited her just fine and she'd hoped he was setting the tone for the whole weekend.

"Let's stop."

A glance in the mirror showed her that his laptop was now shut. Working, he was remote and safe. It was

when he leaned back in his seat and focused his attention on her that things, in her head at least, became decidedly unsafe.

"Let's not stop." If she was here as more of a friend
than a driver she was allowed to voice an opinion. "It's
not planned. I haven't called ahead."

"They'll cope, I'm sure. I don't know what you're
going to have but I only wanted a coffee. And maybe a
muffin."

"I meant for security. Which you knew. They like to
know in advance where we intend stopping." Now, he'd
decided to tease? She didn't think much of his timing
but the glint in his eyes and the lift to his lips made her
stomach give a funny little lurch.

"It'll be okay," he said. "If we didn't know we were
stopping, no one else could have. This whole weekend
is going to be as low-key and as off-the-radar as possible."

"In that case, we shouldn't stop where people will
see you and recognize you." The café loomed ahead.
One more minute and they'd pass it.

"Stop the car, Danni."

Repressing a sigh, she pulled off the road and into
the parking lot. There was only so far she could push
the friend-versus-driver split.

"You wanted me to be more spontaneous."

So now this was her fault? "I don't think I said that,
Your Highness." She used the "Your Highness" deliberately. She was desperate to get the formality back
into their relationship because something fundamen-
tal had shifted that night in the library with him. When
he'd kissed her hand, the press of his lips igniting a low
forbidden heat. Actually, it had shifted in the seconds

before when she'd touched his nose, when her eyes had met his as she did so. She'd been slammed by a desperate desire to kiss him. Properly. To slide into his arms, press herself against him and kiss the bejeebers out of him. Really, she'd been no better than Anna and hadn't even had the excuse of alcohol. If that was spontaneity, it was a bad, bad thing.

"Call me *Your Highness* again and I'll sack you on the spot."

He was joking. About the sacking part anyway. She was sure of it. Just not the "Your Highness" part. He hated that from her. "Fine. I didn't say I wanted you to be more spontaneous. Adam."

The twitch of his lips stretched into a smile. She hadn't realized it before but that smile of his could be irritating, especially when the smugness of someone who'd gotten his way—again—gleamed in his eyes. Even so it made her own lips curve in response.

"No. But you implied it," he said. "So I'm going to be spontaneous. And we're going to stop for unplanned coffee."

"Paul won't like it." Paul was the head of palace security. They'd had a half-hour meeting together before she'd picked up Adam this morning.

Everything was shifting. Even the fact that he'd insisted she not wear her uniform disturbed her. She wasn't used to driving Adam wearing jeans and a sweater. It felt…disconcerting, like she didn't quite know who she was or what role she filled. It blurred the boundaries in her mind. It allowed her to think of Adam and kissing in the same thought. Perhaps she should have packed the uniform just to be safe.

"Paul will cope. Now, are you going to come in with me, or are you going to sit out here in the car and sulk?"

"I don't sulk."

"Good. Let's go get coffee."

Danni got out and muttered a "yes, Your Highness" under her breath. By the time she'd got round to Adam's side of the car he was already standing, breathing deeply of the crisp air. "One day…" she said.

He waited for her to continue, a smile still tilting his lips.

"Yes?"

"One day I'm going to outmaneuver you."

The smile widened and stole her breath. "And on that day Satan will swap his pitchfork for a snow shovel."

She shook her head and turned away, breaking the direct line of fire of that smile. She'd forgotten, or maybe never realized because she'd known him forever, how attractive he really was. Especially when he smiled. But now wasn't when she wanted to be noticing things like that. Now, when she already felt the ground slipping and tilting beneath her. Irritation was the emotion she should be after. Irritation that he thought he could so easily best her. Irritation that it was so often true.

Inside the café they ordered drinks and chocolate muffins and sat at a booth with a view over the pine-forested hillside and up to the snow-covered mountains.

"You can see these mountains from my office in the palace," he said, leaning back in his seat after his first sip of coffee. "Every time I see them I remind myself that I ought to come up here. Rafe and Lexie have been up to the Marconi chalet several times and even Rebecca and Logan have visited. But it's been years since I made the time. So, thank you."

Danni shrugged. "Pleased to be of assistance." More pleased than she could let him know. Already he looked different, a little less strained. This could be her service to the country. Though right now she didn't care about the country, just about him and that this would be good for him. He looked relaxed and open. "So, who's the date?" She needed to remind herself what was really going on here because she was in imminent danger of forgetting. He hadn't told her anything. Just that whoever she was would already be up at the chalet.

"Claudia Ingermason."

"The figure skater?" The Claudia Ingermason Danni was thinking about had won a medal for San Philippe two winter Olympics ago and had since launched her own brand of top-of-the-line winter and ski gear. She was also stunningly beautiful with the looks of a Swedish supermodel.

He nodded. "Rebecca set it up. Claudia's an old school friend of hers. You said to try dating someone I could have fun with. We both enjoy skiing. So it should be...fun."

"You've met her before though?"

"Not exactly."

"So, this is a blind date?"

"No. I know who she is."

"Did you bully Rebecca into setting you up with someone?"

"I resent the implication that I bully people. And even if I tried, Rebecca would be the last person to stand for it. I asked her if she could think of anyone and she came up with Claudia."

"Sounds perfect." Danni set down her coffee. "So why don't we get going? The sooner I get you up there, the sooner you and Claudia can start having fun."

"There's no rush. She's tied up in a photo shoot for her next season's line. It's running behind schedule. She'll be an hour behind us at least." Adam's hands were wrapped around his mug and he didn't appear in any hurry to go. "There's just one thing I don't understand."

"What?"

"Why this still feels like work?"

"Because you're making it work. You're trying to force it."

"I'm just trying to speed things up."

She shook her head. "Relax. If you remember how. If it's meant to be with Claudia, it'll work out. And if it's not, at least you still got to go skiing. But either way I think we should get going because I don't like the look of the weather." The distant clouds seemed to have grown darker in the time they'd been sitting here.

Adam frowned. "You've had a weather update?"

"It's not supposed to snow till much later this evening or possibly tomorrow."

"That's what I thought." He shrugged and took a sip of his coffee. His eyes drifted closed in a long slow blink. And given that this was the most relaxed she'd seen him in years, Danni wasn't going to hurry him along. He'd been out till the early hours of the morning at a state function and from a comment he'd made earlier, it sounded as though he'd scarcely gone to bed because of calls to the other side of the world he'd had to take.

* * *

"What are you doing?" Danni asked, horrified, fifteen minutes later as Adam got into the front seat beside her. She'd been looking forward to the subtle reprieve from his company. Company she could like too much. Now he was beside her instead of in the back, preventing her from putting things into their proper perspective. Me driver, you passenger. Me commoner, you royalty.

Now, as he sat beside her, she had bad thoughts like me woman, you man instead.

"What does it look like?"

"It looks like you've forgotten where you're supposed to sit."

"Where I'm *supposed* to sit? It's *my* car. I can sit anywhere I want."

Definitely man, and one who thought he could do whatever he wanted. Probably because he usually could. Time for diplomacy.

"And a very nice car it is, too. But I'm your driver. And the point of having a driver is so that you can sit in the back and work. Use your time efficiently. Not have to worry about conversation." Like he had done for the first hour of their trip when he was completely oblivious to her. They had each had their space.

"We agreed that this wasn't a normal driving role. You're also here as a friend and adviser. Besides, I've finished what I need to do for the time being. Now, I thought I'd sit up here. The view's better." He looked at her as he spoke so she kept her gaze where it ought to be, trained on the road as it wound up into the mountains. Though if she was able to look at him, she might be better able to gauge what he was playing at. Or not.

She never knew with Adam. By all accounts no one did. She'd often heard his brother and sister, and even once his father—from whom he'd inherited the trait—complain of that very same thing.

He opened the glove compartment.

"What are you doing?"

"I like seeing what you keep in here."

"Nothing."

He pulled out the thriller she was reading, turned it over. "Doesn't look like nothing."

"Nothing you'd be interested in. Adam?"

"Yes?"

"You're sure you haven't got work you should be doing?"

With a smile he closed the glove compartment. "I'm sure. The truth is I'm having second thoughts about this date. Not the skiing part, but the having to get to know another woman."

"It's because you're still looking at this as work."

"It's partly that but worse than that, I've realized that if the chemistry's not right, it's just going to be a waste of my time, like getting stuck in an unproductive meeting."

"Nothing like anticipating success."

"What if it's blatantly obvious there's going to be nothing between us? I should have stuck to dinner. There's an easy escape. So, just so you know—" he folded his arms across his chest "—I'm blaming you if this goes badly."

"If that makes you feel better."

"You know I wouldn't blame you," he said a few moments later.

"I'm not so sure of it. But I can live with it."

She loved the little smile that played at his lips.

They lapsed into silence, and finally Adam seemed content to sit and absorb the beauty and serenity of their surroundings. Snow blanketed the ground and weighed on the branches of the fir trees that stretched back from the road. He spoke only once, to point out the tracks of a deer disappearing into the forest. She could almost feel the tension leeching from him.

His phone rang. The call was brief. He gave assurances to whoever was on the other end of the call that everything was fine and that there was no need to apologize. When the call ended he tipped his head back in the seat. "That solves that. Turn the car around."

Danni flicked a glance at him.

"We're going back."

"Is something wrong?"

"Claudia can't make it. The art director walked out and the photo shoot's in chaos. If she's not going to be there, then there's no point in me going. Besides now I can attend tomorrow's meeting of the Prince's Trust."

"I thought you were pleased to have a good reason not to attend."

"I was, but I don't have that reason anymore."

"But the skiing?"

"The mountain's not going anywhere. I'll come up some other time."

"You haven't in how many years?"

"I will." He wouldn't, and her heart sank on his behalf. Partly because Claudia wasn't going to be there but mainly because he'd miss out on the first day he'd taken off in nearly a year. The lines of tension and weariness showed around his eyes. "You've got competent people at the meeting for you?"

"Yes."

"Then why not stick to your half of the plan and enjoy the skiing? If you take care of your own needs, you're a better leader because of it."

"There are more important things I should be doing."

"But—"

"What?"

"Nothing." It wasn't her place to comment on his private life. He'd ignore her anyway.

"No. What were you going to say?"

"Just that I can't turn around here. There are too many blind corners. There's a place up ahead just a few minutes."

"Good." He tilted back his seat and closed his eyes. Within minutes his face softened and his breathing slowed and deepened, and now, finally asleep, he looked almost to be smiling.

It was an hour later before he opened his eyes again. And for the last half hour Danni's regret over her decision had been growing. Especially the last ten minutes during which snow had begun to fall. Earlier and more heavily than forecasted.

Adam adjusted his seat to a more upright position and looked around, frowning. "Danni?" A low warning sounded in his voice.

"Yes."

"The light is fading." He glanced at his watch. "And it's snowing."

"Yes. It's nothing the Range Rover can't handle." But she didn't like it all the same.

"And we still appear to be going up into the mountains."

"Ahh, yes, so it would seem."

"So it would seem?"

She didn't like the heavy sarcasm or the annoyance underlying his words.

"Why are we still going up?"

"Because…"

He waited—far too silently—for her to finish her explanation.

"Because that's how we get to the chalet, and now we're not so very far from it."

"The Marconi chalet?"

"You keep repeating my words."

"In an attempt to see if they make any more sense when it's not your mouth they're coming out of. Sadly, they don't. And you're going to have to explain."

"You fell asleep."

"I'm aware of that."

"And you looked so tired."

"Danni."

She couldn't ignore the warning in his tone. "And there really wasn't anywhere to turn around."

"For the last hour there's been nowhere?"

She didn't answer.

"Turn around. Now."

"I don't think it's a very good idea." They were only twenty-five minutes from the chalet.

"Clearly you don't think it's a good idea. But that doesn't concern me. What concerns me is getting back to the palace. Tonight. So that I can sleep the night in my own bed and do the things I'm supposed to be doing tomorrow." His voice was lethally quiet.

"I thought that you'd appreciate the enforced break. I thought you could use it."

"You thought wrong."

"Adam, I—"

A jolt shook the car. It shuddered and pulled to the right and at the same time an alarm sounded on the dashboard computer. All three things told her the same thing. The very last thing she wanted to happen.

A flat tire.

She pulled off to the side of the road. For a moment she sat there not daring to look at Adam. She held the wheel. "This will just take a couple of minutes. And then we'll be back on the road." She'd have it changed quicker than another vehicle could get here for assistance or to pick up Adam. She radioed in her intentions and got out.

By the time she reached the back of the car, he was already there, pushing his arms into a down jacket. "What are you doing?" She hitched up her own jacket onto her shoulders.

"I'm going to change the wheel." He spoke in a tone that indicated he would tolerate no disagreement.

She disagreed anyway. "No, you're not. I'm the driver. I'm going to change it. That's what I'm here for." Danni opened the back.

"You're here to drive me where I want to go and you weren't doing that."

"That's different."

"I'm not going to get into an argument with you." He spoke gently but implacably. "This is my car. I'm going to change the wheel." Adam reached in front of her and lifted out the spare tire.

"If I was a man, would you insist on changing it?" She grabbed the jack and the wrench and followed him to the wheel that sat heavily on its rim.

Adam set the tire down. "If you were your father I would."

Danni put the jack beside it and turned to him. She knew, and didn't like, the obstinate look in his eyes. "And he'd be just as insulted as I am."

"Deal with it. I'm not going to stand by and watch while you change the tire. What do you take me for?"

He stepped toward the jack and she insinuated herself into the sliver of space between him and the car, blocking his way.

"But you expect me to stand by and watch you? This is my job, Adam. It's what I'm here for."

"What you're here for is completely separate." He sidestepped but she moved with him.

"Not separate, because, in case you've forgotten, I drove you here. Your Highness." The title was supposed to remind him of their respective roles. It was also intended to let him know how irritated she was with him right now.

Snowflakes drifted between them. "Looks like you just solved our problem. I warned you what would happen if you called me Your Highness. You're fired. Which means you're not my driver, so stand aside."

Her temper flared. "You can't fire me without written warning." She had no idea if that restriction held true for the palace, a world that operated with its own rules. She only hoped Adam didn't know either—terms of employment for staff not being a major diplomatic concern. "So, as far as I'm concerned," she pressed on, "I'm still your driver and I'm going to change the wheel."

"No. You're not my driver and you're not going to change the wheel." He stepped closer, intimidating her

with his size and his very nearness. Another inch and
they'd be touching. She looked up and met the obstinate
light in his eyes with what she hoped was its equal in
hers. His breath mingled with hers. His warmth surrounded her. And a very different kind of warmth
leaped deep within her. Her heart beat faster, her breath
grew shallower. It took her a moment to register and
recognize the sensation.

Desire. Need.

No. This couldn't be happening. Not with Adam. It
was just the proximity. It was his very maleness, it was
the insular life she led, lately devoid of male relationships that weren't purely about camaraderie.

The light in his eyes changed and darkened, the
anger and stubbornness replaced by something she
couldn't name. Time hung suspended. Slowly, he lowered his head. She breathed in his scent, and without
meaning to, moistened her lips and swallowed. He was
going to kiss her, and she shouldn't want it.

But she did.

In a single deft movement he slid his hands beneath
her armpits, picked her up and set her to one side.

He smiled. Then dusted off his hands. Victorious.
Satisfied with his win. Damn him.

It took seconds for her equilibrium to return, for her
to get past the fact that she'd thought of Adam that way,
and not just in some dim imagining, but with him right
here where she could have, and almost had, reached for
him. Because he was right there. She'd ached to know
the taste of his lips on hers. It had seemed imperative.

And he had seen her thoughts and shunned her.

He crouched beside the wheel, positioned the jack
and reached for the wrench, relegating Danni to the

position of observer or at best support crew unless she wanted to tackle him out of the way. Which would get her precisely nowhere. She was left alternating between mortification at her reaction to him, and frustration at the fact that he'd so easily brushed her aside both as his driver and as a woman.

"If you fire me you'll have to drive yourself home. You'll lose all that time you could have spent working."

"With pleasure," he said, sounding as though he meant it. "At least I'll know I'll get where I want to go."

"You'll have to help yourself with your dating issues. Help yourself unwind and lighten up."

He raised his eyebrows and looked about them. "If this is your idea of helping me unwind, I can live without it."

He had a point. All she'd succeeded in achieving was to make matters worse.

Adam set to work on the wheel and Danni stood to the side and watched him. Snow dusted his head and shoulders. Petty as she knew it was, she silently tried to find fault with even the tiniest detail of how he changed the tire. He gave her no opportunity.

Usually she found strength and competence attractive. In Adam, now, coming after everything else, these traits were irrationally annoying. As he set the old tire on the ground she reached for it.

"Leave it," he said. "I'll get it when I'm done."

It sounded like an order. She ignored him, and to the sound of his sigh, wheeled it to the back of the car.

Sacked. She'd been sacked. Again. That was three times now.

If they were no longer employer and employee and they weren't friends, then what were they? Two acquaintances temporarily stranded on the side of the road as the snow began to fall more heavily. Everything was too unpredictable. Including Adam.

Maybe she should have expected his annoyance at her decision to override his request, but she hadn't expected his obstinacy over changing the wheel, and never could she have predicted that flash of awareness that passed between them as they'd faced off. Out of everything, that bothered her the most. The sudden fierceness of it had come out of nowhere.

No traffic passed by on the road. She walked back and continued watching, trying to figure him out. Adam was older, though not that much older; it had just always seemed that way. But because of that and, more importantly, their respective positions, he was untouchable. He was also supposed to be imperturbable, safe and predictable, a touch on the staid side, considered and considerate, dependable. Anything listed in the thesaurus under *safe* would do to describe him. That's who he was.

Until now.

And if Adam wasn't being Adam, it turned her world upside down.

She tucked her gloved hands beneath her arms and bounced on her toes, trying to keep warm.

He lowered the car back to the ground and began giving the wheel nuts a final tightening. "Get back in the car. You're cold."

"I'm fine." She crouched beside him and reached for the jack.

He glanced at her steadily. "Anyone ever tell you that you're stubborn?"

"A lot of people as it happens, but it's a bit rich coming from you."

"Insolent?"

"I might give you that one."

He shook his head. "Provoking?"

"No more than you."

He stood. "Exasperating?"

She stood too, glaring up at him. "Pot and kettle."

Adam looked skyward, as though seeking help from the gray and darkening sky, before his eyes met hers again. Apparently he hadn't found the help he sought because frustration tightened his features.

And there it was again, that something else in his gaze. That something that did ridiculous things to her insides, made the world seem to tilt. She studied him, trying to hide her reaction and trying to figure out what it was that had changed. If she could pinpoint it, she could deal with it.

"Way more than me," he insisted, incredulous.

"No, because I—"

His hand snaked out, cupped the back of her head and drew her to him.

Adam's lips covered hers, stealing her words, replacing them with the taste of him, overwhelming her with the feel of him, the exquisite heat of his mouth against her cold skin, and the answering heat it ignited within her. He coaxed and dominated and she gave back and gave in, welcoming and returning his fervor.

This was what she'd wanted.

He was what she'd wanted.

Danni slid her arms around him, held him and angled her head, allowing him to deepen the kiss. Allowing him to draw her deeper under his spell. She welcomed the erotic invasion of his tongue. And the flames within her leaped higher as though he'd touched a match to gasoline.

The flash point of her response told her how much more she'd wanted this than she'd ever admitted. She lost herself in sensation. Enthralled, enraptured, ensnared.

In seconds he had her backed against the car, his hands cold and thrilling against her jaw. A counterpoint to the heat of his mouth. His fingers threaded into her hair. Fierce, possessive. His body pressed against hers and she arched into it, breasts to chest, hips to hips. Meeting and matching him. Governed by hunger. Slave to sensation. He was everything she wanted and more and he was everything she'd thought—almost hoped— he wasn't. Cool reserve replaced by searing passion.

He kissed her as though starved for her and awakened the same hunger within her.

Danni groaned, weakened and empowered, aflame.

Abruptly, he broke the kiss and drew back. His eyes, passion-glazed, met hers, and she watched as shock and regret replaced that passion. He snatched his hands from her head as though burned and clenched them into fists at his side.

A terrible silence welled.

Her frantic heartbeat slowed and she fought to calm her breathing. Adam swallowed. "Danni, I—"

"Don't." She turned away from him and picked up the jack and the wrench and strode to the back of the car. She couldn't bear to hear him apologize, to voice the regret written so clearly on his face. She didn't want to hear the word *mistake* from his lips.

Gritting her teeth, she stowed the tools in the back,

mortified by her untutored and revealing response to him. And despite everything she knew, all the things about Adam that would make it impossible for him to want her, or let himself want her, she waited, hoping against hope, that he would speak—not words of regret but something else.

But she could wait only so long.

In silence, Danni headed for the driver's door. Since protocol had clearly been abandoned and left twitching in the snow, she was going to make sure she was the one behind the wheel. It was the only chance she had of control. It would remind them both of who they each were.

He got in beside her, bringing strained silence with him.

There were no guidelines for this scenario.

Danni started the car and took a deep breath as she looked out into the near darkness and the now heavily falling snow. Just as Adam was remembering who he was, she had to remember her role, too. This was not the weather to be driving back in. Visibility would be almost non-existent and the road would be icy and soon snow-covered. Common sense, much as it pained her, had to prevail. She wanted nothing more than for this to be over. She was no coward, but she wanted to run and hide. Instead she took a deep breath and said, "I don't think we should head back to the palace this evening."

Six

Adam glanced at Danni sitting stoically behind the wheel, all her attention focused ahead. The atmosphere inside the car was more frigid than outside, and it wasn't because of the snow coating her hair and shoulders. A new tension tightened her jaw that had nothing to do with the deteriorating driving conditions and everything to do with that kiss.

She'd smelled of pine and snow and tasted of the mints she kept in the car, and for a second she had melded with him, her lithe body pressing into his even through the barrier of their clothing. He'd felt her surprise. He'd caught her reciprocated desire. As surprising for her as it had been for him. And for a moment nothing else had mattered.

She had come alive in his arms, fire and light. But

perhaps that was just Danni. She probably made love that way. His groan almost escaped out loud.

He had to stop remembering and reliving the kiss.

He'd messed up. Royally. And he had to make it right. He had to find a way to get things back to the way they were before he'd kissed her.

The kiss that should never ever have happened. The kiss that, in the moment, had seemed like the only right thing in the world. The kiss that had wrenched control from him and plunged him into a place where there was no thought, only sensation and desire.

But as he watched the snow falling outside he knew they had a more immediate issue to sort out first. "How far are we from the chalet?" he asked, his question more brusque than he'd intended. The control was difficult to reclaim. Even now traces of the consuming need lingered, pulsing through him, refusing to be suppressed.

But she was Danni and he would not let himself want her.

The kiss, the desire, was an aberration.

"Twenty-five minutes," she said quietly, pressing her lips together as soon as she'd spoken.

Those lips. The compulsion to taste her had overwhelmed him. The feeble justification flitting into his mind, that, as of a few minutes ago, she was no longer officially his driver had seemed a valid excuse. And stopping that kiss had been one of the hardest things he'd ever done. Only her groan of pure desire had cut through the fog of passion, allowing a moment of sanity.

Sweet, sassy Danni kissed like a dream. The most erotic of dreams. The way she'd responded, the way her mouth had fit his, the feel of her body against his—all had felt...perfect. All had promised forbidden pleasure.

It was afterward that regret had surged in. Once that last shred of sanity had warned him to end the kiss, he'd seen the shock in her eyes and realized what he'd done, the boundaries he'd trampled over, the very wrongness of kissing Danni, no matter how right it had felt.

His responsibility, much as she'd disagree, was to protect her, not to claim her, to assault and insult her. "Let's go to the chalet." Going to the chalet was the best option given the deteriorating weather, though it carried its own risks being alone with her there. But if he kept duty to the forefront, perhaps it offered him a glimmer of a chance to make it right with her. To get things between them back to a place that was as close to normal as possible. Because otherwise once they got to the palace, they would go their separate ways and he would lose her—their relationship irreparably damaged. Because of him.

He studied her profile, searching for words. He was reputed to be diplomatic. It was failing him now. Had failed him already because that talent ought to have stopped him from getting into this situation in the first place.

He always thought before he acted or spoke.

Always.

Until that moment. And it was all to do with Danni. She stirred him up in ways he couldn't like. She made him forget to think.

"Danni—"

"I don't want to hear it, Adam."

She had to. They had to clear the air. "It was an accident."

"What, you slipped and fell and your lips landed on mine?" She shook her head and a slight smile touched her lips.

"I—"

"Just don't. I know everything you're going to say and you don't have to. It shouldn't have happened. We both know that. You're going to try to take all the blame yourself, as though it had nothing to do with me. As though I hadn't wanted it, too. Just once. Just to know. You're going to say we should forget it happened, put it behind us and move forward."

He wanted to refute her words. But she'd gotten it right.

"So let's do that," she said. "We'll forget it." She clenched her jaw and glared at the road ahead.

One of the things they had in common was that neither of them liked to admit an injury or a weakness. Perhaps that would work in their favor here. "Do you really think it's possible? That was no ordinary kiss." His head still spun, the blood still surged in his veins.

"I'll give you that, it wasn't ordinary. Far from it. And I should probably retract my implication after your date with Clara that there must be something wrong with your technique. Because clearly there's not. But we can leave it at that."

"Can we?" It was the right thing to do, the only way forward.

"Of course we can. It was a heat-of-the-moment mistake and that moment has passed. It was one minute out of all the years we've known each other. The years should count for more than the minute, don't you think?"

"Yes."

"So, if you're going to apologize for anything it should be for sacking me."

"You called me Your Highness."

"You were being a pompous ass."

"Good thing you're already fired."

She grinned, and that small flash of smile lifted a weight from him.

"That's three times now you've sacked me. Each time unjustified."

"You made me spill coffee on my shirt."

"I didn't want to hit the pothole."

The truth had nothing to do with the coffee and everything to do with the look that had passed between them when he'd taken off his shirt. The surge of desire he'd felt for her. She'd only been twenty-one, and his friend, and he hadn't wanted to feel that for her. But he'd stepped away from the friendship anyway. And he'd missed it. Not often, but sometimes in the quiet moments he thought of her.

"So can we talk about something else? Please?"

If she was prepared to try, if she was prepared to move on, then he could, too. "Tell me about the Grand Prix."

"Thank you." She sighed her relief, and filled him in on the latest developments in bringing a Grand Prix to San Philippe. And while at first there was an obvious strain to her words, over time, as they talked, it really did become easier, a little more natural. Neither of them had forgotten the kiss, but the conversation, the finding of common neutral ground, gave him hope that the damage wasn't irreversible.

After ten minutes their headlights picked out a sign through the swirling snow. It advertised an inn he didn't remember seeing before. He glanced at Danni. She wore driving gloves but he was certain that if he could see her hands, her grip would be white-knuckled. And they had another fifteen minutes of driving to go, at least, possibly longer given the speed with which conditions were deteriorating. "Let's try here."

"But—" Her argument died on her lips and she did as he suggested.

She stopped beneath the portico in front of the Austrian-style chalet. It was smaller by far than the Marconi chalet but offered respite from the driving and shelter from the weather. That was all they needed. That and somewhere he could put some space between them.

"I'll go in and check that they have rooms," she said, in the guise of chauffeur not friend, as she reached for her door. And maybe chauffeur was safer.

His hand on her arm—a new but hardly significant breach of protocol given what had already happened— stilled her before she could open her door. Despite the thaw of the last ten minutes, he at least, couldn't move on without actually apologizing.

She turned back but only enough that she could look straight ahead through the windshield. "Don't," she said, reading what was on his mind. "It never happened. We're moving on."

A sharp tapping on her window startled them both. They turned to see a hulk of a man blocking the window, his face shrouded by the hood of his coat. Danni glanced at Adam and waited for his nod before lowering her window.

"You finally made it," the man shouted against the gusting wind. "Drive around to the side. I'll open the garage door." Without waiting for a response he disappeared back inside.

Danni looked at Adam again, her eyebrows raised in inquiry, hesitation in her gaze, making it his call. He knew he should be grateful that at least she was looking at him with something other than appalled horror. He nodded. "Let's go in."

"He must be expecting someone else."

"Well, he's got us. Drive round. Unless you have a better suggestion?"

She radioed their location to the palace and then eased the car around the side of the building and into the garage.

Their host stood waiting. He'd shed his coat but he looked no less of a bear of a man than he had outside. Tall and broad, in need of a haircut and with a furrowed brow. The furrows eased as Danni and Adam got out of the car, and he smiled. "I was beginning to worry you might not make it tonight."

"We're not who you're expecting." Adam waited for recognition to dawn on the other man's face.

"That's okay. So long as you can cook."

From the corner of his eye he saw a flicker of a smile touch Danni's lips. Adam wasn't often expected to be able to cook when he arrived at an inn. "I know a couple of dishes but I have to admit, cooking's not my strong point. We were heading for a chalet further up the mountain—" he didn't say which one "—but saw your sign. And the weather's atrocious out there."

"Oh." The single word was disappointment itself. "You're not Simon?"

He shook his head. "Sadly, no."

"Well, you're here. And you can't go back out. But

the food's not going to be very good." A hint of an accent colored his words. "My name's Blake by the way. Your accidental host. Should have said that first. It's in the list of instructions in my notebook. But I keep forgetting them." He absently patted at his pockets. "I'm just looking after this place for a few days so it's all new to me and there are too many things to remember, too many proper ways and wrong ways of doing the simplest of things. They have some high-falutin' guests stay from time to time who apparently have the pickiest expectations. Everything has to be just so, and done in convoluted ways." His glance took them both in and a smile broke out. "I can tell you two aren't like that." The smile faded. "Are you?" he finished hopefully.

"Not at all," Adam said, grateful for their *accidental* host's warmth and rough charm. It covered and eased the tension. "I'm Adam and this is Danni," he said before Danni could say anything, because she'd taken a deep breath as though about to launch into an explanation. If Blake didn't know who he was, Adam was happy enough to keep it that way. Already the anonymity, when he'd been prepared for any number of different reactions, felt like one less issue to deal with.

"Come on inside. Can't have been pleasant driving in that. I'll get you a drink." Blake smiled. "That's the one instruction I never forget."

"I'll just get our bags," Danni said.

"Wouldn't hear of it. I'll get them." Blake was at the back of the car retrieving their bags before either of them had time to object. "Here, you take this one." Blake passed Danni's bag to Adam. He saw her mortification and shook his head. She didn't like him car-

rying her bag. But unless she wanted to fight him for
it—and for a moment it looked as though she might—
she'd just have to deal with it.

"What do you mean by accidental host?" he asked
Blake, trying to deflect her attention.

"Crikey."

That one word told him that Blake was, as he'd suspected, Australian. Danni's smile grew.

"You wouldn't believe the rotten string of luck that's
led to me being alone here," he said as he crossed the
garage. "The place is owned by my sister-in-law. It's
been in her family for years. She's been coping on her
own these last two years since my brother died and has
turned it into an inn. I was only coming over for a holi-
day and to give her a hand when Sabrina—"

He reached an internal door and looked back. "Nah.
You don't want to know all that. All you need to know
is that people have been breaking their legs and having
babies when they shouldn't, and now getting waylaid
by weather, so you've got me."

He led them up a flight of stairs. "We don't have
any guests booked in for a couple days. I was expecting the new chef and his wife. The chef was a friend
of my brother's. But I have a suspicion that if he was
a friend of Jake's—and yes, I know, *Blake and Jake*,
what were my parents thinking?" He barely paused for
breath but his voice had a surprisingly melodic quality
to it that was easy to listen to and Adam tried to focus
on that rather than Danni, and the sway of her hips, as
she walked up the stairs ahead of him.

Blake reached the top, set Adam's case down and
turned to wait for them. "Anyway, if he's a friend of
Jake's, chances are he's found himself a tavern and

holed up there. And if I'm right and he has found a tavern, there's no telling when we'll see him, regardless of what the weather does. The useless—"

Blake stopped himself and grinned as Danni and Adam halted in front of him. It was a surprisingly sheepish expression for such a big man. He reached to take Danni's case from Adam. "You should know that at the very top of the list of the instructions Sabrina left for me was to not talk too much. And never ever to swear in front of guests. Written in red. Because I wasn't supposed to deal with the public, really. Simon's wife's going to do that. So, let's just get that drink I talked about. And don't worry, there'll be dinner for tonight and it'll will be warm and tasty if not fancy." He glanced from the cases at his feet to another set of stairs. "I'll take these up to your room in a jiffy."

"Rooms." Adam said with an emphasis on the s. "We'll need two." He said it before Danni had to. Though for a second the thought of sharing a room—a bed—with her, had stirred something fierce within him, something that had catapulted his mind back to when he was kissing her.

The kiss and the associated sensations had imprinted on him and he didn't think it was going to be possible to erase them. They would, he was certain, haunt him for a long time to come.

"Two?" Blake looked between them, frowning.

"That's not a problem, is it?"

"No," he said drawing the word out. "But seeing as I was expecting the chef and his wife, I only have one room ready. But it won't take me long to sort out. I'll do it while you're drinking your mulled wine. You will have a glass of mulled wine, won't you?" He trained a look of earnest concern on them. "I have some ready."

"We'd love to, thanks," Danni said with a smile that wiped the concern from Blake's face.

He showed them into a cavernous living room with high wooden-beamed ceilings and a roaring fire in a stone hearth. "You stay by the fire. I'll be back in two shakes of a lamb's tail."

Danni looked from Blake's departing back to Adam. "I haven't apologized for overriding your request to go back to the palace. For us ending up here."

And if she hadn't done that he wouldn't have kissed her and they wouldn't be in this mess. "It's okay. I appreciate your reasoning." He knew she'd done it for him because she'd thought he needed to take some time for himself.

"We don't have to stay here if it doesn't suit you."

"What do you mean?"

She looked around the room. "This is nice but it isn't going to be what you're used to, especially with no staff. I can get us to the Marconi chalet if you'd like."

"Okay, so now I am annoyed. What do you take me for, Danni? *This isn't what I'm used to.* You know I served in the military. I had plenty of accommodations during my time that were far less salubrious than this. Almost all of it, in fact."

"I know but…"

"I thought you were one of the few people who saw beyond the title."

"I do."

"Yet you think I'd rather send us both back out into that weather, not to mention insulting Blake, for the sake of what? A higher thread count? Someone to open doors?"

"A better meal," she suggested.

"I don't care about the food."

She looked away. "You're right. I know you're not like that." Had his kiss driven such a wedge between them that she couldn't even meet his gaze?

Another thought occurred to him. "You don't have a problem with Blake?"

"Me? No." She looked as horrified as he'd been when she'd suggested he might not consider this place up to his usual standard. But then a sudden merriment flashed in her eyes as she added, "He's gorgeous, mate."

Relief flooded through him. That was the Danni he remembered.

Her grin faded too soon. "We should tell him who you are."

Which in turn dimmed his own enjoyment in her response. "Why?"

"Because he has a right to know."

"Can you imagine what that will do to him? He's already flustered."

"But—"

"He doesn't need to know."

"Is that an order?" She raised one eyebrow.

Why did she always have to challenge and question him? He'd never figured it out. Never figured *her* out. "I don't give you orders, Danni. I never have. And not just because you wouldn't have followed them."

She did a funny little head tilt that he took to be grudging acknowledgment of the truth. "But sometimes your requests do sound a lot like orders."

He shrugged. That was his acknowledgment that

maybe there was also an element of truth in what she said. He'd learned to be careful about how he expressed his thoughts and wishes because they could be taken too seriously. But it also meant that if he wanted something done, a subtle remark was usually enough to see it accomplished.

Blake came back in carrying two cinnamon-scented glasses of mulled wine. "Here, get these down you and I'll sort out your other room. That is, if you're sure you don't want to share."

"We're sure," they said in unison.

They watched him go and Danni laughed. "I'd bet my life's savings that no one's ever handed you a drink and told you to 'get it down you' before."

"Your savings are safe." Adam raised his glass to her and looked about the room. His gaze took in an antique chess set positioned between two armchairs. The pieces set up for a game. "Do you want to play?" Anything to keep her distracted, to pull things back to where they ought to be between them.

She looked from the board to him. "I've barely played since the last time with you."

"Me neither."

"Are you lying?" she asked, suspicion narrowing her eyes.

"I might have played a time or two. What about you?"

Her lips twitched. "A time or two."

They could move on. He knew it. She'd never been one to hold grudges, preferring to live in the present.

"I'm not sure that now's the best time to get back into it though, because in all our matches that summer and the few afterward, I never won a game off you."

"I wouldn't remember."

"You remember. You're too competitive not to. But that last time I had you in check twice."

"Once. And it only lasted until my next move when I put you in checkmate."

"It was twice and it took way more moves than one to make it checkmate. I almost had you."

"Prove it." He nodded at the set.

She hesitated.

"There's nothing else for us to do. Unless you want to talk about what happened before?"

"I'm white," she said with a false cheerfulness.

Adam waited for her to sit and watched as she touched and aligned each of the intricately carved pieces. "It's a beautiful set," she said, picking up a finely carved knight and turning it slowly.

"I'm guessing it's an original Staunton." He lifted his king and looked at its base. "Ebony and boxwood made around the 1860s. And it's your move."

"I knew it would come to that," she muttered. She opened with her king's pawn. "The trouble is you taught me. You know how I play because it's how you taught me to play. It seems like an unfair advantage."

"Which means you know how I think and play, too. But you quickly developed your own strategies. Unconventional but occasionally effective."

She shook her head. "The difference now is I'm not going to let your gamesmanship put me off."

"Gamesmanship?" He feigned outrage. That had been one of the things he'd enjoyed about playing with her. The way she tried to match wits with him verbally as well as strategically.

"Gee, Danni. Are you sure you want to do that?" She

mimicked him. "'Are you sure you've thought through all the avenues? The obvious move isn't always the best one.' You turned me round in circles, like that labyrinth at the palace."

"I never gave you bad advice. Besides, you were more than capable of thinking your way out of it. And you always liked the labyrinth."

"You were five years older than me."

"You wanted to play." He mirrored her move.

"I always thought I could beat you—one day. And then we stopped playing, just as I was getting better and coming close to matching you."

"I was letting you think you were coming close because, like you said, I had five years on you. It was only fair to give you a chance."

"Says the man who taught me the French proverb, *you cannot play chess if you are kindhearted*. You weren't *letting* me come close to winning. I was doing that on my own. In fact that's probably why you stopped playing with me."

"And of course it had nothing to do with me going back to boarding school."

"That might have been a factor." She grinned.

"And if we're talking sayings, I lost count of how many times you reminded me that after the game, the king and the pawn go back in the same box."

"Still true."

And he was just as grateful now as he had been then that she thought that way. He paused with his hand on a knight. "Those chess games helped me get through that vacation."

"Only because winning makes you happy. Don't expect it tonight." Challenge and anticipation lit her eyes.

And the same sensations stirred within him. "Okay, Kasparov. Show me what you've got. But I'm thinking you're still going to make me a happy man." He hadn't intended the double entendre. But he could see by the way her eyes widened before she looked quickly back at the board that she'd read more into those words than he'd intended. And he too had thought more than he ought as soon as they were out of his mouth. In that fleeting instant he'd thought of ways Danni might make him happy and of ways he might please her, and of how she would look in the throes of pleasure. Forbidden thoughts. He had to stop them.

And he had to get his head into the game or she'd beat him. She made her next move and they played in the silence of concentration for fifteen minutes until Blake came back.

"Glad to see that being used." He nodded at the chess set. "It belonged to my grandfather. Only Jake ever played and even then not much." He stood a short distance away, his hands behind his back, and surveyed the board. "Who's winning?"

Danni met Adam's gaze then looked at Blake. "Hard to say at this point." Adam agreed with her assessment. Already she'd surprised him a couple of times. He was going to have to work for a win.

"Do you want to finish the game before I show you up to your rooms?"

Adam looked at Danni whose attention was back on the board, her hand hovering over her bishop. "This game may not finish anytime soon."

Blake shook his head. "That's the trouble with

chess," he grumbled. "Takes too long and you can't even tell who's winning."

Danni made her move and then with one last look at the board, stood and smiled at their host. Blake gestured to the door. "It took me a while to find everything. But I think I've done it right. Ticked off everything on the list anyway." The crinkling of paper sounded as he patted his pocket. "I'll show you up now and then fix your dinner. Like I said, it won't be fancy, but it'll be tasty and there'll be plenty of it. I'm more used to cooking for a shearing gang than couples on vacation. I hope you're hungry."

"I could eat a horse?" Adam said tentatively.

Clearly the right answer. Blake clapped him forcefully on the back. "That's what I like to hear," he said as he led the way up the stairs. "I've put Danni in here." He opened a door to a bedroom with a canopied four-poster bed in the center draped in a white linen coverlet, with a heart-shaped chocolate wrapped in red foil on the pillow. "It's the best room," he said proudly.

"Bathroom's over there," Blake pointed to a far door and then walked to another. "This is the adjoining door. It can be locked from either side. Or not." The man clearly thought there was something going on between them. Or that there would be soon. An idea that teased at Adam's senses no matter how he tried to repress it. But repress it he had to. There could be nothing between the two of them for a whole host of reasons. Her age and the fact that he was looking for a wife being the first two that came to mind. A wife to stand at his side now and when the time came for him to fill his father's shoes as monarch of the country. A role that wouldn't suit the adventure-loving Danni and one which he couldn't imagine her suiting in return. He knew what he needed in a partner—he had his list.

So, anything with Danni, as tempting and insistent as the idea suddenly was, would be wrong because it wouldn't be fair to her. And would ruin a relationship that he was only now coming to properly value.

She was out-of-bounds.

The room revealed by the opened door was similar though smaller than the one they stood in. The bed was a standard bed, the covers were somewhat rumpled in a testament to Blake's bed-making skills. Though here too in the center of the pillow sat a foil-wrapped chocolate.

Danni looked at him, her narrowed gaze revealing her discomfort. He was assuming the discomfort was over the disparity in their rooms rather than the proximity. He only wished he could say the same for himself. He'd never have thought having Danni St. Claire so close could be disconcerting, but he knew without a shadow of a doubt that he'd be lying in bed tonight and thinking about her on the other side of that door.

That kiss had a lot to answer for. *He* had lot to answer for. And she hadn't let him apologize for it.

Then again, maybe he'd kissed her just to stop her arguing.

No. Not true.

He'd kissed her because he'd suddenly wanted to. Needed to so badly that he hadn't been able not to. And there was a part of him, a traitorous rebellious part, that couldn't regret it, that triumphed in it.

Worst of all was the fact that she'd responded. Unequivocally. An encouragement he would have been much better off without. That instantaneous connection and heat had been like no other kiss.

Usually he made quick irrevocable decisions and seldom revisited them, seldom regretted them. This confusion, the indecision and second-guessing that assailed him was uncharted and disturbing territory.

Danni opened her mouth to protest over the room arrangement. He silenced her with a hand on her shoulder. "These look terrific," he said. "Thank you."

"I knew you'd appreciate them. Sabrina knows how to do things nicely." Their host kept talking, oblivious to the sensation rioting through Adam, and all because of the feel of her slender shoulder. "And those chocolates," Blake pointed to the pillow, "are delicious. Just had one when I was making your bed. I couldn't help it." He clapped his hands together. "So, dinner now?"

"Can you give us fifteen minutes, please?" Danni asked, stepping away from Adam's side.

"That's even better. Of course you'll be wanting a bit of private time. And I'll be able to make sure it's all properly ready and hot. Sing out if you need anything. Just come down when you're ready."

As soon as Blake left, Danni turned to Adam, her gaze earnest. He missed the feel of her close to him.

"We're swapping rooms," she said as she started for her suitcase.

Adam blocked her way. "No. We're not."

"Yes. We are." She sidestepped.

He matched her, again blocking her way with his body. "No. We're not. And that *is* an order."

"Ha. Remember what you said about me not being likely to follow your orders. You were right. My room's twice the size of yours. I wouldn't be able to sleep in it. You're the one who's a prince."

"You're only here because of me. It's very right. All it is is a bed to sleep in anyway." And no matter which bed he was in he wouldn't be getting much sleep. Not with her so close. "I'll bet you've always wanted to sleep in a four-poster bed."

Her irrepressible grin lifted one side of her mouth. "Actually, when I was younger my fantasies ran more to a racing car bed."

"But what about now? Where do your fantasies run to now?" His fantasies suddenly included her laughing lips.

They were standing close. He could see flecks of gold in her eyes. He could see the tips of her teeth revealed by her parted lips. He took a step back. "I'm sorry. That was inappropriate and not something I need to know." Her mouth closed and she bit her lip, drawing attention to its soft fullness.

He should turn and go, but he stood there staring at her, wanting her. And he could see the mirror of his wanting in her eyes.

Hope twined with desire inside him. *Hope* that she felt something of what he did, and *desire* for her, here and now. He didn't want either. He *shouldn't* want either. And together they were a fearsome combination.

Where was her outrage over his earlier kiss? The overstepping of bounds, the abuse of power? He'd settle for sympathy and a gentle admonishment that she didn't think of him that way, or even for her to laugh in his face. He could deal with any of those. Anything to remind him that the sudden attraction laying siege to him was one-sided and had to be vanquished, that kissing her could never be allowed to happen again. Because that was what was right and safe.

But it wasn't one-sided. He could see that now. It hadn't been just him in that kiss. The attraction simmered between them.

He should step away, not want to pull her closer. Her lips had a newfound power over him. He wanted, so much that it was a need, to kiss her again.

He looked away from her—her eyes, her lips, her hair, her feminine curves, everything that tempted him—so that he could think clearly. But instead he saw that big four-poster bed and pictured Danni in it. With him.

It was insanity. Lust—that's all it was—was gaining the upper hand.

He was alone here with Danni, when he'd planned a weekend with no work, no distractions, so now he was fixating on her. If his date, Claudia—he struggled to remember her name—was here that wouldn't be happening. Although he could scarcely remember what Claudia looked like. She was ostensibly a beauty but she had none of Danni's spirit and sass. And everything going on in his head was just plain wrong and he couldn't, wouldn't allow it.

Even if he'd correctly interpreted the way she'd melted into him. Even if she hadn't wanted him to stop that kiss.

His thoughts refused to be suppressed.

Danni's expression as she watched him turned thoughtful. She knew he was battling with himself. And as that realization registered, the light in her eyes changed, desire shone through. The desire that had sprung to life between them, more powerful for being mutual and forbidden. The hunger for her gnawing at him almost undid him. He could pull her to him now....

He might not have control over his thoughts or his desires but he still had control over his actions and he removed his hand from her shoulder and turned away from her.

It felt like the hardest thing he'd ever done.

He crossed the room, putting necessary distance between them. "We need to talk about what's happening here. We're alone together for the first time and I don't know how or why, but somehow it's changing things. But not everything. And what remains constant is the fact that anything between us would be wrong. It's not that I don't want...it's just all kinds of wrong."

"You think I don't know that? That you're stuck here without your duties to occupy you, or the woman who should have been here, so you're focusing on me. A convenient substitute."

She waited for him to disagree. "Yes," he said. Though it wasn't that. Not by a long shot. This attraction to her was anything but convenient. Danni was all the things that were missing in his life, things she'd pointed out, spontaneity, honesty, and this felt like his last chance to grab them. But, and it kept coming back to this, it would be wrong. Unfair to her when she deserved so much more. "So let's just go to dinner. And we are not swapping rooms." He spoke as coldly as he could. "Tomorrow we're going home. Things will be back to normal."

He crossed to the door, each step away from her heavy and determined, as though he was fighting gravity.

"Adam?"

He shouldn't respond, but he turned. And she was right there. Her hands went to his head and pulled him down and she rose up on her toes and kissed him. A kiss of contradictions. Sweet and hard. A kiss that challenged and dared, and the press of her lips to his, of her body against his, the taste of her, filled him with fire.

The kiss undid all of his resolutions, weakened him. She took and she gave and left him mindless of anything other than her.

Then she broke the kiss and strode away.

Relief and regret tore through him as he sagged against the wall.

Seven

Danni woke to a soft tapping on the door. She had no idea what time it was other than early. So she rolled over and ignored it. The tapping grew louder. "I'm fine. I don't need anything." Except maybe a glass of water but she could get that for herself.

Blake had knocked just like that last night as she was about to get into bed because he'd forgotten to check that her bathroom had everything it ought to. And although those few minutes of Blake's garrulous company after the strained torture of dinner with Adam had been a blessing, she didn't want to see him, or anybody, right now.

Adam had been polite during their meal. Too polite. And charming. Too charming. There had been nothing real or honest about their conversation. The manners and the charm masked a remoteness that seemed impossible to bridge.

She'd all but told him that she wanted him. And he'd turned her down. Supposedly hell had no fury like a woman scorned, but she wasn't feeling scorn so much as mortification.

A chasm had opened up between them and it was of her making. She'd kissed him and he'd let her walk away. He hadn't mentioned the kiss during dinner. Not once.

She'd hoped that his gentle but undeniable rebuff would quell the insane one-sided lust that had sprung from nothing and nowhere in the space of a few days. But apparently insane lust didn't work that way. And she was still hankering, twisted up on the inside with wanting him.

She'd had wine with dinner in her desperation to forget. Not much, but usually she drank nothing. The wine had given no consolation and no reprieve from her embarrassment.

He was Adam Marconi. Heir to the throne of San Philippe. She was the daughter of one of the palace drivers. He'd known her since she was five. He didn't even think of her as a woman. If only there was a way to get through this day without seeing him.

"Danni?"

Her breath caught in her chest and every muscle tensed. It wasn't Blake at the door. It was Adam. And the tapping hadn't been at the main door to her room but at the adjoining door.

"Danni? I'm coming in."

Danni burrowed farther beneath the covers. "What do you want?" She knew there was no way of completely avoiding seeing him today but surely it didn't have to start now.

He opened the door enough that he could look into the room, his gaze somewhere on the wall above her head. He didn't so much as put a toe past the threshold. "We're going skiing. Did you bring gear?"

"Yes. I'm always prepared for anything, and I wasn't going to twiddle my thumbs while you were off skiing. But I thought we were going back to the palace today?"

He opened the door a little wider. "We're going skiing first. It snowed heavily overnight again and although it's stopped now, it'll be several hours before the roads have all been cleared. So we're stuck here for a while." He was clean shaven, his dark hair slightly damp. "Blake tells me there's a small ski field a five-minute walk from here. I thought we'd try it. It's got to be better than…being cooped up in here." He didn't add, *with her*. She didn't need the reminder of what she'd done last night. "Breakfast will be ready in fifteen minutes. Can you be ready?" His gaze lowered and tracked over her rumpled bed. Rumpled because she'd tossed and turned most of the night.

"Of course I can." He was sounding a degree or two warmer than he had last night, a little more like his usual self, as though he had put yesterday and last night behind him, as though he could pretend it had never happened. Relief washed through her. She couldn't forget what she had done, her madness. But perhaps they could get back to a place of…comfort between them. A place where they both pretended. She just had to show him that she could be normal. And if normal meant spending the morning on the slopes with him to prove herself, she could do it. Skiing would be the perfect distraction and a much better alternative to staying indoors alone and stewing.

* * *

The only sound in the still morning was the quiet crunch of their boots on the snow. Danni focused on the trail lightly trampled by the few people who'd come this way already this morning. Ahead, she could make out the next three orange-tipped trail markers before their path disappeared in a gap between the pines.

The chalet had a snowmobile but she'd only been half listening to Blake's convoluted explanation as to why it wasn't available this morning. But the walk, Blake had assured them though he hadn't done it himself, was short.

"It's beautiful," Danni said. The beauty, the serenity, helped give her perspective. Her turmoil was just that, hers. And not important. Or at least she knew that one day it would seem unimportant even if that day wasn't quite here yet.

"It is," Adam agreed easily, his step keeping pace with hers.

Breakfast with him had been marginally better than dinner. They were both valiantly pretending the kisses had never happened, both trying to act normally with each other. They were managing. Just. Like bad actors in a play. She could believe it if she forced herself to.

Through a gap between some pines, Danni glimpsed the rustic buildings of the ski field farther up the hill and guessed that Blake's five-minute estimation of the trip was optimistic. "I'll bet you don't usually have to walk to your ski fields lugging your own gear," she said. She tried for a teasing tone but guilt over the fact that it was her decisions that had put him in this predicament gnawed at her. If she hadn't ignored his wishes yesterday, none of this would have happened.

"Not usually, no." He glanced at her. "But I'll bet you don't, either."

"Good point. I guess not." She looked at the markers ahead. "You know, if we skip that next marker and head straight for the one beyond it, it'll be quicker. Some of the footprints already go this way." She headed in the direction she'd suggested, not waiting for Adam to agree. Because he wouldn't. He played by the book. He didn't take shortcuts.

"Why is it you have such a poor opinion of me?" He spoke across the few feet of snow that separated them.

She glanced at him, but with his hat and glasses in the way, too little of his face was visible to gauge how serious his question had been. "I don't."

"You do. You think I'm soft and spoiled and arrogant. Not to mention boring and uptight."

"I never said those things, especially not soft." She tried to remember what she might have ever said about him.

He laughed. Loud and deep. "But that's how you think of me."

His laughter was a relief and a balm. "You're a prince Adam. You've had a life of utter privilege. Apart from a few years in the military."

"You grew up on the palace grounds. You had a lot of those same privileges and, might I add, none of the responsibilities."

Danni said nothing. She couldn't totally agree with him but she also couldn't totally disagree with him.

"It helps you, doesn't it?" he said.

"It helps me what?"

"You prefer not to see me as a normal man. It wasn't

always like that. But I am normal and that's why I have to keep my distance."

She laughed but hers was a little forced. "You're not normal. Nothing about you is normal." She didn't want to hear whatever explanation he'd come up with for rejecting her. "You wouldn't know normal if it jumped up and bit you on the—"

He waited for her to finish but she held her tongue. Too late, but she held it anyway. "You see," he said. "You won't even use words you'd usually use because you're with me. And you used to not be like that. I know that's my fault and I need to fix it. I just don't know how."

If she'd changed it was because she did see him as a normal man now. One who might have needs, one who could fill needs she didn't want to own. She deviated a little farther off the visible path, wanting to put more space between them.

"Bit me where, Danni? Go on, finish your sentence."

There was too much of a challenge in his voice for her to refuse, too much of an assumption that she wouldn't. "Bit you on your fine royal ass."

He smiled. "Thank you. For that openness and for calling my ass fine."

The way those ski pants fit him, there was no doubt about that whatsoever. Not that she was going to admit it to him. "You can also be a royal pain in the ass."

"Again, thank you."

She laughed. "You were like this when Rafe used to tease you, too. Imperturbable, unfathomable. It was totally exasperating. We jumped off the groundsman's shed roof that time just to see how you'd react. You barely batted an eyelid."

"It used to drive him nuts."

"He has my sympathy."

"He always did."

There was something she couldn't quite grasp in his tone. "Meaning?"

"Nothing. But you two were quite the team when you were younger."

"United in tormenting you."

He nodded.

"We were doing you a favor." She looked across the few feet that separated them, trying to see how he'd take that assertion.

"I don't think I ever thanked you for it."

"There's no need for sarcasm." She hid her smile. "We kept you real, and grounded. Stopped your head from getting too full with all that rubbish you insisted on cramming into it."

"By rubbish you mean…?"

Danni paused. "Maybe it doesn't seem so much like rubbish now."

"So you mean my studies? Languages?"

She nodded. "Like Latin."

"You made me teach you some of it."

"I was young and impressionable."

"It may be a dead language but it lives on in other languages it forms the basis for—"

He caught her smiling and grinned back before he looked away, shaking his head.

"See, you just can't help yours—" She squawked as she stepped into a snow drift and sank down to her thighs. She tossed her skis and boots ahead of her and tried to work her way out. Adam stopped to watch her floundering. Finally she held out a hand to him.

He set his things down beside hers, took a few steps closer and looked at her outstretched hand. "Ah, so now I can be of service to you. Now I'm not so boring for preferring to follow the trail markers. And perhaps not quite so useless, hmm?" The light teasing in his voice was invigorating.

"I'm hoping not. But it's not anything you learned in Latin that I need from you now."

"Adsisto." Testing the snow he eased forward and reached for her hand.

"Gratia," she said as she accepted his clasp. He pulled her up and toward him. In two steps she stood pressed fully against him, and he steadied her with an arm around her back. And all the sensations, all the memories, came flooding back. Time stood still. His gaze dipped and flicked up again, then he blinked, long and slow, and stepped back. Away from her.

"Do you ski much?" he asked as the field came into view a couple silent minutes later. "I should have asked earlier. I just assumed."

"You assumed right." Her heartbeat had settled back to somewhere around normal. "I go whenever I get the chance." Even her voice sounded normal, revealing nothing of the breathless, and as it turned out point-less, anticipation she'd felt pressed against him. "I love skiing. The freedom, the speed, the exhilaration." She'd wanted his kiss, had almost been able to taste it. She'd learned nothing from last night.

"I guess that's why I assumed you did. Anything that involves speed and exhilaration and the risk of break-ing your neck."

"You like it, too," she reminded him.

"Yes. I do," he agreed.

"I never thought we'd have anything in common. We're so different. Or at least you pretend you are."

"It's not me pretending I'm not like you. I freely admit who I am. It's you who's in denial. You're more like me than you want to admit."

"I'm nothing like you. You're royalty, you're a scholar, multilingual and let's face it, a bit of a geek."

"A geek? As in I like things like…chess?"

"Yes," she said slowly, seeing immediately where he was going with this, "but I only ever learned because we were both laid up that time, you with your leg and me with chicken pox. I was bored and had gone through all the other games and you'd gotten banned from everything electronic for crashing the palace network."

"The excuses won't work, Danni. Admit it, you enjoy chess."

"Yes," she admitted. "But that doesn't mean anything."

"The Lord of the Rings." Adam had given her the books and insisted she read them prior to the first of the movie adaptations coming out. He'd re-read them at the same time and they'd had many lengthy discussion about them.

"Face it, Danni. Underneath the Action Woman exterior you're part geek, too. And it's not geeky but we have skiing in common."

She focused on the buildings ahead and the chairlifts stretching up the hill before them. "Yes, but—"

"And don't forget cars. You may not like who I am and what I do, but that doesn't mean you're not like me, that we don't have things in common."

She swallowed her shock. "I never said I don't like

who you are and what you do." He couldn't possibly think that. Could he?

"No?"

They reached the periphery of the clusters of skiers waiting for tickets or chairs. "No. I totally admire who you are and what you do. I always have. I can't imagine anyone better suited to it."

"I'm not sure that's a compliment."

"It is," she said quietly.

He stopped walking but because of his glasses she couldn't read what was in his eyes. He'd opened his mouth to say something when the sound of a sob caught their attention. Danni looked down to see a girl of about five or six looking woefully around, her eyes wide and panicked. She dropped to her knees in front of the child. "What are you looking for? Have you lost someone?"

The girl nodded, the rabbit ears on her ski hat bobbing. "I can't find my daddy." Her bottom lip and her voice trembled.

"That's okay," Danni said brightly, "because I know how to find lost daddies."

"Do you?"

"I sure do." She passed her skis to Adam.

"There's an information kiosk just over there," he said quietly to her.

She turned back to the girl. "Hold my hand and we'll go to that little building." She pointed to the kiosk, where a number of people were milling around. "They have a special place for lost fathers."

The girl put her gloved hand into Danni's. "What's your name?"

"Georgia."

"Come on then, Georgia. Let's go find your daddy. I'll bet he's really worried." Danni quietly prayed that Daddy had noticed the missing child and would also have gone to the kiosk.

Adam walked ahead of them, cutting a path through the crowd. At the kiosk he tapped on the shoulder of a tall man gesticulating wildly, who stopped and turned. Adam pointed out Danni and Georgia and the man came running. "Is that your daddy?" Danni asked the girl.

Georgia saw her father, said "Daddy," and promptly burst into tears. The man scooped up Georgia, enfolding her in a hug. "Are you okay, honey?"

Georgia nodded into her father's shoulder, her sobs subsiding. "The pretty lady knew how to find lost daddies."

He swung an arm around Danni and pulled her into a fierce embrace. "Thank you, thank you. I only turned around for a moment. And then she was gone." His voice was marginally steadier than his daughter's had been earlier.

"She's fine." Danni disentangled herself from father and daughter. "And a lovely girl. Enjoy your skiing." She wasn't even sure he heard, he was so busy hugging his daughter.

She turned to find Adam standing close by. "You handled that well," he said, admiration in his eyes.

"Thanks."

"Pretty lady."

"Enough with the sarcasm."

"I don't think Georgia was being sarcastic."

"I didn't mean Georgia."

"Neither did I."

And she wanted too much to believe him. "Let's see if you're still calling me *pretty lady* when I beat you to the bottom of the first run."

He tipped his head to the side. "It's all right to accept a compliment, Danni."

No. It wasn't. It wasn't all right to accept or believe in Adam's compliments. It wasn't all right to have this conversation with him. "Frightened of losing? Is that why you're being nice? So I'll go easy on you in return?"

He sighed. "Come on then. Show me what you've got."

It was late afternoon before they got back to Blake's chalet. They'd intended to return at noon. But the conditions on the slopes had been perfect. As they'd skied they'd slipped into the easy camaraderie they'd once had—at times teasing, at times earnest, always effortless. For the second part of the afternoon, when they should have been packed and departing the chalet, each time they'd made it to the bottom of a run, they'd looked at each other and one or the other of them had suggested, *one more.*

Technically Adam was a better skier than she was, a joy to watch as he swerved and swooped effortlessly down the runs, but while she couldn't quite match him in sheer skill and grace she made up for it in determination and what he'd laughingly called recklessness as she'd skidded to a stop mere inches from him at the bottom of a run.

For the afternoon, she'd allowed herself to forget who he really was, helped by the fact that if they recognized him nobody on the ski field called attention to

who he was. So, it was a day without cameras or protocol or excessive politeness and deferential or preferen-
tial treatment. He'd waited in line with her at the small
cafeteria, his hat low on his forehead and his glasses on,
and sat outside at the picnic table where they'd sipped
their hot drinks and eaten pizza before taking to the
slopes again.

"We'll head back tomorrow morning," he said as
they approached Blake's chalet.

She questioned him with a look but he gave no explanation. He never did. Not to her and, she was guessing,
seldom to anyone. Their plan, when they'd stretched out
their time on the slopes, had been to head back straight
away once they were finished. She didn't want to ask
whether he now wanted to stay because he wanted the
day—with her—to continue. Like the day at Disney-
land she'd once had as a kid, a day that she couldn't
bear to end. But perhaps he was just tired and didn't
feel like the drive, or perhaps he didn't want her driving after a day's skiing. Assuming they were ignoring
the whole *you're fired* thing and that he would let her
drive anyway. Always with Adam there were so many
questions in her head because he let no one see what
was going on in *his* head.

And the weak part of her that she'd denied for so
long was just grateful that she would get to spend more
time with him. Every minute delighting her. She wasn't
going to question that. Not yet.

They stepped inside and stowed their gear in the
drying room. But with the divestment of their outer
layers, Adam seemed to put on an invisible layer of reserve, something that had been blessedly missing all
day. He'd put it on as she'd taken off her jacket, and it

became even more noticeable as she passed by him to exit the drying room. He backed almost imperceptibly away from her.

They walked silently to the living room.

Blake welcomed them with his customary verbose good humor, insisting that he'd have mulled wine ready for them in front of the fire as soon as they'd—and he used his fingers as quotation marks—freshened up.

So she showered and thought of Adam. Thought of the deep pleasure she'd found just being with him today. She'd sat on the chairlift with him, the hum of the wheel on the cable the only sound interrupting the deep quiet that was peculiar to snow. Sometimes they'd talked on the chairs, and sometimes they'd just sat. Both ways were easy. Both were blissful.

She was a fool. And she didn't know how to stop it.

She'd had relationships before, but they'd been mutual. And clear. Superficial and uncomplicated. Nothing like this.

This one-sided wanting was so much harder to deal with, so much harder to hide. She knew he did what he thought was best for her—but he had no idea. His definition of *best* and hers were poles apart.

He was passing her door when she left her room, self-conscious in a dress and heels.

Adam, as always, looked totally at ease. A soft black cashmere sweater stretched across his shoulders and hinted at the definition of his chest. He held out his arm for her, as though it was the most natural thing in the world.

And maybe for him it was. Doubtless he had held out his arm to women to escort them to dinner almost every night. But for her, just sliding her hand onto his forearm filled her with new sensations. Made her blood rush faster. It made no sense. They'd spent the whole day together. And she'd thought she'd put yesterday's insanity behind her. They'd been close the whole day. And though she'd had wayward thoughts, they hadn't had the intensity that gripped her now. She'd been able, so long as she wasn't looking at his lips, to put their kisses from her mind and not crave more.

But they'd also had on layers and layers of clothes. And she was acutely aware that she'd never touched him before in this supposedly neutral fashion, not since she was a kid when touch meant nothing except friendship, when touch didn't light fires of connection and possibility within her.

Resting her palm on the softness of his sweater, feeling the strength and warmth beneath it, well, it did bad, bad things to her. Made her think bad, bad thoughts. She wanted to lean in, inhale more deeply of his scent, the scent of freshly showered male. And she wanted his lips on hers, and his hands on her. She wanted to know so much more about him than he let her see.

What she needed, on the other hand, was to get farther away from him. So that her brain could start functioning properly again, so that she remembered who she was. And who he was. And that he was looking for a wife. One who met his criteria. Not a temporary fling with his temporary driver.

But, a little voice whispered, *that wouldn't be so bad, would it?*

His step slowed and she looked up to see his gaze on her. "What is it? Do I have toothpaste on my lip?" She ran her tongue around her lips to check. He shook his head and looked away.

"You look—" he cleared his throat "—nice. That's all."

"Nice?"

"Lame compliment, I know. But I don't think the right word to describe you exists. And in that dress…" His gaze swept over her; it didn't linger but there was something in it that warmed her. "Your legs…I scarcely knew you had any."

Danni laughed at his uncharacteristic awkwardness. She'd brought the simple black dress because it traveled well and still made her feel feminine, as did the glint of male appreciation in Adam's eyes. "I hope that's not supposed to be a better compliment." She tried to make light of the reaction to him that was sweeping through her.

His laughter was little more than a breath. But it warmed her further and compensated somewhat for the "nice." Not the best compliment she'd ever had. But coming from Adam, who doubtless had a wealth of sophisticated flattery at the tip of his tongue, it felt honest. And making him laugh always felt like a triumph.

The laughter was still there in his eyes as they held hers for a second.

He started walking again. Oh yes. She knew how he thought of her. As a kid. Almost a sister. That was why his "nice" had felt honest. Danni slid her hand from his arm on the pretext of adjusting her dress. And didn't put it back. *Nice.* It made her realize how much more she wanted from him.

Blake met them as they came down the stairs and insisted they sit in front of the fire while he brought the mulled wine. Adam tilted his head toward the chess set and when she nodded, he shifted it so that it sat between them.

He adjusted the pieces on his side of the board and looked up. "I owe you an apology and my thanks."

"An apology *and* thanks. Wow. That's a big day for you. I'm a little shocked."

"I'm serious, Danni."

"So am I."

He shook his head but a grin tugged at his lips. "Wait till you hear me tell you that you were right."

She slapped her hand to her chest and gasped. This was how she was supposed to behave—the teasing friend, not a woman whose mind was steaming down a one-way track that ended with his bones being jumped.

His grin widened briefly before disappearing. "I haven't had a day like that, as good as that, in…I don't know how long. I skied and forgot about almost everything. Forgot about brewing diplomatic crises and security concerns and upcoming engagements and speeches. Forgot about looking for—thinking of the future." Had he been going to say looking for a wife? "And I owe you for that. You made a good decision when you brought me here."

"Thank you."

"Nobody else would have seen that or done that."

"Because they're all too scared of you."

"Scared?" He sat back in his chair, his brows drawn together. "No they're not."

"In awe, might be a better word. Though I fail to see why." He was just a man doing his job. His job happened to be fairly high profile. But it was still just a job. And a demanding one that he needed time out from occasionally. Who was she kidding? Even she felt the awe occasionally. But in her case it was because of who he was, not what he was.

"I can live with awe," he said with a faint smile.

"It's not good for you. You'll lose touch with reality. You'll get a big head."

"A big head?"

Big Head was what she used to call him when he got all superior on her when she was younger.

Now he was laughing at her. Not out loud. But inside. She just knew it. And she felt her lips twitch in response.

"Thankfully I have you to keep me humble."

And scarily, she wanted to do far more than keep him humble. Things she wasn't supposed to want to do to a prince. It was there somewhere deep inside her, a humming attraction to him. Stronger when she was closest but always there. And she didn't know how to make it go away.

"I needed today. So thank you."

He'd needed today. He'd needed the time out. But he didn't need her. She bit her lip. She shouldn't want him to need her. But wanting her, just a little, wasn't she allowed to want that?

"What about you?"

"Me?"

"You enjoyed today?"

"Yes." Way too much.

"You seem thoughtful."

"I'm fine," she said a little too brightly. "Tired. In a good way. And hungry." In a bad way.

It had happened again. Since coming back here, the ease she'd felt with him had turned to dis-ease. The stiffness and politeness that he used to keep people at a distance was creeping back.

"So, are we going to play?"

"Sure. Can't wait to whip your..."

"My?"

She loved it when he smiled like that, knowledge in his eyes. "Your fine royal ass."

"Have at it."

If only.

They'd scarcely started when Blake returned with their drinks. "Dinner will be ready in half an hour. And you'll be relieved to know that the chef finally turned up. And whatever it is he's cooking, it smells good."

They sat in front of the fire, the chess set between them. The game gave her something other than Adam to focus on. But it wasn't enough of a distraction to keep her from noticing his hands as he moved his pieces and wanting those hands on her, or the deep concentration on his face when she stole looks at him while his attention was focused on the board, and wanting it focused on her.

She was contemplating the curve of his ear when he suddenly shifted his gaze to catch her studying him. His dark eyes trapped and held hers. "Your move," he said slowly.

If it was truly her move, she'd leave her seat and trace the shape of his ear, maybe run her fingers through his hair or over his shoulders, and definitely, definitely kiss his lips, seeking the taste of him, needing to feel that softness, to inhale something of him.

They were both leaning forward over the board. His face was close and she was trapped by the depths in his eyes.

Desire. It bloomed within her. And she recognized its match in the darkening of Adam's eyes. She tried to look away. Tried and failed. And she couldn't say for certain which of them closed that small distance. She'd thought so hard about it that maybe it was her. But it didn't matter because his lips were on hers. She closed her eyes and savored the onslaught of sensation. His lips, firm yet soft, the taste of cinnamon from the mulled wine, and his encompassing warmth. She gave herself over to the kiss. Let the sensations wash through her, claim her. She felt his hand at the back of her head, his fingers threading through her hair.

Unlike their earlier desperate kisses this was achingly tender.

Eight

"**D**inner's ready." They broke apart at the sound of Blake's voice. "Oh, sh—sorry. I didn't mean to interrupt."

"You weren't interrupting," Adam said.

"Looked like I was, to me. Dinner can wait if you like."

"No." Adam who was never outwardly fazed by anything spoke almost curtly. He took a breath. "We're ready now," he said a little less abruptly.

"This way. If you're sure." Blake looked from Adam to Danni.

"We're sure," Adam said.

He led them to the dining room where it would be just the two of them with candles on the table between them and soft music playing from unseen speakers. Danni, whose biggest problem was usually saying all the wrong things, could think of nothing at all to say.

They focused on their appetizers, though neither of them ate much. Finally Adam set his fork down. "I'm sorry."

And there it was, his apology, an attempt to let her down gently, to take the blame and then reassert the proper distance between them.

"Don't be," she said warily. "It's me who's sorry."

"I shouldn't have kissed you then and I shouldn't have kissed you yesterday. I can't seem to help it. But it won't happen again."

She should say nothing, but instead, "Why not?" slipped from her lips.

His eyes widened. "I don't want to ruin or lose what we have and I won't take advantage of you."

"We don't have anything to ruin or lose." Danni's fork clanged against her plate.

"Yes we do. I trust you and I value you and I like you."

Like. That was at least as bad as *nice.*

"The last thing in the world I want is to do anything to change that."

"You're too late. It's already changed."

"How do we change it back?"

"We don't. We can't. And I don't want to. And it wasn't you who kissed me just then, it was me who kissed you. So you have no right to apologize for it. Ever since we kissed yesterday—"

"We shouldn't have."

"Since before we kissed, if I'm going to be honest." She pushed on before he could stop her. "I've thought of you differently."

"We can go back to how we were."

"I don't want to."

Adam looked stricken.

"I want to go forward."

"Forward?"

"I want to see where these new feelings go. I want you to kiss me and to touch me. All over. And I want to be able to kiss you, and to touch you. All over. And I want more than that, too." She waited, her heart pounding. Why, why, could she never keep her mouth closed?

Sorrow and a shadow of horror clouded his face. "We can't, Danni."

She'd known he didn't want to think of her that way. If she'd just kept her mouth shut, she could also have kept her dignity. "I'm sorry." Heat swept across her face as she picked up her fork and stabbed at a mushroom.

"It's not that I don't want to."

She looked up. His dark eyes were troubled. "At least be honest. Making up excuses would be worse than anything. A simple 'I'm just not attracted to you' will do nicely."

"I'm more attracted to you than I can stand. I kept skiing today—past when we should have stopped and gone home—just because I wanted to prolong being with you. Just being with you. Do you have any idea how extraordinary that is? I'm happiest on my own. Or at least I thought I was. But I've discovered that's not true. I'm happier when I'm with you. I can't stop thinking about you, but…"

There had to be a *but*, because for a while her heart had hoped and soared.

"I'm not going to do anything about it."

"Why not?"

"Because I'm supposed to be looking for a woman I can marry. A woman who can stand at my side and be my princess when I take my father's place."

"And I'm not that woman?" She was the opposite of what he was looking for. She knew it, she'd always known it, so it shouldn't hurt.

"Do you want to be?"

She almost said yes, till she thought about it. Danni laughed. "No. I can't think of anything worse." Except for the part where she would get to be with him in private.

"That's why I'm not going to do anything about it."

"Because there's no future in it."

He nodded.

"What about the present?"

"It wouldn't be right. It wouldn't be fair to you."

"Who are you to decide what's fair to me?"

"I'm not having this conversation with you."

"Do you see this appetizer we're eating?"

"Yes."

"It's not dinner. It's not the main event. It'd never fill you up, but it's very nice. So just because you're looking to start dating seriously so that you can find your perfect woman doesn't mean that while we're both here we can't..." She shrugged then took a deep breath. *Don't do it,* a voice of warning cried in her head. "I want to make love with you."

He shook his head. And in his eyes was hardness. And pity. "We can't. It wouldn't be right."

She'd just propositioned him, something she'd never done to any man. And been turned down.

And still she wanted him.

* * *

In her bedroom she changed into her pajamas—
drawstring pants and a camisole—and sat on the big,
empty, four-poster bed. She had no fantasies of a four-
poster bed, only fantasies of Adam. So real she could
taste them, feel them, so real they beat inside her chest.

Senses alert, she listened to the faint precise sounds
coming through the wall of Adam getting ready for bed.
The bathroom door opening and shutting, taps running.

He was attracted to her. He'd said that much—the
admission wrung regretfully out of him.

But he wasn't going to do anything about it. That
regret was hers.

Because it wouldn't be right or fair to her. Was the
regret, the loss of something not known, never to be
known, fair? Was sitting in here alone and needing,
fair? He would do nothing about that injustice.

But could she?

A sliver of light peeped beneath the adjoining door.
Was he thinking about her? Or had he put her from his
mind? He was good at that. Deal with the issue at hand
then move on to the next, letting no overlap complicate
one or the other. He could be in there reading or working, totally focused.

But he'd said he was attracted to her. More than he
could stand. And Adam was not a man to use words
lightly.

She crossed to the door and put her ear to it but heard
nothing. She touched her fingers to its hard, unreveal-
ing, uninviting surface.

He'd already admitted that her going against his
stated wishes and bringing him here had been a good

decision. She could…seduce him. She swallowed a
laugh that would have been close to hysterical.

Steeling herself, knowing that some regrets were
bigger than others and some opportunities could never
be recovered, she touched the handle. The beating of
her heart precluded hearing anything else.

So few things in life scared her, but this…this terrified her. She deepened her breath till her fingers ceased
their shaking.

She'd already made a fool of herself. She had nothing
further to lose. Slowly, she turned the handle, holding
her breath against the possibility that he'd locked the
door from his side, and on her exhale swung the door
silently open.

He sat at the small desk, his back to her and his
laptop open in front of him but his head held in his
hands. Trying to work? But not.

Drawn to him, to that broad back, that bent head,
Danni crossed the thickly carpeted room.

Adam didn't move.

She stood behind him. His laptop had switched to
its screen saver.

He straightened and held himself still, as though listening. She just had to touch him, one hand to the closest forbidding shoulder but her heart beat so hard she
could scarcely move.

"No."

The single abrupt word was fierce. Sighing heavily,
he rested his fingers on the keyboard and began slowly
to type. A document with graphs and tables sprang to
life on the screen.

That *no* was a message for her. What was she doing?
She was no seductress. She was wearing her pajamas!

She didn't even own anything that could claim to be a negligee. He'd already turned her down. How much rejection did she want? Panic gripped her. She took a step backward, held still and then took another step. She backed halfway across the room on unsteady legs then turned. And she had her fingers on the edge of the door when his hand landed on her right shoulder and the shock waves reverberated through her.

"What are you doing?" His deep voice held both the question and his reluctant awareness of what her answer had to be. Given her earlier admission there could be no other.

"Nothing." She didn't turn to face him. She couldn't. Her heart thudded in her chest. Run. Run. Run. But she couldn't do that, either.

He stepped in closer. She could feel him behind her, surrounding her without touching her, except for that one touch, a heavy hand tight on her shoulder. Its grip invincible.

"Why are you in here?" His breath feathered across her neck sending warm shivers through her with the gently spoken words. Tension, beyond anything she'd known, seized her. A combination of wanting and anticipation and cowardice and fear.

He had to ask? As if her presence here wasn't obvious. She didn't doubt that women had tried to seduce him before. She was certain, however, that he'd never had to ask what they were doing. "I was going to burgle your room." Between that and seduction, burglary was surely the lesser sin.

"What were you going to take?" he asked quietly.

"Your innocence." She'd thought about making it a joke but her words came out a whisper.

His hand on her shoulder tightened and he pulled her back against him. She felt laughter reverberating through him. Okay. So maybe it had sounded like a joke. Apparently a really funny one.

But the silent laughter stilled. "My innocence is long gone, Danni," he said, utter seriousness in his quiet voice. "It's only when I'm with you that I even remember I had any."

She waited. His fingers tightened where his hand still rested on her shoulder. His breath still feathered across her neck though his breathing was shorter. And though the beat of her heart still commanded her to run, his hand and her recalcitrant feet and perhaps that whisper of breath kept her immobile.

"Maybe we should just forget I came in here."

"It's not going to be that easy."

"Nothing ever is with you."

"Why?" His other hand came to rest on her left shoulder.

"Because you never let anything just be easy. You're always analyzing life like it's a chess game."

From the floor below them came a crash and the rumble of Blake's voice.

Adam's hands slid lower till they curved around her arms, his touch gentle but unbreakable. "I meant," he said, and she imagined his smile, "why were you trying to seduce me?"

"How many reasons could there be?"

"More than you could imagine," he said quietly.

"Well apparently I don't have a very good imagination. Because as far as I can see there would only be one reason I would try to seduce you."

"Danni. Go. While you can." He moved. Closer still.

So that she felt the press of him against her back. His hands slid lower still until they wrapped around hers, holding her in direct contradiction to his words. His cheek was beside hers.

She closed her eyes and leaned against him, over-whelmed by him. His nearness, his warmth, his scent enveloped her.

Movement again, and then the gentle press of his lips against her neck. Need blossomed. Drenched her. Stole strength from her limbs so that she melted back against him, her head falling to one side to give him greater access to her neck because she needed this kiss. His kiss.

This moment of weakness might be all she would get from him. So even as the desire and delight en-gulfed her, she tried to catalogue the sensations. But the strength of them made cataloguing impossible.

He just was. And his touch did what it did. And called to something in her that was beyond reason.

And while his lips and touch worked magic on her, magic so powerful it needed access to no more than the bare skin of her neck, his hands moved again, slid-ing from her hands to her waist, sliding beneath her top. Skin to skin. His heat seared her so that her breath shuddered in her chest. She backed more firmly against him.

Hands and lips stilled.

Please don't let him stop.

She leaned farther back, trying to meld herself with him so that he couldn't let her go, couldn't push her away. And she felt the evidence of his need, heard it in the ragged hitch to his breath.

"Danni."

She heard too much in his voice. Regret and blame and apology. His hands started to slip away. He would ignore need and go with his idea of right. She gripped his wrists and his hands stilled. She guided them upward, trailing over waist and ribs till she led them where she wanted to feel them, covering her breasts. He groaned against her neck and his thumbs brushed over hardened nipples.

Her gasp matched his groan as need streaked through her, hot and fierce.

He dropped his hands and as she was about to cry out in protest he turned her around.

And kissed her.

Properly. Finally. The kiss she'd been waiting for all her life. There was no anger or regret this time. No sweet gentleness. There was only need. His lips against hers. His tongue dancing with and teasing hers, clamoring to learn her and please her. His arms wound tightly around her and his body pressed against her.

She returned his kiss. Greedily. She had wanted this for so long even while she'd denied that wanting. She'd imagined it, dreamed of it.

And it was everything that she'd imagined and dreamed only better and so much more.

And now that she was facing him, she too could touch. Lifting her hands to his face, she traced his cheekbones, his jaw, felt the rasp of beard against her palms. She slid her fingers through his hair to delight in its dark silk. But she wanted more, too. As they kissed she found the buttons of his shirt, fumbled them undone so that she could touch the warm hard planes of his abdomen, the contours of his chest, the strength of his back.

She was torn between the delight of slow explora-
tion, the need to learn and treasure every contour, and
the ravenous need to feel all of him, all at once, to fill
her hands with him. She'd waited so long for this impossible reality and knew a fear that it might all vanish.
It felt so much like magic, being held by him, kissed by
him, that surely it could disappear as quickly as it had
appeared, like a mirage in the desert.

Just as she'd feared, his hands came up, framed her
face and he pulled back, breaking the kiss, ending the
beauty.

He studied her and she tried to read his thoughts in
his eyes. She saw turmoil and anguish. But she saw
desire also. Deep, aching desire. It was there in his
darkened eyes, in his parted lips and ragged breathing.

"It's not right," he whispered.

"It's very, very right," she whispered back.

And then he was kissing her again.

His attempt at restraint demolished, she could have
cried in triumph.

He dropped his hands and wrapped his arms around
her and carried her through the door to her bed. He set
her on the floor. Torment clouded his eyes. His hands
gripped her arms, their hold almost fierce. "Don't fight
it, Adam. Just please tell me you have condoms."

A smile flashed across his face and he closed his
eyes. "I give in. I'll be damned for it, but I give in."
Relief weakened her. He was back from his bathroom
within seconds and with slow wonder he peeled her
camisole over her head and her pants down her legs.
She helped him shed his clothes and they knelt facing
each other on the bed. She helped sheath him and then
Danni climbed onto his knees straddling him so that

she could touch his face, trail her fingers along his nose, his jaw, over his lips. She'd wanted to touch him so badly for so long now, had done it countless times in her imagination. And the reality was everything she'd imagined and more. The hardness of muscle and bone, the silk of skin, the rasp of hair.

"Do you have any idea," he said, "how badly I want you?"

She bit her lip as she looped her hands behind his head. "I think I might." She shared that same need.

His hands rose to her breasts and a shudder rippled through her as his thumbs teased her nipples. She arched into his touch and he replaced his hands with his mouth, kissing each breast in turn, pleasuring her with lips and teeth and tongue while his hand roved, cupped her bottom and pulled her closer still so that his erection pressed against her.

He moved abruptly, swept her off him so that she was lying down and he was over her. "You are so perfect," he said, shaking his head and settling himself between her legs.

She wrapped her legs around his back. "Enough with the talking." She lifted her hips so that she felt him at her entrance. His passionate gaze locked with hers as he slid into her, stretching her, filling her as she'd ached for him to. Her body welcomed him. He stopped there, then slowly pulled out before filling her again, the pleasure exquisite. They moved together, perfectly in tune. The bliss built until it was almost unbearable. Sounds escaped her, cries of delight and need. Their rhythm built, became fiercer yet, unstoppable, till he was driving into her and she was meeting each thrust, taking him deeper still till the pleasure raging through her couldn't be contained and her orgasm ripped through her, shattering her. Adam surged against her, crying her name.

They lay, chests heaving, foreheads touching. As their breathing calmed he rolled off her but kept her in his arms. She laid her head on his shoulder, sated and dreamy.

Sanity slowly returned.

She felt and heard Adam take a breath. "Don't say anything."

"Not even, wow."

Danni laughed and he pulled her closer to him.

Adam woke and watched Danni sleeping, bathed in soft morning light. He could scarcely remember seeing her still before. Completely relaxed. Even when they played chess and she took her time thinking before making a move there was a contained restlessness to her as though she was ever ready to leap from her chair. It showed itself in the subtle tapping of her fingers or her toes.

He smiled now. She didn't share a bed well. She lay at an angle across the big bed. One arm was flung up above her head, her fingers curling gently. The pale skin of her arm looked so soft, vulnerable almost. Her eyes, usually flashing fire, were closed. Eyelashes kissed her cheeks.

She stirred and rolled. And the sheet he'd pulled up over her as she slept shifted. So beautiful. She took his breath away. Pale and lithe. More petite than he'd realized—again he blamed that restless energy that radiated for her, always making her seem...more. More than the sum of her parts. More alive than anyone else he knew. Brimming with vitality and humor.

The edge of the sheet lay across her chest, dipping low but not low enough to reveal her pert perfect breasts.

So feminine. He'd been willfully blind to that about her before. He'd focused over the years on how much of a tomboy she was, how she was his friend, at times almost a sister, to help him avoid focusing on the obvious. Danni was gorgeous. Passion personified. Nothing sultry, just an electric sensuality that called to him, like no one else.

Called to him? Like no one else? The thought stopped him cold.

He couldn't entertain thoughts like that. She was Danni. He was a brief pit stop on the race that was her life. And he had a life to lead, too. Responsibilities to live up to.

He should get out of this bed, cross back to his own room and lock the door behind him. Too late, he realized that he suddenly stood on the precipice of something unknown and dangerous.

She opened her eyes and her lips curved into a smile. That's where the danger lay. Those eyes. Just looking into them pleased him. Her smile broadened, she shifted again, arched just a little. He took back his earlier thought. Sultry. There was no other word for it. He rolled toward her. Precipice be damned.

She traced a pattern across his chest with her fingertip. "You know, French is the language of love but you never spoke French to me while we were…"

Making love? Neither of them would want to call it

that. "Because I couldn't think straight in any language. I can try now if you like?"

She grinned and her eyes sparkled.

He caught her lazily circling finger. "I'll speak words to you that will light you on fire. Words you'll understand even though you don't speak French or Italian or German." He brought that finger to his lips and kissed it. "Croissant, Citroen." He found her next finger, kissed that also. "Schnitzel, Mercedes Benz." Her fingers weren't enough. He rolled on top of her, holding his weight from her, and loved the way she wriggled to accommodate him and the heat and anticipation in her gaze.

"Go on."

He brushed her hair back from her face and kissed her forehead. "Pizza, Ferrari."

"Ohh, I think I like Italian best. Give me more."

"Demanding wench."

She rocked her hips.

And he'd give her the world. "Tiramisu, Lamborghini."

"Take me I'm yours."

He touched his lips to hers, and conscious thought, in any language, evaporated.

Nine

Adam stood with Danni and Blake under the portico of the chalet. Satisfaction thrummed through him as smoothly as the idling of the Range Rover's engine.

One night and one morning of perfection, of love-making and laughter. They'd stolen that much for themselves. As he watched Danni talking easily with Blake, he realized it was the laughter that had surprised him. He'd never laughed so much with a woman before. But Danni teased and joked, taking nothing, least of all him, too seriously. She was a revelation.

He hadn't thought she could be right when she'd said a relationship should be fun. It was one of the many lessons he'd learned from her.

Living in the moment was part of her nature. She had refused to talk about the future, about anything other than right now. And it turned out that very little talking at all was necessary and that there were far better ways than skiing to capitalize on snow on the ground outside.

The sheer compulsive energy of her had drawn him in. She'd uncovered a part of himself he'd walled over and forgotten.

He watched her now. Some of that energy had dimmed. Their time of isolated perfection was over. They were heading back. For the first time he could remember he was resisting what lay ahead.

"I hope you've enjoyed your stay," Blake said as though he was reciting lines from a script. He probably was. Several times throughout their visit, he had consulted the little red notebook that contained his instructions. Even absent, Sabrina ran a tight ship.

"Very much," Danni answered.

Blake leaned a little closer. "I didn't say anything, because I didn't want you to know." He lowered his voice. "But you were my first ever guests. I'm relieved it was you two. I don't know too much about this lark and I'll admit I was worried. I didn't know how it would go if someone important had come to stay. Sabrina would have killed me if I did anything wrong or got too familiar with guests. Or talked too much." A sheepish smile spread across his face. He winked. "If you ever see her and she asks, tell her I didn't."

"You didn't," Adam said.

"Anyway, it was a good practice run for me. We're expecting a mayor next week. I won't say who because I'm not allowed to talk about guests, but at least I've got this under my belt as a warm-up. I'll still be nervous having a local dignitary but it won't be so bad."

"Rest easy. You were the perfect host."

Blake slapped him on the shoulder with surprising force. "Thanks, mate. That means a lot to me. Oh, hey, I forgot to get you to sign the guest book."

"It's okay," Danni said. "I signed it." She tossed and caught the car keys. She knew he watched the movement. Challenge lit her eyes. He let the challenge pass. The driving was important to her.

Like him, she'd been reluctant to leave their bed this morning. But once she had, she'd approached the things they'd needed to do efficiently but almost mechanically.

They'd been on the road a few minutes when he asked, "Whose name? In the guest book."

"Just mine. And my signature's almost indecipherable. Don't worry, there'll be nothing to link you here with me." She didn't sound like the Danni of the last few days. There was a new distance and formality to her voice, and a subtle tension about her shoulders. Was this how it was going to go? Had he ruined everything by giving into the overpowering need and making love with her?

"That wasn't what I was worried about."

"No? What were you worried about then?"

"Would you believe me if I said you?"

She sighed but there was a hint of laughter behind it and her shoulders eased. "Yes. I would." The glance she flicked in his direction was almost sorrowful.

The road unwound before them, a dark damp strip between blinding white snow and dark green pines. The GPS in the dash showed what lay ahead. But there was no road map for what came next for them. And as a man who lived by plans and goals and schedules, the uncertainty and the changes they would face bothered him.

He didn't know if she realized what they'd be up

against. "You're the one who has the most to lose if this becomes public knowledge," he said. Hers was the life that would be turned upside down, its quiet privacy obliterated. He didn't want that to be the legacy for her of their brief time together.

"It won't become public knowledge. It can't. It was just one weekend." She sounded blithely unconcerned with her own fate. "Only you and I know, and I'm not telling anyone. And if you can curb your tendency to run off at the mouth," she said with pure Danni sass, "we'll be fine. Blake knows we were there together, but he doesn't know who you are. And even if he did I don't think he'd tell. Not deliberately."

"And there's always Sabrina to keep him in line." Blake had showed him a photo of the absent Sabrina, a tiny, sweet-looking woman.

"Exactly," Danni agreed with a smile. "One snow-bound weekend. We were allowed that much."

But the possibility of what they'd shared becoming public was only part of what was bothering him. The other part, the purely selfish part, was the prospect of losing her, and what they'd found, so soon after discovering it. He'd been closer to her this weekend than anyone else. Ever.

"You're saying that's it, that this is over between us?" That was supposed to be his line, but hearing it acknowledged by her made him want to fight it. He wasn't used to this kind of confusion. Usually the right thing to do was obvious, or at least felt right. But ending things with Danni, when they'd scarcely started, felt wrong in his heart at the same time as he knew in his mind it was right.

She flicked a worried glance at him. "Yes. It has to

be. You know that. We have no future. We go back to life as normal."

That was the trouble. He did know. And yet she'd turned him upside down and inside out until he couldn't think straight. Because of her, he might never think completely straight again. But what he did know was that what he used to consider normal would no longer be enough. "I'm not sure it's possible."

"We'll manage." She spoke fiercely.

Did she really believe that? They'd come together so quickly there had been no slow anticipatory buildup, no courtship. None of the romance Danni herself had once informed him women wanted. Didn't she deserve that?

"And I'm supposed to be okay with just using you for a one-night stand? You're okay with that?"

"Absolutely. And you have to be okay with me using you. It was probably wrong of me but..." She shrugged.

He shook his head. Her voice held a brittle note of falseness. "I don't know, Danni. Things have changed so quickly and so absolutely. I need time to think it through."

"No, you don't. I can see where you're going with this. You think you haven't done right by me. But you have. Very, very right."

He didn't like the sudden stubborn lift to her chin, the narrowing of her eyes.

"You'll forget about the weekend and move on." She kept her voice low and easy but he thought perhaps she had to fight for that calm. "We both will. You're being honorable. I know you don't like the thought of using anyone."

"I wasn't using you. You know I wouldn't." But had he?

"Then I guess I owe you an apology, because you wouldn't. Not intentionally. But I was using you."

"I don't believe you." He recognized the tough kid who always came up fighting in the woman beside him.

"Believe me. I thought it was mutual or I wouldn't have…"

Wouldn't have what? There had been no forethought in what had transpired between them, no stopping to consider consequences.

She swallowed. "So while your protest is sweet, it's not necessary."

He couldn't see beyond the bravado, couldn't fathom what was going on in her head. And he owed it to her to find out. Despite what she said, he did need to do right by her. It was imperative.

"Danni, we need to talk this through."

"No we don't." She looked fixedly ahead. He couldn't see her eyes, and he needed to have some idea what she really felt. Her eyes, so expressive, always gave her away. "Let's stop at that café. The one we stopped at on the way up."

"I don't think that's a good idea." And still she didn't so much as glance at him.

"If what we have is over—"

"It has to be." She made his "if" an absolute.

"Then we'll be going to go back to how it used to be between us?"

"Yes."

"So, I'll cease being your lover and go back to being a prince to you, nothing more?"

"It's for the best."

"In that case, stop at the café. It's an order. And if you really want to prove things can go back to how they were, you'll follow it."

Danni took a deep breath and consciously relaxed her shoulders and flexed her fingers before resetting them around the wheel. Adam would come to his senses soon. All she had to do was to *keep calm and carry on*. It was either that or panic and freak out. When the café came into view she slowed and pulled in to the parking lot. An obedient driver. Nothing more.

Inside, the scent of coffee filled the air and an open fire blazed in the hearth. Only a couple tables were occupied, but at first one table, and then the other, heads turned. Then each of those few people leaned in closer to their companions. And whispered.

She could have kicked herself. Getting away without Adam being recognized the first time they'd been here had been more luck than she should have hoped for. A second time was too much to ask.

But, she reminded herself, the first time they had nothing to hide, and this time needn't be any different. She was his driver. Taking him home from his weekend break. *Of fantastic sex,* a wicked, insidious voice whispered. No. She was Adam's driver for the weekend. Period. If she repeated it enough times she could almost believe it. He was a prince. She was returning him to the palace. To his life. She should have worn her uniform. Because although it made her stand out, it also made her invisible. People saw it and then dismissed her.

Without her uniform she worried that people might see the woman who had spent the weekend in bed making love with a prince. She felt so different, so sexually satisfied, it didn't seem possible that the difference wasn't obvious.

Adam's nod and smile took in the occupants and the staff, earned him smiles and gasps in return. Somehow—through years of practice most likely—he'd mastered the art of looking warm and approachable while at the same time discouraging anyone from testing that approachability. He stood at the same booth they'd occupied during their first visit and waited for her to sit.

Danni slid onto the dark leather seat. Adam sat beside her. Too close. Too intimate. She scooted around so that she sat opposite him. Like a driver might. No. Not a driver. A driver would never sit like this with a royal client. But perhaps a friend. She could live with friend.

They ordered drinks from an effusive waitress who looked as though she might almost curtsy. When she'd turned her back, Adam leaned in. "Just a few hours ago we were making love." He kept his voice low, so as not to be overheard but it made it even more seductive than normal.

Danni didn't need his reminder. It was too easy looking at him to remember all that they'd shared. But she couldn't think about them making love. And he couldn't be allowed to, either. Or at least he couldn't be allowed to talk about it.

Deep down she knew she couldn't be just friends with him. Not after they'd been so much more. So her pending grief would be for the loss of both a lover and a friend.

In the space of days, things had gone further and deeper than she should ever have let them. She should

have run far and fast that first night she leaned into the
car to wake him and met his gaze and felt that insistent
tug of attraction, the kick of desire. She should have run
before she realized how very much more lay behind it.

"I just want to know that we've thought through our
options before we consign 'us' to an impossibility," he
said.

"We don't have any options and there is no 'us.'"

"There are always options."

"Not always. Not this time." They couldn't have options. It ended now. She could have no part of his life.
She'd remember this always as something magical. But
that was all it could ever be. A memory.

She had to be ruthless with the naive unthinking part
of her that craved options and possibilities, that wanted
to dream of a future, no matter how short, that wanted
to steal all the minutes and hours and days and nights
they could. Regardless of right or wrong. Regardless
of the consequences because in this case they wouldn't
be hers alone.

Adam belonged to their country, he wasn't hers and
he never would be.

She thought she saw a shadow of the sorrow besieg-
ing her in his eyes. Beneath the table his foot brushed
against hers. A small point of contact, toe to toe,
through leather. They weren't allowed even that much
and yet she couldn't move her foot away.

If they weren't in a public place and he reached for
her, she would too easily succumb. As it was, he rested
one hand on the table near hers and she ached to hold
it.

"The trouble is that I can't bear for this—" he gestured between the two of them "—to end. And I don't think you can either."

"We don't always get everything we want in life."

He sat back as the waitress approached with their coffees but his gaze never left her face.

"Don't you see," Danni said once the waitress had gone again. "It has ended. It ended when we walked out of that chalet."

His frown deepened, as though he might argue. But he knew who he was and what he owed his country and his family. He was returning to a world of responsibilities. Responsibilities that included looking for a woman to stand at his side as princess.

"I can't stand by while you search for the perfect royal wife. I'm strong, Adam, but I'm not that strong. Or that much of a masochist."

He jerked as though she'd slapped him. His hand clenched into a fist on the table. "And I'm not that much of a bastard. How could I look at another woman after you?"

"You have to."

He sat up straighter. The silence stretched and stretched, till finally he spoke quietly. "I'm stopping my search for the perfect wife."

The bottom dropped out of Danni's world.

No. She wouldn't be responsible for her country's prince postponing his search. She'd be reviled throughout the principality.

She stood, her legs far from steady. "Then you definitely don't need me."

Ten

The drive back to the palace lasted an eternity. Adam sat as silent and inscrutable as a sphinx next to her. She just wanted the trip to be over. She needed to get away from him, because being this close when she could no longer have him was torture.

She would drop him off and aides would come running with crises for him to negotiate. He would move on.

But when she finally saw the longed-for towering sandstone building, it was loss rather than relief that swamped her.

This was it. This was their goodbye.

She drove to the entrance to his wing. He turned to her as she pulled to a stop. "Have dinner with me to-night?"

"No. I'm going to spend this evening with Dad." She took a deep breath. "Adam, don't do this."

"So when I kiss you now you'll be kissing me good-bye?" His dark beautiful eyes were steady on her, drawing her inexorably toward him. Desperation for this one last kiss. It was the desperation that told her she couldn't allow even this kiss. Especially this kiss.

"No. Yes. I mean, I can't kiss you, but if I did I would be kissing you goodbye."

Rational thought disintegrated as he leaned closer. She caught his scent, saw his lips—lips she knew so well. Every cell in her body yearned for his touch. One kiss. One memory to take away. She wasn't strong enough to deny herself that.

"You want this, too," he said softly.

"No, I don't." She was inches from him and she knew everything about her contradicted his words.

He laughed, the sound low and rich. And more than anything she wanted those laughing lips on hers. She pulled back and looked straight ahead, anywhere rather than at Adam. Adam, whom she could never have again. "You should get out now. We both have things to do. Lives to get back to."

"I'm not getting out. Not until you kiss me."

"That's blackmail." She couldn't let him win. If he was going to be stubborn then she could be, too. She got out, striding round the car to open his door and hold it wide.

As he got out, she walked quickly to the rear of the car and removed his suitcase. She carried it to the recessed entrance to the palace. She turned and found him right there. He lifted his hands to frame her face.

Just that touch of his palms along her jaw rendered her immobile, stole her breath. Made her ache. Her lips parted with need for him. She felt the familiar insistent tugging low within her.

"Tell me you don't want me to kiss you, every bit as badly as I want to kiss you. If you tell me that, then I won't."

She fought for long seconds over her answer, drowning in his eyes, aching with the need to touch him. "I don't want you to kiss me."

He lowered his head and brushed his lips across hers.

"You said you wouldn't." The feebleness of her protest echoed the weakness of her willpower.

"You lied when you said you didn't want me to. So that made my lie okay, too. Tell me you don't want me to kiss you again."

His breath mingled with hers in the cool air. She swayed toward him, her body betraying her mind. "I don't."

"Liar." He kissed her again, this time the way she needed him to, his lips slanting over hers, tasting her deeply, and filling her with the taste of him. Her arms slid around him, pulling his body closer, holding him to her, and any last scraps of reason fled. She was lost to him, lost to the sensations. His warmth, his scent, the exquisite pressure of his lips on hers, the way his tongue teased.

Finally, at a nearby sound, they broke apart and he rested his forehead against hers. His thumbs stroked her jaw. "This is wrong." His words whispered across her lips.

She knew he had to see and admit it sooner or later. But still the admission, when she was blinded with the need stirred by his kiss, hurt. "I told you."

"I should be dropping you at your door, not the other way around."

"That's not how it works. I was the driver."

"No, you weren't. I fired you, remember. I was only letting you drive as a favor. I know how you like it. So get back in the car and I'll drive you to the gatehouse."

"No."

"Yes. Or we go inside." He glanced at the palace. "I have a big bed in there, Danni. And I can't stop thinking about having you in it. This is your last chance before I pick you up and carry you inside. Maybe then I'll have you worked out of my system and can let this be over."

Danni saw the calculation in his gaze and knew she had only seconds before he acted on his threat. She strode from him and got into the passenger seat, shutting the door behind her. If this was how he wanted to play it… If it made him feel better, gave him the illusion of control, she would do it.

He drove her to the gatehouse and cut the engine so that all was silent before he turned to her, his eyes darkening, soulful and sinful. "Kiss me again."

She wanted to do so very much more than just kiss him. He was some kind of sorcerer making her forget what was good for her, what was right. And she had to break his spell without giving him the chance to weave a new one.

She leaped out of the car, shut the door with hasty, choked words of thanks and goodbye and ran into the house.

"You're sure everything is all right?" Her father asked for the second time that evening as she looked into the fridge trying to decide what to cook for their dinner.

"Fine, Dad," she said as brightly as she could manage. But she was far from all right. Adam had said he was stopping his search and it was her fault. "I'm just a little tired. I'm looking forward to a quiet and early night." Her first night of getting used to not being with Adam. Given that they'd only had one night in each other's arms it shouldn't be that difficult. What was one night out of a lifetime? Even if that night had been blissful perfection. There was no reason for this awful weight pressing on her heart.

"Oh."

She didn't like the sound of that "oh" and looked at her father. "What's up?"

"I must have misheard him."

"Misheard who?"

"Adam."

A knock sounded at the front door.

"Dad? What's going on?"

"Adam called earlier. He said he was going to come around to see you."

Danni strode to the door, her father's voice catching up to her as she reached for the handle. "Is there something going on between you and Adam?"

Her fingers stilled and she turned back. "No, Dad. There's not." Not anymore. On one hand he'd think she was breaking ancient unwritten rules if there was something between them; on the other, there was probably nothing in the world her father would like better. It would be a dream come true for him.

But this was her life and she had to live it to best suit herself, not her father.

Danni pulled open the door and came face to face with the man she didn't want to see. And all the memories of what they'd shared and being with him came flooding back, swamping her. The oppressive weight lifted from her heart and it soared like a bird unexpectedly freed from captivity. She stared at his face and it reflected some of the same hunger she felt.

She'd missed him. Damn it.

She'd only been away from him for a couple hours and she'd missed him. It was so good just to look at him. And despite the fact that he was forcing her hand in coming here, there was a trace of uncertainty and need in his eyes as he watched and waited. She should have capitalized on it; instead, that uncertainty and need undid her.

"Adam." She meant to say his name without feeling. Instead her voice was filled with yearning.

She drank in the sight of him. A sight she had to deprive herself of. Soon. But not yet. She needed just a couple more seconds first. Time to imprint in her memory just how he looked—his eyes, his nose with that bump, his lips, his jaw. She had to clench her hands at her sides to keep from reaching for him.

From behind his back, he produced a bouquet of flowers.

"You shouldn't have." The gesture was romantic.

"You don't like them?"

She lifted the bouquet to her face and inhaled the fragrance. "They're beautiful. Nobody's ever given me flowers before."

He reached for her shoulders and pulled her toward him. His eyes searched her face.

She tried to be strong. Difficult when desire swept

through her, overwhelming good sense, overwhelming everything.

He pulled her closer still and waited. Leaving her anticipating. Wanting.

Finally it was she who gave in and closed the distance, needing the touch of his lips on hers.

He released her too soon from the kiss that should never have happened. His hands had traveled to loop around her waist and he kept them there, kept that bond between them.

She should pull away.

She stayed where she was.

On a soft sigh Adam kissed her again. This kiss was full of the promise of delight and pleasure. It was long blissful seconds before he lifted his head.

"I spent the entire meeting with the Spanish ambassador thinking of doing that."

"But we agreed," she protested. Too little, too late.

"We didn't agree to anything."

Danni laughed. A mix of exasperation and despair. Why did it have to be Adam? The one man above all others she could never have. The one whose whole existence was so far removed from hers. He needed a woman who was her opposite, cultured and sophisticated, diplomatic and beautiful. Someone who would make a good princess.

And she needed to forget about him.

But at this instant, cradled in his arms, she could only be grateful that he was making a liar out of her and taking what he—and she—wanted rather than what was right for him.

"Come out with me tonight. We need to talk."

"No. I have work in the morning. A press conference to prepare for later this week."

"Don't leave him standing out there, Danni. Ask him in." Her father's voice came from within the house.

"No." There was no strength, only panic, in her voice. She couldn't let him do this.

"Come and watch this, you two," her father called. "They've got coverage of the Brazil race."

Adam lifted an eyebrow. "Watching Formula One with your father, what harm could there be in that?"

"All sorts of harm."

A hint of a smile touched his lips. "Frightened of me, Danni?"

"No." Liar. She was terrified of what he'd done to her heart, of the havoc he could wreak.

"Good, then you won't mind."

"Why won't you take no for an answer?"

"It's a failing. Weren't you supposed to cure me of my flaws?" He looked over her shoulder. "Evening St. Claire."

Danni's heart sank. If her father was here, there would be no getting rid of Adam. "Evening, Adam. Are you two coming in or are you going to stand out there in the cold all night?"

Adam watched her and waited, appearing to leave the decision—now when it was too late—up to her.

"We're coming in," Danni said on a sigh. She had no strength to resist. Her earlier attempt had been a bluff—and he'd known it. There would be time enough for strength tomorrow. After just this one evening, in the company of her father. What harm could there be in it? A little voice in the recesses of her mind echoed her earlier answer—all sorts of harm. Because she wanted so desperately just to *be* with Adam—near him, able to watch and hear him, to laugh with him for one more evening.

Tomorrow she would leave. Go stay with a friend. Go somewhere Adam wouldn't follow her. She would force a clean break on herself.

"Have you eaten?" Adam asked as she put the flowers into a vase.

She shook her head.

"Takeout?" He pulled his phone from his pocket. "Is Chinese still your father's favorite?"

She nodded. Her acquiescence complete. She might as well just roll over and present her stomach for him to scratch. Oh, wait. She'd already done that.

He followed her to the living room. Her father sat in the armchair, leaving her and Adam the couch. They sat close, but not touching, which was its own kind of torture. As her father added his commentary to that of the announcers, Adam's hand, out of her father's line of sight, found hers and closed around it. And this touch was too much and not enough.

The three of them watched, intent, conversing only occasionally, shouting at the screen at times. And despite knowing that she shouldn't allow it, Danni found so much pleasure in sharing this with Adam and her father that it hurt, this taste of what could never be.

After they'd eaten, she made coffee, needing an excuse to get away, a chance to regroup, to grow a spine. But in the kitchen she stood at the counter and stared out into the night.

Adam came to stand behind her. His arms wrapped around her. "The times I spent here with you and your father were as close as I got to ordinary growing up and

you have no idea how much they meant to me. I knew
my father loved me but it was your father who spent
time with me, who had no expectations. I've always
been grateful."

"I liked how you were when you were here. You
were so different from when you were with Rafe or the
other kids. You were so serious, so remote, as though
even with them you had to remember who you were."

"I must have been insufferable."

"We suffered you." She smiled, remembering those
times. She'd seen the barriers he erected, they all had,
but she'd seen the chinks and breaks in the invisible
armor he cloaked himself with. She'd seen them when
he'd been here, or when it had been just the two of
them, and he'd thought she was too young to really understand what was going on, and too devoted to him to
reveal the secrets he sometimes revealed to her. She'd
reveled in her perceived status as his favorite. She
wanted it still.

She stepped out from the shelter of his arms.

What if I fall in love with you? She wanted to scream
the words, the real reason for her fear. Instead she
locked them deep inside her. Because she knew the
answer to that question. It would be a terrible, terrible
thing.

Eleven

Something was off.

Danni had been coordinating the biannual press briefings since the start of the process of bringing a Grand Prix to San Philippe. The feel in the room today was different. And it wasn't just her and her confusion over her feelings for Adam and her sorrow over what could never be.

The last official press release two weeks ago, back when her life had been normal, had contained promising developments. But not promising enough to justify the crowd in the small room that usually had more empty chairs than full ones.

She caught an enquiring glance from Michael Lucas, the head of San Philippe motorsport, and gave a small shrug. As well as the usual motor racing commentators, and representatives from tourism, who expected a Grand Prix to have a major influence on visitor numbers, there were reporters and journalists she didn't recognize. There was also a new sense of energy and excitement in the room.

As she stood to the side of the stage, she reviewed her notes again, including the emails that had come in last night and this morning. Nothing surprising there. She could only be glad that, after a drop-off in interest over the last few months while proceedings slowed down in talks about safety and scheduling and disruption to residents, awareness appeared to be picking up again nicely.

She tried to keep her thoughts on task, tried not to think about Adam, who she had missed so desperately in her bed this last week. She'd ached for his presence, his scent, the weight of his body next to hers. Missed the way he made love to her.

The first thing she'd done at work the Monday after her ski weekend was to make arrangements to move forward her trips to other Grand Prix host countries. She was getting out of San Philippe. It was the only way.

The sound of Michael clearing his throat recalled her attention. The panel, including drivers, and manufacturers' representatives were all ready. Michael looked for her nod then began the conference with the latest updates, then opened the floor to questions.

He took a couple of questions about the race course then chose one of the journalists Danni didn't recognize to ask her question. Danni could see the woman's press accreditation but from this distance couldn't tell which publication she was with. But if interest in the

Grand Prix was spreading to mainstream media she could only be glad.

"I have a question for Ms. St. Claire."

All heads turned toward her. Danni hid her surprise, but suddenly she wasn't quite so glad. As she reached for the microphone the end panelist held out for her, she had a very bad feeling.

"Is it true that you're romantically involved with Prince Adam?"

Danni clamped shut the jaw that wanted to fall open. Not interest in a Grand Prix. Interest in a grand prize. A grand prince. Gossip about her and Adam.

She'd really thought they'd got away with it, a weekend of anonymity. But it had been naive to hope they might evade speculation and that their time together would be something she could treasure and keep to herself. Just one weekend. Did Adam not deserve that? Whether or not he deserved it, he wasn't going to get it.

Interest in the room picked up palpably. Journalists, presumably the ones who hadn't known already, sat up straighter. Initial surprise and disbelief turned quickly to curiosity. Danni glanced at Michael, who was frowning but whose head was tilted inquiringly, waiting for her to deny the accusation. Her breath caught in her throat. She looked back at the reporter. "That's not something we're here to talk about," she said with a brittle smile. She signaled for Michael to take the next question. They needed to divert the reporters' interest. A distraction like this one was the last thing she wanted.

But the journalist wasn't about to let it go at that. "How would you characterize your relationship with the prince?" She called out her question, not waiting to be asked.

Danni paused, needing to shut this down and move on. She was about to issue a categorical denial—after all what she and Adam had was over, it had to be— when she looked up and saw a solid, dark-suited man standing at the back of the room. Wrightson, one of the palace drivers. What was he doing here? He gave his close-cropped head the smallest of shakes.

No? No, what? Don't deny it? Do deny it?

Danni took a deep breath and looked back at the woman. "How would I characterize my relationship with the prince? To you, very carefully. And that's all I have to say on the subject."

A murmur of laughter spread through the room. The motorsport journalists were no more pleased about the presence of tabloid reporters than she had been. Imposters in their ranks. Though undoubtedly many if not all of them were scenting new angles for their stories, angles that might sell more papers or subscriptions or ad space on websites. They might not all like it but they knew what paid their wages. She just had to keep the focus where she wanted it. "Now let's move on. Robert?" Robert Dubrawski, a newscaster with a background in finance, would be wanting information on the economic impact of a Grand Prix.

Through a mix of firmness and humor, she kept the rest of the briefing relatively on track. And when the allotted time was up, she took a back exit from the room and into the side streets walking quickly, wanting to put distance between her and impending disaster.

She knew a quiet little restaurant in the old part of the city. She could get a corner table and figure out what was happening and what she needed to do about it. She was hurrying toward the restaurant when a sleek dark Jaguar pulled alongside her, slowing to a stop.

The window slid down to reveal Wrightson behind the wheel. "Prince Adam wondered if you could spare some time to meet with him?"

Only if Prince Adam could wind back time itself and stop this from happening. She was about to refuse when she heard her name called out. The reporter from the briefing and a photographer were running up the street toward her.

Danni hopped into the car.

The breaking of their story changed everything.

They had to come up with a joint strategy, an excuse for why they'd been seen together. And doubtless, if they needed it, Adam would have the very best PR advisers at his service.

She switched on her phone, found a message from Adam asking her to call him and another more recent message from the receptionist at work advising her not to come back after the briefing because photographers were swarming the building.

Danni didn't speak as the car rumbled over the cobbled streets, crossed an arching bridge and headed sedately for the palace. She did her best to tamp down the anticipation that seeing Adam inevitably stirred. Fifteen minutes later they drew up outside Adam's wing. Before the car had quite come to a stop, Danni opened her door and got out. As she looked around, unsure of what to do, the door to Adam's wing opened and he strode out.

And despite all her resolutions, her determination that everything had to be over between them and her annoyance that what should have been private had been made public, her heart leaped at the sight of him. So confident, so intense. The concern in his eyes for her.

He strode toward her and caught her shoulders. "You're okay?"

She nodded.

"I'm sorry about the press." Regret and anger tinged his voice. If the press had wind of their story, there were only two ways it could go. They'd revile her for stopping him from finding a suitable woman or they'd expect him to confirm it was serious with Danni.

He wouldn't accept either of those outcomes. He understood his duty.

"It's not your fault."

He pushed a lock of hair behind her ear. "Actually it is. It's because of me they're interested in you. I never wanted them to get to you." Along with the regret and anger she recognized resignation in his voice, his eyes.

He knew, finally, that what they'd shared had to be over.

Even with all her attempts to convince him of that simple truth, his acceptance of it opened up an emptiness inside her that filled with a great welling sorrow.

"As soon as my secretary told me there were pictures, I tried to get word to you. Your phone was off."

"I'd put it to voice mail."

"I know. So I sent Wrightson. I would have gone myself but…"

"Fuel to the fire. I get it. Thanks for trying though."

"I'd have stopped it if I could."

"I know. But you can't and so we need a strategy. Is it too late to say there was never anything between us?"

"They have photos of us skiing and photos of us

leaving the palace grounds together. The skiing ones have only just come to light. But combined with the others…"

"Can they be explained any other way?"

He lifted a shoulder. "They could be."

"Then let's—"

"It's best to be honest." He brushed his knuckles across her cheek. "At first you were labeled a mystery woman. Unfortunately, but not surprisingly, it didn't take them long to figure out who you were."

"No. It wouldn't have." She thought of the reporters' tenacious questions.

"I heard you handled the press well."

"I managed. I think. The questions caught me by surprise. I was about to deny any relationship when Wrightson shook his head."

"Like I said, it's best to stick to the truth. It always comes out eventually."

"If we have to stick to the truth," she said, "we tell them we had a weekend together but that it was a mistake."

"I don't make mistakes. And you definitely weren't one."

"Then we tell them that it…didn't work out."

"Seemed to me that it worked pretty well."

"It did." For that one isolated weekend.

"So have you come up with a way to handle the publicity?"

"I've spoken to the palace advisers."

"And?"

"I also spoke to my father and to Rafe."

"Oh." Of course it was inevitable that his father and brother would find out and have an opinion. She shouldn't be surprised or dismayed. "What did they say?" She held up her hand. "No, wait. Don't tell me. I know what they said." Adam had needed to hear their views, but she didn't. It was surely them who'd finally convinced Adam that there could be no relationship with her. She should be grateful for that. "What's the strategy."

"As unoriginal as it is, 'No comment' seems to be the preferred strategy. That combined with no further contact between us. When there's no fuel, the fire soon dies out."

His gaze searched her face and he shook his head. "I've missed you." He pulled her to him. Acting on pure conditioned response, she rose up for his kiss and welcomed the touch of his lips to hers.

How could this be over when he kissed her like that?

How could she walk away from him?

His kiss, as always, sent sensations spiraling through her, weakening her legs, trampling over rational thought. That was why she was having such trouble walking away from him, she thought with a half laugh—weak legs.

She'd been too long without him.

He was her addiction.

As her hands, of their own volition, slipped around his waist, he pulled her closer still. Enveloped her in his warmth. Warmth that turned rapidly to heat.

Once more, a voice whispered.

Once more before it was over.

"Can you do one thing for me?" she asked.

"I'd do anything for you."

"Make love to me once more." She would take this and then nothing more.

He pulled back. She read the hesitation in his eyes and then his capitulation. He caught her hand in his again and strode wordlessly for the palace. He hurried up to the second level, past the library and along a hallway hung with portraits. The next door they passed through led into a bedroom. Unmistakably masculine.

Her gaze took in the room. He hadn't been lying when he'd said he had a big bed. There'd be room to turn cartwheels across it. Or make love lying any which way across it. She could turn cartwheels but she'd much rather make love.

A lock clicked into place as Adam pushed the door shut behind him. For one long delirious second they looked at each other. Awareness and unbearable hunger hummed in the air between them. Then he tugged on the hand he still held and she went to him. With no thought of talking she reached for him, undoing buttons and belts and zips, finding her way inside his clothes, needing skin on skin contact, the male heat of him, her addiction needing to be fed. One last fix. This close she could breathe in the intoxicating scent that was his alone. The one that called every cell in her body to attention. And the touch of him, the warmth that spread through her, were enough to reassure her that satisfaction was close at hand. Her craving would be satisfied.

Her only consolation for her senseless weakness for him was that he seemed as desperate as she was—lost to the haze of desire. Tugging and pulling at her clothes, with none of his legendary finesse. He eased her back onto his bed and lay down over her.

All the world narrowed to this one moment, this one man. All her thoughts, every sensation was centered on him and what he gave her.

He rose up, his broad shoulders and corded neck straining. Ready for him, needing him, she arched against him. He accepted her body's plea and in one long stroke drove in deep and fast, filling her so that her "yes" came out as a low satisfied moan, mingling with a similar inarticulate sound from him.

So good.

He felt so good. So right. So perfect.

And then he was moving within her, slowly at first but she didn't want slow and he responded to her needs, driving in harder and deeper and she reached for his hips, clasping the bunching muscles, moving with his rhythm, pulling him still harder and deeper, her legs around his back. Because she needed this. She needed him.

They strove together, swirling into the same vortex of wanting, racing for a release that demanded completion. Sensation, like licks of fire, swept through her, curling her toes, setting her aflame for this, for him, carrying them to that other mindless place till sensation couldn't be contained and the power of it surged through them as it crested and shattered.

Leaving her shaken and spent.

He held her in his arms as their breathing slowed and minds and bodies adjusted to the fact that they were no longer one. Aftershocks rippled through her as sweat cooled on her skin.

"Funny," he said later as he pushed a lock of hair from her face. "Whenever I dreamed about making love to you here in this bed, I imagined it to be slow and exquisite. I thought we'd take hours."

The awareness of Adam losing his ever-present restraint with her, thrilled and humbled her. "At least you got the exquisite part right."

His arm tightened around her. "And maybe we could try…"

She didn't know where she would find the strength to walk away from him because she hadn't known, hadn't let herself believe, that they could be this good together. That she could want more than his body or to give him more than hers. That he could make such a deep impression on her heart.

No, not an impression, he owned it. All of it.

The heart in question sank with the dawning awareness.

Love.

She'd fallen in love with Adam.

He was like no other man she'd ever known. She loved his seriousness, his complexity, his kindness. She loved him and everything about him.

A man she couldn't have. The irony was that he was the one person she wanted to share the appalling realization with. The Adam who was her friend as well as her lover in whose arms she now lay. The Adam who understood her, who always had.

But she couldn't admit her love. All it would do would be to make him feel guilty. He'd never asked for her love. She'd been an interlude in his search for a wife.

Maybe she should just be grateful that they'd taken as much as they had. More than they should have been allowed.

It was hard to be grateful when her heart was breaking.

She sought the temporary solace of making love with him again.

A long time afterward, a long slow exquisite time afterward, she rolled out of his bed.

Love wasn't supposed to hurt like this.

She found strength along with her clothes.

It wasn't till she was dressed that she turned back to Adam to find him watching her. Those now serious eyes had been fierce with fire and passion. For her.

This was it. The end. They both recognized it.

She turned away from those beautiful brown eyes and crossed to the window. Seconds later she saw his reflection in the glass. He'd come to stand behind her. Outside, darkness was falling. Her life had once been so uncomplicated. She leaned her forehead on the window.

Fifteen minutes later they sat in a nondescript sedan belonging to the palace's head of security. "I did your one last thing. Will you do one for me? Will you let me show you something?" He'd asked and she'd agreed. How could she refuse him? They skirted the city, crossed the river and several blocks later turned into an industrial area on the outskirts of the city filled with warehouses and light manufacturing. "Where are we going?"

"You told me once there were rumors that I had a mystery woman."

"Yes. And you laughed."

"You'll see why soon. We're almost there."

At the entrance to a light industrial complex, he pressed a code into a keypad that opened an enormous gate. Inside, he drove slowly past a series of closed roller doors, finally stopping in front of one. He pressed a button on his key chain and one of the doors slowly rose. He looked at her. "I haven't shown this to anyone before."

"You don't have to show it to me now." She almost didn't want him to. She had no idea what was behind that door, only that it was deeply personal to him.

"I want to." He drove into the dim interior. Danni instantly recognized a workshop, tools neatly lining the walls, and saw straight away the shape of a low, covered car. They parked alongside it and the door closed behind them.

She looked from him to the covered car. "Why would you keep a car out here when you have all that space at the palace?"

"This is private. It's nothing to do with the palace or being a prince. It's my escape from both of those things. Through that door over there—" he pointed to a wall "—are stairs to the top level. I had it converted to an apartment, just a bedroom and a bathroom. It's utterly private."

He tilted his head toward the shrouded car. "Let me show her to you. My mystery woman." They approached the car and he peeled back the cover. Her first glimpse of gleaming wheel spokes confirmed what she'd suspected as soon as she'd seen the shape of the low-slung car. "Dad's Bugatti. You're the collector?" She looked from the car, its engine exposed, to him. "How is that possible?"

"Your father did so much for me for so many years. Especially after my mother died. I wanted to do something for him in return. I knew he was selling the car at least in part for your college fees and that he'd never accept outright financial help. So I bought it through an intermediary. Don't get me wrong, it wasn't truly altruistic, having the car to work on has given me peace and much pleasure over the years."

"Dad doesn't know?"

Adam shook his head. "I wanted to finish it and then give it back to him. It's nearly ready. I steal an hour here and there."

Danni touched his face—her fingertips to his beautiful strong jaw. "That's a lovely thing you're doing."

He opened the nearest door. "Hop in."

Danni let him hand her into the car. Into the driver's seat. He took shotgun. "Do you remember—" she began.

"Yes. And I'm embarrassed about it."

"You said a girl couldn't drive it. That girls weren't good drivers."

"Thanks for reminding me. Did I ever apologize for that?"

"Not as such. But you let me drive for you. I figured that meant something."

"It did. And if it will mean something to you now you can drive the Bugatti. The detailing isn't finished but it runs like a dream."

Half an hour later they were parked on top of a hill looking back over the lights of the city gleaming like diamonds strewn across the night. A full moon hung partially obscured in the sky.

"I could sit like this with you forever." Adam's low voice reached across the darkness between them.

Danni looked away and surreptitiously wiped a tear from her cheek. She tried to swallow the ache in her jaw.

"I hope you find a good man, Danni."

She turned to him. "Would you be insulted if I wished you success in your search for a suitable wife?"

"To my core."

"So, don't…"

"I won't." He reached for her hand, held it with a clasp more fierce than gentle. "But I want you to be happy."

"And I want the same for you."

He tipped his head back and closed his eyes. He opened them again and looked at her with that intensity that was unique to him. "You know that if I didn't love you as much as I do, I'd ask you to marry me."

"You love me?" The words reverberated within her, filling her with joy and sorrow, her greatest wish and her greatest fear.

"With all my heart. I don't know when or how it started. And I don't know how to stop. You can't possibly know how vital you are to me. But I couldn't ask you to share a life that would make you miserable. Rafe made me see that."

A silence stretched between them. He loved her. He loved her.

Finally, she spoke softly. "If I didn't love you as much as I do I'd accept."

"You love me?"

"With all my heart. And I do know how it started. It began when I was five and you got that book down from the shelf for me. And I don't know how to stop either, or believe that you can possibly know how vital *you* are to *me*. But I'm not what you need. I'd be a terrible royal wife."

His hand tightened on hers. "The constant glare of

publicity, the tedium of royal engagements. I couldn't bear to see your joy in life diminished."

She allowed another small silence, turning his words over in her head. "People cope," she said quietly. "I coped with the press today. But what about my lack of sophistication, my lack of diplomacy? I couldn't bear to discredit you."

He freed her hand, shifted his to caress her face. "There are far too many sophisticated and diplomatic people in royal circles. What I need in my life is vitality and plain speaking. Someone who's honest with me. Someone I can be with in the quiet moments. And I've been told I need to learn to have fun. To be more impulsive. I need a lot of work. I could use help with that."

She wanted so desperately to help him with that. "I meet none of your criteria for a royal wife."

"That's not quite true. You meet plenty of the criteria on that list. You're good with the press, you're good with children and you're beautiful beyond belief, but none of those matter anymore because I drew up a new list."

"A new list? When?"

"When you first tried to tell me that we were over. I thought it might be wise." He lowered his hand and pulled a folded and crumpled piece of paper from his pocket and passed it to her. "I didn't do too well with it. I couldn't come up with much."

Danni spread the paper out on the steering wheel. There was just enough light to make out that there were a few words on the paper but not enough to read them. "It's too dark. I can't read it."

"It says, 'Item One—she must be Danni.'" He blew out his breath. "And that's it."

The moon rose up from behind the clouds, shining enough light that she could make out her name on the paper. "You're right. It's not much of a list."

"It was the best I could do."

"I'd say you need help with it."

"I probably do."

"You should add to it that she must love you. Because if she loves you, whatever she has to give up will be less of a sacrifice than giving up on love."

"And I guess you'd tell me I should love her in return? With all my heart? And be willing to do whatever it takes to make her happy?"

"Absolutely."

"So that's three simple criteria." He turned in the seat and lifted his hands to her face. "She must be Danni, she must love me and I must love her in return? Will you help me find her and help me convince her to marry me, to never leave me?"

"Yes," she sighed. "But only if you kiss me now."

Epilogue

"Have I told you how beautiful you look tonight?" Adam stood and held out his hand to Danni.

"Yes." She put her hand in his, stood and walked to the dance floor with him, stepping gladly, gratefully into his arms.

They were the third couple to occupy the floor. The bridal couple, Rebecca and Logan, danced, eyes for only each other. Their wedding had been beautiful, full of pomp and splendor, but with human touches and laughter and most of all love.

Their love for each other had shone through every moment and every syllable of the service from the time Rebecca had taken her first step on the long walk up the cathedral's aisle.

Rebecca had looked amazing in her ivory silk and

lace gown and Logan had been visibly stunned as he watched her walk toward him.

Danni and Adam were among the very few who knew that beneath Rebecca's gown the first addition to their family already grew.

Rafe and Lexie danced now too, holding tight to each other. Their baby, Bonnie, had punctuated the service with her laughing gurgles, a delightful counterpoint to the beautiful solemnity of the occasion. Bonnie had stayed through the official luncheon but had been taken home by the nanny before this more intimate dinner and dance for a mere three hundred. But if they followed the pattern Danni had quickly become aware of, Rafe and Lexie would soon head home, too. Wanting to be with each other and their child had suddenly become a singular priority. The playboy prince had become a doting husband and father, completely besotted with the two women in his life.

At the head table, Prince Henri and Danni's father sat back in their chairs, sipping cognac and watching over proceedings with obvious fatherly pride.

Adam hadn't taken too long to bring his father round to the idea of their marrying. He'd had several meetings alone with him before bringing Danni to meet him officially. The main thing Prince Henri had wanted to be certain of was that they were resolute in their love for each other—because there would, he assured them, be trials. But once he was convinced of their love, he'd insightfully predicted that the country too would grow to love Danni. They would see her as just like them, an ordinary citizen, a commoner whom they could claim as one of their own and love. She would be the fairy tale come true.

And he'd been right. The press had quickly decided they were on Danni's side and made much of the work she'd done in bringing a Grand Prix to San Philippe. And they frequently pointed out how refreshing she would be for the royal family. Already it seemed that their prince, who they acknowledged could sometimes seem a little reserved, looked more relaxed and open. It helped that every photo they printed showed both Danni and Adam radiant with happiness.

Gradually, other couples joined the dance floor. So much had changed for Danni and Adam in the last month. They'd announced their engagement at Christmas. They'd considered waiting until after this wedding but speculation had been so intense that it seemed easiest to admit the truth, that yes they loved each other and wanted to marry.

Their wedding wouldn't be for another eight months. It was the soonest that it could be arranged given the pomp and ceremony that was apparently necessary, more even than there had been today. But, after all, it wasn't every day the heir apparent got married. The country wanted to celebrate, just as, after being robbed of a wedding by Rafe and Lexie eloping, they'd anticipated and then celebrated today's occasion.

Already a provisional guest list was being drawn up. Many of the names on it would be dictated by protocol and etiquette, with attention paid to international considerations. She and Adam were content to leave much of it to their aides, though they had made sure to insist that Blake be on it.

The only thing that really mattered to Danni was that she got to be with Adam. For the rest of their lives.

He danced with her, holding her closer than decorum suggested was proper, their bodies pressed together from shoulders to toes. Almost heaven, Danni thought as she swayed in his arms. Moving with him, being held by him. Every time she thought it couldn't get any better, it did.

"You look stunning in that dress." The dress in question had been made for her, a beaded evening gown, with simple flowing lines, in deepest purple.

"Thank you, but you know as soon as we get home I'll be kicking off these shoes and getting changed." She was gradually getting used to the formality of dress that was now often required of her, but she still liked her jeans best of all.

"You'll be getting out of the dress, do you mean? I'll be happy to help you with that." He pulled her closer still and spun her.

"So long as you're more help than you were when I was trying to put it on."

"The trouble is, as beautiful as it looks on you, it looks even better off you." He leaned down and whispered in her ear. "Though I guess you could keep the shoes on if you like."

Danni laughed. She couldn't believe she'd once accused him of lacking fun and spontaneity. In public he was seriousness personified. In private he was anything but. And she loved every facet of him.

* * * * *

LET'S TALK
Romance

For exclusive extracts, competitions
and special offers, find us online:

MILLS & BOON

MODERN

Power and Passion

Prepare to be swept off your feet by sophisticated, sexy and seductive heroes, in some of the world's most glamourous and romantic locations, where power and passion collide.

Eight Modern stories published every month, find them all at

millsandboon.co.uk/Modern